Mary Nichols is [...] stories, family sag[...] Historicals. She w[...] Novelists Associat[...]ry day at her computer pr[...] novels and divided the rest of her time between reading, research, gardening, playing golf and, when it became necessary, housework! Mary passed away in Feb 2016 having written well over 100 books.

Regency Scandals

Regency Scandal:

Outrageous
Propositions

MARY NICHOLS

MILLS & BOON

First Published in Great Britain 2020
By Mills & Boon, an imprint of HarperCollins*Publishers*
1 London Bridge Street, London, SE1 9GF

REGENCY SCANDAL: OUTRAGEOUS PROPOSITIONS
© 2020 Harlequin Books S.A.

Scandal at Greystone Manor © 2014 Mary Nichols
The Hemingford Scandal © 2004 Mary Nichols

978-0-263-28221-4

MIX
Paper from
responsible sources
FSC™ C007454

This book is produced from independently certified FSC™ paper to ensure responsible forest management.

For more information visit: www.harpercollins.co.uk/green

Printed and bound in Spain
by CPI, Barcelona

SCANDAL AT
GREYSTONE MANOR

Chapter One

April 1817

'Stand still, Issie, do,' Jane said. 'How can I pin this hem if you will keep dodging from one foot to the other? And stop admiring yourself in the mirror. We all know what a beautiful bride you will make.'

It had taken weeks of indecision about colour and style before the heavy cerise silk had been bought and then they could not decide on who was to make it up. 'You do it,' Isabel had told her sister. 'You are every bit as good a seamstress as any London mantua-maker and a great deal better than poor Miss Smith.'

Jane laughed at the compliment. 'Very well, but we'll ask Miss Smith to do the plain stitching. She could do with the work.' The elderly spinster came from the village three times a week to make petticoats for the ladies as well as repair torn garments and mend the household linen.

Jane had been doing as much as possible towards the wedding to save a little on the expense. Her mother was determined it would be the wedding of the year, in spite of Sir Edward's pleas they should not be too extravagant. Jane was perhaps the only one of the family to take any notice of him, but that did not mean Isabel's wedding would be anything less than perfect if she could help it. She had taken great pains with the gown, making sure it fitted perfectly. It had the fashionable high waist, long sleeves, loose at the top but tight from the elbow down, a heart-shaped neckline and a flowing skirt, trimmed with lace and embroidered with white-and-pink roses. All that was left to do now was stitch up the hem and add the decoration to the neckline and sleeves—yards of ribbon and lace, interspersed with tiny coloured beads. Sewn on by hand with minute invisible stitches, they were going to take some time to do. She did not begrudge the time, nor her sister her happiness, not even at the sacrifice of her own.

Isabel was to marry Mark Wyndham, heir to Lord Wyndham, who lived with his parents less than three miles away at Broadacres. The families had known each other for years and often visited each other, so the girls and their brother had grown up in close proximity and there was no formality between them. A marriage between Mark and Isabel had been talked about for years as if it were a foregone conclusion, though Mark had not formally proposed until he came back from the Peninsular War, where he had distinguished himself as an aide to Sir Arthur Wellesley, now the Duke of Wellington. The engagement pleased both families and it had relieved the girls' father, who did not want Isabel to go the way of Jane and become an old maid. To have two unmarried daughters was not good for his self-esteem, and nor, come to that, his pocket.

Jane was perhaps the only one of the family, apart

from her father, who realised that they were living beyond their means, trying to maintain a status and life-
style not commensurate with income. The estate was run
down, fences needed mending, ditches needed cleaning
out, some of the cottages needed repairs and the house
itself was in urgent need of refurbishment. Greystone
Manor was a lovely old house, solidly built to withstand
the ravages of the east wind that blew in off the German
Ocean, but that didn't stop it being draughty. Its large
withdrawing room was icy in winter and cool in summer;
its huge kitchens and dairy with their stone floors were
hard on the servants' feet. The family tended to use the
smaller parlour as a sitting room and the breakfast room
as a dining room except on formal occasions. Today the
girls were working in Isabel's bedchamber, whose window overlooked the front drive. Outside the spring sunshine was warm and inviting and everyone hoped that
this year there might be a good harvest, which would
make up for the terrible failure of the year before.

'There, that's done,' Jane said. 'You can take it off now
and I'll get Miss Smith to stitch the hem while I gather
the flounces for the skirt.'

She helped Isabel out of the gown and carefully folded
it ready for the seamstress when she came that afternoon.

Isabel hugged her. 'You are so good, Jane, I wish I
could be more like you. You are clever at whatever you
do, sewing, cooking, managing the servants and you have
such a way with the village children. You ought to be
getting married, too, and having children of you own.'

'We can't all be wives, Issie.' At twenty-seven, everyone, including Jane herself, knew she was well past
marriageable age. Her role in life was to be a helpmate
to her mother, to busy herself with the arrangements for

her sister's wedding, to calm her other sister's excitable nature and try to curb her brother Teddy's profligacy. Added to her good works in the nearby village of Hadlea, it was enough to keep her occupied. She had little time to bemoan her single state.

'But you must wish for it sometimes?'

'Not really. I am content with my life.'

'Did you never have an offer?'

Jane smiled, but did not answer. There had been someone once, ten years before, but it had come to nothing. Her father had disapproved on the grounds that the young man had no title and no fortune, no family of any standing and no prospects. She could do better than that, he'd told her. But she never had and the only other man she had come to have feelings for had not reciprocated and her foolishness was a deeply held secret which she had never told a soul. She was not beautiful and, compared with her younger sisters, she was plain Jane.

How their parents had managed to produce three girls so different from each other, Jane could not fathom. Jane and Isabel were both dark haired, but there the similarity ended. Jane was taller than average; she had strong features, well-defined brows and a determined chin. Isabel, six years younger than Jane, was considered the beauty of the family. She was a little shorter and more curvaceous than Jane, and her face was rounder and very expressive; she was not one to hide her feelings. Tears and temper were often displayed, but she soon recovered and became her usual sunny self. Jane was more circumspect and kept her feelings to herself. As for Sophie, she was fair-haired and blue-eyed and, at seventeen, had not yet shed what her mother chose to call her puppy fat.

'I am doing the right thing?' Isabel asked suddenly, sinking on to her bed in her petticoat.

'Whatever do you mean?'

'Marrying Mark.'

'You are surely not having doubts now, Issie?'

'It's such a big step. I keep wondering if I shall make him happy, or if I shall be content with him.'

'But you have known him all your life. You know he is tall and handsome, that he is thoughtful and considerate, that he has deep pockets and likes nothing better than to indulge you. What more can you ask?'

'That's just it. Perhaps I know him too well. And perhaps I've missed someone else, someone for whom I could feel the grand passion.'

'Isabel, you are talking nonsense, the grand passion is a myth, dreamed up by romantics. It's much better to marry someone dependable, someone you know won't let you down.' Isabel's sudden doubts were having a strange effect on Jane. It had taken all her resolve to wish her sister happy when the engagement had been announced and she had entered into the preparations for the wedding with as much whole-hearted enthusiasm as she could muster. Her sister's doubts worried her.

'Mark is dependable, that's true,' Isabel said. 'But he is almost like another brother.'

'Mark is nothing like a brother.'

'No, of course not. I'm being silly. He's not a bit like Teddy, is he?'

'God forbid! One of Teddy is enough.'

They laughed at this and the tension eased. Jane helped her sister into her day dress and was just brushing her hair and tying it back with a ribbon when they heard the sound of someone arriving. Isabel jumped up and went to the window to see who it might be. 'It's Teddy,' she said. 'My goodness, where did he get that coat? He looks like a bumble bee.'

Jane joined her sister at the window. Their brother, three years younger than Jane and three years older than Isabel, had just descended from the gig he had hired at the Fox and Hounds, where the stage from London had no doubt deposited him not half an hour since. The coat Isabel had commented on was of yellow-and-brown stripes. It had a cutaway skirt and deep revers. His trousers were fawn and his waistcoat yellow with red spots. 'Papa will have something to say about that,' she said.

They were descending the stairs as a servant opened the door to admit him. He flourished a brown beaver topper at them both. 'Jane, Isabel, I hope I find you both well.'

'Very well,' Jane said.

'Where did you get that extraordinary coat?' Isabel demanded.

'Gieves, where else? Do you like it?' He twirled to show it off. 'Where is Papa? I need to talk to him. Is he in a good mood?'

'Oh, Teddy, do not say you have come to wheedle money out of him?' Jane said. 'You know what he said the last time.'

'Well, a fellow can't live decent on what I earn at Halliday's.' Halliday and Son was an eminent firm of lawyers who had a practice in Lincoln's Inn Fields. Teddy had gone to them after leaving university at the behest of his father, who did not believe his son should pass his days in idleness. He was still very junior and could not command the large fees his mentors did.

'Then take a little advice from me, Brother,' Jane went

on. 'Change that coat and waistcoat before you see him. It will not help your cause.'

'Wise words, as always, Jane,' he said. 'I'll go up to my room and put on something drab.' He picked up his portmanteau from the floor where he had dropped it and ran up the stairs two at a time.

'He doesn't change, does he?' Isabel said.

'No, unfortunately. I fear we are in for an uncomfortable dinner time.'

In that she was right. Even though Teddy had changed into a dark grey coat and a white cravat and waistcoat, he had evidently not been successful with their father. He was resentful, Sir Edward was angry and Lady Cavenhurst upset. Jane and Isabel tried to lighten the heavy atmosphere by talking about the wedding and the doings in the village and were only partly successful, not helped by Sophie demanding to know what was the matter with everyone, why the gloomy faces. 'Anyone would think there had been a death in the family,' she said.

'Death of me,' Teddy said morosely, which made his father snort derisively and his mother draw in her breath in distress. But no one commented and they continued to eat their roast beef in a silence broken only when someone asked politely for the sauce boat or the salt cellar.

After the meal ended, the ladies repaired to the withdrawing room, where a maid brought in the tea tray. 'Is Papa very angry with Teddy?' Jane asked their mother as they arranged themselves on sofas.

'He is more disappointed than angry,' her ladyship said. She was still a handsome woman, with an upright figure which belied her forty-nine years. 'Teddy promised him he would limit his extravagance, but it seems not to have happened. But we will not talk of it. No doubt it will be resolved somehow.' It was typical of their mother to shut her eyes to problems in the firm belief someone else would solve them.

They had not been seated many minutes when Sir Edward and Teddy joined them, but Teddy soon made his excuses to leave. Jane rose and followed him. 'Teddy,' she said, taking his arm. 'Are matters very ill with you?'

'Couldn't be worse. And the old man refuses to stand buff.'

'Oh, dear, what will you do?' They strolled into the book room where there was a comfortable sofa and sat down side by side.

'I don't know what to do. You can't help me out, can you, Sis?'

'How much do you owe?'

'Well…' He seemed reluctant to go on. 'It's mostly gaming debts and they simply have to be paid.'

'Go on, how much?'

'Five thousand or thereabouts.'

'Five thousand! Oh, Teddy, how did that come about?'

'You know how it is—you win some and you lose some and I kept thinking I would recoup. Luck was against me.'

'Who do you owe the money to?'

'Lord Bolsover holds the biggest of my gambling debts, about three thousand. He's the one making the most noise about it. There are a couple of others. Gieves and Hoby and the vintner can wait.'

'Wait for what? Until you have another winning streak? And I would have thought it was more important to pay your tailor and bootmaker who have a living to make. Gaming debts are not enforceable by law. You should know that, working in a law firm as you do.'

'All the more reason to pay them. It is a question of honour.'

'Honour! Teddy, if you had any honour you would heed poor Papa, who has always done his best for you. He is not made of money, you know.'

'So he told me.' He heaved a sigh. 'He suggests I find myself a rich wife, preferably a widow, old enough and independent enough to curb my excesses.'

Jane could not help laughing and was relieved to see a slight twitch of her brother's lips in response. 'He only said that because he was cross with you.'

'He was in earnest, Jane.'

'You do not like the idea?'

'Oh, I like it well enough, always supposing the wealth came with a pretty face and figure. But where am I going to find such a one who'll have me? Even if I did, it would take time and I haven't got the time. Hector Bolsover wants his blunt.'

'Oh, Teddy, what a mess you are in.'

'I know. Can you help me out?'

'Where do you think I can find so much money?'

'You still have the bequest Aunt Matilda left you, haven't you?'

'That is meant to be my dowry.'

'But, Jane, you are never going to marry, are you?'

Only a brother would be so blunt. It hurt, but she didn't show it. 'Maybe not, but I have other plans for my inheritance.'

'More important than rescuing your only brother from the River Tick?'

She sighed heavily. She had a dream of opening an orphanage for some of the children of men lost in the recent war. The idea had come about when she had been in London the year before. She had seen some ragged, barefoot children running about the streets begging and when she spoke to one of them, to the dismay of her mother who had accompanied her, she was told a tale which made her heart bleed for him. His father had been killed in a battle in far-off Portugal, his mother had been forced into service where children were not welcome and because she was obliged to live in, she had to give up the tenancy of their two tiny rooms. He slept in doorways or under the trees in the park. 'I do well enough,' he told her, holding out his hand for money.

How many more were there like that? she had asked herself, how many children were there without homes, without adequate clothing and enough to eat? 'Surely the government should do something about them,' she had said to her mother, as they left the child clutching a sixpence. 'Their fathers fought for king and country and that is how they are rewarded. It's a disgrace.'

'I do not see what we can do about it.'

'We can speak to Sir Mortimer for a start.' Sir Mortimer Belton was their local Member of Parliament. 'If the problem is put to him, he might bring it up in Parliament. We could make a fuss, bring it to the public's attention. Raise a subscription to provide the children with homes.'

'Oh, dear,' her mother had said. 'That sounds like a crusade.'

And a crusade it had become, but trying to make the government move was like tickling a tortoise. Jane had decided that she must set an example—not on a grand scale, she could not afford that, but she could do something locally. A small boarding school for about a dozen orphans of soldiers in their own vicinity was what she had in mind. It might encourage others to do the same in their own localities. The five thousand pounds she had would not be enough and she had enlisted the help of the Rector, the Reverend Mr Henry Caulder and his wife, to raise funds. They had decided that the best way to do it was to find philanthropic sponsors. To encourage them, she would put her own money into the venture, she had told them. If she gave her inheritance to Teddy, it would put an end to her plans before they had even begun to take shape.

'Can you not ask Lord Bolsover for more time, so that we can think of something?' she queried.

'You don't know his lordship, or you wouldn't even suggest it.'

'If he is such an unpleasant man, why do you associate with him?'

'He is in the group I play with.'

'Teddy, you are a fool and I do not wonder that Papa is angry with you.'

'Do you think you can bring him round? He always listens to you. I will be for ever in your debt.'

She laughed. 'You are in enough debt without adding me to your list, Teddy, but I'll see what I can do with Papa. Not tonight, though. Give him time to calm down. How long will you stay?'

'I cannot show my face back in London until at least Bolsover is satisfied.'

'But what about your position at Halliday's?'

'What position?'

Even the almost-unshockable Jane was taken aback

by that. 'Oh, Teddy, don't say you have been dismissed? No wonder Papa is furious.'

'He don't know about that. Daren't tell him. If you can't help me, I will have to go abroad, the Indies or India or something.'

'That will break Mama's heart. And the disgrace will be hard to live down. And there's Isabel's wedding in a month's time. What do you think Mark will say about a scandal like that hanging over the nuptials? Go away, Teddy, go and make yourself useful somewhere and let me think.'

He stood up and left her. Her thinking led her nowhere, except to the realisation that she would have to forfeit her inheritance. The thought of all those orphan children continuing to suffer because of her brother's selfishness was more than she could bear. She had always been tolerant of Teddy's foibles, but this time he had really angered her. If it were not for her mother's distress and her sister's wedding, she would let him stew.

'If it isn't Drew Ashton,' Mark exclaimed when he saw his old friend striding towards him along Piccadilly. 'Where have you sprung from? It's years since I saw you.'

'I've been in India, just arrived back.'

'And looking very prosperous, I must say.' Mark looked the other man up and down, taking in the perfectly fitting coat of clerical-grey superfine, the embroidered waistcoat, the diamond pin in his precisely tied cravat, the pearl-handled quizzing glass hanging on a chain from his neck, and the gold pocket watch. His trousers were strapped below his polished city shoes. 'You didn't used to be so elegant.'

'I did pretty well out there. You don't look so bad

yourself. What have you been up to? How are your lady mother and Lord Wyndham?'

'They are both well. As for me, I've been campaigning with Wellington. Came home after Waterloo and now about to be married. I'm in London to call on my lawyers about the finer points of the marriage settlement and to buy a suit of clothes for the wedding.'

'You've time to join me for a meal at Grillon's, surely.'

'Yes, of course. Glad to.'

Mark turned back the way he had come and they walked a little way down the street to the hotel, where they were soon settled at a table and ordering food and wine.

'Tell me,' Mark said, while they waited for the repast to arrive. 'Why the sudden urge to visit India? I recollect you left Broadacres in somewhat of a hurry. I hope it had nothing to do with Mama's hospitality.'

'No, certainly not. Lady Wyndham's hospitality is of the best. She made me very welcome. It was a family matter that came up suddenly and had to be attended to. I did explain that at the time.'

'So you did. I had forgot. So, what are you going to do now you are back in England?'

'I am thinking of buying a share in a clipper and continuing to trade. It has served me well so far.'

'Trade, Drew?'

'Why not? I am not so top-lofty as to turn my nose up at a good way of making a fortune'. He stopped speaking as a waiter brought their pork chops, succulent and sizzling with fat, together with a large bowl of vegetables. They helped themselves and tucked in.

'A nabob, are you?' Mark queried. His friend certainly gave that impression. It was the only way he could have come by such finery without inherited wealth, which Mark knew he did not have.

'You could say that. I went out with the intention of making a fortune and in that I succeeded. I am no longer the poor relation to be pitied because no young lady of any standing would consider me.'

'I'm sure that isn't true, Drew.'

'Oh, it is, believe me. The young lady I wanted to marry turned her proud nose up at me. Not good enough, you see.'

Mark detected a note of bitterness in his old friend's tone 'There are plenty more fish in the sea.'

'Indeed, yes, although, unlike you, I am in no hurry to become leg-shackled.'

'I am not in a hurry. We have known each other since childhood.'

'Tell me about her. Is she beautiful? Does she have a pleasing temperament?'

'Yes, to both questions. You have met her, Drew. Her name is Isabel Cavenhurst.'

'Cavenhurst!'

'Yes, you sound surprised.'

'No, no,' Andrew said hastily. 'I do remember the name. Don't the Cavenhursts live close to Broadacres?'

'Yes, on the other side of the village at Greystone Manor. We went there several times while you were staying with us. Surely you remember that?'

'Yes, now you remind me, I do. There were three young ladies, I recall, though the youngest was no more than a child and the middle one, still at her lessons. The elder was seventeen or eighteen. I recall her name was Jane. I misremember the other names.' He spoke nonchalantly, as if it were a matter of indifference to him.

'Isabel is the second daughter. She is by far the most beautiful of the three, but Sophie is young and may grow into her looks. As for Jane, she has some very good qualities I can admire, but good looks is not one of them.'

'So you have taken the pick of the bunch and not the eldest. Isn't that a little unusual?'

'We are not in the Middle Ages, Drew, my parents would never presume to tell me whom I should marry. I was able to please myself. Anyway, Jane would not have welcomed my advances even if I chose to make any. I believe there was some sort of disappointment. I don't know the details, but she withdrew from society and I saw more of Isabel. Then of course I went to Portugal and was away six years. Isabel and I became engaged when I returned.'

'So when is the wedding to be?'

'Next month. The fifteenth.'

'Then I wish you happy.'

'Thank you. You must come down for the wedding.'

'Oh, I don't know about that.'

'Why not? You do not have a prior engagement, do you?'

'No, I am as free as the air until I find my clipper.'

'Then why the reluctance?'

'It is surely up to the bride's family to issue the invitations? They may not wish to include me.'

'That's a feeble excuse if I ever heard one. I can put forward my own guests. Besides, there is something you can do for me…'

'Oh, and what might that be?'

'Jonathan Smythe was to be my groomsman, but he had to go to Scotland to visit an elderly relative who is dying and as his inheritance hangs on his attendance at the death bed, he has abandoned me to go to her. I need someone to stand up with me at the altar.'

'I haven't seen Jonathan since we were at school together. The terrible trio, they called us, do you remember?'

'Yes. Always into mischief, the three of us.'

'My great-aunt and Jonathan's second cousin live in the same area of Strathclyde, both of them dragons.'

'I know, but dragon or not, he has been summoned and I am left without a groomsman.'

'I am flattered, Mark, but why me?'

Mark looked at his friend, his head a little to one side. 'Because I am sure you will do the job admirably and you are one of my oldest friends, so who better? As soon as I saw you coming down the street, I knew my problem was solved. You will do it, Drew, won't you?'

'I'll think about it.'

'Don't think too long. I have to go back to Norfolk the day after tomorrow and before that I have to bespeak me a suit of clothes fit for a bridegroom. Will you help me find it? You can help me choose gifts for my bride and her attendants, too, if you've a mind. It is always good not to do these things alone. A wise counsellor is what I need.'

Andrew laughed. 'From having nothing to occupy me but a good dinner and a game of cards, I suddenly find my time filled with onerous tasks.'

'Helping me buy a wedding outfit is not onerous. I am not short of blunt. I can afford the best and, if it helps, I will undertake to have a hand of cards with you. We can go to White's. Are you a member?'

'No, I haven't been back long enough to join any clubs and without sponsors I am unlikely to be accepted.'

'No matter, I will introduce you. So, do we shake

hands on it?' He put down his knife and held out his right hand.

Andrew took it. 'Very well. Tomorrow we go shopping. I make no promises about attending the wedding though.'

Mark grinned. He was satisfied for the moment. He did not doubt that he would be able to persuade his friend to Broadacres and then he might find out the truth about why he had disappeared so suddenly. He did not believe the tale of family business because, as far as he knew, Andrew's only family was an elderly spinster great-aunt who had had no wish to look after the orphan when his mother and father both died within weeks of each other. She had put him out to foster parents until he was old enough to go to school. From the odd things Drew had told him, he had been subject to physical abuse and mental torment. Mark had always felt sorry for him when they were at school, because when all the boys went home for the holidays, he had been left behind. He had invited him to Broadacres, but until Drew was old enough to make his own decisions he had been forbidden to come on the grounds it would give him ideas above his station. It was when they'd left university that he had been prevailed upon to spend some time at Broadacres before looking for a way of earning a living. Why, if it was family business that had called him, did he make such haste to go to India?

When they had finished their meal, which Andrew insisted on paying for, they parted, promising to meet again soon. Mark hired a hackney to take him to Halliday and Son to consult the son, Mr Cecil Halliday, about the marriage settlement. Mark was a careful man, but he was not ungenerous; he wanted to be sure Isabel had enough pin money to buy whatever she liked in the way of gowns and fripperies without having to appeal to him every time. He was not unaware that Sir Edward was struggling— it was obvious by the state of the house and grounds— and he had waived the dowry he had been offered. He knew how much of a sacrifice that would have been for the others—her ladyship, Jane and Sophie—who might suffer as a consequence. It was the last thing he wanted.

He was surprised when he arrived at the lawyer's premises not to encounter Teddy, who was usually scratching away in the outer office. There was another man sitting at his desk.

'Where is Mr Cavenhurst?' he queried after he had been shown into Cecil Halliday's office and they had exchanged greetings and handshakes.

'Mr Cavenhurst is no longer with us.'

'Not working here? Where has he gone?'

The man shrugged. 'I have no idea, back to his lodgings or home to Norfolk, perhaps.'

'What happened?'

'That's not for me to say, sir.'

'I understand your reticence, but he is to be my brother-in-law. Am I to assume you dispensed with his services?'

'You may assume that,' the man said, tight-lipped. 'I shall say nothing.'

'Very well. I'll not embarrass you by asking any more questions. Shall we get down to business?'

They spent the next hour fine-tuning the agreement and then Mark set off for Teddy's lodgings. The young man had flitted owing rent, he was told by the concierge in aggrieved tones. Mark paid the back rent and returned to his hotel. He had known Teddy all his life, they had played together as children and gone to the same school, although Teddy was four years younger and they'd had very little contact while there. They had not attended the same university and afterwards Mark had joined the army in Portugal and Teddy had subsequently taken up the position of junior clerk to Halliday and Son. It was only recently, because of the wedding, they had seen more of each other.

Mark wanted to like Teddy for Isabel's sake, but he had always found him brash and insensitive, which had come about, he supposed, because he was the longed-for son and heir. Born between Jane and Isabel, he had been thoroughly spoiled by his doting mama. So what had he done to make Halliday give him the bag? Whatever it was would not please Sir Edward.

He was able to make an informed guess later that evening when he and Drew met at White's and were joined by two others in a game of whist. One was Toby Moore, an erstwhile army captain whom Mark had known slightly during the war, and the other was Lord Bolsover. They were not two he would normally have chosen to play with, but all the other men present were already settled at their games and he could hardly refuse a polite request to make up a four.

'You are affianced to one of the Cavenhurst girls, are you not?' Bolsover queried, while they waited for a new pack of cards to be brought to the table. He was a year or two older than Mark, extravagantly dressed. His dark hair was worn short and curled forward over his fore-head and ears. His skin was tanned, which was surprising since, as far as Mark was aware, he spent long hours at the gaming tables.

'Yes,' Mark said. 'I have the honour to be engaged to Miss Isabel Cavenhurst.'

'The wedding to be soon, is it?'

'In a little under a month. Why do you ask?'

'Curiosity, my dear fellow. I am well acquainted with Cavenhurst.'

'Sir Edward?'

'No, never met him. I meant the son. We have had a few hands of cards together. I am afraid he is a poor loser. I believe he has run home on a repairing lease. I do hope he recovers quickly, I am not in the habit of waiting for my money.'

Mark could well believe that and wondered where the conversation was leading. 'No doubt he has gone home for the wedding.'

'So soon? I think not. It is to be hoped his father can come up trumps because at the moment I hold all the cards. I have bought up all the man's debts and they were spread far and wide. I do not think Teddy Cavenhurst ever bought anything with cash.' Everyone knew that creditors who could not make their debtors pay often sold the debts for a fraction of the original figure, in order to be rid of them.

His heart sank, but he hid it with a laugh. 'Sir Edward has always stood buff for his son. Have no fear.'

'I had heard the estate was in a poor way and Sir Edward hard put to come about.' Bolsover spoke nonchalantly as he picked up the pack that had just been put on the table in front of him and broke the seal.

'Where did you hear that? I know nothing of it.'

His lordship gave a cracked laugh. 'Worried that the lady's dowry is at risk, are you?'

'No, of course not. I do not know where you obtained your information, but I suggest you tell whoever it is that they are in error. Now, as we have the cards, shall we play?'

'To be sure.' His lordship finished shuffling the pack and put it on the table. 'Will you cut for trumps, Mr Ashton?'

The subject of Teddy and his debts was dropped, but it worried Mark. From the way Bolsover had spoken about the dowry and the Greystone estate, the amount must be substantial. Surely not enough to ruin Sir Edward? How much was it? He could ask Isabel, or better still Jane. She would be bound to know and also the extent of Sir Edward's problems.

'You are not concentrating,' murmured Drew, during the break between one game and the next as the pile of coins at Bolsover's elbow had grown. 'I had already won that second trick, you did not have to waste a trump on it. That is a beginner's mistake.'

'I'm sorry. It won't happen again.'

'Dreaming about your bride, are you?'

Mark smiled, but did not answer. He picked up the cards Toby Moore had just dealt. This was better; he had a good hand. They played in silence and recouped some of their losses. Drew was a very good player; he seemed to know where all the cards were and by the end of the evening they were in profit.

'A satisfactory evening,' Drew said, as they strolled to Jermyn Street where he was lodging.

'I think you must be a seasoned gambler,' Mark said. 'Hector Bolsover has a reputation as a sharp, but you made him look clumsy. He won't like that.'

'What do you know of the man?'

'Not a great deal. I believe he is unmarried and spends all his time in the clubs and gaming hells. I have heard he does not always play fair, though no one has seen fit to challenge him. If he has Teddy's vouchers, it could go ill for the Cavenhursts.'

'So that was what you were in a brown study about?'

'It is worrying.'

'Are you concerned about the dowry?'

'Good heavens, no! It is the least of my worries.'

'So, we are still going to look for wedding finery tomorrow?'

'Naturally we are.' They stopped outside Drew's lodgings. 'And you are going to come back to Broadacres with me, aren't you?'

'Have I said that?'

'No, but you will. I want you to meet Isabel again before the wedding. We will invite the Cavenhursts over for supper.'

Drew laughed. 'In the face of such a prospect, how can I refuse?'

Mark went on his way to the Wyndham town house in South Audley Street well satisfied.

Chapter Two

'Papa, can you spare me a minute?' Jane had found her father in the estate office where he worked most mornings. The desk in front of him was scattered with papers. He had evidently been raking his fingers through his greying hair; some of it was standing up on end.

'Oh, it is you, Jane. Come in and sit down. I thought it was that reprobate son of mine and I can hardly be civil to him at the moment.'

Jane advanced further into the room and sat on the chair placed the other side of the desk, a position usually occupied by the estate manager, but she had just seen him leave and knew her father was alone. 'I am sorry to hear that, Papa. It is on his behalf I am come.'

'So, he has descended to sending his sister to plead for him, has he?'

'He feels that you have not fully comprehended the trouble he is in and that perhaps I can explain it better than he.'

Sir Edward managed a humourless laugh. 'I comprehend it only too well, Jane. What *he* does not comprehend is how impossible it is for me to comply with his outrageous demands without impoverishing the rest of the family.'

Jane gasped. 'Surely it is not as bad as that?'

'It is every bit as bad as that. My investments have failed. Last year's ruined harvest and the demands of my tenants for repairs, not to mention Isabel's wedding, have been the last straw. We are going to have to retrench. I am sorry, but Teddy will have to find his own solution. I warned him the last time he came home that it was the last time. He must learn I meant it.'

'But what is he to do, Papa? He is young and impressionable, it is only natural he wants to spread his wings and keep up with his friends.'

'Then he should choose his friends more wisely.'

'But, Papa…'

'Jane, you will displease me if you continue. You have a soft and gentle heart and it is to your credit, but in this instance you are backing a lost cause. You would do better to put your mind to ways of retrenchment, ways that your mother will accept as reasonable.'

'Very well, Papa.' She rose to go, then turned back. 'Isabel's wedding is not in jeopardy, is it?'

'No, I think we can manage that.'

She left her father, but did not immediately seek out her brother. She needed a little time to herself and she needed to think about the task her father had set her. One thing was very sure: her inheritance was going to have to be sacrificed and the sooner she accepted that the better. She went up to her bedchamber, put on a light shawl and a bonnet and set out for the village.

But for the problems that weighed her down she would have enjoyed the short walk. The sun was shining, the birds were singing and the hedgerows were bright with blossom. Hadlea village, set in the north Norfolk fenland, was not a large one. There was a church, a rectory, a windmill, two inns and several cottages grouped around a triangular village green on which there was a pump and some old stocks, though no one had been put in those in her memory. Side roads from the green led to a farrier and harness-maker who also mended shoes, a butcher and a tiny front-room shop that sold almost anything the village women might need from salt to sugar and soap to candles, working boots to plain cotton tick. For anything like muslin and silk, ribbons and bonnets, they had to make a trip to Norwich or King's Lynn or wait until the travelling salesman came round, usually at the end of the harvest when his customers had a little money to spend.

Jane made her way to the rectory and was greeted cheerfully by Mrs Caulder. 'Come in, Jane, I will have some tea and cakes brought into the parlour. It's time Henry came out of his study. He has been in there all morning, working on tomorrow's sermon.'

Mrs Caulder was very plump, a testament to a love of her cook's cakes. She fussed around, giving the orders and calling her husband to join them, while Jane sat on one of the chairs and wondered how she was going to explain that the five thousand pounds she had promised for their project would not be forthcoming. She could not divulge the true state of affairs.

'How are you my dear?' Mrs Caulder asked. 'Did you walk here? I did not hear the pony and trap.'

'I walked. It is such a lovely day.' Even as she spoke, she wondered if the pony would have to go, or perhaps the carriage, or the riding horses.

'To be sure it is. Ah, here is Henry.'

The Rector was of medium height, with a shock of grey hair, which he wore long and tied back with a thin black ribbon. He was a jovial man and beamed at Jane. 'What a pleasure to see you, my dear Miss Cavenhurst. I hope I find you well.'

'Very well. But I am afraid I have some disappointing news.'

'Surely not the wedding?' exclaimed his wife, handing Jane a cup of tea.

'Oh, no, nothing like that. It's simply that I cannot give our orphan project the five thousand I promised.' She paused, then resorted to an untruth. 'I find I cannot touch it until either I marry or I reach the age of thirty in three years' time. I have been racking my brains trying to think of a way of going ahead without it.'

'My dear girl, do not look so downbeat, it is not the end of the world,' the Rector said, flinging up the skirt of his coat and seating himself beside his wife to take a cup of tea from her. 'We will contrive somehow without it. We shall have to find a wealthy patron, more than one if need be. I never did feel quite at ease about you giving it in the first place.'

'Oh, I am much relieved,' Jane said. 'I thought it would be the end of all our hopes. You have given me fresh heart.'

'There are orphanages all over the country, some a great deal better run than others. We must ask them how they manage and draw up a list of possible patrons. You, I am sure, could persuade people to donate. It is a good cause and you are so passionate about it.'

Jane laughed at that and the rest of the visit passed cheerfully. She was still smiling as she started out to cross the green on her way home. She had her head down, deep in thought, and did not see the two men until she was almost abreast of them.

'Jane, we are well met,' Mark called out to her.

She looked up, startled, and found herself hurtling back ten years. The man beside Mark was unmistakable. The years had dealt kindly with him. He was tall, broad and muscular and dressed to perfection in a brown coat of Bath cloth and fawn buckskins tucked into shining tasselled Hessians. A gold watch chain hung across his creamy brocade waistcoat and a huge diamond sparkled in his cravat. All this she noted before lifting her eyes to look into his face. It was tanned and the only lines were around his hazel eyes, due either to laughter or squinting in the sun. He was regarding her with a look she interpreted as amusement. Was she a comical figure? To be sure, her dress was plain, but her shawl was pretty and the ribbons on her bonnet were new even if the bonnet was not.

'You remember Miss Cavenhurst, do you not?' Mark said to him. 'This is Jane, sister to my fiancée.'

'Of course I remember,' Drew said, doffing his hat. 'How do you do, Miss Cavenhurst?'

'I am well. And you?' She had often wondered what it would be like to meet him again and whether the old attraction would still be there. He was an extremely attractive man, to be sure, and a great deal more confident than the man she had sent away, but after ten years, it would have been surprising if she had not found him changed.

'I am in good health, Miss Cavenhurst, and happy to renew acquaintance with you. It has been some time.'

'Ten years,' she murmured and then wished she had not mentioned the time. He would assume she had been counting and dwelling on it, which was the last impression she wished to give him.

'Yes, and every one of them devoted to the goal of returning one day, having made my fortune.'

'And have you?'

'I believe so.'

'He is a nabob,' Mark said, laughing. 'But underneath he is the same Drew Ashton I knew before he went away. He has come to stay with us at Broadacres and be my groomsman.'

'I thought you already had someone,' Jane said, turning towards him. He was almost as tall as Drew, but slimmer and his urbane good looks contrasted sharply with the weathered look of his friend.

'So I did, but he has been called away and when I met Drew in London, the solution to my problem was obvious.'

'How fortuitous for you.' She turned back to Drew. 'So, you came to see how we all go on in Hadlea, Mr Ashton. We are a quiet community, little changes here.'

'Except we all grow older and wiser,' he said.

'That is true, of course.' Was that some reference to their youth ten years before or was he telling her his old passion had died a natural death, as surely hers must have done?

'Jane, I need to have a quiet word with you,' Mark said. 'Perhaps Drew will excuse us for a moment?'

'To be sure,' Drew said. 'I will amuse myself exploring the village.' He bowed to Jane. 'Good day, Miss Cavenhurst. I shall look forward to renewing my acquaintance with the rest of your family while I am here.'

She bowed her head in acknowledgement. 'Good day, Mr Ashton.'

She watched him stride away, then turned back to Mark. 'He is much changed and yet he has not changed at all.'

'Except he is richer,' Mark said with a laugh.

'What is it you wanted to speak to me about?' She did not want to talk about Andrew Ashton. His sudden arrival was something else she had to deal with. Would he mention the past or would it be a closed book? She hoped the latter. She did not want to be reminded of it.

Mark's smile died and he seemed to be reluctant to go on, which was so unlike him that she wondered what it could be. 'Jane, I met Lord Bolsover while I was in London. Drew and I had a hand of whist with him and a friend of his at White's.'

'Oh, surely you are not a gambling man, Mark? Gambling is an insidious evil.'

'I only play for amusement now and again and never for high stakes. You play yourself of an evening, do you not?'

'Yes, when we have company and then for counters, not money. But do go on.'

'Bolsover is not a man I would normally associate with, but Drew wanted a game.'

'Mark, you are beating about the bush. You are going to tell me Teddy owes him money, aren't you?'

'You know of it?'

'I am the first person my brother comes to when he is in trouble.'

'I believe he owes Lord Bolsover a substantial amount—will you tell me how much?'

'Mark, I know you mean well, but Teddy would not like me to divulge the figure, not even to you. Why do you want to know?'

'Lord Bolsover is putting it about that Teddy is a welsher and he will have his money by hook or by crook. He even hinted he would have the Manor.'

She gasped. 'It is not so large an amount, Mark. He cannot do that, can he?'

'Not while your papa is alive, but when Teddy inherits, that will be a different matter. Isabel will be with me, of course, but I am concerned for you and your mother and Sophie. Can Sir Edward settle the debts?'

She hesitated. To her shame, she had already told one untruth that day and she did not want to tell another, especially to Mark, but he had truly frightened her with his tale that Lord Bolsover had bought up all Teddy's debts, the full extent of which she did not know.

'Come, Jane, I am soon to be family and would help if I could. I will not repeat what you tell me.'

'Whether Papa can or cannot is not to the point, Mark. He simply refuses.'

'Oh, dear, does he know how deep in Teddy is?'

'I do not know, Teddy may have told him, but if matters are as bad as you say, Papa would have a struggle to settle, I think. Like everyone he has been badly hit by taxes and poor harvests. I shall do what I can for Teddy with my own money and that may hold his lordship off for a time.'

'Jane, you cannot do that. Your money is your dowry.'

She gave him a crooked grin. 'I am never likely to marry, Mark, and we all know it.'

'Nonsense. You would make someone a splendid wife and I know that you love children. I have seen you with them in the village.' He laughed suddenly. 'If I were not already taken, I might offer myself.'

She could not help it, the tears spilled from her eyes.

It was so unlike the down-to-earth Jane, he became alarmed. He put his arm about her and pulled her to him, so that her head nestled on his shoulder. 'I didn't think that would make you cry, Jane. I beg forgiveness.'

Angry with herself, she pulled away from him. 'Oh, it wasn't that. It was…' She gulped. 'It was the thought of Teddy's debts bringing us so low.' She dried her eyes and managed a laugh. 'I could cheerfully beat him.'

'So could I.'

'Isabel knows nothing of it, so please do not say anything. We mustn't spoil her wedding. I have no doubt we will come about.'

'I will escort you home.'

'No, please don't. I shall be fine. Go back to Mr Ashton; he is obviously waiting for you.' She nodded towards Drew, who was idling on the other side of the green.

It was typical of Jane, to be so unselfish, Mark thought as he rejoined Drew. She always thought of others before herself and that blinkered family of hers took her for granted. Even Isabel, while singing her praises, took advantage of her. As for their brother, he was a scapegrace without an ounce of conscience or good sense and to apply to his sister whenever he was in trouble was the outside of enough. He could pay the debt for them, but he was quite sure Sir Edward would be too proud to accept it, though he did not doubt Teddy would take it eagerly and then go on as before. It would be like throwing money into a bottomless pit. Teddy needed to be taught a salutary lesson. But what and how? It needed some thought and he would do nothing until after the wedding.

'If I did not know you better, I would think you were

a little too fond of your future sister-in-law,' Drew said as they turned to walk back to Broadacres.

'Nonsense. I am afraid I unintentionally upset her.'

'Didn't look like that to me.'

'Looks can be deceptive and it is none of your business anyway, Drew.'

'True, and neither is it true of those old biddies standing by that garden gate, but I have no doubt they will make it so.'

Mark glanced in the direction of Drew's nod. Mrs Stangate and her crony, Mrs Finch, were standing at the former's garden gate, watching them. 'Oh, no, the two biggest gossips in the village. They will add two and two and make five.'

'Whatever did you say to her? It must have been something very telling for you to abandon your usual sense of propriety.'

'I expressed the wish to beat her brother.'

Drew laughed. 'Oh, I assume you told her of our meeting with Lord Bolsover.'

'Yes, but she already knew some of what Teddy had been up to but, I suspect, not the whole. It makes me angry the way everyone in that family leans on Jane and expects her to fetch them out of whatever bumblebath they have tumbled into.'

'Is that so?'

'Yes. She has given up everything for them and is now proposing to use her own money to pay off Teddy's debt.'

'Does she know how much that is?'

'I don't think so. Nor do I think she has enough. According to Isabel, their grandmother left each of the girls a little money for a dowry. Isabel has already spent hers on her trousseau, so it cannot have been a great amount.'

'Tell me,' Drew said thoughtfully. 'Why did you choose Isabel over Jane, when you so clearly have a high regard for her?'

Mark hesitated before replying, trying to find a satisfactory answer. 'A high regard is not love, is it? Jane has much to commend her, but I did not think of her in that way. Everyone, and that includes me, simply accepted that she was not going to marry and it became easy to think of her as Isabel's unmarried sister. Unfair, perhaps, but that is the way of it.' How unfair he was only now beginning to realise.

'And Isabel?'

'Isabel is beautiful and lively and she loves me. What more can a man ask?'

'What indeed,' Drew murmured.

'Have you never been in love?'

'Frequently. I have been in love with every mistress while it lasts, but it never does. They always reveal their true colours in the end.'

'Then you have not been in love at all. Love is meant to last a lifetime.'

'Is that so?'

'Yes. I fear you are too cynical, Drew. What has made you like that? Have you been disappointed?'

'I have just said so. Frequently.'

'I was not talking about mistresses and you know it. I meant a proper young lady.' He paused, remembering something Drew had said. 'Oh, the young lady who turned you down. That hurt, did it not?'

'At the time, yes.'

'So have you come back to try again?'

'No. It happened too long ago, we are both changed.'

'Who is she?'

'That would be telling.'

'Then tell.'

'One day, perhaps. Now can we change the subject? I find it exceedingly boring.'

Mark laughed. 'Very well, keep your secrets. Would you like to ride this afternoon? We could go round the estate and across the common to the fen. I can find you a good mount.'

'An excellent idea.'

They turned in at the wrought-iron gates of Broadacres and made their way up the gravel drive to the house. It was a very large house, testament to the wealth of the Wyndham forebears who had built it. Almost a castle, it had a turret on each of its four corners and a cantilevered flight of stone steps up to a huge oaken front door. Four storeys high and with a crenellated roof decorated with carvings, its long windows reflected the sun and shone like a myriad of mirrors. Mark loved it. It was his inheritance and it was to this home he would bring his bride. It was certainly extensive enough to support two families; he did not need or want to find another home for himself and Isabel.

'What do you think of Broadacres?' he asked his friend. 'Is it as you remember it?'

'Yes. Even better. Lord Wyndham has a good estate manager, methinks.'

'The best, but my father likes to involve himself in the running of it and he always tries to include me in any decisions, so when the time comes—though I pray it is a long time off—I will be able to take over with little or no disruption.'

'You have your life planned out so neatly, Mark, does nothing ever upset your equilibrium?'

'Occasionally, but I try not to let it. To be constantly up in the boughs is not good for one's health.'

Drew laughed. 'Then you and I must differ. I like a little excitement, doing something out of the ordinary just to feel I am alive.'

'Was India not exciting enough?'

'It had its moments.'

'Tell me about it. I promised Isabel we would travel widely for our wedding trip and India might be the place to go.'

'It is an extraordinary continent. There is enormous wealth and abject poverty side by side, and there are always battles of one kind or another between the natives and the East India Company. It is also very beautiful if you can tolerate the heat. The best place to be in the summer months is up in the mountains. If you really intend to go and I have bought my ship, you could take passage on her. It will be my wedding gift to you both.'

'That is very generous of you, thank you.'

'Not at all. You and your parents have been generous to me. I have not forgotten that.'

'We shall have to find you a bride.'

'If I need a bride, I will find one for myself,' Drew said. 'I abhor matchmakers. Begging your pardon, my friend.'

Mark laughed and they climbed the steps and entered the cool interior of the house.

Jane walked home with her head in a whirl of mixed emotions. The last few days had upset the even tenor of her life. From helping her sister with her wedding, determined to make it the best she possibly could in the hope that it would settle her demons, she had been flung into

what she could only call disarray. First there was Teddy
and his problems, which were bad enough, then her father's revelation that they were not nearly as comfortable
financially as everyone thought and now the sudden arrival of a ghost from the past which unnerved her. Was
she as immune to him as she had always hoped she would
be if they ever met again? Only time would tell; he had
taken her breath away and made her heart beat fast, but
what did that signify except surprise? How long did he
intend to stay? According to Mark he was down for the
wedding, still three weeks away. And to top it all, Mark
had seen her cry and had taken her in his arms and the
demon that sat on her shoulder had done a little dance of
glee. At all costs she must conquer it.

She took the long way home in order to calm herself
and put her mind to what was important, so she turned
down a quiet lane that led into the ancient wood which
shielded the house from the north wind that came down
from the Arctic with nothing in its way to stop it.

The woods were quiet, but there were sounds if one
took the trouble to listen. The song of the birds, always
stronger in spring; the cooing of pigeons; the rustling of
small animals in the last of the dead leaves; the sighing
of the wind in the tree tops; the distant barking of a dog;
her own, almost silent, footsteps. And there were other
things to see and note: the buds on the chestnut trees; the
unfurling of pale, new bracken stems; bluebells with their
gently nodding heads; the odd browned leaf hanging on
the bare branch of an oak, not yet in new leaf; a butterfly emerging from its chrysalis and drying its wings in a
patch of sunlight filtering through the branches. Spring
was a time of new beginnings, of hope. Where was her
life going from here? Would she go on as she had been

doing for the last ten years, or would it take a different direction? How could she best help her father?

She emerged on to the lane, crossed the narrow road and went through a gate which led to the back of the house. She stood a moment to look at it. It was old, but not as old as Broadacres, having been built just before the Civil War, when it was sequestered by the Parliamentarians and given to her father's ancestors for their service to the cause. They seemed not to have suffered for their allegiance because in the subsequent restoration of the monarchy, they had been allowed to keep the prize. It had all happened a hundred and fifty years before and Sir Edward rarely spoke of it. Jane had deduced he was perhaps a little disappointed that his forebears had not been granted a peerage, which would have set him above the common people. He made up for it with aspirations for his daughters, which was why he had been so against any connection between Jane and Andrew Ashton. Jane, who adored her father and always obeyed him, had sent her suitor away.

It would be untrue to say she had mourned his going ever since. She grieved for a year or so and then pulled herself together to settle into her role as the unmarried daughter and everyone's hopes had turned on Isabel. A marriage between Mark and Isabel had been talked of for years, but he had not formally proposed until he came back from the war. Ever since then everyone's attention had been concentrated on the wedding. But now, it seemed, that was destined to be overshadowed by financial problems. Her father had asked her to think of ways of retrenchment and she had so far done nothing about it. She would do so that very afternoon and draw up a list.

Pulling herself up, she quickened her pace and was

soon indoors. Having shed her shawl and bonnet in her room, she went downstairs to the small parlour where she found her mother and Isabel scrutinising the guest list for the wedding. Most of their close friends and neighbours knew about it already, but there were others further afield that Lady Cavenhurst felt ought to be invited. In that they were at loggerheads with Sir Edward.

'Papa says we do not need to invite so many,' Isabel complained when Jane took a seat beside them. 'He says it is all getting out of hand and we must limit the number to fifty, when I had been planning on a hundred and fifty, at least.'

'Do we really know that many people?' Jane asked mildly.

'Of course we do. Papa is being unreasonable.'

'No doubt he has his reasons. Let me look at the list.'

Isabel handed it to her. 'But there is everyone here you have ever spoken half-a-dozen words to, Issie,' she said, scanning it quickly. 'They would only come to stuff themselves at the banquet and not to wish you well. Would it not be better for it to be a little more intimate, with only close relations and friends who would be happy for you? Mark, I notice, has not asked for a great number to be invited and you do not want his guests to be overwhelmed by yours, do you? It would look like a slight, an effort to diminish him.'

'Would it? I hadn't thought of that. Now you have put a doubt in my mind. Mama, shall we cross some of them off?'

'Perhaps we should take another look at it,' her ladyship said. 'But we really cannot limit our guests to fifty—that would be parsimonious.'

It was evident to Jane that her mother either did not

know or was shutting her eyes to the extent of their financial problems and her father had lacked the courage to tell her. Unless she had badly misjudged the situation he would have to do so soon

'There is one that will not be coming, I have discovered. I met Mark in the village and he told me Jonathan Smythe has been called away to a relation's death bed and he has appointed a new groomsman. No doubt he will tell you when he sees you.'

'Which will be tomorrow evening,' Lady Cavenhurst said. 'We are all invited to Broadacres for supper.'

'All of us?' Jane queried, her heart sinking.

'Yes, of course. Lady Wyndham would not leave anyone out, would she? Did Mark say who his new groomsman is to be?'

'Yes. Mr Andrew Ashton. He was with Mark when I met him.'

'Ashton!' exclaimed her mother. 'Why on earth did he choose him?'

'He is an old friend of Mark's, Mama, so why not?'

'Andrew Ashton,' Isabel murmured. 'Didn't he come and stay at Broadacres years ago?'

'I believe he did.' Jane said. 'He is much changed, having come back from India after making his fortune there.'

'India! Mark has said we may go there for our wedding trip. I shall enjoy asking Mr Ashton all about it. Mama, what shall we wear for this supper party? Is it to be formal?'

'No, dear, Lady Wyndham says informal on her invitation and there is to be music and cards.'

'Then we must contrive to keep Teddy away from the card table,' Jane said, a remark upon which they all agreed.

* * *

The interior of Broadacres was as imposing as the exterior. It had a grand entrance hall where the cantilevered staircase of the outside was repeated with the addition of a wrought-iron balustrade. There was a long gallery lined on one side with paintings, not only of the family, but of landscapes and seascapes, horses, dogs and cattle. There were long windows on the other side, which looked out over the sweep of the carriage drive. Chairs and sofas were placed at intervals and a long Turkish carpet laid down the centre covered the stone flags. Off this gallery were several beautifully furnished reception rooms, a book room, a formal dining room and at the far end, occupying the whole of the ground floor of one wing, a magnificent ball room. Upstairs the bedchambers were equally spacious and well equipped.

'To think this will be your home,' Jane whispered to Isabel as they were conducted down the gallery and along a corridor to the family withdrawing room. Ahead of them marched Sir Edward and Lady Cavenhurst and an unusually subdued Teddy. 'You will one day be mistress of it.'

'Oh, don't say that. It terrifies me. I wish we could have our own place, something smaller and less grand, but Mark will not hear of it. He says it is so big we need never come across his parents if we do not wish to.'

'I am sure you will manage very well.'

The footman who was conducting them opened the door of the withdrawing room and announced them one by one as they entered. As Lady Wyndham came forward to greet Sir Edward and his wife, Jane looked about her. Although it was a grand room, it had a comfortable feel about it, as if real people lived in it and used it, unlike the public rooms at the front of the building which seemed cold and impersonal.

She came out of her reverie when she heard Lady Wyndham introducing Drew to her father and mother and Sir Edward's response. 'I believe we have met, sir.'

'Indeed, you have,' Mark put in. 'Mr Ashton stayed with us for a few weeks when we left Cambridge. That was… How long ago, Drew?'

'I do believe it was all of ten years,' Drew responded. 'So long that I am not at all surprised that Sir Edward has forgot me. I was but a stripling with pockets to let.'

'Now he is a nabob.' Mark laughed. 'As rich as Golden Ball and certainly no stripling.'

'That much is evident,' Sir Edward said. Jane knew he was remembering and wondering if he had come to renew his suit. She had wondered about that herself, but dismissed the idea. Too much water had flowed under the bridge in those years.

Lady Wyndham turned to Jane. 'Do I need to introduce you to our guest, Jane?'

'No, for I remember him very well, but I doubt Isabel and Sophie do.'

'No, I don't,' Sophie said. 'I never met a nabob either. What does a nabob do?' She addressed her last remark to Drew, who was bowing in front of her.

'He trades in India, Miss Sophie,' he said. 'He sends Indian artefacts, spices and jewels back to these islands in fast ships and they return with items of English manufacture, furniture, ornaments, gowns, those sorts of things, and thereby he makes a profit.'

'And have you made a good profit, Mr Ashton?' This came from Isabel, who had been standing beside her sister, staring at Drew in fascination.

He bowed to her. 'Tolerable, Miss Isabel. You see, I do remember you, though you were still at your lessons at the time.'

'Let us sit down until supper is served,' Lady Wyndham said, ushering them towards chairs and sofas.

They arranged themselves about the room and Isabel contrived to be sitting next to Drew. 'Do tell me about India,' she said. 'Mark has promised to take me there after we are married and I would like to learn all I can before we go. Tell me, is it necessary to speak the language and wear... What do they call those gowns the natives wear?'

'Saris, Miss Isabel. They are more intricate than they look, but they are very cool in the heat and the fabrics are superb. I have known European women take to them when the heat has become too much.'

'Oh, I should dearly like to try one.'

'I am sure you would look charming,' he said.

'And what about the language? Is it difficult to learn?'

'There are several languages in India, but you would not need to learn any of them. The native servants speak a kind of pidgin English and, apart from visits to the bazaar, you would not need to communicate with other natives. And you would never go to the bazaar unless accompanied by someone familiar with the language and customs.'

Jane watched this exchange with some misgiving. It was not polite of her sister to monopolise the gentleman, certainly not at the expense of Mark, who was standing by the window watching them. On the pretence of looking out at the terrace and formal gardens beyond it, she went over to stand beside him.

'She means no harm, Mark,' she whispered. 'She is

simply interested because you said you would take her
to India.'

'I know.'

A footman came to tell them supper was served and
they made their way into the dining room. They were
silent while the servants waited on them, but the conversation began again when they stood aside, this time
led by Lord Wyndham and Sir Edward, who began a
discussion about the dire state of the nation's economy.
The year before had been miserable, with no summer to
speak of, the crops failing and labourers and returning
soldiers out of work. There was unrest among them everywhere. At the end of the year there had been a mass
meeting at Spa Fields, addressed by Henry Hunt, who
had a gift for rabble-rousing, and the whole thing had got
out of hand and had to be quelled by the militia. Revolu-
tionary plots were being uncovered everywhere, which
had led the Government to suspend habeas corpus and
outlaw seditious meetings.

'It is a mercy we have escaped here in Hadlea,' his
lordship said. 'I have managed to keep all my men employed and even take on one or two more. No doubt it is
the same with you, Cavenhurst?'

'Indeed,' Sir Edward said, though he did not elaborate.
Jane knew he had not taken on any men for some time,
not even when old Crabtree retired at the age of eighty
and one of the younger men went off to pastures new.

'At least there is some good news,' Lady Wyndham
put in. 'Princess Charlotte is with child again and there
are high hopes that she will carry this one to full term.'

'Let us hope so,' Lord Wyndham said. 'A new heir
to the throne will divert people from their dislike of the
Regent.' An attempt on the Prince Regent's life had been

made in January when an unknown assailant fired at his carriage on the way back from opening Parliament, but fortunately he had been unhurt.

'I am concerned for the soldiers' orphans,' Jane said. 'They are living on the streets, learning nothing but to be beggars and thieves. They need homes and a little education to fit them for work when they are old enough.'

'Yes, it is sad,' her mother said. 'But, Jane, I am sure Lord and Lady Wyndham do not want to hear of your project.'

'On the contrary,' Lord Wyndham said. 'I, for one, am interested and should like to hear about it.' He was a very big man, both in height and breadth, with a round red face, but he smiled a lot and was easy to talk to.

Given a ready listener, Jane launched into an explanation of what she hoped to do, while his lordship and the rest of the company listened intently. She was glad of the audience, it gave her the opportunity to test her persuasive skills. 'I intend to start with something small, taking local children,' she said. 'But even a small home will be costly to run properly. We have to find sponsors.'

'Jane!' Her mother was shocked by this talk of money over the supper table.

Lord Wyndham laughed. 'You daughter is undoubtedly passionate about the subject. I like that and you may count on me for a donation, Miss Cavenhurst.'

'Thank you, my lord, I am indeed grateful.'

'I, too, will add to your funds,' Drew said. 'What about you, Mark?'

'Miss Cavendish explained her plans to me some time ago,' Mark said. 'I have already promised my contribution.'

'Everyone is being very free with their blunt,' Teddy murmured to Jane.

'Yes, isn't it wonderful?' she whispered back. 'It's better than gambling it away.'

Annoyed by this barb, he turned away and concentrated on eating.

'Now let us talk of more pleasant matters,' Lady Wyndham said. She was an excellent hostess and had seen, if not heard, the exchange between Jane and her brother. 'How are the wedding plans coming along, Grace?'

Lady Cavenhurst was glad to answer and the meal ended pleasantly and was followed in the drawing room with the girls taking it in turns to play the pianoforte and sing, while a card table was set up for those who wished to play. It was late when the party broke up and Sir Edward's carriage was brought to the door to take them home.

Chapter Three

'Mr Ashton is a fascinating man, don't you think?' Isabel asked Jane. 'He has been everywhere and done everything and is so interesting to talk to.'

It was the day after the supper party and the girls and their mother were sitting in the small parlour. Jane was sewing tiny beads on to the skirt of the wedding gown, while Lady Cavenhurst and Isabel sat at the table, writing the invitations on cards.

'So he may be,' Jane said, 'but I think it ill of you to monopolise him in conversation and ignore poor Mark.'

'Oh, Mark did not mind it. He knows how much I want to travel.' She picked up one of the invitations. 'There, I have made a blot on that one. Pass me another, Mama, please.'

'How many have you crossed off the list?' Jane queried.

'About a quarter. We could not take any more off without giving offence and we don't want Papa to look a pinchcommons, do we?'

'I do not think catering for fifty is mean, Issie. Papa is worried about the cost. You know what he said this morning.'

Earlier that day Sir Edward had come in from going round the estate with his steward and found his wife and daughters in the morning room, talking about the wedding. Seizing the opportunity of finding them all together, he had delivered a homily on the need to economise. It was a word unknown to Lady Cavenhurst and Isabel. Jane had produced the list she had made, beginning with the notion that they could all spend less on clothes, bonnets and shoes, which had raised a cry of protest from Isabel and Sophie. A second suggestion was that they often wasted food and that Cook should be instructed not to buy exotic produce like lemons and pineapples and only to use fruit and vegetables grown in their own kitchen gardens and to cook no more than was needed for the numbers sitting down to eat. Her ladyship had said that Cook would not like that at all and the provisions for the wedding feast had already been ordered.

'Unfortunately, even that will not be enough,' Sir Edward had said. 'I am afraid there will have to be serious retrenchment.'

Jane had consulted her list again. 'Then we could cut down on the number of servants. We do not really need three chambermaids and three parlourmaids, and if we helped in the garden ourselves we would not need so many gardeners. I, for one, would not mind doing that. And we could do without the carriage if we had to.'

'Do without the carriage!' her mother protested. 'How are we to go about without one? Tell me that.'

'We could keep the pony and trap,' Jane said. 'One pony is cheaper to keep than four horses and then we would not need more than one groom; Daniel can manage on his own. If we needed to travel further afield, we could go by stage.'

'Go by stage!' Her mother was affronted. 'Impossible.'

'Perhaps I could take paid employment to help,' Jane went on, ignoring her mother's exclamation. She wondered if her mother really understood the gravity of the situation or was simply shutting her eyes to it.

'Heaven forbid!' her ladyship exclaimed. 'You have not been brought up to work, Jane. And what can you do in any case?'

'I can sew.'

'Like Miss Smith, I suppose.'

'No, not like Miss Smith, though there is nothing wrong with what she does. I meant designing and making high-class gowns. Or I could teach. I think I should find that rewarding.'

'Bless you, Jane,' Sir Edward said. 'I hope it will not come to that.'

'Well, I will not hear of it,' his wife said. 'You will make paupers of us.'

'There is no question of that,' he said, trying to smile. 'But we do have to find ways of making substantial savings and the longer we put off doing so, the harder it will be.'

'What about my wedding?' Isabel had wailed.

'I am not proposing to curtail your wedding, Isabel,' her father told her. 'But please limit the guests to fifty and try not to be extravagant over the banquet.'

'We will postpone any decision about savings until after the wedding,' her ladyship said firmly. 'Once Isabel is married, no doubt Sophie will follow shortly afterwards and our expenses will not be so great. We may come about without all these measures.'

Sir Edward gave up and left them. No one had mentioned Teddy's problems, but he was going to have to mend his ways whether he liked it or not. There was no question in Jane's mind that her inheritance would have to go.

She set the gown aside on a nearby chair. 'Let me look at the list.'

'No,' Isabel said. 'You will cross everyone off and Mama has approved it. You shall not spoil my wedding, Jane.'

'Will it spoil it if you have only fifty guests?'

'Of course it will. I want everyone to see me in my wedding gown, marrying the most eligible bachelor for miles around.'

'The wedding is not the be-all and end-all of a marriage, Issie. It is only the beginning.'

'I know that. Do you take me for a fool? And what do you know of it?'

'Girls, do stop brangling,' her ladyship put in. 'It is not becoming and I cannot see how a handful of guests can make you so up in the boughs, Jane dear. It is so unlike you.'

The arrival of a maid to tell them that Mr Wyndham and Mr Ashton had arrived and were asking if the ladies were at home put an end to the conversation and set Isabel in a panic. 'Mark mustn't see the dress, Jane. It is unlucky before the day. Put it away quickly.' She jumped up from her seat and knocked over the ink bottle. Its contents ran across the table and over the chair on which Jane had put the dress. Isabel's terrible shriek brought the two gentlemen running into the room.

'What has happened?' Mark demanded. 'Are you hurt, Isabel?'

'Go away. Go away,' she shouted in a paroxysm of angry tears.

'But, my dear, you are distressed.'

'We have had a little accident with the wedding dress,' Jane told him. She was trying to be calm, but the sight of that black stain on the skirt of the dress had made her heart sink. The beautiful fabric and all those hours of work were ruined. She could have cried herself, but one sobbing woman was enough. 'I will calm my sister, if you will excuse us for a few minutes.'

'Of course, we will go away and come back later.'

'That would be best,' Lady Cavenhurst said, as she put her arm about her younger daughter to comfort her.

As they bowed their way out Jane rang the bell for a maid to come and clean the table, then she spread the gown out to inspect the damage. 'It might wash out if we are quick,' she said.

'No, it is ruined,' Isabel cried. 'How can I go to my wedding in a gown that has been washed? It is a bad omen, a very bad omen.'

'Do not be so melodramatic, Issie,' Jane scolded. 'I will see if there is enough material left over to replace that panel.' She doubted if there was, but she had to console Isabel somehow.

'There,' her ladyship said. 'Jane does not think it is irretrievable. Do dry your eyes and go up to your room to wash your face, while Jane sees what can be done.'

'It was her fault,' Isabel said with an angry pout. 'She should not have been sitting so close to the table where I was writing.'

Jane was taken aback and opened her mouth to protest, then shut it again. Isabel was in no mood to be reasonable.

'I do not know what is the matter with you girls today,' their mother said. 'I have not heard you quarrel so much since you were tiny children. This wedding is setting everyone at odds with each other.'

A servant arrived to clean up the table and the carpet where some of the ink had spilled and her ladyship helped Isabel from the room, leaving Jane to gather up the gown, being careful not to smear the ink on any other part of it. She carried it up to Miss Smith's workroom, to find the leftover material.

There were several small pieces but not one large enough for a whole panel. She would need some ingenuity to refashion the skirt to make use of them. A join could perhaps be disguised with a band of ribbon, but she would have to put it on all the panels to make it look as if it were meant it to be like that. She would have to unpick some of the embroidery and redesign it around the ribbon. It could be done, but what worried her more and had been doing so for some time now, was her sister's attitude to the wedding. She did not seem to be able to look beyond it to what married life would really be like. 'But what do I know about it?' she murmured to herself, as she sat down and began unpicking. 'An old maid with no prospects of ever enjoying the role of wife.'

She had been working there perhaps half an hour when her mother joined her. 'I have given Isabel a tisane and she has gone to sleep,' she said. 'She was a little calmer and is relying on you to rescue the gown.'

'I think I can, but I will need to have a join halfway down the skirt. I thought of disguising it with ribbon. I am unpicking the skirt now.'

'It was very naughty of her to blame you. I am sure she will apologise when she wakes up.'

'It doesn't matter.'

'Jane, are you very unhappy?'

'Unhappy, Mama, what makes you think that?'

'I thought perhaps the arrival of Mr Ashton might have cast you in the suds.'

Jane managed to laugh. 'After ten years, Mama? Certainly not.'

'I am glad. I know he is now wealthy and sure of himself, but his wealth has come from trade; he is still not a gentleman, nor ever can be.'

'Not in the sense you mean it, Mama, but gentlemanly behaviour and good manners can be learned and I doubt Mr Ashton's antecedents, or lack of them, will make him any less popular in the *ton*.'

'So, you do still have feelings for him?'

'No, Mama, I do not. I was simply trying to be fair to him.' She realised suddenly that what she had said was true. It was not Andrew Ashton who disturbed her heart, but someone much closer to home.

'It is so like you to see the good in everyone, Jane. But if it is not Mr Ashton, what is troubling you?'

'It is Isabel. She seems not to be able to look beyond the wedding day itself and I am afraid she is in for a rude awakening.'

'I cannot think why. Mark is the best of men, he can be relied upon to do his best to make her happy. You must not begrudge her her day, just because...' Her ladyship stopped in mid-sentence.

'Because I will never have one of my own, is that what you were going to say, Mama? Do not think it. I do not. I am content with my life as it is.'

'But every young lady dreams of being married.'

'Not every young lady, Mama.' She was firm on that score, as much to convince herself as her mother.

'You are a good daughter and a good sister, Jane. I would not change you for the world. Teddy tells me you are going to help him out of the coil he is in, since his papa will not, in spite of my pleading.'

'I didn't exactly say I would, I said I would think about it. It will take all of Aunt Matilda's bequest and I so wanted to use it for my orphanage.'

'Papa will make it up to you, when he has calmed down, I am sure.' She watched as Jane detached the stained skirt panel and set it aside. 'Now, put that away and come downstairs for nuncheon. I have no doubt the gentlemen will be back later this afternoon and we must offer our excuses for Isabel and make little of this morning's episode.'

Jane had done as she was bid and was back at her sewing in the parlour while her mother finished off the invitations when Mark and Drew returned.

'Forgive me for returning so soon,' Mark said, bowing to her ladyship. 'But I was concerned for Isabel. She was so distraught, I feared she was going to make herself ill.'

'It was the shock of seeing the ink on her lovely wedding gown,' her ladyship told him, beckoning the young men to be seated and instructing the maid to bring refreshments. 'She is calm again now that she knows Jane can put it right.'

'I am working on it now,' Jane said. 'I am hopeful that no one will ever know it has been altered.'

'Dear Jane,' Mark said. 'So dependable, so calm in a crisis. We are indebted to you.'

Jane felt the colour flood her face. 'You are a flatterer, sir. I beg you to desist. I only do what any sister would do.'

'That is for others to judge.' To have calmly said she would rescue the gown after Isabel herself had spoiled it and blamed her for it was unselfish to a degree. Isabel had not bothered to lower her voice and it had carried clearly as they were leaving. Delightful Isabel might be, delightful and beautiful, but she also had a fiery temperament, which took no account of other people's feelings. Yet Jane was always thinking of other people before herself. Why was he comparing them? He had been doing too much of that lately and it did not bode well.

'I had better put this away.' She folded the gown in its tissue and laid it to one side. 'Now we can have tea without fear of another spillage.'

'How did it happen?' Drew spoke for the first time.

'Isabel is convinced that it is unlucky for the bridegroom to see the wedding dress before the bride joins him at the altar. She was in haste to have it out of sight before you were shown in and so managed to overturn the ink bottle.'

'I thought it might be that,' he said. 'I am glad the gown is not ruined, but I brought this for your sister in the hope it might make up a little for her loss.' He picked up the brown paper parcel he had been holding on his knee and handed it to Lady Cavenhurst. 'If you would be so kind as to allow her to accept it?'

'What is it?' her ladyship asked, a little doubtfully.

'It is nothing very much, my lady. A length of silk for a sari. Miss Isabel expressed an interest last evening. If she does not wish to use it as a sari, I believe there is enough material to make a gown. Call it a wedding present.'

'How very kind of you.' Her ladyship unwrapped the parcel to find a length of silk in a deep pink that was very similar to that of the wedding gown. There was yards and yards of it but, because it was so fine, it could be folded into a very small parcel.

'It is beautiful,' Jane said, reaching forward to touch it. 'Isabel will be thrilled with it. Mark, what do you say?'

'Oh, undoubtedly,' he answered.

'I brought it from India,' Drew said. 'Not only that one, but several others. When I knew I was coming here, I put them in my baggage as gifts for the ladies.' He grinned suddenly. 'It is good business, you know. The ladies wear gowns made of the silk and when they are asked where they came by them, they refer to me. I chose that one for Miss Isabel because I noticed the colour of the one that had been spoiled.'

'How thoughtful of you,' murmured Lady Cavenhurst. 'And if Mark has no objection, I will make sure she has it.'

'I have no objection, why should I?' Mark said. 'Drew has already presented my mother with one.'

'Would you care for one, Lady Cavenhurst?' Drew asked.

'That is very kind of you, sir, but I think not. I do not have the figure for such a thing.'

'As you wish.' He turned to Jane. 'What about you, Miss Cavenhurst? Would you like one?'

'As Mama said, it is very kind of you, but I could not possibly accept such a gift. It is enough that you have promised to donate to my orphan charity.' It was the answer expected of an unmarried lady, but she could not help feeling a pang of disappointment. She had never seen or touched so fine a fabric.

Isabel, who had heard and seen the gentlemen arrive from her bedchamber window, had hurriedly renewed her *toilette* and came to join them. Both men stood up and Mark hurried to take both her hands in his. 'Are you feeling better, my dear?'

'Yes, don't fuss, Mark. I was upset because I thought my gown was ruined, but Mama told me Jane can fix it, so all is not lost, after all.' She turned to Drew. 'Good afternoon, Mr Ashton. I am sorry I did not greet you properly earlier. Please forgive me.' This was said with a dazzling smile.

He bowed to her. 'It is understandable, Miss Isabel. Gentlemen sometimes do not understand the importance of a lady's dress.'

She gave a tinkling laugh. 'But you do, is that so?'

Jane was shocked at her sister's offhand treatment of Mark and her obvious attempt to flirt with Drew. 'Sit down, Issie,' she said. 'The gentlemen cannot be seated again until you do.'

Jane was sitting beside her mother on one sofa, so Isabel sat on the other. Mark seated himself beside her and Drew found a chair. It was then Isabel noticed the silk in her mother's lap. 'What have you there, Mama?'

'It is a sari, my love. A wedding present to you from Mr Ashton.'

'A sari! Oh, Mama, may I accept it?'

'Mark has said you may, so I have no objection.'

Isabel was on her feet again and letting the material cascade over her arm in shining ripples. 'It's lovely,' she said, bright-eyed. 'Oh, thank you, Mr Ashton. You are so thoughtful, I am overwhelmed.'

'I thought it could be used for a new wedding gown if the other was ruined.'

'But it is not ruined and I want to keep this as a sari. There are yards and yards of it. How is it worn?'

'I think you will need the help of your maid. There is a knack to it.'

'Bessie would not have any idea. Can you show me?'

'Isabel, I am sure Bessie will manage it when you are in your own room,' her mother said. 'The parlour is hardly the place to dress, especially with gentlemen present.'

'Mr Ashton can show me on himself.'

'Isabel!' Her mother was shocked.

'I am too big and too clumsy,' Drew said, laughing. 'I have printed instructions with illustrations for the benefit of European ladies. I will have a copy sent over for your maid to study.'

'That will serve admirably,' her ladyship said. 'Isabel, I suggest you fold it up and take it to your room before you knock your tea all over it.'

'Anyone would think I was clumsy,' she said.

'No, but you are somewhat excitable,' her mother said. 'I beg you to calm yourself.'

Isabel disappeared with the sari and the others drank their tea in silence for a minute or two. Jane was shocked by her sister's behaviour. She would not blame Mark if he gave her a put down when he managed to find her on her own. What motive did Mr Ashton have for making the gift? Was it simply as he had said, a wish to help over the accident with the gown, or was there more to it? He was evidently attracted to her sister. Was Isabel aware of it? Was Mark? He would never believe ill of Isabel. Or was she herself seeing more than was really there?

'The weather is set fair for the next few days,' Mark said. 'I promised to show Drew more of our county and we plan an excursion to Cromer tomorrow. I wondered if

Miss Cavenhurst and Isabel might like to join us, if you and they agree, my lady?'

'I can see no harm in it,' her ladyship said. 'What do you say, Jane? Do you think Isabel would like it?'

'I am sure she would,' Jane answered. She was not so sure about wanting to go herself, but if her sister went then she would have to go, too, or their mother would never allow it.

'That's settled then,' Mark said, rising to leave. 'We will come at ten o'clock tomorrow morning with the carriage.'

The men bowed to the ladies and left.

'When did you think of an outing to Cromer?' Drew asked, as they walked back to Broadacres. 'You did not mention it before we came.'

'I thought the ladies might like it. It might serve to put Isabel in a calmer frame of mind and give Jane a little reward for the hard work she does. You have no objection, have you?'

'None at all.'

Wyndham's carriage was as comfortable as any well-sprung travelling coach could be; there was plenty of room inside for four. Hadlea to Cromer was not above twenty miles and they arrived in a little under two hours, having spent the time in idle chatter, most of it led by Isabel quizzing Drew about India and his travels.

They pulled up at an inn in the lower part of the village near the church, where Jeremy, the coachman, and the horses would be looked after while they strolled along the beach. It had been warm in the coach, but as soon as they were out of it, they felt the cool breeze blowing off the sea. 'I am glad we decided to bring warm shawls,' Jane said, wrapping hers closer about her. Like her sister, she was wearing a muslin gown and a sarsenet pelisse. Hers was striped in two shades of green, Isabel's was white. They both wore straw bonnets firmly tied on with ribbon.

'Would you prefer to stay in the carriage?' Mark asked her. 'Or go to a hotel?'

'Certainly not,' she answered. 'I came for the bracing sea air and that is what I mean to have. What about you, Issie?'

'Me, too. I am sure the gentlemen do not want to be cooped up indoors and I am not a bit cold. I want to go down on the sand.'

'Then you shall,' Mark said, offering her his arm.

She took it, leaving Jane to walk beside Drew, though she did not take his arm. They strolled down a narrow cobbled road at the end of which they had their first view of the beach and the sea. 'It looks cold,' Jane said.

'It nearly always is,' Mark said, turning to her with a chuckle. 'There is nothing between Cromer and the Arctic, except sea. But at least that is calm today. Would you like to go bathing? It is supposed to be beneficial and there are machines down there if you would like it.' It was early in the summer, though a few brave souls were taking a dip.

'No, I do not think so,' she said. 'I shall be content to watch.'

'It must seem even colder to you, Mr Ashton, after the heat of India,' Isabel said.

'Oh, I am a hardy soul, Miss Isabel. I might take a dip myself. What do you say, Mark?' There were men in the sea a little further along the beach, but the girls would not go near them, for they nearly always took to the water naked, unlike the women who were hampered by voluminous clothing and did not stir far from the bathing machines where they changed.

'I think I should stay with the ladies,' Mark said. 'But do you go if you have a mind to.'

Drew would not go alone and all four made their way down a cliff path on to the sand. The beach was not crowded and they walked towards the water's edge. Jane was more inclined to stride out when they reached the firmer wet sand and Mark kept up with her. Drew, behind them, stooped to pick up a flat round stone and threw it into the sea in such a way it bounced along the waves two or three times before it disappeared.

Isabel clapped her hands. 'Oh, how clever of you, Mr Ashton! Do show me how to do it.'

He picked up another stone and put it into her hand. 'You need to throw it quite hard and keep the trajectory low,' he said. 'Set it spinning flat as it leaves your hand.'

She tried and failed and tried again. 'No, do it like this,' he said, taking her hand and closing her fingers round the stone. Mark and Jane, who had gone a little ahead, turned to see why the other two were not close behind and were greeted with the sight of Drew with his arms about Isabel, trying to direct her aim. And they were both laughing.

'Oh, dear,' Jane said. 'Isabel has no sense of propriety at all. It is as well there is no one on the beach who knows us.'

'It is not her fault,' Mark said. 'Drew sometimes forgets he is not still in India where no doubt such familiarity is allowed.'

Jane did not know how accurate that statement was, but it was so like Mark to see no harm in his beloved. She hurried back to her sister, followed by Mark.

'Drew has been teaching me how to make a pebble bounce,' Isabel called to them. 'Do come and try it.'

Jane could not rebuke her sister in front of others, but as they walked further along the beach she contrived to draw her out of earshot of the gentlemen. 'I hate to scold, Issie, but really, you should not have allowed Mr Ashton to put his arm round you, nor should you have referred to him by his given name. Surely, you know better that that.'

'Oh, don't be such a fusspot, Jane. There was no harm in him showing me how to spin a pebble and Mark always uses Mr Ashton's given name. It just slipped out.'

'I am sure it did, but do try to be more careful.'

'You are a fine one to talk. You have been seen in the village with Mark's arms about you. Sophie had it off her friend, Maud Finch. Mrs Finch saw you with her own eyes.'

Jane had a vague memory of seeing Mrs Finch talking to Mrs Stangate when she met Mark and Drew on the village green. 'I stumbled and he prevented me from falling,' she said. 'You may trust Mrs Finch to make a mountain out of a molehill and Sophie should not have repeated it.'

'You have quite ruined my day with your scolding.' Isabel pouted. 'I was having such fun.'

But it was not long before she was holding her skirts up in her hand and racing over the sand to the water's edge, laughing as the waves rippled over her kid shoes, which would undoubtedly be thrown out when they arrived home. Jane felt unhappy about the rebuke. It had made her sound a killjoy and she had not meant it to be like that at all. Her concern was for Mark. He had said nothing and even tried to excuse Isabel, but underneath he must have been feeling hurt. And if Mrs Finch's gossip reached his ears he would be doubly embarrassed.

Further along the beach they watched some fishing boats unloading their cargo of crabs and Mark bought two for the girls to take home for their cook and then they returned to the promenade for refreshments in the Red Lion. A short walk along the cliff top followed when they all used Drew's telescope to scan the beach and the horizon.

'How close everything looks,' Jane said. 'Why, I can see the sailors on the deck of that ship and its name quite clearly. It's called *Morning Star.*'

'That is the vessel that brought me home from India,' Drew said. 'It is a very good ship, well run and fast. It is something like that I have a mind to purchase.'

'And then Mark and I will go to India on it,' Isabel said. 'Three more weeks to go. I can't wait. Will you be sailing on her, too, Mr Ashton?'

'It depends on what turns up,' he said. 'Perhaps.'

'I think it is time we made our way back to the coach,' Jane said. 'Mama will be wondering what has become of us.'

The coach deposited them back at the Manor at five o'clock. Jane and Isabel said goodbye to their escorts and carried the parcel of crabs into the house. They were tired but happy, ready to regale their mother with what they had seen and done. No one that evening thought about tragedy and Isabel had ceased to moan about bad omens and suchlike fancies.

They had not expected to see Mark again so soon, but he arrived at an unheard-of hour next morning, looking so sorrowful that Jane immediately wondered what was wrong. Sir Edward had gone out to the stables to check on one of the horses that seemed lame, but the ladies were still seated at the breakfast table.

He bowed to them all. 'I am sorry to disturb you so early,' he said. 'But I am afraid I bring dreadful news and I did not want you to hear it from anyone else.' He paused and gulped, then went on. 'My father passed away in his sleep last night.'

Lady Cavenhurst was the first to recover from the shock. 'Oh, you poor man,' she said. 'What a dreadful thing to happen. His lordship seemed so well when we dined with you the other evening.'

'His valet found him when he went to wake him this morning and immediately alerted me,' he said. 'I sent for Dr Trench, though I knew it was too late to do anything for him. His heart just gave out, the doctor told me. As you can imagine, my mother is distraught.'

'Poor Lady Wyndham,' Jane said. 'Is there anything we can do?'

'I do not think so. Later, perhaps, she might appreciate a visit.' He turned to Isabel, who was staring at him as if he were an apparition. 'Isabel, I am so sorry, but the wedding will have to be postponed while I am in mourning.'

'Postponed,' she echoed, then burst into tears.

Jane ran to comfort her. 'Hush, Issie, you must be brave for Mark's sake. He will have a great deal to do in the next few weeks.'

'That is true,' he agreed. 'And I am afraid I must go. I will let you know about the arrangements for the funeral later. Isabel, will you accompany me to the front door? That is if her ladyship agrees.'

'Of course. Go along, Isabel. And please offer my condolences to your mother, my lord.'

He managed a wry smile. 'I suppose I will have to get used to that, but please don't stand on formality, my lady. I was Mark, I remain Mark to you.' He reached out a hand to Isabel. 'Come, my dear, I wish to talk to you.'

Isabel took the hand and together they left the room. Jane and her mother were left looking at each other, not knowing what to say.

'This is dreadful news indeed,' her ladyship said. 'I feel for poor Lady Wyndham. Theirs was a true love match. I wonder how long a period of mourning there will be?'

'A year is usual, Mama.'

'I know. We shall have to help Isabel bear up. And I suppose I had better make a start on cancelling the wedding invitations and ask Cook to cancel the orders for the banquet.' She smiled suddenly. 'At least your father will be spared the expense of it for now.'

Jane supposed someone had to think of the practicalities, but she was more concerned with how Mark and his mother were feeling and her heart went out to them. To lose one so dear so suddenly must be very hard to bear.

Chapter Four

Mark returned to Broadacres, overwhelmed by misery and the weight of responsibility that now rested on his shoulders. There was so much to do and a wedding was the last thing on his mind. Isabel had been upset, which was understandable, he supposed, but he had managed to calm her before he left, telling her the time of mourning would soon pass and then they would have the wedding she dreamed of.

'We might not be able to have the long wedding trip we planned,' he had told her. 'There will be much to do on the estate. But perhaps we will be able to go later when I am settled into my new role. It has come so suddenly, I cannot take it all in.'

'Mama called you "my lord". That really brought home to me what has happened and how your life will change. You might not be the same person at all.'

'Nonsense. I shall not change just because I have inherited a title and an estate. You, of course, will become Lady Wyndham when we marry.'

'And shall I be mistress of Broadacres?'

'Naturally, you will.'

'I am not sure I shall be any good at it. I might let you down.'

'Oh, you silly goose,' he had said, dropping a kiss on her forehead. 'Of course you will not let me down and you will have the mourning period to become used to the idea. Now I must go. I shall see you again when you and your mother call on my mother.'

Lady Wyndham, he was told when he arrived home and enquired for her, had been given a tisane by her maid and was resting in her room. He did not disturb her, but spoke to the steward about matters of the estate, telling him to carry on as usual, then he set about writing letters to everyone who needed to be told of his father's demise. It was sad work and he had to stop frequently to overcome his emotion. His father had been the best of fathers, spending time with him as he grew up, teaching him to shoot, fish and ride, making sure he had a good education, instilling in him a sense of what was right and proper, and showing him by example to care for those around him. 'High and low, we are all human beings,' he had said once. 'We should treat everyone with the dignity they deserve whether they be the poorest labourer or the king of England.' Now he was no more.

Already the news was becoming known in the village and people were going about with long faces. Many of the servants and even the hardy outside staff were openly weeping. Lord Wyndham had been a popular figure, known for his humanity and fairness. Mark prayed he would be able to live up to his father's ideals.

Drew came to him as he was finishing the last of the letters. 'I assume there will be no wedding yet a while,' he said. 'And now is not the time for house guests. I plan to leave for London by tonight's mail.'

'I shall miss you, Drew.'

'And I you. But I will return for the funeral, if you would like me to.'

'Of course. Next Thursday, here in Hadlea.'

'Please convey my gratitude to Lady Wyndham for her generous hospitality. I have written her a note, which I have asked her maid to pass on to her when she is feeling up to receiving it.'

'That is kind of you.'

'And express my good wishes and condolences to Miss Isabel. It is going to be hard for her to have the wedding postponed and cope with a very different life from the one she envisaged. How did she take the news?'

'She is very sad, of course, but took it well enough, all things considered. She has the support of her mother and Jane, for which I am grateful, for I cannot give her the attention I would like just now.'

'I am sure they understand. Now, if you will excuse me, I shall go and pack.'

'There is something you can do for me,' Mark said, as they shook hands. 'Will you make sure my letters go on the mail?'

'Gladly.'

'I've just one more to write. I'll send them to you when they are ready. Jeremy will drive you to the Fox and Hounds.'

Drew left and Mark pulled another sheet of notepaper towards him, dipped his pen in the ink and resumed writing.

An hour later he was free to receive Lady Cavenhurst and her three daughters. All four bent the knee and addressed him as 'my lord', which made him feel thoroughly uncomfortable and he begged them not to change towards him.

'How is your dear mother?' Lady Cavenhurst asked. 'I would not intrude on her grief if she does not wish it.'

Even as she spoke Lady Wyndham entered the room. She was dressed in unrelieved black, but was dry-eyed and upright. 'Grace, thank you for coming,' she said.

Lady Cavenhurst hurried towards her and took both her hands in her own. 'Helen, I am so very, very sorry. If there is anything we can do for you, you have only to ask.'

'There is nothing that I can think of. Will you be seated?'

They sat in a little circle, not knowing what to say until Jane spoke. 'Lord Wyndham will be sorely missed by everyone who knew him,' she said. 'He was such a good, kind man, always ready to listen and so generous, too.'

'Yes, he was, wasn't he?' Lady Wyndham smiled suddenly. 'I remember when he found Jeremy as a child running about the streets of London and brought him home. He was filthy and verminous, but nothing would do but he should be given a bath and new clothes and fed. He slept in the stables and has been with us ever since.'

'You mean Jeremy, your coachman?' Isabel queried.

'Yes, he has grown into a fine man and would do anything for my husband and for Mark, too.'

'That is why his lordship listened to my tale of wanting to set up a home for war orphans,' Jane said. 'He understood.'

'His promise will be honoured, Jane,' Mark said quietly.

She turned to him and noticed the sparkle of tears in his eyes and her heart went out to him. The pity of it was that she could not tell him so. 'Thank you, Mark, but you have more important matters to deal with, I am sure.'

'Have you decided on the funeral?' Lady Cavenhurst asked him.

'Yes. It is to be in St Peter's in Hadlea next Thursday. The Bishop of Norwich and the Reverend Caulder will officiate. There will, of course, be refreshments here afterwards and the reading of the will.'

'I shall mourn for the rest of my days,' Lady Wyndham said. 'But we will not keep Mark and Isabel waiting too long for their wedding. I want to see grandchildren playing about the place before I leave this world. I think six months will be enough for the official mourning.'

'Thank you,' Isabel said. 'You are very kind.'

'I have no doubt you have much to do,' Lady Cavenhurst said, rising. 'We will take our leave. Please do not hesitate to send for us if there is anything we can do for you.'

As they were leaving they met Drew on the gravel in front of the house. He was about to climb into the gig which was to take him to the Fox and Hounds. He bowed to each of them. 'Ladies, I regret I cannot stop and talk. The mail is due in twenty minutes.'

'Are you leaving?' Isabel asked with something like dismay in her voice.

'Yes, Miss Isabel. I would not intrude on the household grief, but I shall come back for the funeral. Lord Wyndham was very good to me, when I was struggling to make my way.' He bowed again, climbed into the gig and was driven away.

The pony and trap in which Jane had driven them to Broadacres was waiting for them at the door. It was just big enough to seat four comfortably. She was a competent driver and enjoyed bowling about the village in it, though her mother and Isabel much preferred the coach.

'It was considerate of Lady Wyndham to think of you, Issie,' Jane said, skilfully turning the pony towards the entrance gates. 'In the midst of her sorrow, she is still thinking of others. Six months is not so long to wait and the time will soon pass.'

'I knew spilling that ink on my gown and letting Mark see it was a bad omen,' Isabel said. 'And I have been proved right.'

'That is just a silly superstition,' her mother told her. 'Do not think of it.'

'It is not the only one about weddings,' Sophie piped up. 'It is said a postponed wedding never takes place.'

'Sophie, how could you?' Lady Cavenhurst remonstrated as Isabel burst into tears. 'There was no call to repeat such nonsense. You have upset your sister, for no good reason.'

'Sorry,' she mumbled.

But nothing would comfort Isabel and she continued to weep all the way home.

'Issie, do dry your tears,' Jane said as gently as she could, though she was fast losing patience with her sister. 'If Lady Wyndham and Mark can bear up, so should you. Their loss is the greater.'

'It's all right for you, Jane,' her sister grumbled. 'You have not had your wedding snatched away from you.'

'Isabel, it has not been snatched away,' her ladyship said. 'It has merely been postponed for six months. It is to be hoped that by that time you will have learned how to be more dignified. Think of the position you will have as Mark's wife. You will be Lady Wyndham and mistress of Broadacres. Everyone will look to you to set a good example. Mark does not want a wife who bursts into tears at the slightest setback.'

Isabel did not answer and Jane pulled up in front of the stables and they all dismounted, leaving Daniel to unharness the pony and rub him down. They met Teddy in the hall, as they were going upstairs to take off their bonnets.

'Teddy, where have you been?' his mother asked him. 'We have just been over to Broadacres to offer condolences. You should have been with us.'

'I had business in Norwich. I will go over later.'

He did not elaborate on what the business might be. Jane had little hope that he had been looking for a way out of his dilemma. She knew their father had spoken to him about the need to make savings, but she had no idea what her brother's reaction had been. She sighed as she continued upstairs to her own room. She must write to the bank manager to ask him to release her savings. And then what? Would Teddy turn over a new leaf?

The funeral had been attended by almost the whole male population of the village and distant relatives and friends of the Wyndham family came from far and wide, including Drew. Although it was not usual for ladies to attend funerals, but to wait at home for the menfolk to return, Lady Wyndham had insisted on being present at the interment of her husband. She had been dry-eyed throughout and regally upright in her widow's weeds. She had maintained the stance throughout the service and even afterwards when everyone gathered for refreshments in the long gallery at Broadacres. Helped to a seat by Mark, she sat accepting condolences and listening to the mourners recounting tales of what Lord Wyndham had said and done, some of which raised a wry smile. Mark was here, there and everywhere, being the perfect host, but Jane could see the strain in his eyes. To be suddenly catapulted into his inheritance years before he expected it must be a daunting prospect for him.

One by one the mourners began to leave until only the family and servants remained for the reading of the will. Mark caught Jane as she was preparing to leave with the rest of her family. 'Stay, Jane,' he said. The look of dismay on Isabel's face made him add, 'And you, too, Isabel.' He turned to Sir Edward. 'I will see them safely home afterwards, Sir Edward.'

Leaving their parents, Sophie and Teddy to go home in the family coach, the girls took seats near Mark and Lady Wyndham as the lawyer cleared his throat to begin. There was nothing remarkable in the will. There were bequests to all the servants commensurate with their status, small bequests to nephews and nieces, a generous allowance for his widow and three thousand pounds to Jane to use for her orphans. The amount made her gasp. His lordship had promised a donation, but she had never dreamed it would be so much. It made her realise that she would have to go ahead with it; there could be no backing out now. Mark, who had been standing by his mother's chair, bent and whispered in her ear. 'I will match that, Jane. You shall have your orphanage.'

The lawyer was coming to the end. 'Finally, to my beloved son, Mark, I leave the estate of Broadacres and all its lands and holdings, the London house in South Audley Street, the overseas investments and the residue of monies after all other bequests have been fulfilled.' He looked round at his audience, but, as no one had any comments, he gathered his papers up and prepared to leave.

Some of the relatives, who had come a distance and would be staying at Broadacres overnight, went to their rooms to rest and change for dinner and those living locally took their leave of Lady Wyndham and Mark, leaving only Jane and Isabel.

'Drew, will you be so kind as to escort the ladies home?' Mark asked. 'I must stay with my mother and my guests.'

'It is not in the least necessary,' Jane said. 'It is a fine day and we can easily walk.'

'Then I shall walk with you,' Drew said. 'I am staying at the Fox and Hounds. The Manor is not so very far out of my way.'

'Oh, thank you, sir,' Isabel said before Jane could protest again. 'I, for one, shall feel more at ease with an escort.'

This was a strange statement from one who was accustomed to walking about the village with only Jane or Bessie as a companion. Jane looked sharply at her, but did not comment. With Drew between them they set off. No one spoke as they made their way down the drive and out of the huge iron gates on to the road to the village.

'It has been a sad day,' Jane said. 'We were all very fond of Lord Wyndham. Her ladyship stood up to the occasion very well, don't you think, Mr Ashton?'

'Indeed, yes. She showed enviable stoicism, but underneath I am sure she was suffering. They were so devoted, an example of what a marriage should be.'

'Yes, it is a pity all marriages are not like that,' Jane said. 'But I suppose it is down to finding your soulmate, someone you wish to spend the rest of your life with. So often marriage becomes a matter of convenience. Husband and wife lead almost separate lives, each with their own interests and circle of friends.'

'Unfortunately that happens all too often' he said.

'You have never been married?' Isabel queried.

'No.' He laughed. 'I never found my soulmate. I thought I had once, but it was not to be.'

'Why not?'

Jane held her breath for his answer, praying he would not mention her name. He looked at her and smiled. 'We were both too young, too immature and I had yet to make my way in the world.' He laughed suddenly. 'Since then I have been too busy making my fortune to think of marrying.'

'Would you go back to her if you could?'

'Isabel,' Jane remonstrated, 'you should not quiz Mr Ashton in that fashion.'

'Oh, I do not mind it,' he said. 'To answer your question, Miss Isabel, I thought I would. I thought that if we met again and she saw how prosperous I had become, she and her papa might think differently and I would win her. But I have thought better of it since.'

'Why not? Is she not as beautiful as you remembered?'

'Oh, more so. It is not that—'

'Issie, did you notice how strained Mark was looking today?' Jane interrupted the conversation, which was becoming too embarrassing to be borne. 'It is hardly to be wondered at, but I hope he manages to sleep tonight. He will need his strength in the next few weeks.'

'There will be no wedding,' Isabel said, ignoring Jane's attempt to divert her. 'Did you know that, Mr Ashton?'

'I knew it had been postponed, but it will take place later, will it not?'

Isabel sighed. 'I am no longer sure of anything.'

'Isabel, what are you saying?' Jane exclaimed. 'Surely you have not changed your mind about marrying Mark?'

'I don't know. I am so confused. Watching how everyone behaved today, especially Lady Wyndham, I thought I shall be expected to be like her, to direct that huge household and remain calm whatever the crisis and I do not think I can manage it.'

'It has been a trying day,' Jane said, wishing her sister had not voiced her doubts in front of Drew. 'You will think differently when you have had a night's sleep and are more yourself.'

'It's not just today. I have been worried about it for ages.'

'Oh, Issie, I am losing patience with you. This is all because of the ink spilled on your gown and that ill-considered remark of Sophie's.'

'What remark was that?' Drew asked.

'It was nothing,' Jane said. 'A silly superstition our sister picked up from somewhere.'

'Postponed marriages never happen,' Isabel told him.

They had been walking side by side, but now he turned to Isabel. 'I am inclined to agree with Miss Cavenhurst. It is silly.'

'Oh, I would not mind it if I had not already been having doubts,' she said.

'Now is hardly the time to express them, Issie,' Jane remonstrated. 'Think of poor Mark. He has enough to contend with without that.'

'He knows how I feel.'

'And what did he say?'

'That I would have the mourning period to get used to the idea.'

'There you are, then.'

'Jane, I wish you would not try to be a second mother to me. You are always telling me what I should and should not do and I am tired of it. You can know nothing of how I feel. I do not believe you have a heart.'

Jane was hurt as she was often hurt by her sister's thoughtlessness, but she would not show it, certainly not in front of Drew. 'Issie, you knew that if you accepted Mark one day you would be Lady Wyndham and mistress of Broadacres. It is not something new.'

'I didn't think it would be for years and years when we had grown quite old. And now it has happened.'

'But if you truly love Mark, that would not matter in the least. Now, let us speak no more of it. I am sure Mr Ashton does not want to hear it.'

They continued in silence. Jane was appalled at what Isabel had said and in front of Andrew Ashton, too. Did Mark really know how Isabel was feeling? It must have added to his sadness over the loss of his father. The bride he had chosen did not want to become the sort of wife a man in his position needed. Was he expecting Isabel to become used to the idea or was he really worried about it? The pity of it was, that she, the unmarried sister, could not speak to him on such a private matter. What could she say if she did? Nothing. Her own feelings, locked away in the heart Isabel declared she did not have, could never be brought into the open.

She stole a sideways glance at Drew, wondering if he would pass on what he had heard. He looked sombre as if debating the issue within himself. He turned his head towards her and caught her looking at him. 'Do not worry,' he murmured. 'Your secret is safe with me.'

She looked away in confusion. What secret? Isabel

had said Mark knew how she felt, so that was no secret. That she and Isabel had been arguing about it? That was hardly a secret either. Surely he had not guessed how she felt about Mark? That would be too mortifying.

They arrived at the front door of the Manor. Drew declined Isabel's invitation to come in for refreshment, bowed and took his leave. Jane and Isabel went indoors and rejoined their parents and siblings. Nothing was said of the conversation on the road.

Jane had been promised enough money to buy a house for her children's home without the need to use her aunt's bequest, so she had agreed to hand that over to her brother.

'I do it for Papa's sake, not yours,' she told him, a few days later when she caught him coming into the house in the middle of the morning. He looked dishevelled, as if he had been up all night and she wondered if that had been the case. He was rarely at home. 'I have asked the bank to pay it into your account, but it will be the last. Use it wisely and no more gambling.'

'Thank you, Sis.' He grinned. 'I suppose a jobation is a small price to pay for it, but you know you are sounding more and more like Papa.'

'It is because we both worry about you, Teddy. You do not seem to have any sense of responsibility.'

He heaved a melodramatic sigh. 'I am a sore trial to you, I know. How much is it, by the way?'

'Five thousand pounds and I begrudge every penny of it and make no bones about it. If it had been for anything else but gambling…'

'It will pay my way out to India and keep me going

until I make my fortune.' He stopped her before she could begin scolding him again.

'India! What are you talking about? No one has mentioned India.'

'Well, it might be the West Indies. I haven't made up my mind.'

'Teddy, that money is meant for you to pay off Lord Bolsover and your other debts. It was not given to you to fund your travelling.'

'Unfortunately I have no choice. Five thousand is not nearly enough to see me clear and Hector Bolsover, for some reason of his own, has been going round buying up all my debts, not only the gambling debts, but everything else. I don't know what his game is, but it ain't good to have all one's debts in one pot. Spread about a bit they can be managed by paying off a little here and there, robbing Peter to pay Paul, as it were, but as it is I am trumped. There is nothing for it—I must emigrate.'

She was appalled. 'Teddy, have you been gambling since you returned home?'

'I've only been trying to recoup my losses. I thought it would save you having to stand buff for me...'

'Now you are in deeper than ever.' She was exasperated that he never seemed to learn.

'Sorry, Jane.'

'Have you told Papa and Mama you are leaving?'

'I am about to.'

'And when will you go?'

'On tonight's mail. Wish me luck, Jane.'

'Luck! I would sooner box your ears. You have brought disgrace on this family, Teddy, with all this talk of luck. I can only hope that a spell abroad and some real work will bring about a miracle.'

'Oh, Jane, give over your lecture. You will not see me again for some time, let us not part at odds with each other.'

His engaging grin was still evident and she relented enough to hug him and tell him to take care.

The family was all at odds, she reflected as he hurried away. Her brother was a scapegrace and her sister, Isabel, was having serious doubts about a marriage that had been talked about for years and welcomed by both families. Her father was worried to death about his finances and her mother blind to it. So far there was nothing wrong with Sophie except a tendency to speak without thinking. As for her own thoughts and feelings, they were as much in disarray as everyone else's. The best cure for that, she decided, was to occupy herself with something worthwhile.

She was determined to make her orphanage a success and although she had enough to start looking for premises, she would still need a regular income to run it. To find that she must raise more money and the best place to do that was London. Her father would never allow her to go alone and he was too preoccupied to take her. It would need some thought.

Jane consulted the Rector and Mrs Caulder and though the Reverend said he would enquire about premises, he cautioned her not to consider travelling to London without a male escort. 'Instead you could make a start by writing letters to influential people,' he said.

'Begging letters?' she queried in dismay.

'Well, yes, but in a very good cause. Shall we give the organisation a name so that you are not asking for yourself, but on behalf of everyone connected with the idea? I would ask Lord Wyndham to put his name to it, but it is too soon after his bereavement. I will sound out one or two others.'

They spent some time suggesting and discarding names for the project. Jane did not want the word orphanage to be used. 'It will be a home,' she said. 'A home and a school.' In the end they decided on the Hadlea Children's Home and she would spend a little of the money having headed notepaper printed.

She was walking home, turning the phrases of her letter over in her mind, when Mark caught up with her. 'Jane, I was on my way to visit you.'

Long practice had made her adept at calming herself when she met him. She turned and smiled, taking in his dark suit and black cravat, the bleakness of his countenance, and wished she could comfort him. There was no one to do that, except perhaps his mother, who was too immersed in her own grief to do it. Isabel seemed incapable of it.

'My lord,' she said.

'Oh, for goodness' sake, Jane, let's not have any of that "my lord" nonsense, or I shall become very cross with you.' He fell into step beside her. 'What were you so deep in thought about, that you did not hear me?'

She told him about her plans for the Hadlea Children's Home. 'Thanks to you and your father, we have enough to look for premises, but we need a few wealthy philanthropists to pledge future income,' she said. 'Papa cannot take me to London at present, so I must write letters. If I could mention one or two influential people, it would help.'

'You may use my name, Jane.'

'Oh, I didn't mean… Oh dear, it sounded as if I was

asking…' She stopped in confusion because he was laughing.

'Oh, yes, you were, and blatantly too.'

'But you did ask what I was thinking about.'

'I did, that is true, and it is also true I would have offered in any case. I will help in any way I can.'

'But you have so much to do, sorting out the estate and getting used to your new role.'

'It is not that difficult, Jane. My father involved me in the affairs of the estate as soon as I was old enough to understand. He groomed me well for the job and the workers are all good men who know what is expected of them. The difficulty arises because my father is no longer here to advise me and I miss that. Mother looks after the house and the indoor servants, but she has never taken an interest in what is happening on the estate. I am on my own there.'

'You have our support for what it is worth.'

'It is worth a great deal, Jane.'

She felt the colour flood her face. 'You said you were on your way to call on us.'

'Yes. I have to go to London on business and wondered if Sir Edward or Lady Cavenhurst had any little commissions I could do for them while I am there.'

'That is kind of you.' She paused, as an idea came to her. 'You could do something for me, though.'

'Gladly. What is it?'

'Take me with you. I am sure Papa would allow me to go if you were to escort me. I could stay with Lady Cartrose, widow of my mother's brother. She lives in Mount Street. All you need do is take me to her.'

'I am not sure…'

'Please, Mark. I could do my fund-raising so much

easier in the capital, make appointments to meet people, have the notepaper printed, that sort of thing. Aunt Emmeline is well up in society and could perhaps introduce me to people. I am sure I could be more persuasive face to face than by correspondence.'

'Oh, I am sure you could,' he said. 'And I would take you willingly if I thought it could be accomplished with propriety.'

'And why would it not? You are to be my brother-in-law, are you not?'

'I am not sure that guarantees anything, Jane,' he said with a wry smile. 'Let us see what Sir Edward thinks, shall we?'

Sir Edward, when he was approached, was dubious. 'My daughter thinks she is mature and independent,' he said. 'And to some extent she is, but we cannot flout convention. It is bad enough that Teddy... No, we will not speak of him.' Teddy had departed in a welter of tears from his mother and anger from his father, who had told him he had washed his hands of him.

'It would be perfectly proper if Isabel were to go, too,' Lady Cavenhurst said. 'Then Jane would be their chaperon.'

'Oh, yes, yes,' Isabel said, eyes shining. 'I should like that very much.'

'Yes, that would serve,' Sir Edward agreed, turning to his wife. 'Do you think your sister-in-law will have them?'

'I am sure she will. She is always asking when we are going to pay her a visit. I will write to her at once. My lord, will you take the letter to the mail office on your way home?'

'Gladly, my lady. There is something you could do for me in return. Would you call and bear my mother company while I am away? She is still feeling very down and I do not like leaving her.'

'Of course I will. When do you go?'

'I was planning to make a start tomorrow, but I will defer it until the day after to give the ladies time to pack. I mean to be on the road betimes, so I will call for them with the coach at half past eight if that is not too early.'

'We will be ready,' Jane said.

He bowed his way out, leaving Isabel jumping up and down in excitement.

The journey was accomplished in two days with frequent changes of horses at the various staging inns along the way and an overnight stay at the halfway point. Isabel spent much of her time looking out of the coach window and exclaiming at what she saw, while Jane and Mark discussed Jane's fund-raising.

'There are several orphanages in London,' he said. 'Some good, some downright bad. You should visit a few of them and find out how they are run and how they raise their money and perhaps learn some of the pitfalls to avoid. They might give you some ideas. Once my business is done I will be happy to escort you. Perhaps tomorrow afternoon.'

'Yes, that will be convenient, thank you,' Jane said. 'It will give me time to prepare some notes in the morning.'

'How boring,' Isabel said.

'You do not have to come, Issie, dear,' Jane said. 'I am sure Aunt Emmeline will find something for you to do more to your taste. You know what a busy social life she leads.'

'But you will be taking Mark from me.'

'I will make it up to you, Isabel,' he said. 'You must allow your sister to have her children's home. After all, you have your wedding to look forward to.' He smiled. 'Already two weeks of the six months have passed.'

'Yes. I am a crosspatch, aren't I?'

'Not at all,' he said. 'Shall you like to visit Bullock's Museum? I believe they are displaying Napoleon's coach captured at Waterloo. We could all go one afternoon.'

She had been mollified by this idea and had recovered her good humour by the time the coach drew up outside Lady Cartrose's house in Mount Street. Mindful of his escort duties, he bade Jeremy take the coach on to Wyndham House and entered the town house to hand his charges and their maid over to her ladyship, who had received her sister-in-law's letter and was expecting them. Since Jane had last seen her she had put on a great deal of weight and was now a roly-poly of a woman. She was dressed in a dark-purple gown and wore a white cap on dyed red hair.

'Come in and let me look at you,' she said, as the maid who had conducted them to the drawing room disappeared to fetch refreshments and Bessie was conducted up to their rooms to unpack. 'My, you are quite grown up now and so elegant. I did not know I had such beautiful nieces. Do present your escort.'

'Aunt Emmeline, this is Lord Wyndham,' Jane said.

'And am I right in thinking he is your betrothed?' She turned a round, smiling face to Mark.

Jane was dismayed. 'On, no, Aunt. Lord Wyndham is Isabel's betrothed, not mine.'

'Oh, dear, what a foolish mistake to make. I must have misread you mother's letter. My lord, please forgive me.'

Mark bowed to her. 'My lady, it is of no consequence.'

'Do let us be seated.' She waved her hand in the direction of two sofas and some chairs. 'Then we can have a comfortable coze over some refreshments and you can tell me all about yourselves.' She sat on one of the sofas as a maid brought in the tea tray and another appeared with two plates loaded with cakes and pastries.

It soon transpired that her ladyship was very deaf and they were obliged to repeat almost everything they said in very loud voices, while her ladyship munched her way through two large pastries and several cakes. The girls ate one cake each and Mark felt duty bound to manage more than that in order to please their hostess.

An hour later, when her ladyship had satisfied herself that she had learned all she needed to know about their lives and aspirations, Mark prepared to take his leave. 'I shall be occupied on business affairs during the morning tomorrow,' he told her ladyship. 'But I shall call in the afternoon, if I may. I promised Jane to take her to visit some orphanages.'

'Then you should go to the Foundling Hospital,' she said. 'It is open to the public and has raised considerable sums for its upkeep with artwork and musical evenings.'

'Yes, I have heard of it,' Jane said. 'I should like to do that.'

'In the meantime I will invite as many wealthy acquaintances as I can squeeze into my drawing room for music, cards and refreshments two evenings hence, so that you might be introduced to them and talk to them about your children's home. It will not be easy to extract money from them, however. Everyone is complaining of hard times. The war cost everyone dear in taxes and last year's dismal summer and the poor harvest means their estates and investments are not producing the income they have come to expect.'

'All the more reason for people to think about the poor orphans,' Jane said. 'If times are hard for the wealthy, they are even harder for the poorer people.'

'I am sure that your silver tongue will do the trick,' Mark said. 'Until tomorrow, then.' He bowed and was gone, leaving the ladies to discuss social affairs and exchange gossip.

The Foundling Hospital, set up by the philanthropist Thomas Coram over seventy years before, was much bigger than Jane had imagined it would be. Most of the children were the offspring of unmarried women, though there were some orphans. The children were well clothed and well fed and appeared happy in their way, but Jane could not agree that giving them new names and cutting them off from their real parents, even if there was only one, was the way she would go. It was done, she was told, so that the mother could repent of her sin and make a new life for herself unburdened by children.

'I would rather encourage the children to meet and talk about their kin,' she said as she and Mark returned to Mount Street. 'Especially widowed mothers. Families are important.'

He had been supporting her all the way, standing beside her as she spoke to the Governor of the home and asking pertinent questions she might not have thought of herself. This time alone with him was precious, so precious, that it was difficult to give her mind to the purpose of their visit. Every time her arm had brushed his sleeve or he put his hand under her elbow to help her up a step, she had felt the warmth flood her whole body. She really must make herself concentrate on the conversation and not the fact that they were alone together in his carriage.

'I think you are right,' he said. 'Poor Drew's relations did not want anything to do with him when he was orphaned. They sent him to a good school and believed that was the end of their responsibilities. It is one of the reasons I befriended him and brought him to stay at Broadacres.'

'Yes, I remember him telling me. He has done well for himself since.'

'Yes, and I heard him say he would help with your project. You must keep him up to it.'

'If I see him again.' She paused. 'Mark, do you trust him?'

'Naturally I do. Why do you ask?'

'No reason.' She took a deep breath and changed the subject. 'The Coram has given me other ideas for raising money besides writing letters. We could arrange musical evenings with talented musicians for which the wealthy audience would pay handsomely and we could put on a fair in the village and ask for donations for the stalls and prizes for competitions, charging a small entrance fee.'

'A fair would not attract the wealthy,' he said. 'It would mean a great deal of work for a small reward.'

'I know, but it would give the people of Hadlea the opportunity to become involved. I want the home to be part of the community, not cut off behind hedges and walls. And every little helps. I thought the last Saturday in August would give the best chance of good weather and allow time to arrange it all.'

'Then we could do it on Ten Acre Field on the far side of Broadacres estate.'

'But, Mark, would that be wise? You are so recently bereaved. What will your mother say?'

'I will consult her, but she will say it was what my father would have wished. Your project was close to his heart, as it is to mine.'

'What would I do without you?'

'I am sure you would manage admirably.' He turned to smile at her, making her heart flip. Did Isabel realise how fortunate she was?

They arrived back at Mount Street to hear from Isabel that she and Lady Cartrose had been riding in her ladyship's open carriage in Hyde Park and they had stopped frequently so that she could be introduced to some of her ladyship's many acquaintances. 'I am sure it was more interesting than visiting an orphanage,' she told them. 'And guess who we chanced upon, riding in the Row? Mr Ashton, no less. When he heard you were in town, Mark, he said he would call on you. And Aunt Emmeline has invited him to call tomorrow. There was talk of an outing together.' Her face was alight with enthusiasm and excitement, which filled Jane with a kind of foreboding.

Strangely Mark did not appear to see his danger. He smiled and said he would have called on Drew in any case and he would certainly make time for an outing if that was what the ladies wished. Then he bowed his way out.

Chapter Five

The outing was arranged the next morning when both men arrived at Mount Street at the same time. They would visit Bullock's Museum that afternoon and attend a concert in the Chinese Pavilion at Ranelagh Gardens in the evening, a plan which pleased Isabel. As soon as they had taken their leave she began discussing the dress she would wear.

'My green-and-pink-striped sarsenet,' she said. 'With a pink bonnet and gloves.'

'Issie, you must remember that Mark is in mourning and that you, as his betrothed, should be a little more sombre in what you wear.'

'You mean I should go into mourning, too? We are not married yet. His late lordship was not kin to me. I do not see the necessity.'

'Not mourning, Issie, but something quieter out of respect for Mark's feelings.'

'You are always worrying about Mark's feelings, Jane. I begin to wonder if you are not a little in love with him yourself.'

'Nonsense.' Her reply was sharp, but she turned away

so that her sister could not see the consternation on her face. 'Aunt, what do you think?'

'Think about what?' the lady asked vaguely. It was obvious that her deafness had prevented her from following the conversation.

'I was saying that Isabel should not wear bright colours in deference to Mark's state of mourning,' Jane said very loudly.

'You may be right,' her ladyship said. 'But there are some lovely shades of lilac and dove grey to be had.'

'The only thing I have in grey is that plain old carriage dress I wore to come here. You do not expect me to wear that again, do you?'

'It would serve,' Jane said.

'Well, I won't. How can I shine in society in something as drab as that? The gentlemen will not like me in it.'

'Gentlemen?' Jane queried. 'What gentlemen?'

'Why, Mark and Mr Ashton, of course.'

She would not be moved and it was a resplendent Isabel in pink and green who greeted the gentlemen when they arrived. Jane was in a plain lilac trimmed with white lace. Both carried parasols for the day was warm.

Bullock's Museum was housed in the Egyptian Hall in Piccadilly, only a short distance away and they elected to walk. There were strange, often bizarre exhibits in the museum, things like skeletons and animal bones, weapons and armour, uniforms with bullet holes in them, and unusual plants. They wandered round the exhibits, then moved on to inspect the magnificent travelling coach used by Napoleon on his campaigns. He had abandoned it after his defeat at Waterloo and taken to his white riding horse to make his escape. When he knew escape was not possible he had appealed to King George for asylum in England, but this had been refused and since the island of Elba could not hold him, he had been sent to St Helena, way out in the Atlantic. His coach had been bought for the museum and people flocked to see it. Painted blue with gold ornamentation, it was very large and luxuriously appointed, with a folding bed, even a desk with pens, paper and ink, and compartments for maps and telescopes. It had bulletproof doors and blinds on the windows. It obviously needed a team of strong horses to pull it.

'Did the Duke of Wellington ride about in a carriage like this?' Jane asked Mark.

'He had a carriage, though it was nothing like as ostentatious as this,' he answered. 'In any case, he preferred to ride.'

'Did you meet him?'

'Yes, several times, though I do not think he deigned to notice me.'

'I shall write one of my letters to him. He is supposed to be in sympathy with the plight of his men and their families.'

'I don't know how you dare,' Isabel put in.

'Nothing ventured, nothing gained,' she said, laughing.

'Well, I think you are wasting your time,' her sister went on. 'It is a national problem. What can one woman do?'

'If we all thought nothing could be done, nothing would be done,' Mark said.

'I sympathise with the children, of course I do,' Isabel said. 'And I always give a few coppers to beggars, but you are talking about thousands of pounds. You are becoming obsessed with it, Jane, and I, for one, am tired of hearing about it. If you and Mark wish to continue the conversation, Mr Ashton and I will find something else to talk about.' She took Drew's arm. 'Come, Mr Ashton, show me the animals.'

Drew looked towards Mark, who answered with a slight nod and Drew allowed himself to be led away.

'Mark, ought we not to follow them?' Jane asked, staring at their disappearing backs in consternation.

'She is bored, Jane.'

'That is no excuse. I am appalled by her behaviour and can only apologise on her behalf.'

'Dear Jane, there is no need for you to apologise for anything. You are not your sister's keeper.'

His endearment meant nothing to him, but everything to her, but she must guard against letting him know that. 'No, but I am concerned that she is not showing proper regard for your feelings.'

'And do you know what my feelings are, Jane?' he queried with a smile. 'Can you read my mind?'

'No, of course not.' She felt the colour flare in her face and wished to end the conversation. 'But I still think we should follow them for propriety's sake.'

He laughed suddenly and it was the first real laugh she had heard from him since his father died. 'Whose reputation were you thinking of, Jane? Theirs or ours? Who is the pot and who the kettle?'

She was obliged to smile at that. 'Then, for all our sakes, let us rejoin them and endeavour not to discuss the Hadlea Children's Home.'

The stuffed animals were in a separate part of the museum for which they had to pay an extra shilling. The entrance was a narrow corridor made to look like a rocky cave, which opened out into a tropical rainforest where the stuffed animals were set in lifelike poses among the vegetation. Drew and Isabel were not to be found there or in any other part of the building. Worried about what had happened to them, they went outside to find them standing on the walkway. Isabel was clinging on to Drew's arm with both hands and had her head on his shoulder.

'There you are,' Drew said. 'Miss Isabel felt faint and begged me to bring her out in the fresh air. I dared not leave her to fetch you.'

'Oh, dear,' Jane said, gently detaching her sister from Drew's side and putting her arm about her shoulders. 'Do you feel better now?'

'Yes, a little.'

'Do you think you can manage to walk back to Mount Street or shall we ask Mark to find us a hackney?'

Mark turned to a little crossing sweeper, who was waiting anxiously to see if they wished to cross the road, gave him a penny and bade him run for a hackney. He sped off and was soon back with the hire vehicle.

Thus they returned to Mount Street and in the few minutes the journey took, Isabel recovered her spirits. Jane found herself wondering if her sister had truly felt faint or if it had been act put on for Drew's benefit, then upbraided herself for her uncharitable thought.

'Issie,' she said as soon as they were alone, 'you should not have asked Mr Ashton to take you away from us. It was very embarrassing for Mark and it put me to the blush to think you could behave in such a forward manner, and to compound it by hanging on to Mr Ashton's arm in that fashion was the outside of enough. I dread to think what Mark made of it.'

'I nearly fainted and I don't care what Mark thinks. And I will not have you scolding me.'

'Issie!' Jane was lost for words.

'Well, I won't. I wish I had not said I would marry Mark.' And with that she flounced out of the room, leaving Jane's heart and mind in turmoil. It was so difficult to tell if Isabel really meant what she said, or if it was a tantrum that she would regret.

Her sister was more subdued than usual when they sat down to a light meal with their aunt at five o'clock, but she would not hear of postponing the outing to Ranelagh Gardens on account of not feeling well earlier in the day.

'I am perfectly recovered,' she said. 'We are only in town for a few days and heaven knows when we will ever come again if Papa is so determined we must economise, so I intend to make the most of it.'

It was with a heavy heart Jane prepared for the evening when they would again be escorted by Mark and Mr Ashton. She wished the latter would go away, back to where he came from, but her wish was not to be granted.

Drew and Mark arrived promptly at eight o'clock in Mark's town carriage and all four of them were soon on their way to Chelsea.

The gardens were a popular place where the aristocracy mixed with anyone able to afford the two-shillings-and-sixpence entrance fee. It had a Chinese Pavilion, an ornamental lake and several walks. Outdoor concerts were also staged there. Mark and Drew, with the ladies between them, made their way to the pavilion to listen to the music, which did not finish before it became dark. The area around the pavilion was lit by lanterns strung among the trees, but the surrounding tree-lined walks with their little arbours were in darkness and were therefore a popular place for romantic assignations.

In the crush of people leaving at the end of the concert, Jane became separated from her companions. She wandered round for several minutes trying to find them and was beginning to think her best plan was to make for the exit and wait there for them to find her, when she encountered Mark. 'Where are Mr Ashton and Isabel?' she asked. 'I have been looking for you all for ages.'

'I don't know. I thought they were with you.'

'No. I lost sight of them soon after everyone started to leave. Where can they have got to? If they have been separated, Issie will be frightened; she never liked the dark.' She did not add that if they were together, it was one more indiscretion on her sister's part.

'Our best course is to go to the carriage lines and see if they have made their way there, before we do anything else.'

'Then I will stay here and continue looking.'

'No, Jane, we stay together. I don't want you to become lost, too.'

They went to where the carriages waited, but Jeremy had not seen Mr Ashton or Miss Isabel. They returned to the gardens, now in darkness because almost everyone had left, and began a systematic search of all the paths, taking one of the lanterns from the pavilion to light their way. 'They must have missed their way trying to find the exit,' Jane said. 'Though how that could be when almost everyone was making their way out and they had only to follow, I do not know.'

They walked down one path after another, with Mark

swinging the lantern to and fro and in the process managing to disturb more than one pair of lovers to their dismay or indignation, but there was no sign of Drew and Isabel. They turned back towards the pavilion and here they encountered Drew. He was alone.

'Where is Issie?' Jane's anxiety made her speak sharply.

'I have taken her to the carriage. She is waiting there for you.'

'She wasn't there half an hour ago.'

'No. She fainted and fell among the crowd. I picked her up and carried her back into the pavilion to recover, then I escorted her to the carriage and came looking for you.'

'Then let us make haste and take her home,' Mark said. 'That is twice today she has felt unwell. I do hope she is not sickening for anything.'

They returned to the carriage where Isabel sat waiting for them with Jeremy standing by. Jane rushed to join her. 'Issie, what happened?'

'There was such a crush of people, all pushing and pulling, and I could not move and you all left me and I fainted and would have been trampled underfoot if Drew had not seen what happened and rescued me.'

'Then we are indebted to him,' Mark said, taking his seat opposite her. Drew joined them and they were driven at speed back to Mount Street. The gentlemen did not stay long after delivering the ladies safely into the care of their aunt, who fussed round Isabel and suggested the physician should be called, but Isabel would not hear of it. 'I am perfectly well now,' she said. 'It was the heat and the crush of people made me faint, nothing more than that. I am going to bed. Tomorrow we are going riding in Hyde Park. I would not miss that for the world.'

Jane went to her own bed, but she could not sleep. Her sister had a robust constitution and had never fainted in her life, so what was happening now? Was she deliberately throwing herself into the path of Andrew Ashton? Did she really wish she had not accepted Mark's proposal? It would cause the most dreadful scandal for her to back out now. It would break Mark's heart and he would be tainted by it, too. He was too good a man to be treated in that fashion.

Mark was occupied with his lawyer all the following morning and Jane spent it writing more letters, while Isabel and their aunt went shopping. They did not return until it was almost time for the gentlemen to bring the riding horses to the house. Jane went to her room to change into her riding habit, which was the one she always wore for riding at home. It was plain and serviceable in a dark-green grosgrain. She heard the men arrive as she was slipping into her boots. After fastening a green hat on her dark hair with a hat pin, she went downstairs to greet them.

They were standing in the hall, when Isabel came from her room and down the stairs. She was wearing a new riding habit in mauve velvet, cut in the military style with lines of braiding and gold-fringed epaulettes. Her head was crowned with a tall beaver hat with mauve feathers curling round the brim and touching her cheek. Her feet were encased in kid half-boots. Jane could only stare at her.

'Here I am, gentlemen,' she said cheerfully. 'How do I look?' And she twirled to show off her ensemble, though the very long skirt hampered her.

'Lovely, as always,' Mark said.

'Magnificent,' Drew added.

Jane was silent as they made their way to the front of the house and mounted. The road was busy and they could only ride in single file until they entered Hyde Park, when they walked their horses at a sedate pace along the Row. It was not Jane's idea of going for a ride, but she could not leave Isabel who was intent on seeing and being seen.

They had been riding for perhaps half an hour when another rider coming towards them stopped when he reached them. 'Wyndham, good day,' he said. He was a tall, elegant figure with dark curly hair and almost black eyes, which looked Isabel over appreciatively, then turned towards Jane and then to Drew. 'Ashton, we meet again.'

'Indeed,' Drew said.

'Wyndham, are you not going to present me to the ladies?' the newcomer asked.

Mark seemed reluctant, but he turned to Isabel first. 'Isabel, may I present Lord Bolsover. My lord, Miss Isabel Cavenhurst, my future wife.'

Bolsover swept off his tall beaver to her. 'My felicitations, Miss Cavenhurst. My friend Mark is a fortunate man.'

Isabel replied with a ready smile and a nod. 'My lord.'

Mark turned to Jane. 'And this is Miss Jane Cavenhurst.'

His lordship bowed again, but Jane could not bring herself to smile at him. She inclined her head without speaking.

'Daughters of Sir Edward, I assume,' he said. 'And sisters to Teddy. I am indeed glad to make your acquaintances.'

Isabel, who had never heard of Lord Bolsover in connection with her brother, was inclined to be friendly towards him. 'Oh, are you a friend of Teddy's?'

'I know him well,' he said. 'But I have missed him of late. I do hope he is not ailing.'

'Oh, no, he has gone to India to make his fortune.'

Bolsover laughed aloud. 'So that is where he has hidden himself. No matter, there are other ways of skinning a cat.'

'Isabel, I do not think we should detain Lord Bolsover,' Jane put in quickly. 'And we must be on our way.' She gathered up her reins to move off.

'No doubt we shall meet again,' he said, touching the brim of his hat. 'I have business with Sir Edward.'

'I do not like the sound of that,' Jane said to Mark as they resumed riding. 'It sounded almost like a threat.'

'Don't worry, he can do nothing while Teddy is out of the country.'

'He could threaten Papa.'

'I doubt he plans to leave London to go to Norfolk in the middle of the Season, Jane. He can make a fortune fleecing the young bloods who come to town to enjoy themselves. He would not forgo that.'

'Are you really his friend?'

'Certainly not, no more than he is mine. I detest the man.'

'Why?' Isabel demanded, catching the end of the conversation. 'I found him very civil.'

'He is the one to whom Teddy owes money,' Jane said. 'It is that man who drove our brother to emigrate.'

'It was Teddy's own fault, if you ask me,' Isabel said. 'He did not have to gamble.'

'You are right, of course, but I fear Lord Bolsover has not finished with us yet.'

'What can he do?'

'Nothing,' Mark put in. 'Let us forget him and enjoy the rest of our ride.'

'Yes, let's,' Isabel said and kicked her horse into a trot and then a canter. 'I'll race you to that tree over there.' And she was gone at a crazy gallop.

There was nothing they could do but follow, led by Drew, who was the only one riding his own mount, which gave him the advantage. Jane was a good horsewoman, but on a hired hack could not catch her sister, let alone keep up with the men. She was well behind them when she saw her sister ride under the tree she had pointed out. In an effort to pull up, she was caught by an overhanging branch with such force it threw her to the ground.

Drew was off his horse in an instant and kneeling beside her. He had her head cradled in his arms when Mark and Jane arrived and dismounted. Jane fell to her knees beside them.

Isabel was unconscious, her face paper white. 'I fear she is badly hurt,' Drew said, with an unaccustomed tremor in his voice. 'We must get her back to Mount Street as swiftly as possible and have a doctor fetched.'

He turned from addressing Mark to look down at Isabel and the expression on his face filled Jane with alarm. It was more than just the concern of a gentleman towards an injured lady, more than that of a friend. He loved Isabel. She looked up at Mark to see if he had noticed, but if he had, he betrayed nothing of his feelings as he prepared to remount his horse and go for help.

'Issie, wake up,' Jane said, tears filling her eyes. 'Please, Issie, please wake up.'

Isabel's eyelids fluttered and then she opened her eyes wide. 'Where am I?'

'You came off your horse,' Drew said.

She turned her head towards him. 'Oh, it is you.' Her eyelids fluttered and closed again with a soft sigh.

'Wake up, Issie,' Jane implored her. 'Tell us if you are hurt. Are you in pain?'

'My head aches.'

'It is not to be wondered at,' Drew said. 'You hit your head and there is already the beginning of a lump, but I do not think there are any broken bones. We must get you home and send for a doctor to make sure. Mark has gone to fetch a carriage.'

She struggled to sit up, but he gently pulled her back. 'Lie still or you will make your head worse.'

She subsided, leaving Jane to worry about the inelegant position in which her sister lay and the fact that Andrew Ashton was cradling her in his arms in a most loving way. Did Issie know what was happening? Did Mark?

A hired carriage drew up beside them and Mark jumped out. Drew picked Isabel up and carried her to it. He put her gently on the seat and Jane climbed in beside her.

'We will bring the horses,' Mark said, addressing Jane. 'Do not attempt to leave the carriage until we arrive to help. We will be right behind you.'

'We'll soon be home, Issie,' Jane said when the jolting of the carriage as it moved off made Isabel cry out. 'Put your head in my lap, if it helps.

Isabel did that and Jane sat cradling it, noticing the bump on the side of Issie's head growing and turning purple. If she had had doubts about the genuineness of

Issie fainting at the Museum and at Ranelagh Gardens, she had none over this. She would not have fallen from her horse deliberately, even if taking off like that had been meant to cause a stir. *Oh, foolish, foolish Issie,* she thought as she prayed there would be no permanent damage to her lovely sister.

The two men were right behind them when they drew up outside the Mount Street house. Mark dismounted and ran to the carriage to help Isabel from it. She was too unsteady to walk, so he carried her up the steps into the house followed by Jane and Drew. The footman who admitted them ran off to fetch Lady Cartrose, who immediately took in the situation. 'She must go to bed at once,' she said, turning to dispatch a footman to fetch her physician.

Mark had put Isabel on a chair, but picked her up again to carry her to her bedchamber. Bessie was sent to help Jane undress her while Lady Cartrose and the two men waited in the drawing room. Neither felt like leaving until they knew the extent of the injury.

'What happened?' her ladyship asked, indicating that they should take seats. 'How did Isabel come to fall from her horse? I understood you were only going out for a gentle hack in the Park.'

'That was the intention,' Mark said. 'But Isabel's horse bolted with her. Drew and I galloped after her to try to bring it to a halt, but before we could do so, she was hit by the overhanging branch of a tree which knocked her to the ground. It was so sudden no one had a chance to prevent it.'

'She was knocked out of her senses,' Drew put in.

'What made the horse bolt?'

'I really do not know,' Mark said. 'I wish we had been watching more carefully.'

'I wish it, too,' Drew said. 'I sincerely hope there is no permanent damage. I should never forgive myself.'

The sound of voices in the hall told them the doctor had arrived. Her ladyship rose to conduct him to the patient's room, leaving the two men facing each other in a silence which last several minutes. 'Someone ought to see to the horses,' Mark said in a flat voice. 'We can't leave hired horses on the street.'

'I will do it.' Drew jumped up and left the room, leaving Mark musing on his own. He was sorry Isabel had been hurt and would not for the world have wished it on her, but if she had not spurred her horse in that reckless fashion the accident would never have happened. Why had she done it? Why was he having to make excuses for her and pretend the horse was to blame? Would life with her always be like that? What did that augur for their future happiness together?

Lady Cartrose came back into the room. 'She is comfortable and the doctor has prescribed something for the headache. He said she needed to rest for at least a week, but he did not think her life was in danger.'

'Thank the lord for that,' Mark said.

'Jane is sitting with her. She is blaming herself.'

'Whatever for?'

'I do not know, something about not curbing Isabel's exuberance.'

'Exuberance,' he mused aloud. 'Is that what it's called? I would have called it wilfulness. Isabel set off to gallop and the mare got the bit between her teeth and bolted. It had nothing to do with Jane.'

'You are very fond of Jane, are you not?'

'Indeed I am. I admire her greatly for the way she tries to keep the family together, making sacrifices for them, which they seem to take for granted. She is always making excuses for their bad behaviour. If it isn't Teddy, it's Isabel.'

'You make a good champion of her, Lord Wyndham.'

'There is no one else to do it.'

'Not even Mr Ashton?'

'Drew?' he asked, puzzled. 'No, I do not think so. She always behaves coolly and correctly towards him. What made you think it?'

'He is so often in your company, the four of you together.'

'Why not? Drew is my friend.'

'Oh, I see. I did not quite understand.'

He was not one to analyse his own feelings too closely, but the events of the past few days when he had been more in Jane's company had opened his eyes to the differences between her and her sister and what he saw and felt filled him with doubts. Drew returned before he could ponder that more deeply.

'How is she?' he asked, after bowing to Lady Cartrose.

'Awake and sitting up,' her ladyship answered. 'She will recover, but must have a week in bed.'

'Thank goodness it is no more than that,' he said, taking the chair her ladyship indicated.

'Did you manage the horses?' Mark asked.

'Lord Bolsover turned up just as I was rounding them up and offered his assistance. He said he had seen what happened and was on his way to ask after the invalid.'

'What on earth is the man playing at?'

'I've no idea, but I was glad of his help. Four horses on a busy street are not easy to handle. We each rode one and led another.' He turned to Lady Cartrose. 'When will we be able to visit Miss Isabel?'

'I think perhaps tomorrow Mark may see her, if she feels up to it.' It was plain she did not think it fitting that Drew should see the young lady while she lay in bed.

'Then we will take our leave,' Mark said, rising to bow to her. Drew followed suit.

'I had not intended to stay in town above three or four days,' Mark said, as they walked to South Audley Street. 'And I ought to go back to Hadlea and inform Sir Edward what has happened. No doubt Jane will want to stay with her sister. I can come back for them when Isabel is well enough to travel.'

They separated on the corner of Mount Street and South Audley Street, arranging to meet at White's for supper that evening. Mark went to the mews to order his carriage to be ready to return to Norfolk the next morning and then went into the house to change and deal with some paperwork. But he could not settle to it and found himself pacing backwards and forwards, his mind on Jane and Isabel. The latter was lovely, charming and sensitive in many ways, but in others, completely selfish. Not until recently had he realised that.

As for Jane, she was far from the plain Jane she was purported to be. Her beauty was in her inner self, in her compassion and selflessness which shone through in everything she did. Why had he not seen that before? Was it because everyone else overlooked her and treated her as if she did not matter, was as familiar and static as the furniture? He had been as guilty as anyone. It was not that she lacked confidence; she was more independent than most and able to hold her own in an argument when the subject was something she felt passionate about, especially the orphans. Not everyone needed to be lively and flirtatious—indeed that could sometimes pall. There he was, comparing them again. Did that mean he had made the wrong choice? He stopped his thoughts abruptly before they carried him away where it was best not to go.

On his way to White's he stopped at Mount Street to enquire of the invalid and was told by her aunt that she was comfortable and resting. 'Jane is sitting with her,' the old lady said. 'But the medicine the doctor prescribed has made her sleep and there is nothing we can do but watch over her. What her father will say of my guardianship of his daughters I dread to think. I have written to my sister-in-law and told her Isabel will have the best medical attention available.'

'I must return to Hadlea tomorrow,' he said, 'and will call at the Manor to apprise Sir Edward and Lady Cavenhurst of what happened and reassure them that Isabel is recovering. I assume Jane will stay with her sister? I will return to take them home when Isabel is well enough to travel.'

'Thank you, my lord. I do not know what we would have done without you.'

'I did nothing. Please convey my good wishes to both ladies and tell Isabel I wish her a speedy recovery.' He picked up his hat, bowed and left the house for his rendezvous with Drew.

If he had hoped for a quiet supper and then home to bed, he was thwarted by the arrival of Lord Bolsover. 'May I join you?' his lordship asked. Not waiting for a reply, he sat down at the table where Mark waited for Drew to arrive. 'I would hear how Miss Cavenhurst goes.'

'She is recovering at the home of her aunt.'

'I am glad to hear it. I was fearful that she had sustained a serious injury. A rather headstrong girl, I believe. Has no one told her that the terrain of the park away from the Row is too uneven for a lady riding side-saddle to attempt to gallop? Most unseemly, but courageous, all the same.' He smiled suddenly, but it was the smile of a tiger. 'Undoubtedly Andrew Ashton thought so, for I could see he was most solicitous of her. I helped him take the horses back to the stables, you know.'

'So I heard. We are indebted to you, my lord.'

'He bears watching, that friend of yours.'

'What do you mean by that?'

'Why, you are in danger of losing your bride, or I miss my guess.'

Mark was furious, but contained his temper with an effort. 'You, sir, are impertinent.'

'I am merely stating a fact. It seems to me all the Cavenhursts are untrustworthy.'

'Why are you so interested in my fiancée, Bolsover?'

'I am interested in all the doings of that family. Her brother has deprived me of a considerable amount of money and I cannot let that go unchallenged.'

'What do you propose to do? Neither Sir Edward nor, come to that, either of the Misses Cavenhurst, is responsible for Teddy's gambling debts.'

'Not in law, perhaps, but I am sure Sir Edward would wish to avoid the scandal of a scapegrace son welshing on his debts.'

'I believe Sir Edward considers a spell in India will set him to rights.'

'Only because he does not have the blunt to pay his son's dues, or so I have heard. It is a pity I did not know that earlier before I acquired all the debts. Now, I shall have to rethink my strategy.'

'I do not know how you came by that piece of tittle tattle, but you have been misinformed.'

'I think not. Ah, here is your friend, Mr Ashton.' He stood up. 'I leave you to make what you will of what I have said, but rest assured, by hedge or by style, I will have my revenge.'

'What did he want?' Drew asked as he sat down and beckoned a waiter.

'He was enquiring of the invalid. I do not think he cares a groat how Isabel is, he was simply trying to garner information about Teddy.'

'You can hardly blame him for that. He's lost a deal of blunt.'

'Then why spend more buying up the rest of Teddy's debts? I do believe it is Sir Edward he is after and he means to do it through his son or his daughters.'

'I do not see how.'

'Neither do I, but he spoke of revenge, which puzzles me, since I cannot see that he has been harmed by Teddy or anyone else in the family. There is more to it than debt.'

The waiter came to take their order and they left off their discussion while they decided what to eat.

'Would you like me to try to discover what it is, while you are gone to Hadlea?' Drew asked as the waiter disappeared. 'Bolsover may have confided in some of his associates, who might not know my connection with you.'

'Yes, please do that. He appears prodigiously wealthy, which is surprising because the estate he inherited from his father is only a moderate one in Northamptonshire, not enough to support the kind of life he leads.'

They talked about how the information could be achieved and used while they ate. Not once did Mark mention Bolsover's hint that he might lose Isabel. Andrew Ashton was an honourable man, a long-term friend and he would not betray him in that fashion. But all the same, he could not quite dismiss the idea, not least because Isabel herself had been behaving strangely ever since she met him. If only she had not had that accident, they would all be on the way back to Hadlea the next day and out of harm's way.

Chapter Six

Mark called the next day before he left town and was allowed a short visit to the sick room, where Jane sat reading to her sister. Jane put the book down and went over to the window to look out on the busy street and give them a little privacy. She heard him ask Isabel how she was and her sister's low answer, but then the conversation stopped. They were silent for so long, she risked a glance. Mark was sitting on the chair she had been using and Isabel was propped up in bed, with the covers up to her chin. They were simply sitting there with nothing to say, both looking down, both unhappy.

'I am going back to Hadlea immediately,' he said at last. 'Have you a message for your parents?'

'Tell them I am doing well and no harm has been done,' she said. 'Tell them not to worry. Jane is looking after me.'

'Ah, the inestimable Jane.' He turned to her. 'You are looking tired, Jane. Has no one thought about how you feel?'

'I feel fine,' she said. 'Do not worry about me. Tell Mama and Papa I shall stay until Issie is well enough to travel.'

'I will come back and fetch you.' He rose, picked Isabel's hand off of the coverlet and kissed the back of it. 'I'll be off then. Don't do anything rash while I am away.'

Isabel laughed. 'I can't do much stuck here in bed, can I?'

He bowed to Jane and left. He was no sooner gone than Drew arrived, but Lady Cartrose did not think it fitting to allow him into the sickroom. She received him in the drawing room and gave him an account of the patient's progress and he had to be content with that.

Day by day Isabel recovered and though Jane spent some time sitting with her, trying to cheer her up, she was quiet and withdrawn. Drew called regularly to ask after the patient; Isabel did not see him, though Jane did. He was most concerned for the invalid, more than was warranted in Jane's opinion, considering Isabel was engaged elsewhere. She might not have thought of it if she had not seen the look on his face as he cradled her sister in his arms. She wondered whether to confront him about it, but decided against making an issue of it. Once they returned to Hadlea it would die a natural death.

When she was not sitting with her sister, Jane returned to the matter of raising funds and continued to write letters and invite people to Aunt Emmeline's soirée. Her aunt had wanted to cancel it altogether, but Isabel, feeling guilty about what had happened, insisted it go ahead a week later than planned when she was sure she would have recovered enough to play her part. Jane encouraged her to walk about her room to strengthen her muscles and, on the sixth day, Bessie helped her to dress and she went downstairs for the first time. She was there when Drew arrived on his daily visit.

'I am pleased to see you looking so well,' he said, after

bowing to Lady Cartrose and Jane. 'I feared you might have sustained a serious injury.'

Isabel laughed. 'A bump on the head, that was all, and it is quite gone now. I am my old self.'

'Then I am, indeed, relieved.'

'Are you going to come to Aunt Emmeline's soirée tomorrow evening? I think it will be a very grand affair.'

'It is not meant to be a grand affair,' Jane said. 'It is to raise funds for my orphanage.'

'Well, I know that, but Aunt Emmeline has invited a great many wealthy people so it is bound to be grand.'

'Whatever it is I would not miss it,' Drew said. 'If Mark is not back in time, I shall stand in for him.'

After he had left, Isabel went back to her room to rest, but as she no longer needed anyone sitting with her, Jane went to walk in the garden where she rehearsed under her breath the words she would use to persuade people that the soldiers' orphans were a worthy cause for their charity.

It was there Mark found her on his return. 'Jane, how are you?' He took both her hands in his own and leaned back to look at her. 'You are looking pale. Have you not been sleeping?'

'I am perfectly well, thank you.' His touch was sending shivers into the very core of her. Her love for him was something that could never be cured and must never be spoken of, so every tiny touch, every short private conversation, was secretly treasured. 'You should be asking about Isabel, not me.'

'I imagine she is fully recovered,' he said drily. 'Bessie has just informed me she has gone out with Lady Cartrose and Drew.'

'Gone out?' Jane echoed. 'I thought she had gone to

rest before changing for dinner. I did not even know Mr Ashton had arrived. I hope it will not exhaust her.'

'Your aunt and Drew will make sure she does not become too tired.'

'Will you wait for them?'

'Of course.'

'Did you see my parents?'

'Yes, I did. They are naturally very concerned about Isabel, but I was able to reassure them. They are looking forward to having you both safely home again.'

'I shall be glad to go home too,' she said. 'But there is the soirée tomorrow evening. I must stay for that.'

'You are going ahead with it, then.'

'Yes, Isabel would not have it cancelled on her account, so we simply informed everyone it would be a week later. I have been rehearsing what I will say to persuade people to part with their money.'

'While we wait, will you tell me what you are planning to say?'

They seated themselves on a bench in an arbour, shaded from the sun. 'I thought I would begin by telling everyone about the little beggar boy that set me thinking and how I felt not enough was being done for the soldiers' families. The men left their homes, wives and children to risk their lives and die for king and country and we should not forget that. The least we can do is remember their sacrifice and help their children. After that I will tell them about the Hadlea Children's Home and how we plan to run it and how much it will cost. I have worked out some expenditure: buying the home, furnishing it, taking on staff, running expenses like food, clothes, heating.'

'Would you like me to check the figures?'

'Would you? That would be a great help, but can you spare the time?'

'For you, Jane, I will always spare time.'

'Oh.' She was taken aback, but pulled herself together to laugh. 'You want to know how your money is being spent?'

'No, of course not. I trust you implicitly.'

'I was only joking.'

'I know, but other contributors might be more demanding and it is as well to have the answers at your fingertips.'

'If I get any other contributors.'

'I am sure you will.'

'Shall we go indoors? My notes are all there.'

They rose and went into the morning room, where Jane had left her papers spread out on the table.

They were absorbed in the calculations when Lady Cartrose and Isabel returned, accompanied by Drew.

'Mark,' Isabel said as he rose to greet them. 'I was not expecting you back so soon.'

'I came in order to attend the soirée tomorrow evening and to take you home. Your parents are anxious to have you back.'

'I am not sure I am recovered enough.'

'You were well enough to go out,' Jane said.

'We did not go far and we went in the carriage.'

Lady Cartrose summoned a maid to bring refreshments and they sat down to converse until they arrived. 'I wanted some pink ribbon to match my gown for tomorrow,' Isabel went on. 'And Drew bought us ice creams at Gunter's. Then we saw the Regent riding by in his carriage. He deigned to smile and lift a hand in salute to us, but there were others on the road who booed him. He is enormously fat.'

'He is known to eat prodigious quantities,' her ladyship put in, demonstrating her own ability in that area when a maid brought in the tea tray and a plate of cakes.

'And that when half his people are starving,' Jane added, accepting a cup of tea, but declining anything to eat. 'No wonder he is booed.'

'There are rumours he means to divorce his wife,' Lady Cartrose put in. 'He wants an heir, but if Princess Charlotte manages to bring her latest pregnancy to term, we might have one sooner than we think.'

'I have a good mind to write to him and point out the desperate straits of the soldiers' orphans,' Jane said.

'I do not suppose a letter would ever advance beyond a second or third secretary,' Mark said, smiling at her. 'You would do better appealing to others further down the social scale.'

'Like the Duke of Wellington,' Isabel said with a giggle. 'Do you know, Mark, Jane had a reply from his secretary.'

'Did you, Jane?'

'Yes. He said the Duke was cognisant of the problem and would enter into anything the Government might do to alleviate it,' she answered, 'But he did not feel it fair to subscribe to one small charity above others, especially in a part of the country with which he is unfamiliar. His Grace could not give to all and therefore must decline.'

'An evasive answer if ever I heard one,' Mark said.

They finished drinking their tea and the men took their leave, walking swiftly in the direction of South Audley Street. 'You have been a constant visitor to Mount Street, I believe,' Mark said.

'I go to enquire of the invalid and, in your absence, to see if I can be of service to the ladies. Is there anything wrong with that?'

'No, of course not, but I did notice Isabel referred to you as Drew.'

'A slip of the tongue, no doubt. She often hears you call me that. I do not mind it, if you do not.'

'No, we are all friends. Will you come to the soirée tomorrow evening?'

'Indeed I will. I think Miss Cavenhurst will need all the support she can get. I fear she is going to be disappointed—there are too many people, like the good Duke, who think the problem is for others to solve.'

'I doubt His Grace ever saw Jane's letter.'

'You are probably right, but it is not only that. There have been rumours…'

'What rumours?' Mark asked sharply.

'That Miss Cavenhurst is using whatever funds she gathers, not for the benefit of orphans, but to help solve her father's financial difficulties.'

'Good God! Who is spreading such tales? No, let me guess. Hector Bolsover.'

'You are right. He is saying that none of the Cavenhursts can be trusted with money.'

'I was right, was I not? This is not about Teddy and his debts. Have you managed to discover what is behind it?'

'No, but I think Toby Moore might know something, so I am cultivating the gentleman. He is a very poor card player.'

Mark laughed. 'It is more the case that you are an exceptionally good one.'

'However, when he owes me a great deal of blunt I

shall magnanimously offer to waive it for information. I have undertaken to play tonight. Do you come?'

'No, I have Jane's figures to check and suggestions to make ready for tomorrow.' He tapped the folder of notes he carried. 'I want to give her the best possible chance, especially in view of what you have told me.'

They parted on the corner of the road. Mark walked half the length of South Audley Street, dwelling, not on Jane's figures, but on Isabel and Drew and wondering if Bolsover, for all his nastiness, had been right in his insinuation. He should have felt angry and jealous, but surprisingly did not, or only in so far as the gossip would harm both families if the engagement were broken. It would be decidedly dishonourable to consider breaking it himself and so he must remain passive and await events. The alternative would be to tackle Drew and call him out. But what would that achieve? The death or injury of one or the other and a great many unhappy people. And maybe he was reading more into it than was actually there. He shrugged his shoulders and entered his house.

The following evening, with wine and refreshments ready in the dining room and the drawing room cleared of most of its furniture and ornaments to make room for people, Jane prepared herself for what she knew would be an ordeal. Her gown was a pale sea-green silk of a plain design, trimmed with dark green velvet ribbon. Bessie, who dressed her hair, threaded it with more green ribbon and she wore the pearls her father had bought for her on her twenty-first birthday.

Her head was buzzing with the speech she meant to make, which she intended to be brief in favour of circulating among the guests and speaking to them individually.

Mark arrived early so that they could take a last look at her figures and the notes she had made. At eight o'clock friends of Lady Cartrose began arriving and, being plied with refreshments, stood about eating, drinking and gossiping. They were followed by others, less well known, and by nine o'clock the room was full. It was then Isabel made her entrance, wearing her sari and causing something of a stir, which, of course, she had known it would. Jane could do nothing about it as her sister drifted over to Drew and asked him if he approved. Neither Mark nor Jane heard his reply.

'Let us make a start,' Mark said, turning away from the sight of his fiancée flirting with his friend. He called for attention and said a little about the reason they were gathered together and introduced Jane. Then he helped her stand on a stool so that she could be seen and heard.

She was shaking with nerves, but was so passionate about her subject, she forgot everything else and was soon in full spate. At first the audience were silent, but as she went on the murmurs grew until she was forced to stop to deal with them. 'You have questions?' she asked. 'I will answer them in due time.'

'Answer them now,' one gentleman called out.

'Very well. Who is to be first?'

'I will,' the same man said. 'How can we be sure the money you collect from us will be used for the purpose you state? I have heard your father is close to bankruptcy and the money will go to settle his debts.'

'That is a monstrous accusation,' Jane retorted angrily. 'Even if my father were bankrupt, which is a downright lie and which, were I a man, I would call you out for, it would have no bearing on the Hadlea Home, whose finances will be kept entirely separate.'

'So you say.'

'Toby Moore,' Drew had left Isabel talking to her aunt and come to Mark's side. 'He has no doubt been sent by Bolsover to disrupt the meeting. Let us throw him out.'

They moved towards the questioner. Seeing them approach, the man backed away and, reaching the door, bolted through it. But the damage had been done. Jane could not finish her speech for the heckling, as one question after another was fired at her, not about the home, which she could have understood, but about her father and brother. She did her best to parry them, but in the end it was Mark who rescued her, helping her down from the stool and climbing on it himself.

'If you will not listen to Miss Cavenhurst, then listen to me,' he shouted above the din. 'Most of you know who I am, but for those who do not, I am Lord Wyndham of Broadacres, close by the village of Hadlea. My family has been in residence there for hundreds of years and is well respected both in Norfolk and in London. I and my late father have both subscribed to the Hadlea Children's Home and I will personally guarantee Miss Cavenhurst's integrity.'

'You have an interest, you are betrothed to her sister,' someone commented in a loud voice.

'So I am, but that is all the more reason to make sure my good name is not brought into disrepute. I will appoint my own man of business to set up a trust and oversee the funds. This home is important for the little children who need it and I think it is shameful that so good a cause should be sullied by innuendo and downright calumny. Now, if you would like to make a donation, Miss Cavenhurst is here to take it. If not, I bid you goodnight.'

He stood and watched as several people made their

escape, but one or two came forward to ask Jane more about what she planned to do and she was able to make the points she had been prevented from making earlier.

Only when they had all gone and she had some pledges, though not nearly as many as she had hoped, and a small pile of jewellery to which she had added her own pearls, was she able to breathe freely and thank Mark for his timely assistance.

'You were magnificent,' she said. 'I could not have managed without you.'

'It was my privilege and pleasure.'

'What did that man mean about my father being bankrupt? Where did such rumours start?'

'From Lord Bolsover, I imagine.' He paused. 'Jane, has anyone in your family ever come up against him before?'

'Besides Teddy, you mean?'

'Yes. Perhaps some time ago, something that might explain the grudge he seems to have.'

'Teddy owes him money and has escaped his clutches, is that not grudge enough?'

'I am not sure it has anything to do with Teddy. I think getting his hooks on Teddy was only a means to an end.'

'What end?'

'That I do not know, but I will endeavour to find out.'

'I cannot think of anything. Papa has always been straight and true. I am sure you must be mistaken.'

'Perhaps.' He paused. 'You are looking tired, Jane. This has all been too much for you after looking after Isabel as well.'

'I am a little tired, but a night's sleep is all I need.' She paused, motioning to the pledges, the money and jewels.

'Will you take charge of these? I do not want to bring any more accusations down on my head if I keep them by me.'

'Yes, of course. If you are agreeable, I shall call tomorrow morning and we will go to Halliday and have a trust set up and open an account at the bank in the name of the trust. That way everyone can see it is all above board.'

'Yes, please.' She picked up a canvas bag, put everything into it and handed it to him. 'I knew something like that would have to be done, but I had not thought it was urgent. This evening has made me see so how naïve I have been. I needed you.'

'My pleasure.' He smiled and touched her hand. 'Away to your bed, Jane. I shall bid goodnight to Isabel and her ladyship and be off.'

When he had gone, she said goodnight to her aunt and sister and went to her room, undressed and tumbled into bed. It had been an eventful and troubling day, but it was over and she had made a start on her big project. She could not have done it without Mark's help. Those rumours being spread by Bolsover were worrying, too. They could be very damaging especially if it became known that the Cavenhursts were having to economise. As always happened in such cases, every creditor who had been prepared to wait for his money would now be knocking at their door.

Mark had said he would try to find out what lay behind Bolsover's animosity and she could trust him to do his best, but it was unfair of her to lean on him so heavily. She should be more self-reliant and that meant tackling Lord Bolsover herself. If only she could make him see reason about Teddy's debts and retract his calumny, they might all live in peace and her father's money troubles need not be made public. It would have to be the next day because Mark was taking them home the day after. But how to do it? She did not know his lordship's direction and, even if she did, it was certainly not the thing for an unmarried lady to visit a gentleman in his quarters. He gambled at White's and probably other clubs, but she certainly could not venture into St James's.

Before she could decide what to do, she had drifted off to sleep.

Jane woke next morning very early with the problem still in her mind and it had not been solved by the time Mark arrived with his tilbury. She did not think that she needed a chaperon, but her aunt insisted on one and, as she was far too fat to squeeze into a vehicle meant for two, Bessie was told to accompany her.

Even so, it was a tight fit and Jane found herself so close to Mark, his trouser-clad thigh hard against hers, that she could feel its warmth through her dress. It was so unnerving she could think of nothing else and found herself almost lost for words when Mark spoke to her. When they arrived, he jumped down to hand her out and she pulled herself together to precede him into the building.

Going through the front office, where the juniors worked at their desks, Jane was reminded that her brother had once been a junior here and had left under a cloud. Would that make Mr Halliday less inclined to help her? A clerk conducted them up to the younger Mr Halliday's office, where Mark was greeted cordially.

'I have brought Miss Cavenhurst to meet you, Cecil,' Mark said. 'She would do some business with you.'

Jane bobbed, shook the outstretched hand and was offered a chair.

'The Cavenhurst affairs are usually handled by my

father,' the lawyer said as he and Mark also seated themselves. 'If it is about Mr Cavenhurst...'

'It is not about Teddy or my father,' she said. 'Lord Wyndham will explain.'

As Mark spoke, the lawyer's initial wariness vanished and he became interested in Jane's project and readily agreed to set up the trust. 'Who had you in mind for trustees?' he asked.

'Miss Cavenhurst, of course,' Mark said.

'It is unusual for an unmarried lady to serve in that way,' Mr Halliday said.

'Yes, but it is Miss Cavenhurst's project, she is its leading light, so I think we should allow it,' Mark said. 'But there must be others who are not connected with the family. Would you be one, Cecil? And perhaps we could ask our bank manager.'

They had gone on to discuss the details and, an hour later, left with everything in hand and without the canvas bag containing the money and jewels. The latter would be auctioned and the proceeds added to the funds and Mr Halliday had undertaken to make the arrangements for that. Mark escorted her out to the carriage and saw her safely in. 'I have a little business of my own with Mr Halliday, Jane. I won't be long.' He went back into the building, leaving Jane sitting beside Bessie.

The street was busy with people hurrying to and fro on the pavement and vehicles of all kinds passing up and down, from gigs to grand carriages, from coster barrows to heavy drays. She was so engrossed in watching a skirmish between a skinny terrier and a spitting ginger cat, she did not see the man who approached the carriage and stopped.

'We meet again, my dear Miss Cavenhurst.'

She looked round to find Lord Bolsover doffing his hat to her. 'My lord.'

'All alone? No stalwart knight to defend you?'

'Lord Wyndham is with me.'

'I do not see him.'

'He has gone back inside for a moment, but I am glad we have met.'

'How flattering!'

'I did not intend to flatter, my lord. I wish to speak to you about the rumour being spread about my father being bankrupt.'

'Rumours? Dear, dear, that is unkind.'

'I believe you perpetrated them to discredit me and prevent me raising money for my orphans.'

'Now, why would I do that, Miss Cavendish? I am as sympathetic as the next man to the orphans' plight, but I doubt you will be able to do anything about it.'

'Why not? Someone has to if the children are not to grow up thieves and beggars. All I want is to give them a chance.'

'The reason is obvious, Miss Cavenhurst—you are a woman trying to get along in a man's world and you will meet resistance at every turn. Women are not built to fight with reason. They fight with their emotions.'

'And what is wrong with that?'

'It inclines then to make wrong decisions. You will find out the truth of that in due course.'

'My lord, that sounds like a threat. I wonder why you have taken such an aversion to me. We have only recently met and until a few weeks ago I had never heard of you.'

'Had you not? That is surprising.'

'If my brother had not been so foolish as to play cards

with you, I should still be in ignorance of the kind of man you are.'

'I venture to suggest you are still in ignorance. There are two sides to every argument and you have heard only one.'

'Perhaps, but if you value truth and justice you will let it be known that you were mistaken, my father is not bankrupt and you have no reason to believe I will not conduct the affairs of the Hadlea Children's Home honestly.'

'You are assuming that it was I who started the rumour. You have no proof of it.' He smiled suddenly. 'But if the rumour is true, then I would be a fool to deny it.'

'Of course it is not true.'

'I should ask your father when you get home, Miss Cavendish, or you could go back inside that building and ask Mr Halliday senior, who is the Cavenhurst lawyer, I believe.'

'I will do no such thing!'

'You know,' he said, still smiling, 'you are quite beautiful when you are angry and your eyes flash defiance. I find myself strangely in sympathy with you and that is a weakness I cannot allow myself to indulge in.' He bowed to her, replaced his hat and strolled away.

She watched his departing back in fury and was fighting back angry tears when Mark rejoined her. 'I hope I have not been too long,' he said, climbing in beside her. 'Shall we have an ice cream at Gunter's? It is a warm day and... Jane, are you crying?'

'I am angry.'

'Why, because I left you? I am sorry for that, but I was gone only a few minutes.'

'No, it is not that. I have had an argument with Lord Bolsover. He is an odious man and refuses to admit it was he who spread the rumours about my father and he said my project can never succeed because I am a woman ruled by emotion.' She gave a cracked laugh. 'And here I am, proving it.'

'Oh, Jane, why did speak to him at all? You should have cut him.'

'I wanted to plead with him to stop the rumours.'

'You do not plead with men like Bolsover, Jane. They would see it as weakness. Now let us go and have that ice cream and forget about him.'

But she found it difficult to do that. The man's words ate into her brain and would not go away. She longed to go home, to the peace of Greystone Manor and the comforting presence of her parents. More than anything she wanted reassurance.

The ice cream was refreshing on a very warm day, but they did not linger long at Gunter's. 'My sister and Aunt Emmeline will be wondering what has happened to us,' she said.

Far from wondering what had happened, the ladies had gone for a carriage ride, they were told by a servant. 'Mr Ashton came and they went with him.'

'Then I will not stay,' Mark said. He drew the pearls from his pocket and put them into her hand. 'These are yours, I believe.'

She stared at them. 'How did you come by them? I left them with everything else to be auctioned.'

'I know you did, but I think it would hurt your father to know you had given them away. Keep them safe, Jane.'

'Other people were giving their jewels.'

'Perhaps, but not those they treasured. Your self-sacrifice does you credit, Jane, but the trust can do without them.'

'Thank you,' she said simply and reached up to kiss his cheek. It was an impulsive gesture of gratitude, no more.

'I will bring the travelling carriage here at nine o'clock tomorrow morning, if that is convenient, Jane, and if you think Isabel is strong enough for a long ride. Otherwise we could start later and go slower. It would mean spending two nights on the road instead of one, but I do not mind that.'

'I shall ask her, of course, but I think Isabel is strong enough and we will not need to prolong the journey. I am anxious to be home again as I am sure you are. We will be ready.'

He left and she went to join Bessie, who had gone up to her room to begin packing. Jane had not brought a great many clothes with her and it was soon folded neatly into the trunk she and Isabel shared. 'I will do Miss Isabel's this afternoon,' Bessie said. 'But I do not know how we shall get it all in, she has bought a great many new clothes.'

'I expect Lady Cartrose will lend her another trunk.'

Lady Cartrose, Isabel and Drew returned soon after this. Drew did not stop, saying he was sorry he had missed Mark because he needed to speak to him before they all left for Hadlea. 'I will go and seek him out,' he said. He bowed to her ladyship, then to Jane and finally Isabel, who looked woebegone. 'Goodbye, Miss Isabel,' he said. 'Have a safe journey and my felicitations on your forthcoming nuptials.' Then he was gone.

'That was a strange thing to say,' Jane said. 'It sounded as if he were not going to be at the wedding.'

'He isn't.' Isabel was openly crying. 'He is going away. I am never to see him again. He said it was for the best.'

Jane was inclined to agree with that, but refrained from saying so in view of Isabel's distress, but she realised her fears had been justified: Isabel imagined herself in love with Andrew Ashton. How deep and how lasting it was, she did not know. The sooner they were home the better. 'Mark is coming for us at nine in the morning,' she said, turning to more practical matters. 'I have done my packing. Bessie is planning to do yours this afternoon, Issie. Aunt, do you think you can lend Isabel a trunk? She has bought so many new clothes they will not all go into the small trunk we brought with us.'

'I am sure there is one in the attic,' her aunt said and went off to ask a footman to fetch it down.

'I don't want to go home,' Isabel burst out, amid her tears.

'Why ever not?'

'Because everyone will be talking about the wedding and I cannot bear it.'

'How can that be? Less than a month ago you were talking of nothing else and looking forward to your big day.'

'Yes, and I collect you saying that a wedding was not the be-all and end-all of a marriage and you were right. I see that now. I just wanted to be a bride and Mark is so handsome and rich, but it was a mistake to say I would marry him.'

'But you did and I am very sorry if anything I said made you have second thoughts. I only meant that the wedding itself was only the beginning and played only a small part in a marriage.'

'I know what you meant, but it set me thinking about

being bound to Mark for the rest of our lives and I simply cannot see it. And please do not say it is nerves, for I know it is not. I cannot marry Mark. He is not the love of my life.'

Her sister's words were hurting Jane more than she could bear. Her sister could not envisage a life with Mark whereas she could hardly envisage life without him. 'Issie,' she said slowly. 'Is there anyone else?'

Isabel lifted eyes full of misery to Jane's. 'You have guessed?'

'Is it Mr Ashton?'

'Yes. I have fallen in love with him, Jane. I think about him all the time. My heart lifts when he enters the room and drops again when he leaves it. The touch of his hand sets my body on fire and I want to cling to him and never let him go.'

Jane knew that feeling and felt herself sympathising with her sister, but for Isabel to fling off one suitor in favour of another when the announcement had already been made would cause the most terrible scandal. 'Does Mr Ashton share your feelings, Issie? Has he spoken of them?'

'Not directly, but I know he does. I know by the way he looks at me, the way he speaks. But he is too careful of his friendship with Mark to betray him, he told me that. That is why he is going away. I am so miserable, Jane. If I have to marry Mark, there will be three very unhappy people because I could never make him happy.'

Jane reflected there would be four, but that was her secret. 'I do not know what to say, Issie. Perhaps once we are home again and back into our usual routine, you will forget Mr Ashton and remember why you accepted Mark in the first place.'

'You do not understand.'

'Oh, I do. Believe me, I do.' She stood up. 'Go and help Bessie with your packing and then we will have an early supper and go to bed. We have an early start in the morning.'

Lady Cartrose returned as Jane was staring out on to the terrace, her mind in a whirl. 'I have had a trunk sent to Isabel's room,' she said. 'Bessie is packing, but Isabel is sitting on her bed weeping.'

'She does not want to go home.'

'I know, but I do not flatter myself it is because she wants to stay with me.'

'You know?'

'I am deaf, Jane, but I am not blind. It has been obvious to anyone with eyes to see what was happening.'

'It is very worrying, especially for Mark.'

'He seems to be bearing up very well.' She paused. 'I do not think you should force her to go ahead with the marriage, Jane. It would be a disaster.'

'It is not up to me, Aunt. I am hoping when we are home again and our parents take a hand in the matter, Issie will come to see that her *tendre* for Mr Ashton is mere infatuation, a fleeting thing she can put behind her.'

'I wonder you can advocate that, Jane, considering your own feelings.'

Jane was startled. 'My own feelings do not come into it, Aunt Emmeline.'

'Then they should. You are making a martyr of yourself by ignoring them.'

Jane did not answer. She had spent more time than usual with Mark of late, which had done nothing but strengthen her feelings for him. Had it become that obvious?

* * *

Mark was busy giving orders about preparing the carriage, packing and shutting the house when Drew found him.

'How did it go with the lawyers this morning?' he asked.

'Very well. The trust has been set up and the jewels will be auctioned.' He paused. 'After our business was concluded, I left Jane in the carriage to go back inside. I wanted to rescue her pearls from the auction. Her father gave her those for her twenty-first birthday and she ought not to have sacrificed them. I bought them back.' He smiled at the memory of that peck on the cheek. 'While I was away, Bolsover turned up and he and Jane had an altercation about the rumours, which had her in tears. Even Jane is persuaded it is more than Teddy's debts with him.'

'Yes, it is. It cost me the forfeit of a thousand pounds and a top-of-the-trees stallion in winnings, but according to our friend Toby Moore, it is a long-standing grievance, something to do with the fact that his forebears once owned Greystone Manor and were cheated out of it by an ancestor of Sir Edward. He has vowed to get his revenge and establish himself once again as Lord of the Manor of Hadlea. He has not only bought up all Teddy's debts, but is doing the same with Sir Edward's. He is almost ready to make his move.'

'It is worse than I thought.'

'I wonder if Sir Edward knows what is happening.'

'I do not think so. I am sure neither Jane nor Isabel know the story or I am sure Jane would have told me. It is going to cause the most dreadful scandal if it gets out…'

'Which it cannot fail to do.'

'Poor Jane, I do not know how her orphan home will survive it.'

'And there is your wedding.'

'Yes. We must endeavour to resolve the situation before then. I am wealthy, but I do not think I can rise to such a vast sum without endangering my own estate. We must think of something else.'

'If it is money you want, then you shall have it, but it is my opinion Bolsover will refuse it. He is prodigious wealthy and is determined on having the Manor.'

'How did he come by his wealth? He seems not to have a large estate.'

'Gambling for the most part, though whether he cheats is a matter for conjecture—no one has ever caught him at it.'

'Perhaps, if we could prove that…'

'By "we", were you including me?'

'Only if you want to be included.'

'I am off on my travels again, Mark. There is nothing for me in this country after all. I came to bid you goodbye.'

'Is it because of Jane?'

'Jane?'

'Yes. It was Jane who drove you away last time, wasn't it?'

'Did she tell you that?'

'No, I guessed. Did you come back to try again?'

'I wasn't sure, but I was intent on letting Sir Edward know I had made good and that he had made a wrong decision in refusing his permission for us to marry.'

'Did Jane share your feelings?'

'I believe she did at the time, but it is certainly no longer true.'

'So you are going away disappointed again.'

'Not over Jane.'

'Who, then?'

'It does not matter because nothing can come of it. I go away for her sake and yours.'

'Isabel!'

'Look after her, Mark, and be happy.' And he turned on his heel and left.

Mark stood for a minute so confused he could not think coherently. When he pulled himself together to go after his friend, the street was empty.

Somehow the day was got through, with Isabel white-faced and their aunt flitting about trying to be helpful. Jane was glad when all the preparations were complete and she could go to bed. She undressed and crept between the sheets, but sleep eluded her. She was committed to persuading her sister to go ahead with the marriage because not to do so would be unkind to the man she loved and cause him distress. And it would upset her parents. On top of his money worries, it might very well kill her father. Money worries. What was Lord Bolsover playing at? If only Teddy had not gambled so heavily, if only her sister had not flirted with Andrew Ashton, if only she herself did not love Mark quite so much. Dear Mark. He did not deserve to be embroiled in scandal from any direction. How was it all going to end?

Chapter Seven

Throughout that long journey home, Isabel was quiet and withdrawn, Jane was thoughtful and Mark was unusually taciturn. It was evident they all had a great deal on their minds and hardly conversed at all, except to order food and drink at some of the inns where they pulled up for the horses to be changed and to approve the accommodation when they stopped for the night at the White Hart in Scole. The inn was a very old one, which had once provided lodgings for Charles II and Lord Nelson, not to mention sundry highwaymen, standing as it did on the crossroads between Norwich and Ipswich, Bury St Edmunds and the Norfolk coast.

They were offered exceptionally good food while they waited for their rooms to be prepared, but no one was hungry and the conversation was limited to comments about the magnificent fireplaces and the grand staircase, the food and wine, and the time they meant to be on the road the following morning. Jane and Isabel, who shared a room, were too tired to talk and, in any case, had nothing to add to what had already been said. Even so they slept fitfully.

* * *

The second day was spent in much the same manner as the first and thanks to Mark's foresight in arranging frequent stops for fresh horses to be harnessed, they made good time and arrived at Greystone Manor in the early evening. They were home, much to Jane's relief; the responsibility for her sister would now devolve on her parents.

Mark stayed only long enough to oversee the unloading of their trunks and pay his respects to Sir Edward and Lady Cavenhurst before carrying on to Broadacres.

'Oh, it is so good to have you home,' their mother said, hugging them both. 'I have delayed supper and you shall tell us all that you have been up to while we eat. Isabel, are you fully recovered from your fall?'

'Yes, Mama, and no harm done.' She turned as Sophie came hurrying along the hall to greet them.

'Oh, I have missed you,' she said. 'It has been quite boring here by myself. I am longing to hear all your news.'

'Go up to your rooms and change out of those travelling clothes,' her ladyship said to the two older girls. 'Supper will be served as soon as you come down again.'

Sir Edward looked down at the two trunks which had been deposited in the hall. 'As I recall,' he said, 'you only took one trunk with you. Am I to assume you have been shopping?'

'Well, I could not go out and about town with Aunt Emmeline in the shabby gowns I had taken with me,' Isabel said. 'It was different for Jane, she was too busy with her orphans to worry about how she looked.'

'And how did you pay for them?'

'On your account, naturally. I only had pin money.'

He sighed. 'It is evidently useless to tell you to be frugal.'

'A few gowns and fripperies, Papa, will surely not break the bank,' she said.

'You are impertinent, child. Now go and change before I lose my temper with you.'

Isabel was smiling as she went upstairs with her sister. 'Papa has never lost his temper with me,' she said. 'With Teddy, yes, but never with me.'

'But you do try his patience sorely, Issie. He is looking very strained and I wonder how bad things really are.'

'You do not think that odious man at Aunt Emmeline's soirée was telling the truth, do you?'

'No, of course not.'

When she went to her room, Bessie had already unpacked her things and had gone to do the same for Isabel. Jane sat on the edge of her bed, wondering how much, if anything, she should tell her parents about the rumours and Lord Bolsover. It might only serve to upset them. On the other hand, forewarned was forearmed. She would leave the decision until the next day when everyone was less tired and they had settled in at home again.

Supper was a time for catching up, with Sophie telling her sisters what had been going on in the village in their absence, Isabel chattering about all she had seen and done, avoiding any mention of Andrew Ashton, and Jane apprising them of her visit to the Foundling Hospital and the progress she had made with her orphan project. 'Mark was a great help,' she said.

'Yes, he told us about the Foundlings when he called to inform us of Isabel's accident,' her mother said. 'How did that happen? Hacks in the Park are not usually fraught with danger.'

'I ducked to avoid the overhanging branch of a tree,' Isabel said. 'And my saddle slipped and I came off and hit my head.'

'I am surprised Mark did not check the girth before you started out,' Sir Edward said.

'I am sure he did, but it was a hired mount and a hired saddle, which no doubt did not fit properly.'

'And I believe your aunt arranged a soirée for you, Jane. Did you meet any interesting people?'

'Yes, Aunt Emmeline's drawing room was a squeeze. They knew that I would be speaking about the Hadlea Children's Home. I was very nervous at first, but I soon forgot that as I talked.'

'There were all manner of people there and some were very noisy,' Isabel added. 'There was one man who said—'

'Isabel,' Jane put in quickly, 'Mama and Papa do not want to hear that.'

'Hear what?' her mother demanded.

'It was only someone trying to cause trouble,' Jane said. 'Mark and Mr Ashton soon got rid of him.'

'Trouble?' Sir Edward queried. 'What sort of trouble?'

'He doubted my honesty. There are some people who think a woman not capable of handling money and Mark had to explain that the funds for the Hadlea Children's Home would be administered by a trust of which he would be a trustee and that seemed to satisfy most people.'

'That's not all he said.' Isabel ignored the fierce look Jane gave her. 'He said you were nigh on bankrupt, Papa, and the money Jane collected for her orphanage would go to pay your debts.'

'Issie!' Jane admonished her, noting her father's frown and the high spots of colour on his cheeks and her mother's quick intake of breath. 'There was no need to trouble Papa with that. It is of no consequence.'

'It seems to me you have been mixing with a very bad sort of society,' their mother said. 'I am surprised at Emmeline allowing it.'

'Do not blame Aunt Emmeline,' Jane said. 'She was very particular about those to whom she introduced us. The man arrived uninvited.'

'I heard D—Mr Ashton—say he had been sent by Lord Bolsover,' Isabel went on. 'He's the one Teddy owed all that money to. He is evidently angry that Teddy escaped.'

'Well, I am very relieved that you are both home again and away from all that,' their mother said. 'Let us talk of other things. I have been several times over to Broadacres to visit Lady Wyndham. She is bearing up remarkably well and talking cheerfully of the wedding. Jane, you must finish the alterations to the gown now you are home.'

'I will work on it tomorrow, Mama, when I have come back from visiting the Rector and Mrs Caulder. They will wish to know how well I did raising money.'

The sun was warm as Jane walked to the rectory next morning and she wore a simple gingham gown and a light lace shawl. The parasol she carried was a pale-cream silk with a matching fringe. In her reticule she had a record of all the people who had donated to the fund and the notes she had made after her visit to the Foundling Hospital.

Mrs Caulder was in her garden cutting early rose buds from the bush that climbed the archway of the gate. 'Jane, you are back. How did it go?'

'Well, I think. I made some notes to show you and the Reverend.'

'I believe he is in the church. I was going to take these roses for the altar. Let us go and find him. He has some news for you.'

'News?'

'Yes, I believe he has found suitable premises for the home.'

'Oh, that is good news. I am hoping we can have everything in place and the first children installed before the winter weather.'

The Rector was in the vestry, making entries into the register, but stopped when he saw Jane. 'Allow me a minute or two to finish this,' he said after greeting her. 'Then we can go into the house and talk over tea and cakes.'

While he was doing that Mrs Caulder arranged the roses in a vase and put them on the altar and Jane idled the time looking round the church. She knew every nook and cranny of it, having been a regular member of the congregation since she was in leading strings. When she was too young to take part in the service she had feasted her eyes on everything about her. She knew the inscriptions on the tablets on the walls and set into the floor, she was familiar with the lovely stained-glass window depicting Jesus surrounded by children, and the carving on the font. Wandering into the churchyard, she began reading the inscriptions on the gravestones. There was her grandfather and grandmother and their parents and several others with the name of Cavenhurst. And there were the Wyndhams, generations of them, and Stangates,

Pages and Finches, and there, in a far corner on a moss-covered stone overgrown with grass and brambles and fenced off from the rest of the churchyard, was a name that stopped her short.

> Colin Bolsover Paget, beloved son of Lord and Lady Paget, died by his own hand, May 1649, aged twenty-seven years. May God forgive him and allow him eternal rest.

She brushed the moss from the stone to make sure she had read it correctly and then went round all the graves looking for the names Bolsover and Paget. There were one or two Pagets on more recent graves and she knew there was a memorial on a wall inside the church, but no more Bolsovers. Was it significant? Had she been destined by fate to find that grave? She remembered Lord Bolsover saying he would have his revenge and later telling her she did not know him at all. Did he believe that one of her ancestors had wronged the man in the grave? But it was all so long ago.

'Ah, there you are, Jane.' The Rector's hearty voice broke her reverie and she turned to see him and his wife approaching. 'We wondered where you were.'

'I was reading the inscriptions on the graves. Some of them are very moving, especially the children's. And this one, almost hidden.'

'Ah, yes, a suicide which is why it is outside the consecrated ground.'

'Do you know the history behind it?'

'No, I do not. There might be something in the parish records. Let us go indoors and you shall tell me your news and I will tell you mine.'

Jane followed her friends into the rectory and over tea and Mrs Caulder's honey cakes, she put the mystery of Bolsover to the back of her mind while she told them of everything she had done in London to promote the Hadlea Children's Home, although she did not mention the accusations made at her aunt's soirée. 'When I returned home, I found several letters and small donations as a result of my letter-writing,' she said. 'I am optimistic we can go ahead.'

'You have done well,' he said. 'And I have some news, too. I think I have found a suitable house. It is in Witherington and has been empty for some time since its last occupant died. He was an old man, living alone with only one manservant and a housekeeper. When he died, his heirs were difficult to find and the house was left to the ravages of nature. The heirs have recently come forward and put it on the market. It is large, dilapidated and cheap.'

Witherington was a small hamlet about five miles from Hadlea. It was too small to have its own church and was incorporated in the parish of Hadlea. 'I must go and see it as soon as possible. I will ask Lord Wyndham if he will accompany me, since he is one of the trustees and must approve our choice.'

She said goodbye and left them. She was already over halfway between the Manor and Broadacres, so decided she might as well go the rest of the way and speak to Mark.

She found him in the stables, arranging for the last quartet of post horses to be returned and the carriage cleaned. He was in riding breeches and shirt, which showed off his lithe figure and did strange things to her heart and belly. He turned to her with a ready smile. 'Good morning, Jane,' he said, reaching for his coat which hung on a hook by the door. 'Are you recovered from your journey?'

'Oh, it was nothing. I am quite well and a night in my own bed has worked wonders, also the news that the Reverend Caulder has found some premises for our home. I have just come from the Rectory and decided to call to ask if you could spare the time to accompany me on an inspection. The trustees will need to make the final decision as to whether we buy or not.'

'Willingly. Let us go indoors and we can decide on a day and time. I must fit it in with my obligations here and my duty to my mother.'

'If you are very busy…' she began diffidently.

He smiled at her, a special kind of smile she liked to imagine was one for her alone, but which she knew was fantasy on her part. 'Jane, when I took on the trusteeship, I knew what it would entail and I always make a point of fulfilling my obligations, so think no more of it. We will go as soon as maybe. Perhaps Isabel might like to accompany us?'

They did not have to wait to ask her. Lady Cavenhurst and Isabel were sitting in the morning room with Lady Wyndham. The two older ladies were in animated conversation about plans for the wedding, but Isabel was silent and looking glum, which worried Jane. How long before she got over her infatuation for Andrew Ashton? If she went on looking gloomy for much longer, everyone would notice. But she could not altogether condemn her; she knew what it was like to yearn for someone you could not have.

'I did not know you were coming here, Jane,' her

mother said. 'You could have driven the trap, you know how I hate driving it. I am always fearful it will turn over and land us all in a ditch. And your papa positively forbade us to have the horses harnessed to the carriage for so short a trip.'

'I went to the rectory, Mama, and decided to come on here afterwards. Reverend Caulder has found a house for the Hadlea Children's Home and I needed to consult Mark about it.'

'Jane dear,' her mother said gently, 'I do think you should refer to his lordship in a more respectful way. You are no longer children.'

'Oh, no,' Mark put in. 'I should hate that. It means I must call Jane Miss Cavenhurst and Isabel, Miss Isabel. It would be too stiff for words. Let us go on as we always have.'

'Honestly, Jane,' Isabel said, 'do you never think of anything else but that project of yours? I am sure Mark is bored to death with it. I certainly am.'

'I am sorry you think that,' Jane said. 'I was going to ask if you would like to come with us to view the house. It is at Witherington.'

'No, I should not. I have better things to do with my time. I am sure you do not need a chaperon, being too old for courtship, as everyone knows.'

'Dear me,' Lady Wyndham said. 'I fear, Isabel, you are becoming a little nervous. It must be the wedding playing on your mind.'

'Yes, perhaps it is,' she said and lapsed into silence.

Nothing more was said for several seconds while the heated air cooled and then Lady Cavenhurst rose, followed by her daughters.

'I will call at the Manor later,' Mark said, obviously

meaning when Isabel had regained her composure. 'We can arrange the outing to Witherington then.'

Jane followed her mother and sister to the trap, feeling nothing but foreboding. If Isabel continued to be difficult, she feared for Mark's happiness. A calamity was unfolding before her and she could do nothing but watch helplessly.

'Isabel, what is the matter with you?' Lady Cavenhurst asked when they arrived home and her younger daughter had said not a word on the short drive. 'What has put you in the dismals?'

'Nothing,' she muttered, looking at the hall floor.

'Come now, I do not believe that. You have been in the suds ever since you returned home. I begin to think you are not glad to be back and would rather have stayed with your aunt.'

Isabel raised eyes swimming with tears. 'It isn't that.'

Jane put her arm about her shoulder. 'Issie, you had better tell Mama the whole.'

'If there is something to tell, then we will go into the parlour and sit comfortably,' their mother said, leading the way.

Isabel shot a glance at her sister. 'Come, too, Jane.'

Lady Cavenhurst sat on a sofa and patted the seat beside her. 'Sit here, Isabel, and let us hear what is making you so unhappy.'

Isabel hesitated. 'Go on,' Jane said.

Her sister took a deep breath. 'I can't marry Mark, Mama.'

'Can't marry him? Why ever not?'

'I do not love him and I cannot see myself as mistress of Broadacres.'

'Nonsense! Whatever has put that idea into your head? You have been destined to marry Mark ever since you were children. You could not wait to be grown up enough to wed him.'

'I know, but I was young and silly.'

Her mother gave her a ghost of a smile. 'You mean you are no longer young and silly? You have grown old and wise in the space of two weeks? I begin to wish I had not suggested you should go to London with Jane. Your head has been turned by the *haut monde*.'

'It is nothing to do with London or the *haut monde*. I felt like that before I went. Jane will tell you that.'

Lady Cavenhurst looked at her eldest daughter. 'Jane?'

'Issie intimated she was nervous of becoming Lady Wyndham and having to run Broadacres, Mama. She did not tell me she did not love Mark.'

'It is only nerves,' her ladyship said. 'You will overcome them.'

'It is *not* nerves, Mama. If I am made to marry Mark, I shall be miserable and so will he.'

'Well, it is too late to back out now. You have been engaged for over a year and it is a solemn undertaking. You will lay yourself open to breach of promise.'

'Mark would never do that,' Jane put in.

'No, perhaps not, but it would be a terrible blow, not only to him but to his mother, who is not strong enough to withstand it, not after losing her husband so suddenly. It is only the thought of the wedding that keeps her going. She told me that herself. It is why she shortened the mourning period.'

'Mama, I can't go through with it, I simply cannot,' Isabel wailed, tears spilling.

'You will think differently when the time comes. Mark

is not a monster. You could not wish for a gentler, more considerate husband. It is more important than being in love. There are any number of successful marriages that did not start out with being in love. That will come later.'

'It won't.' Isabel was sobbing now. Jane moved over to sit beside her and put her arm about her, but she had nothing to add to what her mother had said and reiterating it would be hypocritical.

'Go up to your room and wash your face,' Lady Cavenhurst said, decidedly cross. 'I am going to find your father. He will have to know, though he has more than enough problems without you adding to them.' She stood up. 'Jane, see if you can make her see sense—perhaps she will listen to you.'

Jane helped her sister to her room where she sat on the bed, not weeping now, but white-faced and red-eyed. Jane poured some water from the jug on the washstand into a bowl and dipped a cloth into it. She wrung it out and gave it to Isabel. 'Wipe your face, Issie. Crying so much will spoil your looks.'

'I don't care. Perhaps that will turn Mark against me.'

'One thing you can be sure of is that Mark will never break the engagement, whatever you do. He is too honourable and the scandal would ruin both families.'

'You do not understand.'

'I assure you I do and I feel for you. In time, you will get over your infatuation for Mr Ashton and wonder what you ever saw in him.' She paused, wondering whether to go on. 'I did.'

'You?' Isabel was so surprised she left off crying.

'Yes, when he was staying with Mark years ago, just after they left university. Papa would not agree to me marrying him. He said Mr Ashton had no family and no prospects and I could do better. He went to India and I got over it very quickly.'

'I didn't know that.'

'No reason why you should.'

'It could not have been true love.'

'No, it was not, but I did not realise it at the time. Now I know Papa was right, not because of Mr Ashton's lack of status and wealth, but simply that I only thought I was in love. It wasn't real.'

'There you and I differ. For me it is real and will last all my life.'

'You did not tell Mama that.'

'What was the point? Drew has disappeared and I don't know where he has gone, probably back to India. I am going to be an old maid like you.'

'You will break Mark's heart.'

'I doubt it. He spends more time with you than with me.'

'That's only because he is helping me with the Hadlea Children's Home, and you could join us and take an interest if you chose.'

'I do not choose.'

They were interrupted by a knock on the door and Bessie came to tell Isabel that her father was in the book room and she was to go there at once.

Isabel rose. 'Jane?' she queried.

'No, you must go alone,' Jane said. 'He will only want you to repeat what you told Mama.'

Isabel left her and Jane went to her own room and tried to concentrate on sewing beads on the wedding dress. But her attention wandered and the needle slipped from her fingers. What could she do? She wanted to help her sister and shield Mark from scandal, but she had a dreadful feeling that, if Isabel persisted, scandal was inevitable and both families would suffer. On top of Teddy's flight from his debts and the accusations of Lord Bolsover, it would be the last straw from which they might never recover. She heard a door slam downstairs and running footsteps and then silence. Isabel had evidently fled. She did not come upstairs and Jane wondered whether to go and find her, but she really could not go on trying to persuade her sister to go ahead with the marriage when all her own senses were crying out in despair. It was one more sacrifice she was being asked to make and she was beginning to feel a trifle rebellious. In any case Isabel, who nearly always managed to have her own way, would not listen to her.

Mark could not understand Isabel's moods. He had never known her to be irritable. She flared up occasionally, but her sunny nature usually soon reasserted itself, yet now it seemed nothing he could do was right. And he was appalled by her rudeness to Jane. He could see Jane had been hurt, although she did not show it, except by the bleakness in her eyes. He hoped when he arrived at the Manor, Isabel would have made her peace with her sister and be ready to come with them to Witherington. The Hadlea Children's Home project was important to Jane and he wanted to help her, so was Isabel jealous? If she would not go to Witherington with them, then he must make up for it in other ways.

He took the route through the woods, which surrounded the Manor. The sun filtered through the canopy of trees, making dancing streaks of light along the path ahead of him. Overhead a blackbird sitting on a branch let it be known he was encroaching on its territory. There were other sounds, too—the soughing of the wind, rustling, squeaking, the distant barking of a dog—but they were only small sounds and did not impinge on the peacefulness. And then he heard another sound that was not peaceful. Someone was sobbing not far away, someone in dreadful distress. He hurried to find the source of the sound and found Isabel lying on the ground beneath an ancient oak, curled up in a tight ball.

He ran forward. 'Isabel, whatever is the matter?' He knelt down, put his arm about her and helped her to sit up. 'Why are you crying?'

'Oh, it's you.' The voice was watery.

He produced a handkerchief from his coat pocket and handed it to her. 'Did you fall? Are you hurt?'

'I didn't fall and I am not hurt, at least, not in the way you mean.' She sniffed and mopped her eyes.

'Then what is it?'

'Nothing.'

'Nothing?' he queried, tilting up her chin, making her look at him. 'You do not weep for nothing, so you had better tell me. After all, I will soon be your husband, the one to whom you turn regarding whatever is troubling you, the one whose privilege it is to solve all your problems.'

'You *are* the problem,' she burst out and began to cry again.

'Me? What have I done? If I have hurt you, then I beg forgiveness, it was not intentional. Are you cross because I spend so much time on Jane's orphanage? I'll make it up to you, I promise.'

'I do not care how much time you spend with Jane and her orphanage.'

'Go on.'

'I cannot marry you, Mark. I don't want to be Lady Wyndham. I should make you miserable.'

'You must let me be the judge of that.'

'And I should be miserable, too.'

'Ahh. There is more to it. Come, out with it.'

'Mama and Papa say I cannot break off the engagement, it will cause a dreadful scandal.'

'Not half the scandal if I were to break it off.'

'Do you wish to?'

'Isabel, my dear, I would never hold you to an engagement you found abhorrent. You may jilt me if you choose and I will not complain, but I would like to know the reason for it.'

'I do not love you, cannot love you.'

He gave her a wry smile. 'Well, that is a blow to my ego.'

'I am sorry. I am very fond of you. You are like a big brother and I would hate to be at odds with you, but the truth is—' She stopped suddenly.

'You have fixed your affections elsewhere, is that it?'

She nodded.

He considered this only for a moment before the truth dawned on him. Isabel had flirted with Drew, had been lively and happy in his presence, and had not wanted to come home. And Drew himself had admitted that was why he was going away. How blind he had been! 'It's my friend Drew, isn't it?'

'Yes, but he said he would not betray you. That's why he went away.'

'Oh.'

'Jane says I'll get over him because she did. He had asked Papa for permission to marry her, but Papa would not allow it on account of his lack of a fortune. It is why

Jane never married. She says she soon got over him, but I'm not so sure, because I cannot believe no one else asked her, not when she was young and marriageable.'

'Perhaps Jane is right.'

'She is jealous. Drew told me himself that there had been someone else, but he had got over it long ago and was glad of it.'

Mark remembered Drew saying something of the sort, but he had had no idea it had been Jane. He found his emotions churning and it had nothing to do with being rejected by Isabel. He stood up and held out his hand to help her to rise. 'Come, we will go and see your papa and thrash this out.'

She stood beside him, only reaching his shoulder. There were bits of grass and dead leaves clinging to her muslin dress and she brushed them off with impatient hands. 'You needn't come with me.'

'I was coming to see you and Jane about going to Witherington, or had you forgot?'

'Oh, that pesky orphanage. Yes, I had forgot.'

Sir Edward and Lady Cavenhurst were in the drawing room with Jane and it was evident they had been talking about Isabel's extraordinary behaviour, but stopped when they saw that Mark was with her.

'Come in and sit down, my boy,' Sir Edward said, indicating a chair. 'I can see by the look of you that my foolish daughter has told you of this silly notion of hers.'

'I do not consider it silly,' Mark said.

'No, you would not, but rest assured it is only a passing fancy. It is nerves brought about by your father's demise and the prospect of becoming Lady Wyndham and the role she will be expected to fulfil. We will school her in what is expected of her and no doubt your mother will do so, too.'

'I think perhaps it is more than that, Sir Edward, and I would not hold her to an engagement that is abhorrent to her.'

'But the scandal,' her ladyship protested.

'We can end it by mutual consent,' he said. 'It will be Miss Isabel's decision, of course, but I shall accept it gracefully.'

'But why should you?' Sir Edward queried. 'She will get over her reluctance by the time you and your mother are out of mourning. If it had not been for Lord Wyndham's untimely death, you would have been married by now. Less than a month ago she talked of nothing else.'

'That was before she met my friend, Drew Ashton.'

'What?' Sir Edward exploded, turning to Isabel who had seated herself on a chair near the door, almost as if she were prepared to flee again. 'Has that mountebank turned your head just as he did you sister's?'

'He is not a mountebank,' Isabel cried. 'He is an honourable man. I love him and he loves me.'

'I will not listen to this,' her father told her. 'I sent him packing once before and I shall do so again. You need not think I will ever consent to you marrying him.'

'I expect that is why he went away,' she said miserably.

Lady Cavenhurst turned to Mark. 'I am sorry you had to hear this, my lord. Isabel is not usually given to tantrums, as you must know. No doubt she will be in a better frame of mind tomorrow.'

'I came to arrange to go to Witherington,' he said. 'I am free tomorrow afternoon, if that is convenient to Jane?'

'Yes, quite convenient,' Jane said.

'Then I will call at two o'clock.' He rose and took his leave, leaving a silent and morose Cavenhurst family. He had no doubt they would continue to harangue poor Isabel. He did not want a reluctant wife and would happily release her. In truth, he felt nothing but a huge sense of relief. On the other hand, the revelation that Drew and Jane had once wanted to marry had come as a shock to him, but on quiet reflection, he remembered how they had seized every opportunity to be alone when Drew had come to stay at Broadacres. Sometimes his friend had gone riding alone. Had he been off to meet Jane? Was Jane still hankering after him? Was she jealous of her sister? Had they quarrelled over him? Jane had been very quiet while everyone else talked. He wished he had quizzed Drew a little more before he left. Now he did not know where he was.

He returned home to seek out his mother, who was resting in her boudoir. He ought to tell her what had transpired. It would be a dreadful shock to her and he hated the idea of upsetting her, but if Isabel did call off the wedding, then his mother would have to know and the news would be better coming from him.

She was sitting in a chair by the window, gazing out over the park. A book lay discarded in her lap. He pulled up another chair and sat down beside her. 'Mama, how are you?'

'There is nothing wrong with me, Mark. I am just a little tired. I like to see Grace, she is a great comfort to me, but Isabel's outburst has upset me. She should not have spoken to her sister like that. I cannot think what came over her.'

'She is worried and afraid, Mama. I have just been

over to the Manor and learned the reason...' He paused, wondering whether to go on.

'You had better tell me at once.'

'Isabel has told me and the rest of her family that she no longer wishes to marry me.'

'Not want to marry you! What are you saying, Mark?'

'Just that. She has changed her mind. She says she does not love me.' He grinned. 'That was a blow to my pride, but I will get over it.'

'Fustian! She is a foolish girl. She has wanted to marry you for years, she cannot have suddenly changed.'

'But she has.'

'What are you going to do about it?'

'Nothing, Mama. It is not up to me, is it?'

'You must talk to her, persuade her of the advantages.'

'Oh, I think she knows the advantages. They are apparently outweighed by the disadvantages. She does not love me and because of that is not prepared to countenance being mistress of Broadacres.' He smiled. 'So, Mama, you will remain in your place here as chatelaine a little longer.'

'You mean you are going to allow her to call the whole thing off? You will be a laughing stock.'

'Better that than take an unwilling bride.'

'She will change her mind. There are some weeks to go before the wedding.'

'Mama, I do not think I want her to change her mind. I am content to let her break the engagement. We could go travelling, you and I, when you feel stronger, that is. The gossip will soon die down when the tattlemongers find something else to talk about.'

'Don't you mind?'

'Do you know, Mother, I don't think I do.'

'But you must marry, Mark. It is incumbent upon you.'

'Perhaps I will, one day, when the furore has died down.'

'And that will be difficult to live down. Every young lady you approach will wonder what is wrong with you.'

'I hope not every young lady, Mama.'

She sighed and put a hand over his. 'As long as you do not mind, I am content. I was beginning to change my mind about Miss Isabel Cavenhurst in any case.'

He laughed and bent to kiss her cheek. 'Then we are in accord.'

He left her to rest and busied himself about the estate, then visited the Rector to learn a little more about the house in Witherington.

Chapter Eight

As Isabel had declined to go with them and the weather continued fine and warm, Mark called for Jane in the curricle the following afternoon, driving it himself. She was ready and waiting, dressed in a morning dress of primrose-coloured sarsenet, trimmed with blond lace, and a matching pelisse. On her dark curls she had tied a cottager straw hat.

'I spoke to Henry Caulder yesterday,' Mark told her as they trotted along the country lanes, now in sunshine, now in the shadow of the trees. 'He told me what he knew of Witherington House. He said it was dilapidated, which is why it is so cheap.'

'Yes, he told me that. By all accounts it will mean a deal of work to make it habitable. Perhaps the cost of repairs will outweigh the low purchase price.'

'That we shall have to see.'

'How much land is there with it? I should like the children to have somewhere to play.'

'Very little. Most of it has been sold to local farmers as arable and pasture, but there is an acre of garden. We should not want more than that or we would have to employ gardeners.'

'The boys could help with the gardening. If you remember, the Foundling Hospital told us the children were allotted tasks as they grew old enough to do them. I think it is a good idea to give them a little idea of the world of work. I want to fit them to earn their living, to make begging and thieving a thing of the past.'

'You will need some staff: a matron, teachers, a housekeeper, a maid or two and an odd-job man.'

'I know. We can use local people who are out of work.'

They continued to talk about the Hadlea Children's Home all the way and Jane was glad of that. It was easier than speaking of the events of the day before, still large in her mind and, she suspected, in Mark's mind, too. After he had left them, her parents had flatly refused to listen to any more of Isabel's pleading and told her she would change her mind and not disgrace the family with gossip. It was bad enough that Teddy had embarrassed them and been forced to flee the country, but this would be worse and they would not hear of breaking it off. Isabel had resorted to weeping all over Jane and begging her to intercede on her behalf. Jane could not do it, could not hurt Mark. He had been very understanding, but she wondered how he really felt, particularly about Issie's confession that she believed herself in love with Drew, but of course she could not ask him.

They passed a few scattered cottages, an inn and a small triangular green where two women gossiped at a pump, then turned into an overgrown drive, whose gates were permanently open and trapped in weeds and long grass. A short ride and the house came into view. It was a large square house, not much smaller than Greystone

Manor, covered in ivy, which hung over the windows in
long strands. There were several slates missing from the
roof and one of the chimney stacks had lost its coping.
Mark pulled up at the front door and they sat surveying
the building in silence before Mark jumped down and
came round the vehicle to help her down. He preceded
her up a dozen steps to the blackened oak door with its
rusty lion's-head knocker and beat a tattoo.

'No one is living here, surely,' she said.

'I am told there is a caretaker.' He rapped again and
waited, but no one came. He tried the door, but it was
bolted from the inside. 'Let's try the back,' he said.

They found an old man in the yard chopping wood.
'Are you the caretaker?' Mark asked.

'Who wants to know?'

'I do. I am Lord Wyndham and this is Miss Cavenhurst. We have come to view the property.'

The man stuck the axe in the chopping block. 'Best
come with me, then, though if you're expecting a palace,
you've come to the wrong place. 'Tain't fit to live in.'

'We know that,' Jane said. 'What is your name?'

'Silas Godfrey, miss.'

He led the way into the house through the kitchen.
There was a woman standing at the table, cutting up a
hare. 'My wife, Dotty,' he said, then to her, 'These folks
have come to view the house.'

She gave them a quick bob and continued her work.
Silas led them from the kitchen into a narrow hall at the
end of which a door led to the front of the house. 'Have
you been here long?' Jane asked him, as they crossed a
black-and-white-tiled hall and entered what would have
been the dining room. It was oak-lined with a deep win-

dow looking out on to a terrace. Weeds were growing in the cracks in the paving.

'All me life. Come here as a nipper, I did.'

'Then you will know what the house was like in the old days.'

'That I do. Grand it were. It were well kept, too, with any number of servants. Sir Jasper and her ladyship useta give dinner parties in this room. There were always sumf'n going on. The hoi polloi from Lunnon useta come down to stay.' They followed him to the drawing room, a large room with lofty ceilings and carved cornices and windows on two sides, one of which looked out on to the terrace, the other on to a tangle of long grass, weeds and overgrown rose bushes, which had once been a garden. 'It all stopped when her ladyship took ill,' he went on while Mark inspected everything, stamping on the floorboards and poking his finger into the window frames. 'She were ill a long time and when she died, Sir Jasper let everything go. He would not have anyone here. Cut himself off, he did, and started acting strange.' They moved to another smaller room, which smelled fusty and airless and made Jane wrinkle her nose. It had obviously once been a parlour, but there was a narrow bed set against the wall by the window. An outer door led on to the weed-infested side garden. 'Shut himself in this here room, he did, and never moved out of it day or night. We'll go upstairs now, but watch out, some of the treads are missing and the banister i'n't safe.'

Up the stairs they went. The old man obviously found the climb an effort because he was breathless at the end of it. He recovered quickly and was soon talking again. 'The servants left one by one. There weren't much point in a-keepin' 'em on. There were only me and Dotty left when he died. The lawyer what come down from Lunnon asked us to stay and keep an eye on the place while he found Sir Jasper's heirs. Seems he didn't have no close family. Place hev got even worse since then. I can't do the work nor can Dotty.' All the time he was speaking he was going from room to room, throwing open doors. The bedrooms were in semi-darkness because of the ivy, which was already encroaching into the rooms through broken windows. At the end of the wide corridor there were more stairs. 'There's another floor,' he said, reluctant to climb.

'We can manage on our own,' Mark said. 'You go down again, we will find you when we are ready to leave.'

He left them and they climbed more stairs to the next floor where the servants would have been housed.

'It is in a parlous state,' Jane said. 'I begin to wonder if it is worth our while to take it on.'

'I think it is solid enough, the brickwork is sound and the damage fairly superficial. A small army of workers would soon have it to rights.'

She laughed. 'Where am I to find an army of workers?'

'Almost anywhere given the unemployment situation. I can set them on and oversee the work, if you wish. If we decided to go ahead at once, we could have everything done by the winter.'

'But, Mark, you already have so much to do. I feel I am taking advantage of you and burdening you with more problems.'

'Nonsense. You have never taken advantage of me, Jane, and if it is a burden, which I dispute, I bear it willingly.'

'I wonder at you being so kind and helpful given the dreadful way you have been treated.'

'Treated, Jane? You mean by Isabel?'

'Yes. I am so sorry. I wish she had never gone to London with us. It all went to her head.'

'I think it is better that she told me now and not after we were married, don't you?'

'But Papa is determined she will go through with the wedding.'

'I hope he will not insist. Isabel can break it off without too much damage being done. I certainly cannot.'

She looked at him in surprise. 'Would you wish to?'

'I do not want an unwilling wife, Jane.'

'Oh.' Did he really mean he wanted an end to the engagement? It was strange if he did, because both families had been talking about it ever since Isabel left the schoolroom. She remembered it especially because she had been suffering herself at the time and it had made her even more miserable. She had been foolish, she knew that now.

He smiled to reassure her. 'I will speak to Sir Edward.'

'Papa won't let her marry Mr Ashton, I know.'

'But Drew is not the man he was ten years ago, Jane.'

'Oh! So you know?'

'Yes. Do you…? Are you—?' He stopped suddenly.

'Am I still in love with him? No, Mark, I never was, not truly. Oh, I pined for a while, but then I came to my senses and was thankful for my escape. He is rich and self-assured and has turned Issie's head. She will doubtless get over it, as I did.'

'Perhaps, perhaps not. Now let us go downstairs again and inspect the outbuildings. And then we shall have a little picnic before we make our way home.' He started to lead the way down the upper flight, talking over his shoulder. 'I asked my housekeeper to make up a little basket of food and a bottle of wine.'

She knew the subject of Isabel and the wedding was closed and he would not refer to it again, but it left her longing to know how he really felt. Was he just being chivalrous or did he mean he no longer wished to marry Isabel? What would happen if, in a couple of months' time, Isabel succumbed to their father's blandishments and agreed to marry Mark after all? She had begun to hope, just a little, but realised how futile that was. Even if he did not marry Isabel, it was no reason to think he would turn to her. There were any number of younger, more beautiful ladies for him to choose from.

She followed him down. His dark hair curled into the nape of his neck in a most enticing way; she felt an inexplicable urge to reach out and pull her fingers through it, to straighten it and watch it spring back when she let it go. Engrossed in that, she did not look where she was going and her foot caught in a broken stair tread. She flung her arms out to save herself, pushing him in the small of the back. He just managed to save himself from falling and in so doing cushioned her fall so she did not go all the way down. He eased her down on to the next step and sat beside her, his arm about her shoulders. 'Jane, are you all right? Have you hurt yourself?'

'My ankle. I think I've twisted it. It was that rotten step.'

He looked down at her foot. The ankle was already swelling. 'Do you think you can get down the rest of the stairs if I support you?'

'I'll try.'

She did try, but winced and uttered a muffled cry when she put her weight on to her foot. 'I'll carry you,' he said. 'Put your arms about my neck.'

'You will stumble with me. I can do it.'

'No, you cannot.' He scooped her into his arms and carried her down to the ground floor and back down the hall to the kitchen. She could feel the hair which had so entranced her, as she clasped her arms about his neck. It was soft and not wiry at all.

Mrs Godfrey had just put the hare into a pot on the stove and was scrubbing the table. She looked up when they entered. 'Mercy me, what happened?'

Mark lowered Jane carefully into a chair. 'Miss Cavenhurst caught her foot in a rotten stair and twisted her ankle. It will need bathing in cold water and binding up.'

'Them stairs will be the death of someone afore long,' the woman said, as she went to a pail and poured water into a bowl which she placed at Jane's feet. 'Here, take your stocking off, miss, and put your foot in that. It'll cool it, while I fetch some binding.'

'I'll wait outside, Jane,' Mark said. 'Mrs Godfrey will call me when it's done and I'll carry you out to the curricle.'

'I feel such a fool,' Jane said when this was accomplished and she was sitting in the curricle ready to be taken home, one ankle heavily bandaged, its shoe on the floor by her feet. 'We were warned the stairs were unsafe, I should have paid more attention to where I was putting my feet. Thank goodness you were there to cushion my fall. Did I hurt you?'

'No, I only wish I had taken more care of you.'

'It wasn't your fault. And we didn't look at the outbuildings after all.'

'I did while Mrs Godfrey was binding you up.' He flicked the reins to start the horse off on the homeward journey. 'There are some stables, a coach house and a shed. Mr Godfrey was in the garden where he had planted a few rows of cabbages and beans and he showed me round. There is a small dower house on the far side of the garden which is included in the sale.'

'Do you think the house is in too bad a state for our purpose?' Her ankle was hurting abominably, but she tried to ignore it.

'Not if the price is right.'

'I have a picture of it, repaired, redecorated and furnished, its windows gleaming and the garden neat and tidy. And children's laughter echoing everywhere. I want the children to be happy.'

'Of course you do, so do I.'

'The first-floor rooms are spacious enough to make dormitories, the upper rooms the servants' quarters and perhaps a small infirmary if any of the children should be unwell. Downstairs could be the refectory and the school rooms.'

'You were thinking all that as we went round, were you not? It's as if it is already yours.'

'Not mine, Mark, the trust's.'

'As you say. Would you like me to negotiate with Mr Halliday for you? I am afraid you are going to have to rest that foot for a little while.'

'Yes, curse it,' she said. 'But please do what you can.' She paused. 'We didn't have our picnic, did we?'

'No, but it is not too late. Are you hungry?'

'A little.'

He turned the curricle off the road into the shelter of some trees where he brought it to a stop. 'Sit there,' he said, jumping down and removing a wicker basket from under the seat. She watched him place it under a tree.

He took off his coat and laid it on the grass, then came back for her.

'I can hop down,' she said, placing her good foot on the step and trying to stand.

'I think not.' He scooped her up as if she weighed no more than a feather and carried her to the tree where he gently lowered her on to his coat and sat beside her, so close she could feel his trouser-clad thigh through her thin dress. It was highly improper, but there was no one to see them and Mark himself seemed unaware of the impropriety. She knew she ought to move away, but she stayed where she was, letting her imagination play with a picture of them as a married couple and it was quite in order for him to put his arms about her, carry her, sit so close they touched.

'Comfortable?' he asked.

'Yes, thank you.'

He pulled the basket closer and began unpacking it, bringing out ham and chicken legs, bread and pastries, two plates, a bottle of wine and two glasses. 'This is a feast,' she said.

'Yes, Mrs Blandish lives in fear that I shall starve, so help yourself or I shall be in trouble if I take anything back.' He was pouring wine as he spoke and handed her a glass.

'It's champagne,' she said as the bubbles tickled her nose.

'Yes, perfect for a summer's picnic, don't you think?'

'It's lovely.'

'You deserve the best.'

She looked sharply at him and realised he was looking intently at her, as if studying her face, waiting for a reaction. For a second or two she wondered if he was going to try to seduce her and what she would do, but then dismissed the idea as preposterous. She was perfectly safe with him. And somewhere in the depths of her, where she kept her most secret thoughts, she wished she were not. She tried a light laugh, but it sounded cracked. 'That's the sort of thing you should be saying to Isabel to make her change her mind.'

'But I might not want her to change her mind.'

'You are hurt and who can blame you? She has been very unkind to you.'

'Not unkind, honest, and that I can admire, but if she does not love me, then there is no way I would try to persuade her to marry me if she does not want to. I do not have to beg for a lady's favour, Jane. I have more pride than that. Now drink and eat and let us not talk of Isabel again, I am becoming tired of hearing her name.'

She obeyed and they ate in silence for a few minutes, but the silence was making her conscious of other things: the warmth of the sun filtering through the leaves; the song of a thrush singing its heart out; the sheep, shorn of their winter fleece, cropping the meadow behind them; his nearness; her yearning and, over it all, the ache in her ankle, which was even more swollen and throbbing painfully. She had to distract herself from it.

'What needs doing to Witherington House first?' she asked, surprised at how normal her voice sounded.

'Once we have possession, you mean? I think the roof must be first, to make it weatherproof, then the stairs...'

'Definitely the stairs,' she said, laughing a little.

'Yes, then any alterations to the rooms and painting and decorating. Then finding furniture and taking on staff.'

'Do you really think we can have it all done by the winter?'

'I don't see why not.'

'And will we have enough money?'

'We must continue to raise more.'

'I can write more letters and organise the fair we spoke of.'

'On one leg, Jane?' he queried, raising an eyebrow to her.

'That will soon mend and I will still be able to drive the trap round the village and round up some help.'

He looked down at the limb in question. There was no doubt it was more swollen. 'I think we had better cool that down before we go on.' He knelt to release the bandage, unwinding it carefully. The foot was beginning to turn purple. 'You must see a doctor as soon as we get back. Sit still. I'll go and soak this in water.'

Sit still! She could hardly move. She ate a little of the bread with some ham and washed it down with wine, which seemed to be going to her head.

He came back with the cloth wrung out in a stream he had found. 'This should help,' he said kneeling to re-bandage her foot.

In spite of his care, she could not stop a squeak of pain mixed with pleasure at his touch. Oh, she was a mass of contradictions.

'I'll be as gentle as I can,' he said.

'You are being gentle, Mark, and I am being a coward.'

'You are certainly not that. Now, is that better?'

'Much, thank you.'

'I think we had better get you home. Have you had enough to eat and drink?'

'Yes, thank you. It was delicious.'

He packed the remnants away and put the basket back in the curricle, then came back for her. Putting his hands under her arms he pulled her upright on one foot, then picked her up. 'I'm sorry to be such a nuisance,' she said.

'You are not a nuisance. It is not often I am called upon to carry a beautiful young lady in my arms and for you it is a pleasure and a privilege.'

Beautiful, he had said. She didn't believe it for a minute; she was plain Jane, always had been, always would be, but it was lovely to hear it. In spite of her injury, it had been a wonderful day altogether. To have him to herself in close proximity was a treat to be savoured and remembered in years to come.

Mark drove very carefully, trying to avoid potholes and bumps in the road, but either she had drunk too much champagne or the pain was making her head swim, but try as she might, she could not keep it upright. Her eyes closed and she lolled on his shoulder.

He turned to smile at her and transferred the reins to the other hand so that the movement of his arm did not disturb her. Why he had only recently noticed how lovely she was, he did not know, and it was not simply a lovely face, she had a lovely temperament, quiet, caring of others, often to the detriment of her own needs, and he loved her. He could not tell her so while he was engaged to her sister, Jane herself would never countenance that, but as soon as he was officially free he would have to speak of it. He wanted her, he wanted her so badly he ached.

He could imagine her as Lady Wyndham, managing his household efficiently and without fuss, standing at his side at official functions, being a wonderful mother to their children, loving him. Was it possible? He was annoyed to think that it all depended on the whim of Isabel. It was a pity Sir Edward was so against Drew. Where was Drew?

* * *

His musing came to a halt as he pulled up at the front door of Greystone Manor. Gently he touched her hand to wake her. 'Home, Jane.'

She looked startled, as if not sure where she was. 'Have I been asleep?'

'Yes. It probably did you good. Now we have to face your parents and they will undoubtedly give me a jobation for not looking after you.'

'Do not be silly, of course they will not.'

He lifted her down and carried her up the steps. 'Can you reach the knocker?'

The door was opened by Ruby, the downstairs maid. 'Lord a' mercy,' she said. 'What happened?'

'Miss Cavenhurst has had an accident,' Mark said. 'Fetch Lady Cavenhurst, will you?'

The maid scuttled off and Mark put Jane down to stand on one foot, but he kept his arm about her. They were standing like that when Sir Edward and Lady Cavenhurst came hurrying towards them, closely followed by Isabel and Sophie.

'What happened?' her ladyship said, looking at the pair and then down at Jane's foot.

'I caught my foot in a broken stair tread at the house,' she said. 'It is a little swollen and painful, but it will be better by tomorrow.'

'I think Miss Cavenhurst should be taken to her room,' Mark put in. 'She can tell you all about it when she has been made comfortable and the doctor sent for.'

'Yes, yes, of course,' Sir Edward said. 'I'll send for a footman and…'

'No need, I can carry her. Lead the way.' He bent to

scoop Jane up again, evincing a little 'oh' from Jane and a bigger one from Isabel.

'I will send someone for the doctor,' Sir Edward said, turning away, leaving his wife to precede Mark with his burden up the stairs. No one spoke until Jane was safely deposited on her bed and the injured foot put on a cushion.

'Thank you, Mark,' she said. 'I could not have managed without you.'

'With your permission, Lady Cavenhurst, I will call tomorrow to see how the patient fares.'

'Of course, you do not have to ask.'

He bowed and took his leave.

'Well, this is a fine state of affairs,' her ladyship said, sitting on the bed beside her daughter. 'You had better tell me exactly how it happened. And I do believe you have been drinking.'

'We had some wine with our picnic.'

'Picnic? I was given to understand you were going to look at a house for your home.'

'So we did, but Mark had brought a picnic basket. After all, we were going to be gone some time. I believe it was Mrs Blandish's idea. She thought Mark would be hungry.'

'And did you stumble before or after you drank the wine?'

'Mama, what are you saying? Do you think I was drunk? How could you? If you will stop quizzing me for a minute, I will tell you exactly how it happened.'

There was a knock on the door and her sisters came into the room. 'Are you badly hurt, Jane?' Sophie asked. 'What was it like to be carried by a man and a handsome one at that? I bet Issie is jealous.'

'I am not,' Isabel protested.

'If you must know, it was humiliating and embarrass-ing,' Jane said.

'Then tell us all about it.' Sophie plopped herself on the other side of the bed, making Jane cry out when her leg was disturbed. 'Sorry, Jane.' She moved away.

'Is it very painful?' Isabel asked, hovering at the bed-side.

'Yes, it is.'

'I always thought that home orphanage idea was a bad one.'

'It is not and this isn't going to stop me. We have de-cided to take the house. It can be made good.'

'By "we" you mean you and Mark, I suppose.'

'And Mr Cecil Halliday. He is also a trustee.'

'If it is in such a sorry state that it has broken stair treads, then it is perhaps not a good idea,' their mother put in. 'You might have been killed.'

'But I wasn't, was I? Mark was in front of me and he broke my fall.'

'It seems we have a great deal to thank Mark for.'

'Yes, indeed. He says the house can easily be put to rights and it will make an ideal home for the children.'

'Mark this, Mark that—do you never tire of saying his name?' Isabel demanded of Jane.

'Hush, Isabel,' their mother said. 'There is no call to be jealous of Jane.'

'I am not jealous, not even faintly, so you can forget that.'

In the silence that followed they heard the front door knocker. Lady Cavenhurst went to greet the doctor and Isabel followed her from the room.

'Don't take any notice of Issie,' Sophie said. 'She has

been a terrible crosspatch ever since you came back from London. Not a civil word out of her.'

'She is unhappy, Sophie, she cannot help it.'

'It is just like you to make excuses for everyone, Jane. Sometimes you are too kind and everyone takes advantage of you.'

Jane laughed. 'And you do not, I suppose.'

'I try not to. The trouble with Issie is that she cannot make up her mind, especially when Mama and Papa keep on at her.'

Before Jane could answer, her mother brought the doctor into the room and Sophie slipped out of it.

While the doctor removed the now-dried bandage, Jane mused on what Sophie had said. Was Issie really being persuaded? If so, how genuine was it? It put the euphoria of her happy day with Mark into perspective. It was an interlude, an intermission, a pause in her humdrum life, a memory, no more, and she was left with the pain.

Mark went home, left the horse and curricle with Thompson, one of the grooms, and went indoors by the kitchen door, carrying the picnic basket. Mrs Blandish was there, preparing the evening meal. 'You are back, Master Mark… Oops, I should have said "My lord", shouldn't I? I can't seem to get used to it.'

'It doesn't matter, Mrs Blandish.' He put the basket on the table.

'Did you enjoy the picnic?'

'Very much, though Miss Cavenhurst had a slight accident on the stairs at the house.'

'I am sorry to hear that, sir. I hope she was not badly hurt.'

'A sprained ankle. But she enjoyed the food and desired me to tell you so.'

'Thank you, sir. It is always good to be appreciated. Your mother is in the drawing room.'

He went on his way. It *was* good to be appreciated and Jane had appreciated his help, too, but did everyone appreciate her? She hardly seemed to notice how much everyone relied on her—brother, father, sisters all made demands on her—but perhaps now she could not do so much, they might come to realise it. One thing he was determined on and that was to help her with her orphanage as far as he was able. There would be some hefty expenses and the trust might run out of money, but he could always assist there, not only from his own funds, but by calling on his many wealthy friends.

His mother turned from gazing out of the window to smile at him as he came into the room and dropped a kiss on her forehead. 'How are you, Mama?'

'I am well. How did it go?'

He sat down near her and launched into a recital of all he and Jane had seen and done, and the fact that Jane had been hurt.

'I must call on the Manor tomorrow,' she said.

'I'll drive you over, Mama. I said I would go and see how Jane is and we need to talk again about raising more funds. Jane has suggested holding a fair in the village with stalls and competitions and donated prizes. I have said we could use Ten Acre Field for the venue, if you agree. It is far enough away from the house not to disturb you.'

'Of course, but you are master here, Mark, you do not have to ask me.'

'And you are still its mistress and I would do nothing to discommode you.'

'Is Isabel still persisting in her foolish notion?'

'I believe so. I have not seen her today, she is bored by the whole project and did not come with us.'

'That is a pity. Going out with Jane unaccompanied is bound to cause gossip, however innocent it is.'

'There is going to be a certain amount of gossip in any case if the engagement is cancelled.'

'All the more reason not to invite more.'

'But Jane needs my help.'

'So she may do, but until you receive word from Sir Edward himself that the engagement has officially been broken off, I advise you to be a little more circumspect. You could even try being a little more attentive to Isabel.' She smiled and patted his hand. 'Now, away with you. I am supposed to be resting.'

He left her and went to the library to write to Cecil Halliday, suggesting the trustees make an offer for Witherington House and followed that by making lists of what needed doing in an effort to take his mind off Jane. He had talked to his mother calmly, but he was feeling far from calm. He felt helpless, waiting for something to happen. It was like a storm gathering on the horizon and not knowing exactly where or when it would strike.

Chapter Nine

Jane was reclining on a sofa in the morning room, talking to her mother and Isabel about her proposals for fundraising when Lady Wyndham arrived with Mark. Isabel immediately rose, curtsied to them both, muttered something about needing to find Sophie and left the room.

'Please do not try to get up,' Lady Wyndham said, putting a hand on Jane's shoulder as she struggled to rise and ignoring Isabel's hurried departure.

The two older ladies kissed each other's cheeks. 'How are you, Helen?' Grace asked, ringing for a servant. 'You look a little better.'

'I am. I do not think I shall ever recover completely from the loss of my dear Richard, but life must go on, you know. We came to see how Jane is. I was sorry to hear of her accident.'

They seated themselves and Mark took a chair opposite Jane and leaned forward. 'How are you, Jane? Did you manage to sleep?'

'Yes, thank you. Doctor Trench left a sleeping draught for me. I have to keep the limb up for a few days and then walk a little to see how I manage.' She was aware that she sounded stiff and formal, but she felt embarrassed by what had happened the day before: drinking too much champagne; his touch, which set her limbs on fire; the way their bodies melded together as he lifted her on and off the curricle; the conversation which had, at times, been perhaps too personal, especially when talking of Isabel. It made her feel guilty, too, as if she had been disloyal.

The maid returned with a tray containing a teapot, tea caddy and cups and Grace began dispensing tea, while continuing the conversation. 'I question whether a house in such a dilapidated state is fit to make into a home, even for orphans,' she said, addressing Lady Wyndham, as if orphans did not deserve a home such as other people enjoyed.

'I did, too, but Mark assures me it can be put to rights, but it is a great responsibility for an unmarried lady to take on.'

'The responsibility is divided between the trustees, of which I am one,' Mark put in. 'And I have told Jane I will help all I can.'

'I appreciate that,' Jane said quietly. 'I will try not to call on you more than I have to.'

'Call on me as often as you like.'

'I do think it is a pity Isabel does not interest herself in the scheme,' Helen said. 'A man needs a wife who takes an interest in the things he is interested in, otherwise they may as well live separate lives.'

'Oh, then…' Grace stopped and looked at Mark.

'Mother knows,' he told her. 'She is of the opinion Isabel will change her mind.'

'Of course she will,' Lady Cavenhurst said briskly. 'It is only a silly fancy because she is nervous of the responsibilities she will have as Lady Wyndham. I have told her your mother will be there to guide her.'

'Naturally, I will,' her ladyship agreed.

'Thank you,' Grace said. 'You are very understanding.'

'Not at all. I remember how terrified I was when I married Wyndham. It was his mother who helped me.'

Jane stole a glance at Mark who had taken no part in the conversation. His face was wooden. He sipped his tea and looked anywhere but at her. She was glad when the short visit came to an end and she could return to the plans for the fair which she had started. She needed to involve the whole village and the Reverend Caulder was the best one to help her. She would ask him to make a reference to it from the pulpit on Sunday. The swelling in her ankle would have abated by tomorrow and she would be able to hobble out to the trap and drive into the village. There was a crutch somewhere in the outbuildings that Teddy had used when he had broken his leg years before; if it could be found it would help her to walk to and from the trap.

She was driving round to the stables on her return from the village next afternoon when she noticed a carriage in the yard and wondered who the caller could be. Not Mark or his mother—she knew their vehicles; not anyone in the village, it was too grand and was dust-covered enough to have travelled some distance. The coachman was giving the horses buckets of water helped by Daniel. She stopped and used the crutch to support her as she climbed down. Daniel saw her predicament and ran to help her.

'Who is our visitor?' she whispered, as he helped her

into the house by the kitchen door. The front steps were beyond her.

'Mr Halliday.'

'Oh.' With the aid of her crutch she hobbled through the house to the drawing room, where she found her mother and sisters.

'There you are, Jane,' her ladyship said. 'We have a visitor.'

'So I perceived.' She sank gratefully on to a sofa beside Sophie and laid the crutch on the floor beside it. Her leg was beginning to ache abominably after her exertions. 'Is it Mr Halliday?'

'Yes. He and your father have been closeted in the book room for hours. We have all been requested to wait in here until they emerge.'

'Do you know why he is here? Did Papa send for him?'

'I do not think so. They were both looking very serious.' She appeared her usual calm self, but Jane could see she was trembling. 'I suspect they are talking about making economies.'

'Ugh, I hate that word,' Isabel said.

'Papa did warn us,' Jane said.

'So he did, but I cannot think he meant it. People like us just do not economise.'

'People like us?' Jane asked, lifting one eyebrow.

'Gentry.'

'Issie, gentry or not, we have to cut our coat according to our cloth.'

'And that is a silly thing to say.'

'How has your morning been, Jane?' her mother asked, changing the subject abruptly. 'How did you manage?'

'I managed very well. Everyone was helpful. The Reverend Mr Caulder is going to speak about the Hadlea

Children's Home after his sermon on Sunday when he makes the usual announcements. He will ask the congregation to offer their services to help run the fair, and for donations for the stalls and the prizes. We have decided to have it on the last Saturday in August on the Ten Acre Field.'

'Are you sure it will not overtax your strength?' her ladyship queried.

'Mama, I am as strong as an ox and my leg will be quite mended by then.'

They heard a door open and close, then their father, followed by the senior Mr Halliday, entered the room. They both looked sombre. Sir Edward invited the lawyer to be seated and then drew up a chair to sit close to his wife. There was silence for a moment while everyone looked towards him expectantly.

He cleared his throat. 'My dear,' he said, addressing his wife, 'the situation is far worse than I thought. I am afraid we have to make changes in our way of life. Big changes.'

'But why?' she queried. 'It is not as if you are a gambler like Teddy.'

'I don't gamble at the card table, it is true, but I gambled on the 'Change. The harvests have been bad for some time, but last year was the worst. The crops failed, the tenant farmers could not afford their rents and the Home Farm has made no profit at all in three years. In truth, it ran at a loss. My capital was dwindling and I thought buying and selling stock might see us through the worst of it. I was ill advised, not by Mr Halliday, but by others.' He sighed heavily and appeared to be on the verge of tears. 'I lost everything and in order to maintain our style of living I borrowed and allowed the debts to mount up. They are being called in and I cannot honour them.'

'What are we to do?' she asked, while their daughters looked from one to the other in shock. 'Must we do as Jane suggested a few weeks ago and get rid of the carriage and horses and dismiss the servants?'

Theodore Halliday interrupted with a gentle cough. 'My lady, I am afraid such economies would not be enough. It is unfortunate that all Sir Edward's debts have passed into the hands of a single person.'

'Lord Bolsover.' Jane had almost been holding her breath and she let it out on the man's name.

'I'm afraid so. He has made no secret of the fact.'

'What has the man against us?' Jane asked. 'Do you know, Mr Halliday?'

'I am afraid I do not.'

'Do you, Papa?'

He shook his head without speaking. His face was white and his hands were shaking.

She turned back to the lawyer. 'Are his lordship's claims valid?'

'I am afraid they are.' He paused. 'Unless it is put out of his reach, he will claim the whole estate.'

'Greystone Manor?' Grace gasped. 'He can't do that, can he?'

'I am afraid he can if your husband makes no effort to recompense him.'

'But it is our home. The Cavenhursts have lived here for generations, ever since the Interregnum.'

'I am inclined to think his motives might go back as far as that,' Jane put in. 'I found a headstone tucked away at the side of the churchyard. It said...' She paused to make sure she had the wording correctly. '"Colin

Bolsover Paget, beloved son of Lord and Lady Paget, died by his own hand, May 1649, aged twenty-seven years. May God forgive him and allow him eternal rest." Do you think that might be significant?'

'Perhaps, but whether it is or not will not help the present situation,' the lawyer said.

'What will help?'

'We have to sell the Manor and move to a smaller house where we can live more economically,' Sir Edward put in, speaking in a choked voice. 'We have no alternative.'

'Then Bolsover has won,' Jane said.

'Not quite,' Mr Halliday put in. 'If it is the Manor he wants, then selling it and paying him off with the proceeds will deprive him of it and leave enough for you to live in more modest surroundings.'

'Where?' demanded Isabel. 'We will never be able to hold up our heads in Hadlea ever again.'

'Why not?' their father demanded. 'You are to be married to Mark Wyndham and will be leaving home. Teddy has already left and no doubt Sophie will soon follow you to the altar, so it is easily put about that your mother and I and Jane do not need so large a house.'

'The Manor is Teddy's birthright,' Sophie said.

'Teddy has forfeited that,' her father snapped. 'If he had not got into Bolsover's clutches, the man would not have thought of buying up our debts, too.'

'I think perhaps Teddy was simply a means to an end,' Jane said quietly. 'I believe his lordship is conducting some sort of vendetta. I have a mind to discover what it is.'

'It will not help,' he said, his dejection evident in every

word. He was a defeated man and Jane's heart went out to him.

'Then we must make plans for the future,' she said brightly. 'Where do you think you would like to go? Bath is a good place for retirement.'

'Too expensive,' the lawyer put in.

'We must go home to Scotland,' their mother said suddenly. 'There is plenty of room at Cartrose Hall.'

Cartrose Hall was the home of her parents, Viscount and Viscountess Cartrose. It was in a remote spot in the Highlands, which had glorious countryside, thousands of sheep, but few people. The family had made frequent visits there when the children were small, but they had not been so often as they grew up and developed other interests. Besides, the journey took several days and Lady Cavenhurst, who was a bad traveller, had come to dread it.

'But that's the other end of the earth,' Isabel wailed

'But you will not be coming with us, will you?' her mother said. 'You will stay here as Lady Wyndham.'

'Then I will never see you again.' It sounded as if she were coming round to that idea after all and Jane wondered what Mark would make of it.

'Nonsense, Mark will bring you to visit us, I am sure.'

'I shan't be going either,' Jane said quietly. In the last few minutes she had been considering how a move would impact on her. She was committed to the Hadlea Children's Home project, she could not abandon it. 'I shall move into Witherington House.'

'On your own, Jane?' Sir Edward queried. 'Out of the question.'

'I shan't be on my own. I shall have a full complement of staff. I have to stay to help run it and keep raising funds.'

'Other people can do that.'

'But it is my project. It is important to me.'

Lady Cavenhurst began to weep and her husband abandoned his altercation with Jane to comfort her. 'Do not cry, my dear. It will not be so bad. Our daughters were bound to marry and leave home at some time and you would have become used to being without them.'

'But not Jane,' she sobbed. 'Not Jane.'

Made uncomfortable by her weeping, Theodore Halliday rose to leave. 'I will put the sale in hand for you, Sir Edward. I do not think we need advertise it widely. I will tell a few select people and the whole thing can be managed discreetly.'

'Yes, do that.' Sir Edward hardly turned from his wife to bid him good day. No one thought about the man's need for accommodation, until Jane mentioned it.

'Oh, yes, you are welcome to stay,' Sir Edward said. 'But we shall be poor company.'

'I thank you, but I have booked a room at the Fox and Hounds in order to make an early start in the morning.'

Jane rose and went with him to the front door. 'I am sorry to have been the bearer of such ill tidings,' he told her, as she handed him his hat from the table in the hall. 'I am afraid your family is going to need your stalwart good sense in the next few weeks.'

'I know.' A footman who was soon to lose his job opened the door and the lawyer hurried down the steps and climbed into his carriage. She sighed and turned to go back to the rest of the family.

'To think it should come to this,' her mother was saying. 'Me, a Viscount's daughter, reduced to charity.'

'Charity, Mama?' Jane said. 'No one has said you are

reduced to that. You are simply moving house for your own convenience.'

'Yes, so I shall say, and for my health's sake, but it will not make me feel any better about it.'

'Lady Wyndham and Mark will have to be told.'

'Oh, no, surely not?'

'They will think it very strange if we do not confide why we are suddenly selling our home, do you not think? Lady Wyndham has been your friend ever since you married and came to live here. It would be discourteous not to tell her.'

'Yes, I suppose you are right. She made me feel welcome when I was new to the area. I shall miss her more than anyone.'

Jane smiled. 'More than me?'

'Oh, you did not really mean you would not come with us, did you?'

'Yes, I did, Mama. I cannot manage Witherington House from Scotland, can I?'

'Let someone else take it on. I need you.'

'But so do the orphans.' She was tired of arguing, tired of going over the same ground again and again, tired of always giving in. 'Shall I drive you over to Broadacres tomorrow?'

Lady Cavenhurst sighed heavily. 'Yes, let us get it over with, though what I shall say to Helen, I have no idea.'

'The truth, Mama. It was you who taught us that untruths will always come back to haunt us.'

'If I could meet this dreadful Lord Bolsover,' her mother said, 'I would certainly have something to say to him.'

'Then I am glad you cannot, Mama, he would undoubtedly laugh at you. He is an odious man.'

'You have met him?' her mother asked in surprise.

'Yes, briefly when we were in London. I did not like him.'

'I hate him!' Isabel declared. 'He has been our ruin.'

'Not unless we let him,' Jane said. 'Now, cheer up, Mama, and let us begin to make plans how the move is to be achieved without loss of face.'

'I do not want to be poor,' Isabel said. 'I won't be poor, I *will* not. I don't want to live counting my pennies and not being able to have a new gown or new shoes when I want them. I would rather marry Mark after all.'

Jane's heart sank like a stone and her bright cheerfulness suddenly lost its edge.

The thought of leaving her childhood home, the place in all the world where she had been most happy, was heartrending for Jane, but she refused to weep as everyone else seemed to be doing. Tears altered nothing and it was better to be positive. When she said that to Isabel the following morning at breakfast, her sister snapped at her, 'It is all right for you, Jane, you are wedded to your children's home. You do not have to worry about husbands and weddings, you are an old maid and must make do with other people's children. I am being forced into marrying a man I do not love because the man I *do* love chose to be chivalrous and leave the field.'

Jane refused to rise to the bait, but she did wonder if there was some truth in what Isabel said. Was she using the children's home to fulfil a void in her own life? She shrugged; if she was, it would also benefit the orphans she meant to help, so what did it matter? She went to the stables to ask Daniel to harness the pony to the trap, so that she could drive her mother to Broadacres.

* * *

'Your papa is going to tell the servants today,' her mother said as they bowled out of the drive on to the village road. 'He has agreed I may keep Bessie, if she is prepared to stay with me when we move to Scotland, but the rest are to be given notice.'

'Perhaps the new owner will let them stay?'

'Perhaps, but we do not know who he will be, do we? Your father says they must be given the opportunity to find new positions, in case he does not.'

Would they be able to find new positions? Jane wondered. Everyone was having to tighten their belts nowadays—having more servants than were needed was a thing of the past, unless you were exceedingly rich. Only stubborn men like her father liked to keep up appearances. She would need some help at Witherington House, perhaps she could take some of them on. It might be seen as a downward step by Saunders, the butler, and Mrs Driver, the housekeeper, who had been with them for as long as she could remember, but it was better than being without a job and a home. The trouble was that Witherington House might not be ready when the time came to move.

Mark heard them arrive and came out to meet them. He was dressed for riding, though hatless. 'Good morning, my lady,' he said cheerfully. 'I did not think to have the pleasure of seeing you again so soon.' He handed her down, then turned to help Jane down. 'How are you, Jane?' he asked, searching her face.

His tender look of concern disconcerted her. 'I am well, thank you,' she said, standing on one leg while she fumbled for her crutch. He picked it up and handed it to her with a smile. It was all she could do to return his smile and thank him.

'Is Lady Wyndham at home?' Grace asked.

'Yes, I will take you to her.'

'I will wait here,' Jane said. She did not want to witness what she knew her mother thought of as humiliation, nor did she think her mother would want Mark to be present. 'I need to speak to you, Mark, if you can spare the time.'

'Of course. Can you manage as far as the walled garden? There is a seat in an arbour there.'

'Yes. I am becoming quite adept at using this.' She lifted the crutch.

He ushered Lady Cavenhurst into the house and Jane made her way slowly to the arbour garden and sat down heavily. Walking with a crutch was not as easy as it looked and made her shoulder ache, but that was the least of her problems. There was a honeysuckle climbing the frame of the arbour filling her nostrils with its scent and she breathed deeply, more to calm herself than to smell the flower. How much to tell him, how much to leave out?

She could see him as he came down the path towards her, and could admire his splendidly muscular figure; the way he walked, not stiffly, but upright with an easy grace; the superb cut of his clothes; the way he smiled. Would Isabel marry him? Her sister would not think twice about changing her mind again, if it meant she did not have to go to Scotland. It pained Jane to think that he would be hurt either way. The gossip would be dreadful if she did not. It might be said that he reneged when it was so obvious there would be no dowry and the family were spendthrifts. On the other hand, if she did marry him, could they be happy?

'Now, Jane,' he said, sitting down beside her. 'What can I do for you?'

'My mama is going to tell your mother a piece of news which will have consequences for all of us,' she began. 'And I have been given the task of telling you because Isabel flatly refuses to do so.'

'That sounds ominous.'

'I am afraid it is.'

'Go on.'

'Oh, dear, this is difficult.'

'My dear Jane,' he said, putting his hand over hers and adding to her nerves. 'Nothing can be so bad that you cannot confide in me, surely? What has your sister done now?'

'Oh, Isabel has done nothing. It is my father. He is in financial straits and must sell Greystone Manor. My parents are going to say they no longer need to live in such a big house and are going to Scotland for Mama's health.'

'Good God!' he said. 'I knew Sir Edward was struggling, but I had no idea it was as bad as that. How did it come about?'

She told him what her father had said the previous day, keeping nothing back; she felt he deserved to know the whole. 'Isabel does not want to go to Scotland and neither do I. I shall go to live at Witherington House. Isabel, of course, will keep her promise to marry you. That is, if you will still have her.'

'Leaving you behind?' She noticed he made no comment on her statement that Isabel would still marry him.

'It is my choice.'

'But Witherington House is not habitable.'

'I am hoping it will be, or at least part of it will be, by

the time the Manor is sold. The home will need a house-keeper, so why not me?'

'Jane, I do not like that idea at all.'

'You do not have to like it. But I would appreciate your help in getting things moving.'

'That goes without saying. I have already written to Cecil Halliday.'

'No doubt he will know our situation. Do you think it will make any difference?'

'I don't see why it should. Your father's affairs are no business of the trust, whose funds are secure.'

'And do you think we could perhaps take on some of the Manor servants if they fail to find positions for themselves?'

'Dear Jane,' he said gently. 'Always thinking of other people and not yourself. This must have been a terrible blow to you.'

She trembled at the endearment. She must not let him see how affected she was by it, she really must not. She forced a smile. 'My path is clear, Mark. I will tread it firmly.'

'Do you think Sir Edward would accept financial help from me?'

'I am sure he would not and I beg you not to mention it. His pride has already been badly bruised. In any case, the debts are all in the hands of one man and selling the Manor to pay him is the only way Papa will have anything left.'

'You cannot mean Lord Bolsover?'

'Yes. He has done exactly what he did to Teddy.'

'The man is evil. I cannot understand his motive.'

'No, but I found something interesting the other day,' she said. 'I believe he has a connection with Hadlea.'

'I have never heard of it.'

'I found a headstone in the graveyard, not in the consecrated area, but just outside it. It commemorated Colin Bolsover Paget, son of Lord and Lady Paget who died by his own hand in 1649. He was only twenty-seven. There were other old Paget memorials, but none with the name of Bolsover that I could see.'

'It was probably his mother's maiden name.'

'But surely it means there is a connection?'

'It could be coincidence.'

'I do not think so. Lord Bolsover talked of the Manor, of revenge, do you remember?'

'Yes.' He paused. 'I doubt it will make any difference, but I am curious enough to want to find out the story behind that suicide. There are old books at Broadacres that my father collected about the history of the area. I will see what I can unearth.'

'Thank you. I do not know what I would do without you.'

'You said that before.'

'I meant it.'

He stood up and held out his hand to help her rise. 'We had better go back to the house. Lady Cavenhurst will be waiting for you.'

'Did you tell Mark?' her mother said as the little pony took them back to the Manor.

'Yes. He deserved the truth.' She fell silent for a moment, then added, 'What did Lady Wyndham say?'

'She was shocked. We cried together. I shall miss her more than I can say, but she says we are welcome to visit as often as we like. After all, Mark will be our son-in-law.'

Jane contemplated this idea, but it made her so miserable she thrust it from her. She really must stop thinking about him; he was not for her and never would be. If she could cut herself off from him, she would, but they were both so heavily involved in the Hadlea Children's Home project, there was nothing for it but do as she had told him she would: tread her chosen path firmly. But, oh, how her heart ached.

'Helen said she would need a butler and a housekeeper when she moved into the dower house and would be happy to take on Saunders and Mrs Driver. Daniel, too, because she would need a coachman and she did not want to deprive Mark of his menservants.'

'That was kind of her.'

'I wish you were not so stubborn about not coming with us, Jane. It is not seemly for an unmarried lady to live alone.'

'I won't be alone. I'll have staff—perhaps some of the Manor staff will come with me. Besides, I am well past the age of needing a chaperon.'

He ladyship sighed. 'If you must, you must, but at least you will be near Isabel and Mark.'

Jane made no answer to that.

The following days at Greystone Manor were unhappy ones. Everyone was going about with long faces and tear-filled eyes while they began tackling the packing up of those belongings they would be taking with them. Lady Cavenhurst had received a letter from her parents telling her they would all be welcome, that if they preferred a home of their own, one of their tenant farmers was moving away and they were welcome to move in to his house.

'It's a barn of a place,' she grumbled. 'With no con-

veniences at all. And freezing in the winter. I am beginning to feel like the poor relation.'

Jane refrained from pointing out the truth of that and
instead suggested her mother should decide what to take
to make it more homely. Her ladyship would have liked
to take everything—sofas, pictures, ornaments, crock-
ery, cutlery, linen—but was warned by her husband he
did not intend to hire more than one large wagon and
she had better make up her mind what was essential and
what could be left behind and sold. He was, Jane noted,
uncharacteristically sharp with everyone and she knew
the strain was telling on him. Sophie was flinging clothes
all over her bedroom and bemoaning the fact that she
could not take her pony. Isabel, who had quite made up
her mind to marry Mark after all, was reviewing her
wardrobe, knowing she could buy whatever she liked in
clothes when she became Lady Wyndham, but she certainly did not look happy about it.

As for Jane, she discarded the use of the crutch and
took the trap over to Witherington House to inspect it
more closely and talk to Mr and Mrs Godfrey about the
future, telling them what she intended and to ask them
to stay on. 'We'll be right pleased to, miss,' Silas said.

'It will be nice to have children about the place again,'
Mrs Godfrey added. 'There were always children about
in the old days, laughin' and getting' into mischief. Sir
Jasper let them have the run o' the place and Lady Paget
always indulged them with treats.'

'Paget?' Jane queried. 'Did you say Paget?'

'Yes, that wor their name. Didn' yew know that?'

'No, when you spoke of Sir Jasper, you did not mention his family name.'

'I thought ever'one knew it.'

'You said there were children. I understood Sir Jasper had no close kin and that was why the lawyers had such a problem finding his heirs.'

'They were the children of cousins. They grew up and moved away. Stopped comin'.'

'Why?'

'I don' know, do I? Not my business and it were a long time ago.'

'Have you heard the name Bolsover in connection with the family?'

'Can't say I hev. Why?'

'Oh, no reason.' She strolled away from them, intending to take the measurements of the first-floor rooms and make a note of how many beds each could accommodate, but she could not keep her mind on what she was doing. She gave up and went out to inspect the outbuildings she had not seen before. Silas was giving Bonny some oats. 'He's a sturdy little fellow,' he said.

'Yes, and very easy to drive.'

'We used to hev half-a-dozen hosses here, one time,' he went on. 'And carriages and the like. I useta help look after them. Sir Jasper got rid o' most on 'em, when her ladyship died, but he kept a couple of mares to hitch to an old chaise, but when he took to his bed, they were got rid of, too.'

Jane was beginning to feel sorry for old Sir Jasper, alone and unhappy in his declining years, but did he have a connection with Lord Bolsover? Would it make a difference to her plans? She could not wait to tell Mark, forgetting her decision not to call on him any more than she could help.

Mark was sitting in the library with his head in his hands. On the desk in front of him were several old books he had taken from the shelves which he had been perusing when a footman had come to tell him Miss Cavenhurst had arrived and asked for him. She was waiting in the drawing room. Thinking it was Jane, he had hurried to go to her, a smile on his face. She would be interested in what he had discovered.

But it wasn't Jane, it was Isabel. He kept the smile, though it was a little fixed as he bowed to her. 'Isabel, do sit down. I wasn't expecting you. How did you arrive? Have you seen my mother? Have refreshments been ordered?'

'Good morning, Mark.' She sat on one of the sofas and smoothed the skirt of her green-silk dress with gloved hands. 'I walked and, no, I have not seen your mother and I do not need refreshments. We have done nothing but drink tea at home all morning. One would think it was the cure for all ills.'

'I am deeply sorry for what has happened, Isabel. If I can help in any way, you know I will.'

'Thank you.' She turned an appealing smile on him. 'I have been very silly, for which I beg your pardon.'

'I am sure there is no need for that.'

'But there is. You see, I told you that I no longer wished to marry you and you were so gallant as to tell me you would not hold me to it.'

'Yes, I did.'

'But as I said, I was foolish, blinded by false sentiment, and on reflection I wish to retract—'

'You mean you no longer wish to break off our engagement?' His gut was churning with a mixture of disappointment, fury and helplessness. If he could have told her that he would not accept her change of mind and that as far as he was concerned the engagement was off and had been off ever since she had first mentioned it, he would have. But such a course was not acceptable. A lady might, with small loss to her reputation, break off a betrothal, but a gentleman could never do so. It would lay him open to the condemnation and disgust of everyone in the *haut monde* and he would be shunned. He was as bound to honour his proposal as if he had said his wedding vows.

'Yes. I am sorry. I should have thought about it more carefully before speaking.'

'What about Drew?'

'What about him? He left me to you, didn't he?'

'But your feelings for him? Were they not sincere?'

'Not sincere enough for me to face penury on his account.'

He laughed without humour. 'You have certainly put me in my place.'

'I am sorry, I didn't mean to do that. I am very fond of you, Mark. We grew up together, I am sure we will deal well together and you will not hold my lapse against me.'

'No, of course not.' What else could he say? He pulled the bell rope beside the fireplace. When a servant arrived, he bade her inform Lady Wyndham that Miss Isabel Cavenhurst was here and would she like to see her.

Two minutes later his mother bustled into the room. 'Isabel, how nice to see you. I did not know you were here or I would have come sooner. Is your mother not with you?'

'No, my lady. I am alone. I needed to speak to Mark.'

'Without a chaperon? Dear, dear.'

'I did not think of it. Jane never bothers.'

'We do not count Jane.' Her ladyship smiled. 'But never mind, you are still engaged to my son, are you not?'

'Yes, Lady Wyndham, I am.'

Mark could bear it no longer. He made his excuses and returned to the library, where he flung himself into a chair and, moaning, put his head in his hands. His mother's words burned in his brain. 'We do not count Jane.' How could they be so disparaging? How could they take everything from her and give nothing in return? He loved her, he loved her quiet nature, her unselfishness, the way she cared for everyone, sacrificing her own happiness to do so, for her lovely expressive eyes when she looked at him, her sweet smile, her down-to-earth honesty, her courage. Whoever married her would be marrying a treasure and he wished it could be him.

He heard his mother taking leave of Isabel, then a footman escorting Isabel down the long gallery to the front door and then his mother came looking for him. 'You left us rather hurriedly, Mark.'

'I couldn't bear to hear you speak of Jane in that offhand way, Mother. She does count.'

'Oh.' She was thoughtful as she sat down beside him. 'So it's Jane. Oh, dear.'

'Mother, you know I was relieved when Isabel said she wanted to break off the engagement, I told you so.'

'Yes, but you did not mention Jane and I thought you were just putting a brave face on it.'

'No, I meant it, but I could hardly jump from one engagement to another, could I? Jane would never have agreed in any case. I needed time. And now it seems I am not to be given time.'

'Does Jane know?'

'Of course she does not.'

'Best she never does. You cannot get away from the fact that you are betrothed to her sister. Perhaps it would be better if you did not see Jane so frequently.'

'That will look odd, considering we are both trustees of the Hadlea Children's Home and have already been working on it for some time. It will look as if we have had a falling-out over it.'

'So, you will go on torturing yourself when you should be making plans for your wedding. Isabel tells me she wants it before her parents leave for Scotland and I have said it would be best. I don't know the date the move is planned, but these things take time and I do not suppose it will be before the six months of mourning is over.'

'Isabel is a selfish little madam. She is only doing this because she doesn't want to go to Scotland with her parents. She has no love for me, only what I can give her— she as good as said so.'

'Oh, dear, I wish you had confided in me earlier, Mark.'

'Why? What could you have done?'

'I could have accepted the situation instead of agreeing with Grace that Isabel would change her mind and assuming she would. Isabel might then have realised there was no going back.'

'Too late, Mama, and I doubt it would have made any difference.'

'Perhaps not.' She rose to leave him. 'What are you doing with those?' she asked, noticing the dusty books on the desk.

'Some research into the Paget family. Halliday has told me Sir Jasper Paget was the previous owner of Witherington House and I thought I had come across the name somewhere.'

'No doubt you have. There are graves in the churchyard and a tablet on the wall inside the church. You must have seen it dozens of times. It is over the pew next to ours.'

'What do you know about them?'

'Nothing at all. The graves are very old. Does it matter?'

'Not at all.'

'Then put them away and walk with me in the garden. It is a lovely day and I have a mind to pick some roses.'

Chapter Ten

Jane stopped at the crossroads in the village, intending to turn towards Broadacres when she saw Isabel walking from that direction. She pulled up and waited for her.

Isabel climbed in beside her. 'I'm glad you came along, Jane,' she said. 'My new shoes are pinching like the devil.'

Jane flicked the reins and the pony trotted on towards home. Telling Mark about Sir Jasper would have to wait. 'Are they the ones you bought in London?'

'Yes. They are fine when I am riding in a carriage, but not when I am walking.'

'Where have you been?'

'To Broadacres.'

'Without Mama?'

'Yes. I needed to speak to Mark.'

'Oh. And did you?'

'Yes. We have come to an understanding.'

Even though she was half-prepared for it, Isabel's words put an end to any hope Jane might have had. More fool her for even entertaining it, she told herself fiercely. 'By that, I suppose you mean the engagement is on again.'

'Yes, it is.'

'And what did Mark say?'

'He was delighted, of course, and forgave me for my doubts.'

'And now you have no doubts?'

'None. We are to be married before Mama and Papa leave for Scotland, so do you think you can set aside your fascination with your orphanage project for a while and finish my wedding dress?'

'Of course. There is little to be done to it in any case.'

They had barely entered the house when Sir Edward hurried towards them. 'Jane where have you been? I have been looking everywhere for you.'

'I have been to Witherington, Papa. Has something happened?'

'There are people coming to view the house this afternoon and your mama refuses to meet them. You will have to take her place.' He turned to his younger daughter. 'Isabel, go and keep your mother company. She is in her boudoir. Sophie is out riding.'

Isabel left them and he turned to Jane again. 'They will be here in less than half an hour.'

'Then I must go and change out of these clothes and have Bessie do my hair. Witherington House is so dusty it is impossible not to get it on one's clothes. I will be as quick as I can.'

Half an hour later she returned to the drawing room, seeing it with a stranger's eyes and realising it would not give a good impression. The furnishings were shabby and there were dark patches on the wallpaper where her mother had had paintings removed. Papa had said she could not take them, but she had not had them put back. They were on the floor, leaning against the wall. The shelves in the cabinet where there had once been a display of china figurines were empty and forlorn looking. And flowers in the vase in the hearth were drooping. She picked it up and put it outside the window on to the terrace, just as they heard the front door knocker.

Mr and Mrs Somerton were undoubtedly *nouveau riche*. He was portly and dressed in a dark-green coat, yellow waistcoat, whose buttons strained across his stomach, and cream trousers, strapped under his shoes. She was even fatter, in puce taffeta and loaded with jewels. She and Jane curtsied to each other while Sir Edward explained he had asked his daughter to receive them because of his wife's poor health. 'It is why we are leaving here,' he said. 'We have already started to gather together our belongings, as you can see.'

'We expected it to be furnished,' Mr Somerton said, looking round in distaste.

The rest of the house, apart from her ladyship's boudoir, were viewed with the same reaction and the couple departed, making it very clear they would not be buying.

It was the same with the next two people Mr Halliday sent to them. Having steeled themselves to losing their home, they now found that no one wanted to buy it. Lady Cavenhurst, Isabel and Sophie were secretly pleased, though Jane was more realistic and Sir Edward was in despair because he knew he could not hold Lord Bolsover off much longer.

Then the dreadful man himself arrived. He bowled up in an extravagant chaise drawn by four superb horses, and banged on the front door with his cane.

Jane was upstairs on the first-floor gallery, having just come from the sewing room where she had been putting the finishing touches to Isabel's wedding gown, when she saw Saunders, on his dignity as usual, admit him and request his name.

'Go and tell your master Lord Bolsover is here to view the property.'

Jane was taken aback. Why did the man want to view the property? Surely Mr Halliday had not sent him? She walked downstairs in as stately and calm a manner as she could manage, though inside she was quaking. He saw her and stood watching her descend. Not until she reached the bottom did she speak. 'Lord Bolsover, good afternoon.'

He bowed. 'Miss Cavenhurst, I hope I see you well?'

'Very well, thank you. Why are you here?'

'I will tell your father that when he deigns to put in an appearance.'

'I expect someone has gone to fetch him. He may be on the estate somewhere. Will you come into the withdrawing room to wait for him?'

'Very well, but I hope he won't be long.'

She led the way and offered him a chair. 'If you had warned us you were coming, we would have been expecting you.'

He laughed suddenly. 'I doubt it. You would all have gone into hiding.'

'We have nothing to hide, Lord Bolsover.'

'No? The fact that Greystone Manor was up for sale? That was an underhand thing to do.'

'What did you expect my father to do? He has debts to pay as you very well know.'

'I doubt the sale will cover them. How much is he asking? Ten thousand, I believe. It is overpriced by at least three thousand.'

'How do you know the figure?'

He smiled. 'I have my sources. I know Sir Edward's debts to the last penny, I know your brother's debts and I know how much Sir Edward hopes to obtain from the sale. Unless my arithmetic is faulty, the figures do not add up.'

She pretended indifference, but could not quell the feeling of despair that overwhelmed her. Was he right?

Her father arrived and saved her from having to answer. 'Papa,' she said, 'this is Lord Bolsover. My lord, Sir Edward Cavenhurst.'

Her father ignored Bolsover's outstretched hand and stood facing him. 'What do you want?' he demanded. 'Why are you here? My wife is unwell and your presence will upset her. Please leave.'

'I will when I'm done. I wish to see over the premises.'

'Why?' Jane demanded. 'You are surely not thinking of buying?'

'I do not need to, do I?' He was addressing Sir Edward. 'Your debt to me easily covers the price you have put on the estate, which I am told is far above its true market value. You haven't been able to sell, have you?'

'There is plenty of time.'

'No, Sir Edward, there is no time at all. I am calling in the debt immediately.'

Jane gasped and her father turned deathly pale. 'Why? Why are you doing this to us? We have done nothing to harm you.'

'Ah, but there you are wrong.' He smiled suddenly, a smile that sent a chill into Jane's veins. 'I need a home and I think Greystone Manor will serve me very well, but I need to look round to see if it covers the eight thousand pounds owed to me.'

'I do not owe anything like that much,' Sir Edward said.

'You do if you add your son's debts to yours and there is the interest being added every day at ten per cent. So, will you show me round, or shall I wander about on my own?'

'Jane will accompany you. I must go to my wife.' He scuttled away, leaving Jane facing Lord Bolsover.

'Shall we go?' she said, leading the way.

She took him from room to room, downstairs and upstairs, avoiding her mother's boudoir where the murmur of voices could be heard through the closed door. Then they returned downstairs and she led him through the kitchen to the stable yard and the outbuildings, which he inspected. 'That's the house and immediate outbuildings,' she said when that was done. 'There is a park of three hundred acres, some woodland, three farms with farmhouses and the usual buildings, and some farm cottages. If you want to see those, I suggest you hire a hack and ride round on your own, but I trust you have seen enough.'

'I was right,' he said, laughing at her sharp tone. 'You are the only one of the family with any fire. I like that.'

'I wish I knew why you were so intent on ruining us.'

'Soon, if all goes well, I shall tell you. Now I wish to speak to Sir Edward again.'

She preceded him back to the drawing room where she left him while she went in search of her father. He was with her mother and Isabel.

'Has he gone?' her mother asked.

'No, Mama, he wants to see Papa.'

Sir Edward heaved himself out of his chair and left them.

'What does that man want?' Isabel asked.

'He says he is calling in Papa's debts forthwith and wanted to be sure the estate covered them.'

'You mean he is not even going to give us time to sell?' her mother queried.

'Not unless Papa can talk him out of it. He has added Teddy's debts to Papa's and is charging ten per cent interest.'

'But that's outrageous!'

'Yes, it is,' Jane agreed. 'I think it is a means to an end. He wants Greystone Manor and is determined to have it and when Teddy got into his debt he saw a way of obtaining it.'

'But why?'

'I asked him that and he refused to say.'

'What are we going to do?' wailed Isabel. 'What about my wedding? What will Mark say? And Lady Wyndham? She can be very intimidating.'

'I am sure it will make no difference to Mark,' Jane said.

'But where will I live until the wedding? I expected to be married from here.'

'Your papa will think of a solution,' her ladyship said with a simple faith in her husband that Jane thought ill founded. 'He will not see us turned out.'

There was a knock at the door which, in their heightened state of nerves, made them all jump, but it was only Bessie with a message for Jane. 'Sir Edward said to rejoin them,' she said. 'They are in the book room.'

Reluctantly Jane went. Sir Edward was seated at his desk, with papers that looked very much like deeds spread out in front of him. Lord Bolsover was standing at the window with his back to the room. He turned as Jane entered.

'Jane, my dear,' her father began and there was a distinct tremble in his voice. 'His lordship has suggested a way out of our dilemma and it concerns you. I want you to listen very carefully to what he has to say.' He stood up to leave. 'You may not agree and I shall not hold it against you if you do not, but I beg of you to think of your poor dear mama and your sisters.' And with that he scuttled away, closing the door behind him, leaving Jane facing Lord Bolsover.

'Shall we sit down? he suggested pleasantly and, taking her hand, led her to the sofa, where they sat side by side.

Bewildered, she pulled her hand from his and said nothing. Her father's words had eaten into her brain and could only have one meaning. She waited.

'I do not wish to see your family beggared,' he began.

'Then you have a strange way of showing it.'

'I have had my eye on Greystone Manor for a number of years—all my life, in truth. I have always considered it my birthright.'

'Why? The Cavenhursts have lived here for generations.'

'I know. Ever since 1649.'

The date echoed in her head. The date on the headstone. 'Colin Bolsover Paget,' she murmured.

'Ah, so you have found it.'

'Yes, but I do not know the reason for it.'

'Colin Bolsover Paget was so foolish as to fall in love with the daughter of a Roundhead. The Pagets were Royalist to the core. They refused to allow Colin to marry his Gabrielle, but he defied them and changed sides. He found himself opposing his Paget and Bolsover cousins in battle. Gabrielle tried to come between them and in consequence lost her life. Colin survived the battle, but he was cut off from his family and his Roundhead in-laws blamed him for their daughter's death and made his life such a misery, he put an end to it. The Roundheads claimed the Paget home.'

'Greystone Manor.'

'Yes. The last Paget lived out his life at Witherington House, which I believe you have discovered.'

'Where do you come into all this?'

'Colin's mother was a Bolsover, daughter to my father's ancestor, the first Lord Bolsover. I heard the tale at my father's knee as every generation has. Each of us has been sworn to vengeance, but none has managed it until now.'

'I have never heard this story.'

'No reason why you should. It is not something of which the Cavenhursts can be proud, is it? The Pagets that were left hoped their property would be returned to them with the restoration of the monarchy, but it was not to be. Colin Paget was not the only one to change sides.'

'And you think this Banbury tale will make me look more favourably on you?'

'I hope it will because I have a proposal to make.'

'Proposal?' she echoed.

'Yes. You must have guessed.'

'Never!' She was almost shouting and lowered her voice. 'Never in a thousand years. I cannot think why you ever thought of it.'

He laughed lightly. 'It came upon me when I met you in London. You attracted me at once. My widowed mother is anxious to see me settled before she departs this life and insists I marry and set up my own establishment. I need a home and a wife and I think I have found both here.'

'What on earth makes you think I would agree to that?'

'Sir Edward asked you to hear me out and it is only courteous to do so.'

She did not see why she should be courteous to him, but for her father's sake she said nothing, allowing him to go on.

'Your father's and brother's debts together amount to nearly nine thousand pounds, considerably more than the value of the estate, so selling it and paying me off would leave him still in debt.' He paused. 'Ah, that shocks you, I see. But I am prepared to count only what I paid for the debts, which is naturally a great deal less than their face value, and will allow the lower figure to be set against the value of Greystone Manor. There will, if the agreement is reached quickly, be enough left for your parents to leave here with a little cash in hand and their dignity intact, which is something your father sets great store by. You, of course, will continue to live here as my bride.'

'No.'

'No? Did your father not ask you to think about it carefully? Surely you can see the advantages for everyone? I will have a home and a delightful wife, whom I shall treat with courtesy and respect, my mother will be satisfied, your parents will have a little money to live out their lives in modest comfort, your brother can return to the bosom of his family and you, my dear, will be able to continue your work for the orphans. I might even help you with it.'

She did not answer. Everything he said was driving a nail into her heart and almost stopping it. The whole idea was repugnant to her and the worst of it was her father expected her to agree. How could he? How could he ask this of her? Did he think she was so anxious to be married she would accept this…this…? A suitable epithet failed her.

'I have shocked you into silence,' he added, 'but I will give you a week to make up your mind. In that time I hope you will consider carefully the consequences of refusing. Your family will be paupers and I shall still possess the Manor. And just in case you were thinking of moving everyone to Witherington, I could stop that sale, too.'

She rose and ran out of the room, determined he would not see her tears. She paused in the hallway. In any other circumstances she would have sought comfort and solace from her father and mother, but she could not do that; this time they were the source of her distress. There was no one to turn to, not even Mark, who would undoubtedly try to comfort her, but he was betrothed to her sister and she had vowed not to call on him more than she could help for Isabel's sake.

She ran out of the front door and round the side of the house with no destination in mind. How she ended up in the stables, she did not know, but she found herself sobbing on the neck of Bonny. He was warm and he had never let her down, never made demands on her; his bright eyes seemed to tell her he understood. Still crying, she found harness and saddle and put them on him, even though he was a draught pony and unused to a saddle. She used an old milking stool to mount and galloped out of the yard, ignoring Daniel's shout.

She did not know where she was going. Did not care. She was not even aware of other vehicles on the road, nor that a carriage had to pull to one side to allow her to pass. She galloped on, past the Fox and Hounds, over the crossroads, ignoring the turning to Witherington and was at the gates of Broadacres and turning up the drive before she suddenly came to her senses. She should not be here! 'Whoa there,' she called out and pulled sharply on the reins, bringing Bonny to a skittering stop. He reared at being so ill used and threw her.

At that moment, Mark turned into the drive in his curricle and only by skilful driving managed to stop before running her over. Horses, pony and curricle were in a tangled heap. He extricated himself and ran to her. Jane was unconscious and deathly pale and dressed in an afternoon gown, not a habit. She wore no hat, which might have offered a little protection for her head. Something dreadful must have happened to bring her out like that.

'Oh, my God!' He fell to his knees beside her. 'Jane! Jane, wake up. Wake up, please.' He resisted the impulse to shake her awake and felt all over her face and head. His hand came away covered in blood. 'Please God, don't let her die,' he prayed aloud. 'Let her live. I need her…' She did not stir. Ought he to pick her up and carry her into the house? Or should he leave her lying in the road until a litter could be brought to carry her? He looked about him. There was no one about to send for one. He stood up, stooped to pick her up and walked the rest of the way up the drive to the house.

He was met by Thompson, who had heard the sound of the crash and the neighing of the horses and was on his way to investigate. Mark told him swiftly what had happened and sent him to take care of the curricle and

the horses, then he carried Jane into the house and sent
for his mother.

'Mark, whatever has happened?' she said, looking at
his burden.

'She was riding up the drive and came off. I almost
ran her over. Send for Dr Trench, will you, please.'

'Yes, of course I will. And Lady Cavenhurst, too.' She
turned to a footman to give him instructions. Then to
Mark, 'If she was riding, why is she dressed like that?'

'I don't know, Mama, but something dreadful must
have happened at the Manor. Perhaps she was coming
to us for help.'

'Grace will tell us when she arrives. Take her up to
the blue room. I'll send Janet up to you.' Janet was his
old nurse, who was long past retirement age, but she had
nowhere else to go and continued to live at Broadacres,
making herself useful in so many ways, especially when
anyone in the household was ill.

In the bedchamber, always referred to as the blue room
on account of its curtains and bedcover being the colour
of a summer sky, he put Jane gently on the bed. She was
still deeply unconscious and he was afraid for her life.
If she died, he didn't know what he would do. It was
his fault; he should not have turned into the drive so
fast. He fell to his knees beside the bed and stroked her
paper-white face. 'Jane, you must live,' he murmured. 'I
love you. Without you, I am nothing. Please, my darling,
wake up.' He reached over and gently kissed her cheek.
She did not stir and gave no hint that she had heard. His
heart was beating too fast and then almost stopping, before thumping on again. He took a deep breath to calm
himself and took her hand.

He had been a fool, letting convention dictate what

he did. Why had he not seen Jane's worth before he proposed to Isabel? Why had he accepted everyone else's
idea that she was plain Jane and not to be considered? She
was far from plain, she was beautiful. She had a depth
of beauty that Isabel had never had; it came from inside
her and shone out in everything she did. 'Jane doesn't
count.' The words seared into his brain. She counted
for him, more than anything else, more than life, more
than riches, certainly more than the opinion of the *haut
monde*. The trouble was that Jane herself would never
accept him, even if he persuaded her to admit she loved
him, too. She would never betray her sister, just as Drew
would never betray him. Where was Drew?

His mother bustled into the room accompanied by Dr
Trench and Janet. 'Has she come to?'

'No.' He rose from his knees and reluctantly left the
room.

Jane's eyes fluttered open, shut again, then opened
fully. Where was she? She was in a bed, but it was not
her own bed. She turned her head to see Mark sitting in
a chair beside her. He looked tired and drawn, but his
smile was wide. 'You are awake at last.'

'Where am I?'

'At Broadacres. You came off your horse in the drive,
do you remember?'

'No. What was I doing?'

'I think you were coming to see me.'

'Was I?' She struggled to sit up, but was surprised at
how weak she felt and her head felt funny. She put a hand
up and touched a thick bandage. 'What about?'

'I was hoping you would tell me.'

'Sir Jasper,' she murmured. 'I found out he was a Paget and related to the man in the graveyard.'

'I know. I don't think it was that. You would not have left home in such a hurry without even changing into a habit just to tell me that.'

'Did I?'

'Yes.'

'Does Mama know I'm here?'

'Yes, she has been every day.'

'Every day?' she echoed. 'How long have I been here?'

'A week.'

'A week!'

He smiled. 'Yes, seven days and in a delirium most of it.'

She was alarmed. 'What did I say?'

'Nothing that made any sense. The only words I managed to decipher were Papa, Roundhead, Royalist, wedding and something that sounded like Bolsover. We had the devil of a job to stop you thrashing about and reopening your wound.'

'Oh. Who's we?'

'Me, my mother, Janet and your own mother when she came. She was distressed as we all were, but Dr Trench said he expected you to make a full recovery, given time.'

'Time!' she cried, as memory flooded back. 'I do not have time. I have to go home.'

'No, you do not.' He pressed her gently back on to the pillow. 'You are not moving from here until I am satisfied you are well enough. You are safer here.'

'Safer?'

'Lord Bolsover cannot touch you while you are here, can he?' It was said with a smile.

'You know?'

'Your mother told us. The whole idea is preposterous.' He had found references in his own library to the Civil War and to the second Baron Paget who had lived at Greystone Manor. He had been a staunch Royalist in an area of East Anglia that was largely on the side of Parliament. When the Royalists had finally been defeated he had lost his Manor to an early Cavenhurst. A second search of the church records had revealed the story of the suicide. Colin Paget's mother was a Bolsover, a family based in Northamptonshire. That might explain Bolsover's determination to regain the Manor, but not the reason he had offered for Jane. It was not love, he was certain of it.

'I have no choice.'

'The longer you are here, out of the man's reach, the longer we have to think of a solution.'

'There is no solution, Mark. Please do not raise false hopes in me. My duty is plain.'

'Duty! Why must you always be the dutiful daughter?' he said almost angrily. 'Why can you not think of what you want sometimes?'

She sighed. 'Mark, I love my family too much to see them brought low if I can prevent it.'

'What about me?'

'What about you? You are my dear friend, my confidant, partner in my charitable endeavours—I cannot imagine losing all that. I hope very much that will continue.'

'Of course it will, whatever happens, but I—'

'Please, no more, Mark. Will you send someone to help me dress? I wish to go home.'

She had to be strong and resolute because it would be all too easy to lie back on the pillows and play the invalid, letting Mark sit beside her and hold her hand when he should not be doing anything of the sort, and hoping Lord Bolsover would give up and go away. It was a forlorn hope and dwelling on Mark's kindness and concern for her only made her want to cry.

'Very well.' He put the back of the hand he had been holding to his lips and left the room.

She rubbed at her hand contemplatively. He had seemed genuinely distressed by her plight and the way he had searched her face and held her hand made her wonder... Had she dreamed he said he loved her? The voice had been far away, like a distant echo, penetrating her unconscious mind. No, she must not think of it, must not strain to make it real. It was not to be. Isabel would marry him in a few weeks' time and he would become her brother-in-law. She shut her eyes, but a tear escaped from under the lid and slid down her cheek.

'Jane is determined on dressing and going home,' Mark told his mother when he found her in the parlour doing the household accounts. They were easily wealthy enough not to worry about the cost of food and candles and things like that which could easily have been left to Mrs Blandish, but she insisted on doing them herself. 'My mother always did hers and her mother before her,' she had told him long ago when he had remonstrated with her. 'And your father approves.' His father was no longer there to approve or disapprove, but he let her carry on.

'Surely not? She is not strong enough yet and Grace asked us to keep her here in any case, to buy them a little time.'

'I know. I tried to tell her that, but she will not listen.'

'Poor Mark,' she said.

'It is not poor Mark, it is poor Jane. See if you can persuade her, Mama. I have a mind to speak to Bolsover.'

'No, Mark, you must not. He will make a game of you. You will end up fighting him and who will gain by that? Besides, there is enough gossip going the rounds already and you will only add to it. Squabbling over a woman when you are engaged to another just will not do.'

'I must do something. If only I had known the true state of affairs at the Manor earlier, I might have been able to do something, lent Sir Edward some money to discharge them.'

'You could not, Mark. By the time your poor dear father passed away and you came into your inheritance it was already too late.'

He knew she was right, not only about the money, but about confronting Bolsover. What he found so difficult to understand was why a man like Hector Bolsover, who enjoyed the life of the capital and spent most of his time at card tables, would want to come and live in a rural spot like Hadlea. It did not make sense.

'Will you go to Jane? I will drive over to Greystone's to tell them Jane has recovered consciousness. I'll bring her ladyship back with me. She will, no doubt, want to see her daughter.'

The damage to the curricle had not been great and had soon been mended and both his own horse and Bonny had not suffered any harm. In no time at all he was bowling along the village street towards the Manor. As he passed the church he saw the Rector by the lych gate, who waved to him to stop.

'How is the invalid?' he asked him, coming to stand with his hand on the side of the curricle.

'Making good progress, I think. She has regained consciousness and is able to speak. I am going over to tell Lady Cavenhurst the good news.'

'That is a great relief to us all. She will soon be back to her old self, then?'

'It is to be hoped so.'

'I heard she was to be married to the gentleman staying at the Fox and Hounds. The people in the village are very excited about it. They say Miss Cavenhurst deserves her happiness.'

'Indeed she does,' Mark said, through gritted teeth.

'I found Lord Bolsover wandering round the churchyard. He made himself known to me and desired me to have the grave of Colin Paget cleared of weeds and the headstone cleaned. He is an ancestor of his, I believe.'

'So I have heard.'

'Perhaps there will be a double wedding. His lordship seemed amused by the idea, but he did not say he did not like it.'

'I'm sorry,' Mark said, anxious to end the conversation. 'I must be on my way to fetch Lady Cavenhurst.'

'Of course. I must not detain you.' He stepped back. 'Please tell Miss Cavenhurst that I am thinking of her and wish her well. Tell her I have recruited some volunteers to help clean up Witherington House when she is ready.'

'I will, but we do not need to wait until Miss Cavenhurst is out and about again, we can make a start on the house. I think it will please her.'

'Yes, that is a good idea.'

'I will speak to you about it when I have more time.'

So that's what his mother meant about rumours, Mark mused, as he continued on his way. Even if they had not been perpetrated by Bolsover, which seemed likely, he had certainly not denied them. There was an almighty scandal brewing and he did not know how to prevent it.

Lady Cavenhurst seemed unaware of the rumours when he was shown into the drawing room at the Manor and delivered the news that Jane was awake and her mental state had not suffered because of the injury to her head. 'She is wishful of coming home,' he said.

'Much as I would like her home, she must not do that,' her ladyship said. 'Lord Bolsover has called every day and is as determined as ever. He has practically accused her of pretending to be ill in order to delay speaking to him. I had to ask Dr Trench to confirm that she was deeply unconscious and incapable of making a decision. I even hinted that she might have lost some of her mental faculties in the hope he would withdraw his suit, but Sir Edward was quite angry with me. He says Jane is our only hope, so we must not tell Lord Bolsover she has come round.'

'Then Jane must stay where she is. Would you like to come back with me and talk to her?'

'Yes, please. I will go and put on my hat.' She left the room and he wandered round, waiting for her. He had not realised until now how shabby everything looked, especially with the pictures down and the shelves emptied.

'Oh, it's you, Mark.' He whirled round to face Isabel. 'I thought I heard a visitor arrive. How is Jane?'

'She woke up about an hour ago. She is very weak, but otherwise none the worse.'

'I am so glad. It is dreadful here without her, everyone going about with Friday faces. I will be glad when she comes home.'

'But then she will have to give Lord Bolsover his answer.'

'Why not? She will have to give in, in the end.'

He was angry. 'Isabel, you surely would not condemn your sister to marrying that dreadful man?'

'He isn't that dreadful, not when you come to know him better, he can be very charming and he is our only hope. She is lucky to find a husband at all at her age and he is very rich.'

He was so annoyed he was speechless, but luckily Lady Cavenhurst returned, wearing her hat and gloves, and he escorted her to the curricle.

He was still seething and wondered if her ladyship had heard and if she agreed with her daughter. Isabel was totally self-centred. He could not marry her, he simply could not. But how could he get out of it with any honour?

Chapter Eleven

Between them, the two ladies and Mark, with the connivance of Dr Trench, persuaded Jane that she ought to stay where she was for another week at least. Jane herself was convinced of the need for it when she attempted to leave her bed unaided and fell to the floor. Mark was passing in the corridor and heard her sharp cry. He rushed in and helped her up, trying not to notice that she wore only a flimsy nightgown that did nothing to hide her curves, nor the soft swelling of her breasts rising and falling with her breathing. He stood, holding her against him, savouring the feel of her in his arms, her body fitting so neatly into his and his hunger for her became almost unbearable.

True, he had held her before, once on the village green when Drew had been with him. *'If I did not know you better, I would think you were a little too fond of your future sister-in-law,'* his friend had said, which was perceptive of him, considering he had not realised it himself at the time. Then when she twisted her ankle on the broken stair, and latterly when she came off her horse in his drive, but she had always been fully dressed. Even when she had been so ill and he lay watching her hour after hour, she had been well covered, Janet had seen to that.

He turned her in his arms and tipped her chin up so that he could look into her face. 'It seems I am destined to be always picking you up off the floor,' he said, attempting humour. And then he kissed her.

It was only meant to be a gentle kiss, a fond kiss to let her know he was on her side, to try to convey he knew not what, but it deepened into something much more and she stood cradled in his arms and let it happen. There was no cry of protest as his lips found hers, no pushing him away in outraged fury. She melted into him and he knew, he knew then, that he could never marry anyone else, no matter what.

'Jane?' he murmured, leaving off kissing her, but continuing to hold her, knowing she would crumple if he did not. Besides, he wanted to. 'Oh, Jane, what are we going to do? I cannot let you go.'

'No, for I should fall down again.'

'I didn't mean that.'

'Neither did I.'

'I love you.'

'It cannot be,' she said, as a tear slipped down her cheek. Telling her that when it was all too late was the greatest torment of all.

'It is a fact.' He kissed the tear away.

'Mark, don't, please don't.'

'Why? Are you going to tell me you do not love me?'

'I…' She stopped in confusion.

'Be honest with me, Jane.'

'I am always honest with you.'

'Well then?'

'Whatever my feelings may be, it still cannot be,' she

murmured. 'There's Isabel and…and Lord Bolsover.' She shivered.

'Damn Bolsover.' He picked her up, kissed her again and put her back on the bed, pulled the covers over her and sat down on the edge, holding her hand. 'We could run away and marry secretly.'

'Mark, you are joking, you must be. Think of the scandal, think of your mother, your friends and the villagers, who look up to you and respect you. Would you forfeit that? And there's Isabel. Would you break her heart?'

He was tempted to say 'Damn Isabel', but refrained. Instead he said, 'I do not think it would break her heart, Jane. She broke the engagement off once, she might do so again.'

'Not with Papa's bankruptcy hovering over us and Lord Bolsover laying down the law. We must do what is right for everyone.'

'Why can't we do what is right for us?'

She gave him a wan smile. 'Mark, I do not feel strong enough to argue with you, please say no more. What happened here this afternoon is our secret, never to be divulged to a soul, though I shall always remember it and think of it in years to come as a time when I knew that I was once loved.' She attempted a smile.

It was all too much. He fled the room before she could see his unmanly tears.

Jane knew she had done the right thing, but, oh, how hard it had been to send him away. He must have realised the rightness of it, too, because he did not come to see her every morning as he had been doing, popping in for a few minutes to see how she was and asking if she needed anything. She missed his cheery smile and the feeling he gave her that she was important. Well, she would just have to live without that. Her head ached and she felt weak as a newborn kitten, but unless she wanted to spend the rest of her life in bed she would have to do something about it. It was time to make a move.

Every day she left her bed and tottered round the room, hanging on to furniture. Round and round she went, stopping when she came to the window to gaze out at the gardeners tending the borders, hoping for a glimpse of Mark. Then on she went again, until she was exhausted. Day by day her legs strengthened until she could walk without support. The bandage was removed from her head, leaving a little bare patch where her hair had been cut away, but the scar had nearly healed and the hair would grow again. Janet had devised a style that used the length of her hair to disguise it.

The next step was to dress and go downstairs to sit in the parlour, sometimes alone, sometimes with Lady Wyndham, either sewing or reading or talking quietly. She began taking her meals in the dining room, which meant she saw and spoke to Mark, but his mother and the servants were always present and they had done little but exchange pleasantries. Even so, she felt the tension in the atmosphere, the constraints that prevented them even looking at each other properly. It was a kind of exquisite torture.

Her mother came frequently to see her, bringing her clothes, and so did Isabel and Sophie. Isabel's moods of cheerfulness alternated with gloominess and Sophie's bright chatter exhausted her.

'Lord Bolsover has gone to Northamptonshire to tell his mother the good news,' Isabel informed her on one visit. 'And he was also going to see his lawyer about the transfer of the deeds and to draw up a marriage contract.'

'But I have not agreed to marry him.'

'He is assuming you will and so is Papa. You cannot turn him down, Jane, you really cannot. Everything depends upon it. He has even promised to pay for my wedding breakfast and we can invite as many as we please.'

'Do you know how long he intends to be gone?'

Her sister shrugged. 'How long does it take to do something like that? I did hear Papa tell Mama that he had withheld some documents about manorial rights and without those his lordship cannot proceed. But he will send for them, no doubt, so it is only putting off the inevitable.'

Jane had decided to go home the next day and was prepared to walk, but Mark would not hear of it and insisted on taking her in his curricle. It was the first time they had been alone together since the day he had picked her up off the floor and kissed her. She sat silently beside him, watching his capable hands on the reins and occasionally glancing up at him, but he kept his gaze firmly on the back of the horse. Instead of going down the main village street when he came to the crossroads, he turned off on to the road to Witherington.

'Why are you going this way?' she asked, breaking the long silence.

He turned to her with a gentle smile. 'So that I may have a little longer alone with you.'

'Oh.'

'And also because I have something to show you.'

'At Witherington?' That he wanted to have time with her both pleased and worried her at the same time. But

if she kept her mind firmly on the Hadlea Children's
Home and remained businesslike she might just manage
to keep her composure.

'Yes.'

'The sale went through, then? I wondered if Lord Bolsover might try to delay it.'

'He was only one of the beneficiaries and the others
were all keen to sell. He is not as powerful as he would
have us think, Jane.'

'Powerful enough.'

'We will not speak of him. Now, what do you see?' He
had turned into the gates of Witherington House, which
had been replaced on their hinges and were standing open
to reveal a drive cleared of weeds. The house itself had
been divested of its festoons of ivy. 'Mark, what a transformation! There's new glass in the broken windows and
they have all been painted.'

'There are fresh tiles on the roof, too.'

'However did you manage it?'

'I didn't do anything except point out what needed to
be done. It was the people of Hadlea. They love and respect you, Jane, and when they heard from the Rector
what you wanted to do with the place, every able-bodied
man and some of the women and children came forward
and spent their spare time here. I simply bought the paint,
glass and tools.'

'They must be paid.'

'They said they didn't want payment, but I insisted on
giving them something.' He drove round the side of the
house and drew up in the yard where Mrs Godfrey was
feeding chickens. These were new, too. 'I thought the
home ought to be as self-sufficient as possible,' he said,

jumping down and helping Jane to alight. 'Good morning, Mrs Godfrey. Where is Silas?'

'He is in the garden somewhere with some of the folks from Witherington. They decided they wouldn't be bested by Hadlea and came to help. Shall I fetch him?'

'No, let him be. I just want to show Miss Cavenhurst what we have done.'

'Made a transformation, that's what,' she said, then to Jane, 'Miss Cavenhurst, I heard you'd had another accident. I hope you have recovered.'

'Yes, thank you. It was entirely my own fault. I am quite well now.'

'I'll make tea, shall I?'

'When we have finished looking round, we will welcome tea, thank you,' Mark said, leading the way indoors.

The interior had also been cleaned and painted in cream and light green and, with the ivy gone, the rooms were light and airy. 'Oh, Mark, to think all this was done while I was idling at Broadacres.'

'You have friends, Jane, a great many friends,' he said softly. 'Not just me.'

She was tempted to say he was more than a friend, but decided it would be unwise. She went from room to room—everywhere was the same. 'It is ready to furnish,' she said, as they made their way up the repaired stairs. 'Do we have enough money?'

'I think so, but we must continue to raise more. There is the fair, of course. And my mother has said she will open the house and grounds and give a musical recital for her friends. I am sure they can be persuaded to give freely.'

'That is very kind of Lady Wyndham, but she is still in mourning, Mark.'

'She says she will wait until the six months is up, but she is sure that is what my father would have wished. He was all in favour of your idea, as you know. In the meantime we can go ahead with the fair.'

They were standing at the window of the largest bedroom, looking out at a group of people clearing the overgrown garden and piling the rubbish into a heap for a bonfire. She was right; concentrating on the home was making her personal unhappiness almost bearable, but she wondered what all these good people would say if they knew the truth.

They had finished their tour and talked about furnishings and the fair while they sat in the kitchen drinking tea, then set off back to Hadlea.

'I can't thank you enough, Mark,' she said. 'You have made a dream possible.'

'There is another dream I would like to make possible...'

'Don't, Mark. Please don't.'

They were passing the place where they had had their picnic and he pulled up, just as he had before. 'Let us walk a little.'

He helped her down and they walked into the field, where a footpath ran round the perimeter. There was wheat growing in it, almost ripe enough to harvest, but even Jane, who was no farmer, could see it would not be abundant and unlikely to be good enough for making bread. But it was not the state of the harvest which occupied her now, but the fact that Mark had hold of her hand and was drawing her into his arms.

'Mark, you mustn't.'

'Yes, I must.' He bent to kiss her. He kissed her lips,

her eyelids, her neck, the round softness at the top of her breasts, peeping above the scooped neck of the striped-gingham dress she wore. It sent a ripple of sensation right through her body and into her groin. She clung to him, not wanting him to stop. It was he who pulled away, breathing heavily.

'I'm sorry, Jane, my love, my dearest love, I have not made it easy for you, have I?'

'No, you have not, but don't be sorry, unless you regret it.'

'Regret it! Oh, my love. How could I?' He went to draw her to him again, but she stepped backwards.

'No, Mark. No more. Take me home before we both do something we regret.'

'Very well.' He put his hand under her elbow to guide her back to the carriage. 'There has to be a way out of this mess, there just has to be and I will find it, I promise you.'

Everyone was pleased to have her home, telling her how well she looked and that the rest had done her good. 'Now, you are not to go dashing about as you have been doing,' her mother said, sitting beside Jane on her bed while Bessie unpacked the few clothes that had been taken to Broadacres. 'It is why you have these accidents. Do take more care in future.'

'Mama, I cannot be idle. It leaves me too much time to think.'

'Ah, I understand. You know Lord Bolsover has left the village?'

'Isabel told me. I suppose it is too much to hope he has given up and won't be back.'

'I am afraid it is.'

'And you still think I should marry him?'

'If it was left to me, I would say no, let him do his worst, but it is not up to me.' She laid a hand on Jane's arm. 'Your papa can see no other way out of our predicament. And there are Isabel and Sophie to consider. Sophie will never find a suitable husband if we are poor. And there's Teddy. I want him home, Jane, I want my son home.'

'I know.' She sighed, then added, falsely bright, 'I intend to enjoy my last days of freedom.'

'Good.'

'Did you know the villagers have been working at Witherington House?'

'Yes, everyone is talking about it. It is good that Lord Bolsover has said you may continue with it, Jane.'

'It will certainly be a condition of my acceptance.' Even as she spoke she wondered if she would be in a position to insist on conditions.

There was still much to be done. In the following days, she formed a committee in the village to organise the fair and wrote more letters asking for prizes and donations, and perused dozens of catalogues, looking for serviceable furniture for her orphans. Mr Halliday junior had written to her, asking when she intended to admit her first orphans. Her reply was that she knew a brother and sister in Hadlea whose father had been lost in the war and whose mother was finding it difficult having to go to work and look after her children. There were others in the neighbourhood she would approach. They would be the first to be offered homes. As for the rest, she would simply visit nearby towns and keep her eyes and ears open.

Her days were full and for a little while she was able to set aside the prospect of marrying Lord Bolsover, but it was different at night. Tired as she was from her daytime activities, she was never tired enough to sleep soundly.

She had nightmares, which involved Lord Bolsover chasing her, sometimes over flat grassland which suddenly became boggy, sucking at her feet and slowing her down, sometimes through woods at night with strange shapes looming out of the darkness, at other times along high cliffs with the sea crashing on the rocks below them. That was worst—with the menace behind her and the menace in front, she didn't know which way to turn. She always woke just as Lord Bolsover reached out to grab her. At other times she dreamed she was wearing Isabel's wedding gown and her sister was trying to tear it off her, shouting, 'It's mine! It's mine!' That made her feel worst of all and she woke with tears streaming down her face and her bedclothes in a tangle.

She had not seen Mark for some time. She had no idea if he had resigned himself to marrying Isabel, but she assumed he had. Isabel herself talked about it all the time: her gown, her trousseau, what had been ordered for the wedding breakfast, how she would reorganise Broadacres once Lady Wyndham had moved into the dower house. It was as if she dared not stop talking.

'Issie, are you sure you want to marry Mark?' Jane asked her one day when they were alone in the morning room. 'Not so long ago, you declared you could not bear the prospect. You said you did not love him.'

'No more I do, but plenty of marriages have survived without love, especially if there are compensations: a handsome husband, wealth and standing. You should think about that yourself.' She paused. 'Don't you dare tell Mark I said that.'

'I won't.'

* * *

The London Season was well and truly over and all the big families had repaired to their estates in the country, where the harvest was being gathered in. All agreed it was a poor one and the price of bread would go up again. The harvest on Broadacres's farms was better than most, but nothing like as good as it ought to have been. Mark had waved the rents of his tenant farmers for the winter term. It was a gesture they appreciated and rewarded him with genuine loyalty, promising to help the fair in any way they could.

But Mark was not in London to sell his grain, but to try to find a way out of his more pressing dilemma. His first call was on Cecil Halliday, who was working on a court case involving the theft of a silk shawl, but left it to greet Mark. 'I wasn't expecting you today, my lord,' he said as they shook hands. 'There is nothing wrong at Broadacres, I trust.'

'No, nothing. My visit concerns Greystone Manor and Lord Bolsover.'

'My father is dealing with that, my lord. I know little of it.'

'Perhaps you could ask your father to join us.'

He disappeared and returned in few minutes with Theodore, who bowed in the old-fashioned way. 'My lord, my son tells me you are interested in Greystone Manor. Are you considering buying it?'

'No, Mr Halliday, I am not. I need to find out all I can about Lord Bolsover. Are you quite sure his claims are just and fair?'

The old man smiled. 'Just and fair? Hardly. But if you are asking me if they are legal, then I must tell you that as far as I can see they are. Do you have information to the contrary?'

'No, I hoped you might have. Did you know he has bullied Sir Edward into allowing him to propose to Miss Cavenhurst—Miss Jane Cavenhurst, I mean—and his lordship intends to take her and the Manor in lieu of the debt?'

'No. I did not know. That is indeed troubling news.'

'I think Sir Edward believes Bolsover has your support. And Jane—Miss Cavenhurst—is convinced she has no choice but to agree.'

'Good God!'

'Do you know anything at all that might discredit his lordship?'

'Only that he is a gambler and plays deep, but if he chooses to live in that way, it is his affair.'

'I would like you to dig a little, see what you can unearth.'

'My lord,' Theodore said with some pomposity, 'Sir Edward Cavenhurst is my client. I cannot do anything without his permission.'

Mark turned to the younger man. 'Then what about you, Cecil? Will you take my instructions?'

'I would,' he said doubtfully. 'If I knew why you were asking.'

'I am soon to be married into the family and would not have them brought low if I can help it. I would pay off Sir Edward's debt myself, even though it would have a damaging effect on my own resources, but Sir Edward is too proud to accept. Besides, if Lord Bolsover is crooked, I want him brought to justice, not to pay him off.'

'I'll see what I can do,' Cecil said.

'Then you must do it in your own time,' his father said.

'I do not doubt we will have trouble getting Sir Edward to settle his account as it is. I am not inclined to spend any more time on his behalf.'

Mark left, annoyed that even Sir Edward's own lawyer was turning against him. Cecil's enquiries might take some time and he was too impatient to wait. His next call was at White's, where he hoped to find Toby Moore, but Toby like the rest of London society had decamped to the country. The man did not have a country estate, but was no doubt going the round of friends. Frustrated, Mark went to Horse Guards where he met his old battalion commander. 'Can you tell me anything about Lord Hector Bolsover and Captain Tobias Moore?' he asked him when they had finished clapping each other on the back and Colonel Bagshott had congratulated him on his elevation while commiserating with him on the demise of his father. 'What regiment were they in?'

'I have no idea. I believe they served in the Peninsula, if not at Waterloo. Toby Moore calls himself "Captain". I met him once just before the battle of Cuidad Rodrigo. Never saw him again after that.'

'It will take me a little time searching the records. How long are you in town?'

'Only today and tomorrow. I must return to Hadlea the day after.'

'Let's meet tomorrow evening for supper. Stephen's at eight o'clock suit you?'

'Yes, I will be there.'

Mark went back to South Audley Street to spend an evening at home. He could have gone to his club but he did not feel like being sociable. He had too much on his mind. If he could only find something to discredit Bolsover, he might save Jane from being forced into marrying him. It would please Jane and her parents, but it was not enough. It did not release him from his engagement to Isabel. That was something else entirely.

The following evening he met Colonel Bagshott as arranged. They spent a frustrating hour and a half, talking about old times and old comrades and reliving old battles, before the subject of Hector Bolsover was broached.

'As far as I can tell Lord Bolsover was never in the army,' the Colonel said. 'I believe he went out to the Peninsula as a civilian, though why I do not know.'

'He is a gambler,' Mark said. 'No doubt he was fleecing the troops. What about Toby Moore?'

'He was cashiered for cowardice after the Battle of Cuidad Rodrigo. He has no right to call himself a captain.' He paused. 'Are you going to tell me what this is all about?'

Mark told him the same story he had told the lawyers. 'I was hoping to discredit Bolsover enough to make him leave the field,' he said, 'but so far have discovered nothing except that he is a mountebank of the first order.'

'I am sorry I could not help you further. If I learn anything else, I will certainly let you know.'

Mark had to be satisfied with that and they moved on to other topics, which diverted him for a time, but the reality was that he had made very little progress. So much for his promise to Jane that he would find a solution.

All the arrangements for the fair had been completed. Mark had sent his men to mow the field, mark out the lines for the races and set up some of the stalls the day before. An archway festooned with bunting had been constructed at the gate where Mrs Caulder would sit at a table to take the entrance money. Others would be manning stalls of produce and overseeing the competitions. Mark had donated a pig as a prize for a skittles competition and others had donated prizes for various races and feats of strength. There would be bowls and apple bobbing and later in the evening dancing to the music of a fiddle and a lute. Lady Wyndham had agreed to open proceedings. All they needed was good weather.

On the day, Jane was woken early by Bessie drawing back the curtains. Sunshine streamed into the room. She rose and went to the window. The sky was an overall azure, not a cloud to be seen. 'A good omen, we have been blessed with fine weather,' she said to Bessie. 'I'll dress and have my breakfast in the kitchen, then I'll drive over to Ten Acre Field.'

'It is still very early, Miss Jane.'

'I know, but there is still much to do. The pale-blue muslin, I think, and the matching pelisse.'

She was not the first to arrive. The villagers were all used to rising early, especially in summer, and were already going about their allotted tasks. Mark was there, in his shirt sleeves, busily helping to erect a dais for the opening ceremony and the prize giving. His coat and cravat hung on a nearby post. He smiled at her, a little sadly, but it was a smile. 'Have you prepared your speech?' he queried.

'Me? Oh, no, Mark, I am not going to make a speech,' she protested, trying vainly to take her eyes from the sight of his bare chest under the open neck of his shirt.

'But it's your project. Without you it would never have happened.'

'It is just as much yours, Mark. You make the speech.'

She moved on, checking this, checking that, speaking to everyone, her spirits rising a little as she went. If nothing else was right in her life, this project was. Mrs Caulder arrived and sat at the entrance to the field, a jar for the money on a table in front of her. 'Henry will be here in good time to conduct the prayers,' she told Jane, who was becoming anxious in case no one arrived.

One by one they came, paid their sixpences and wandered round to see what was on offer. It was not only the Hadlea and Witherington residents, but people from further afield who arrived in an assortment of carriages. Jane had not thought about what to do with all the vehicles, but Mark, as ever, came to her rescue by suggesting they line up alongside the drive at Broadacres and his stable boys would see to the horses, for a small fee to be added to the funds. 'I'll go and tell the lads and bring my mother back,' he told Jane, hanging his cravat loosely about his neck and slipping his arms into his coat.

While he was gone her father, mother and sisters arrived. In spite of the dreadful cloud hanging over them, they were determined to put a good face on it for Jane's sake and the ladies were elegantly dressed and carrying parasols for the sun was warm. 'Lord Bolsover is back,' Sophie whispered to her. 'We saw him arriving at the Fox and Hounds. We stopped so that Papa could get down and speak to him. I think they argued. Papa looked very flushed and his lordship angry.'

'Where is Mark?' Isabel demanded. 'I expect him to escort me.'

'He has gone to fetch his mother,' Jane said, wishing Sophie had not told her about Lord Bolsover and hoping he would not decide to patronise the fair. 'He will be back soon.'

She left her family to make sure everything was ready on the dais for her ladyship. The Rector was there, sitting on one of the chairs provided. 'We shall do well out of this, Jane,' he said. 'Mrs Caulder has already taken three pounds at the gate, though I fear some of the boys have managed to squeeze through the hedge without paying.'

'Never mind. They will need to pay if they want to enter the competitions.'

Mark's curricle drew up and he helped his mother from it and up on to the dais, where she stood, in unrelieved black, looking about her at the colourful throng, regal but not distant. Mark helped her to a seat and then stepped forward, nodding to a boy at the side of the platform who was holding a brass bell by its clapper. The boy began ringing it, watching in glee as people stopped what they were doing and turned towards him. 'Enough,' Mark commanded, as everyone gathered round the platform. The sound stopped on a last echo.

'Ladies and gentlemen,' Mark began, 'we are here to enjoy ourselves, but also to remember the soldiers and sailors lost in the recent war and think of the children they left behind. All the money raised will go towards the maintenance of Witherington House as a home for some of those children. We would not be here today, if it were not for Miss Jane Cavenhurst, whose idea it was and who has worked tirelessly towards it.' He paused and looked round while everyone applauded. 'Miss Cavenhurst.' He beckoned Jane to mount the rostrum.

She was taken aback and wanted to sink into the ground, but he was holding out his hand to her and the people nearest to her were urging her on. Reluctantly she stepped up beside Mark. 'You will pay for that trick, Mark Wyndham,' she whispered.

'The credit is yours,' he whispered back. 'Tell them about the urchin you met in London, touch their heart-strings.'

She began unsteadily, but as her fervour for the cause took over, her voice strengthened and she saw more than one tear wiped away. 'We are fortunate that the late Lord Wyndham gave a very generous donation to start us off,' she finished. 'And others have also donated. The home has already been purchased, as many of you know, but we still need funds to furnish it and maintain it, so please, buy the produce, enter the games and enjoy the day.'

The Rector stood and led them in a prayer and then Mark called on his mother to declare the fair up and running. It was while she was standing beside her ladyship, looking over the heads of the crowd, that Jane saw Lord Bolsover coming towards her. She looked round for a way of escape, but soon realised she could not flee without creating a scene and she did not want to spoil the happy atmosphere of the afternoon.

Mark had seen him, too. 'Courage, my love,' he whispered. 'Don't agree to anything.'

She was shaking as she stepped down from the dais to face the man she held so much in aversion. He smiled and doffed his hat in an exaggerated bow. 'Miss Cavenhurst. You are recovered, I see, and quite the Lady of the Manor. I chose my bride well, methinks.'

She did not deign to answer that. Instead she said, 'What are you doing here?''

'Why, my dear, I have come for my answer. You have kept me waiting long enough. Let us take a stroll.' He picked up her hand and tucked it beneath his elbow. 'There, that is better, now we may act the happy couple. Do smile, my dear. You will have everyone think our coming union is not to your liking.'

'I do not feel like smiling, Lord Bolsover.'

'Now that is to be regretted, but we shall blame it on your accident, shall we? Not quite yourself yet.'

'I wish you would go away and leave my family alone.'

'Now, my dear, you know I cannot do that. Nor would your father wish me to even though he withheld an important document. Very foolish of him. It did nothing more than cause me the inconvenience of coming back for it. My lawyer refused to proceed without it and I would not trust anyone but myself to fetch it. What your papa seems not to have considered is that every day's delay adds to the interest, which is not inconsiderable. I beg you point that out to him when you tell him you have accepted my proposal.'

'I have not accepted it.'

'Oh, but you will, do not doubt it. Shall we get that boy with the bell to give it a go and announce our betrothal to the whole crowd? I am sure they will all be overjoyed for you.'

'No, please don't.' She hated to beg, but she could see Mark marching purposely towards them with a furious expression on his face and she feared a public quarrel. 'It is too soon. I need more time.'

'You have had over a month.'

'I could not help being ill.'

'But you are well now.'

'After my sister's wedding in three weeks' time,' she said, groping at straws. 'I will give you an answer then.'

Mark was almost upon them when Mrs Caulder came hurrying up to Jane. 'I beg your pardon, my lord,' she said, addressing Lord Bolsover, 'but I must speak to Miss Cavenhurst. It is urgent.'

Jane's relief at the interruption was palpable. She

turned to Mrs Caulder with a smile which left her face when she saw how distressed the lady was. 'What has happened?'

'Someone has stolen the gate money. I only turned my back a minute to listen to the speeches and when I turned back it was gone.'

Lord Bolsover laughed aloud. 'I will leave you to sort it out, my dear, but it is only a few pounds. I can easily make it up for you.' And with that, he strolled away, smiling to himself.

Jane's shoulders sagged as the tension she had been enduring seeped away from her. Her hands were shaking and her knees felt boneless.

'I am mortified,' Mrs Caulder went on. 'I really am sorry, but if his lordship is prepared to make it up, we shall not lose by it.'

'That is not the point.' Mark put in. 'It is theft and we must discover who is responsible. We cannot have people thinking it pays to steal.'

'No, I suppose you are right, but I have no idea who it was.'

'Did they take only the money or the jar with it?' Mark asked

'The jar. Everything. There was a five-pound donation from Sir Mortimer Belton, as well.'

Jane had not seen the Member of Parliament arrive. 'That was generous of him.'

'Yes, but now it is lost. Some people gave more than sixpence to come in, too. They said it was for a worthy cause. There must have been nigh on ten pounds altogether.'

'Did you see anyone loitering nearby?' Mark asked.

'Not that I can recall.'

'Leave it to me,' Mark said. 'We will keep it to ourselves for now. We don't want to cause a stir.'

'I won't say a word. Thank you, my lord.' She hurried away, leaving Mark facing Jane.

'What did he have to say?' he asked.

'Who?'

'Bolsover. What did he say?'

'Nothing he has not said before. I begged him to give me more time. I said I would give him his answer after your wedding.'

'My wedding! Did he agree?'

'He neither agreed nor disagreed. Mrs Caulder interrupted us.'

He laughed. 'Oh, well done, Mrs Caulder.'

'It is not funny, Mark.'

'No, but if she has afforded us more time…'

'Us, Mark?'

'Yes, us. You do not think I am going to let you marry that scoundrel, do you? I have tried to find something to discredit him, but though he is not at all liked, no one seems to know anything against him. There are rumours of sharp practices, but nothing to substantiate the rumours. I shall keep trying.'

'Mark, please do not raise my hopes, if they are to be dashed. I don't think I could bear it. Really, you should be escorting Isabel round the fair and buying her trinkets, not talking to me. I can see her over there and she is looking at us. Go to her, please.'

'You have been neglecting me,' Isabel complained as soon as he joined her. 'People are beginning to notice.'

'I am sorry, Isabel, but I have had much to do with the organisation of this event and seeing that everything is running smoothly and I had to escort my mother back to the house; she finds events like this tiring. Now something else has happened that demands my immediate attention, so I am obliged to leave you again.'

'A fine marriage we shall have if you are forever going off and leaving me.'

'If you wish to change your mind about that again, please say so.'

'No, no, I didn't mean anything,' she said quickly. 'Go and do whatever it is you have to do. But I hope it will not take too long. Papa has said we may stay for the dancing, so I shall expect you to stand up with me.'

He had bowed and left her to watch the races with her parents while he spent the next hour and a half going round all the stalls, asking if anyone had been spending unusually freely, but no one had. Perhaps the thief was no longer on the field, perhaps had never been any further than the gate. If that were so, it was going to be doubly difficult to apprehend him. Or her.

He went to the gate to ask Mrs Caulder if anyone had approached and not entered, but the good lady must have decided that there would be no more arrivals and had left her post. He turned away and it was then he saw the woman out of the corner of his eye. She was carrying a jar close to her chest, which looked very like the one Mrs Caulder had been using. He dodged behind the hedge and watched her. She approached the deserted table and, looking furtively about her, set the jar on the table. Mark left his hiding place and confronted her.

'It is Mrs Butler, is it not?'

'Yes.'

'What were you doing with this?' He picked up the jar. It was heavy with coins.

'Putting it back.'

'What were you doing with it in the first place?'

'Nothing. Putting it back, I told you. I found it.'

'Oh, come, madam, you do not expect me to believe that, do you? Shall I tell you what I think? I think your boy took it.'

She gasped. 'He didn't mean no 'arm, sir. He's only a little lad and he wanted to 'elp me. I lost me ol' man to the war, yer see, and now I've lost me job, on account of staying at home to look after Lizzie, who was sick. You in't a-goin' to turn 'im in, are you?'

'No, I do not think so. We have the money safe. Go home and see to your family.'

'Thank you, m'lord. God bless you.' She bobbed a curtsy and fled.

He took the jar back to Jane. 'It is all here,' he said. 'No harm's done.'

'Oh, thank goodness. I didn't want the day marred by something so unpleasant. Who took it?'

He told her what had happened. 'Did you not say you were thinking of offering the Butler children a home?' he asked.

'Yes. I haven't mentioned it to Mrs Butler yet, but I will do so soon. She may not want to part with him.'

'I think she might. She has just lost her job and her chances of finding another while she has two children to care for are slim.'

'She could work at Witherington House, then they could all be together. I need to recruit staff.'

'Good idea. Shall we join your parents and sisters?'

Jane looked round and spied them watching the skittles competition. Lord Bolsover was with them. 'No, I do not think I will. I'll go and see Mrs Butler. You go.'

But he did not want to join them either and went in search of the parson's wife to give her the good news and return the pot to her after emptying its contents into a canvas bag Jane had stowed under the dais for just that purpose. There was money being taken on all the stalls and it occurred to him that it might be a good idea to take temptation out of the way and collect it. He would take it up to the house and put it in the safe until it could be paid into the Hadlea Children's Home account. By the time he had finished the bag was heavy. They had done well, but he would not count it—that was a pleasure he would leave for Jane.

Mark was almost home when he saw a familiar figure coming towards him, a slightly plump figure dressed in a blue military-style frockcoat, embellished with silver braid. 'Jonathan Smythe, you old dog,' Mark said, smiling with pleasure. 'Where have you sprung from?' They clapped each other on the back.

'Scotland, where else? I've been up to the house and your mother told me where to find you.'

'I will be going back there after I have put this in a safe place.' He held up the bag. 'Come with me.'

Jonathan turned and they walked side by side. 'I was sorry to hear of your father's demise, Mark.'

'Thank you.'

'My mother's cousin died, too. I've inherited a pile of stones, as cold as charity, but it comes with a sizeable fortune so I must not grumble. I assume your mourning has delayed your wedding?'

'Yes. Much has happened since you left.'

'If you still want me to be your groomsman, I am yours to command.'

Mark could think of nothing to say to that except to thank him again.

'You'll never guess whom I met while I was up north. Drew Ashton. I hadn't seen him since we were at school together. He's come up in the world by all accounts.'

'Drew is in Scotland?'

'Yes. He was visiting his great-aunt. I must say I was surprised by that. She never bothered with him when he was a boy and he don't need her blunt now. I reckon it was a convenient bolt hole. He was havey-cavey when I asked.'

'He always played his cards close to his chest. You don't happen to have his direction, do you?'

'I think I have it in my trunk. I left it at Broadacres, by the way. I assumed you would invite me to stay, what with the wedding and all.'

'Of course, stay as long as you like. There's a fair on the Ten Acre Field that I've been helping to organise, which is why I am carrying a bag of small change. I have to go back as soon as I've put it in the safe. There's to be a country dance this evening which I am obliged to attend. Come if you like.'

It was incredible how cheerful he suddenly felt. At last he could see a way out of his dilemma.

Chapter Twelve

The field was lit by lanterns on poles for the dance in the evening. Everyone joined in, including the children, and it proved to be the most fun of the whole day, if only because it was impossible to dance properly on grass. Jane and Mark partnered each other in an eightsome, which meant occasionally holding hands in full view of everyone. She was acutely aware that she must in no way betray how she felt about him, but the slight squeeze he gave her fingers every time they met and circled together told her he was aware of it, too. He seemed unusually light-hearted, smiling and joking with everyone. Afterwards she sat with her parents, watching him dance with Isabel while his friend, Mr Smythe, danced with Sophie.

She was quietly congratulating herself on the success of the venture and enjoying the spectacle of everyone amusing themselves when Lord Bolsover stood over her to claim a dance. She pleaded tiredness, but he would not take no for an answer and led her into the throng.

He was clumsy and stumbled more than once. 'I can't get the way of this,' he said, giving up after only a few minutes. 'If this is what you call dancing…'

'It is meant to be fun,' she said. 'This isn't a London ballroom. If that is what you want, I suggest you return to the capital.'

'Not without my answer.'

'I have told you when I will give you that.'

'And I shall hold you to that, never fear. My mother is become impatient to have a grandson.' Still smiling, he bowed and strolled away. Jane let out a long breath of relief.

The result of the fair was forty pounds to add to the funds, which was far more than Jane had dared to hope for. She and Mark spent Sunday morning at Broadacres, counting the pennies and sixpences and the occasional gold sovereign. 'People have been so generous,' Jane said. 'I can buy enough beds and bedroom furniture to fill the dormitories at Witherington. I will ask the Rector to announce the result in church.'

The announcement after evensong had brought gasps of delight and it was suggested it should be an annual event, which had pleased her. There was so little to please her nowadays; she was becoming hopelessly resigned to marrying Lord Bolsover. He was staying at the Fox and Hounds, but was constantly at Greystone, seemingly unaware of how unwelcome he was. He would talk of the alterations he meant to make, the refurbishment, the parties he would host, smiling all the while with that oily smile of his, which sickened Jane, if no one else. The only way she could avoid him was to spend as much time as possible at Witherington House where she could immerse herself in what was going on there and for a little while, forget her coming fate.

Gradually the furniture arrived and was put in place until it began to look like a real home. She was helped by Mrs Butler, who had accepted her offer and moved in with ten-year-old Robert and two-year-old Lizzie, who had been conceived when her husband came home in 1814. He had only come home to die of his wounds within weeks, unaware that his wife was carrying another child. The family had lived on poor relief until Mrs Butler had found a job working in the fields. It was piece work and the poor woman was so exhausted she was unable to earn more than a pittance. Jane heard the tale little by little as they worked together.

Jane and Mark together interviewed several local people for positions and took on a married couple to be master and housekeeper. They came from a school and would have to give notice to their present employers and would not arrive until the end of September. Mrs Godfrey remained as cook and old Silas looked after the outside. Already what they were doing was becoming known and men and women were turning up asking for employment. They would need more staff when more children were taken in, so she took their names and said she would let them know when the time came.

One was a Portuguese man who said his name was Paolo Estaban. He told her he had been a servant of a British officer in the late war and had returned to England with him. The officer had not paid him for several weeks and he needed employment. He was used to looking after horses and he had seen her pony and trap outside. She was about to say they were not hers and did not belong to the home, but then realised she might well need such a conveyance to get about as she had been doing. She would ask Mark if the funds would stretch to buying it from her father. She told the man to come back the following week.

News of what she was doing had spread and she was also approached by several charities asking for places for children. Three of the most needy had already arrived. Harry, Tom and Emma had been begging in Norwich when they had been picked up by a local parson who had heard about her venture and come to see her. The result was the children had been put on a carrier's wagon and arrived filthy, half-starved and dressed in an assortment of rags. They were also very wary of her and their new surroundings and not at all keen to be put into a bath, brought into the kitchen for the purpose. She asked Robert and Lizzie to make them feel at home and this worked better than anything the adults could do. Bathed, with their tangled hair washed and brushed, and dressed in new clothes, they were different children. She began looking for a teacher because they would need to be schooled.

The whole project was keeping Jane so busy she did not have time to dwell on the fact that the six months of mourning at Broadacres was coming to a close, that half the contents of Greystone Manor had been packed up ready for the move as soon as the wedding was over, not only Isabel's wedding to Mark, but her own to Lord Bolsover. She refused to make any preparation for that, praying as she had never prayed before that something would happen to prevent it.

Mark had said he would think of something, but he had not mentioned it again. After the fair he had seemed more cheerful, making jokes with the children and flattering Mrs Godfrey outrageously. She did not ask him how he was dealing with Isabel, but assumed all was well between them. She tried desperately to forget he had ever said he loved her. It seemed he had done so, for he stopped coming to Witherington. She told herself that was as it should be; she could not continue to rely on him for help. He had other matters nearer home to attend to. She must endure the heartache as best she could.

Mark had certainly not forgotten. He was in a state bordering on panic. There were only two weeks to go to the wedding he wanted so much to avoid and Drew had not answered his letter. Supposing he had moved on and the letter never reached him, what then? He would have to do something himself, something drastic like eloping with Jane. He knew she would never agree to that. Could he abduct her? That would be dishonourable and illegal. And whatever he did would have to be done with the consent of Isabel. He could not see her giving it. The euphoria he had felt when Jonathan arrived had long ago evaporated.

He paced the house, watched by his worried mother, went riding with Jonathan, covering mile after mile, exhausting his mounts until, one morning very early, they came to a halt at the edge of the fen. There was a landing stage there and a lopsided dwelling where the ferryman lived. The meadows on either were only dry in summer and were used for grazing cattle, which grew fat on the lush grass. There was a small rise in the ground on the right, not really big enough to call a hill, and on top of it an old hovel which had many years before been a fenman's dwelling. It was a place Mark knew well, for he had often wandered about here as a child, frequently in the company of Teddy and his two older sisters, picking wild flowers, watching for frogs and toads, having imaginary battles in which the hovel was a fort. Happy times in which the future was unknown.

'What in God's name is the matter with you, Mark?' Jonathan said, as they dismounted. 'You are certainly not acting like the happy bridegroom. I am forced to the conclusion you do not want this wedding.'

'No, I do not.'

'Are you going to tell me why?'

Mark sighed and put his head into his horse's neck. 'I suppose I must.' He paused, wondering where to begin. 'I suppose it started when I offered to help Jane with her orphan project.'

'Jane?'

'Yes, Jane.' He went on to apprise his friend of all that had transpired since Jonathan left for Scotland.

'My, you are in a coil,' his friend said when he finished.

'I have done my best to discredit Bolsover and sorely neglected Isabel in order to help Jane, in the vain hope she would tire of me and call the whole thing off, but she seems not to mind. Jane is not a rival in her mind. If you have any idea how I can come about, I shall be glad to hear it.'

'Short of kidnap and leaving your bride at the altar, you mean.'

'I can't do that.'

'No, I can see you can't. You could try throwing yourself on the mercy of Miss Isabel.'

'I thought of that, too, but it will not do. I would be seen as a bigger scoundrel than Bolsover, Isabel could sue for breach of promise and I would never dare show my face in Hadlea again.' He did not add that, worst of all, Jane would hate him for it and would certainly not agree to marry him. Bolsover would win. It was a bitter pill to swallow.

'Come, let us go back,' Jonathan said. 'There are still two weeks to go. Something might turn up.'

They mounted again and walked their exhausted horses back to the stables, approaching the house from the rear. Mark stopped to look at it, taking in the mellow Tudor bricks, the twisted chimneys, the mullioned windows, the stable block with its ornate clock which hadn't told the time in years. He loved his home, every inch of it, outside and in. He loved his mother and owed her his allegiance and he had responsibilities in the village. His honour was at stake and that counted for everything. There was no alternative but to go through with the wedding. *'Jane, forgive me.'* His lips moved on her name, but he made no sound.

With hunched shoulders and head bowed, he rode on, left his horse with Thompson, ordered the curricle to be readied and entered the house. He neither knew nor cared whether Jonathan followed him. He had to change and find Jane. She must be told and told at once while he still had the courage.

Harry and Tom had disappeared. Jane had no idea where they had gone. Neither Robert nor Emma could tell her anything, except they had been whispering together that morning. She searched every inch of the house before going outside to look in the outhouses and stables. Surely they had not run away? Where would they go? Would they try to go back to Norwich?

Silas was coming towards her; the old man was almost running in his agitation to impart some news to her. 'Miss Cavenhurst,' he said between gasps for breath. 'Someone's stole yer trap. I went to tek Bonny some oats and it were gone, Bonny with it.'

Jane could hardly believe it. Could the boys have taken it? Did they know how to harness Bonny? Could they drive it? The answer was yes, they probably could. They hated to be indoors and, ever since coming to Witherington, had spent most of their time outside, following Silas about. They would have watched him with the pony and seen how the old man harnessed him. He had even taken them on short jaunts to pick up supplies for her. 'Have you seen Tom and Harry?' she asked him.

'They were down the garden with me early on, but disappeared after a bit. Don' know where they went.'

'Do you think they could have taken the trap?'

'Why would they do that, miss?'

'For a lark, perhaps.'

'I dunno. It in't hard to drive and Bonny is a placid old thing. I s'pose they could.'

As far as she was aware no one had come to the house that morning, certainly no one who would have reason to go to the stables. It had to be the boys. But where had they gone? And without the trap how could she go after them?

'I am going to fetch help,' she told him. 'If they come back, grab them and don't let them out of your sight.'

Without even stopping to put on a bonnet, she set off on foot for Broadacres. This was an emergency and she needed Mark's help. At every step she castigated herself. Whatever had given her the idea she was fit to look after children, especially children damaged by the life they had been forced to lead? She had been a conceited fool to think urchins living as they had been doing on city streets would settle down to a placid life in the country. She ought to have taken on a teacher to give them something positive to do instead of waiting until she had a full class. If her negligence became common knowledge, the gossip alone would ensure she did not take in any more children.

She was almost running, stumbling in her haste. What would Mark say? What would anyone say? She had been too wrapped up in her own misery to look after the children properly, that's what. 'Let him be at home,' she prayed.

She struck out across the fields to cut off a corner and sped across Broadacres park towards the side of the house. Jeremy was in the yard, harnessing the curricle. Almost too out of breath to speak, she stopped in front of him.

'Miss Cavenhurst, whatever's afoot?'

'Fetch Lord Wyndham, please, it's urgent.'

The man disappeared while she stood with her hand at her aching side, slowly recovering her breath. Mark joined her almost at once. 'Tom and Harry have run away and they have taken Bonny and the trap. We've got to find them.'

He was admirably calm as he helped her into the curricle, climbed up beside her and set the horses off at a fast trot. 'I don't know what possessed them to do it,' she said. 'They have never given the slightest hint they were unhappy.'

'All boys like mischief,' he said. 'I doubt they will have gone far. We'll go back to Witherington House first. They might have returned.'

At the crossroads he was forced to slow down. There was a flurry of activity at the Fox and Hounds as a stage coach turned in to change horses, set down passengers and take others up. The inn's gig was standing by, ready to take incomers to their final destination. As soon as the road was clear he drove on and turned on to the lane to Witherington.

'I am so thankful you were at home.'

'We'll find them, stop worrying.'

'I cannot help it. It is all my fault. I should have taken more care of them. I should have taken on that teacher we spoke of. I shall never forgive myself if anything bad has happened to them. They could have overturned in a ditch and be lying there, unable to move. They could even be...' She could not say it.

'Jane, stop it, stop it at once. You not to blame and they are how old?'

'Harry is ten and Tom is nine.'

'I was driving a gig all over the estate at that age. They are old for their years, Jane. Do not think of them as children, they are very small, very wily adults, used to fending for themselves.'

She managed a smile. 'Let us hope you are right.'

They were almost at Witherington House when they saw the trap turn out of a narrow lane in front of them. The boys were in it, but it was being driven by a man. 'Don't call out,' Mark said as he pulled in a little way behind them, matching his horse's gait to that of Bonny. 'We do not want to frighten the fellow into galloping. When they leave the lane for the high road, I'll look for an opportunity to overtake and stop them. I can't do it here, the road is too narrow.'

But they didn't take the high road, the trap turned into the gates of Witherington House and continued up the drive, closely followed by the curricle. As soon as both came to a stop, Jane scrambled out and ran to the boys, intending to confront the man. He jumped down and bowed to her. '*Senhora*, I believe these belong to you.'

'Mr Estaban!' she exclaimed.

Mark was beside her. 'You know this man, Jane?'

'Yes, he came to me for a job.'

Everyone started to talk at once—Jane expressing her gratitude, the boys excitedly telling of their adventures and Mark accusing the man of abducting the children and stealing the pony and trap.

'I beg your pardon, *senhor*,' Paolo said. 'I deny that. I found the young gentlemen trying to turn the vehicle in a field gate. A wheel had become stuck against the gate post. I recognised the pony and helped them to free it, then persuaded them to allow me to bring them back.'

'Is that the truth?' Mark asked Harry.

'Yes,' he said, shame-faced. 'We only wanted to try driving.'

'Then you had all better come inside and tell us about it,' Mark said, ushering them through the kitchen door.

'Here they are,' Jane told Mrs Godfrey and Mrs Butler, who were sitting at the kitchen table discussing the situation. 'Safe and sound. I am sure they are hungry and thirsty, so could you find us all something to eat and drink and bring it to the little parlour?' The room, which had once been old Sir Jasper's bedroom, had been thoroughly cleaned and was now a comfortable sitting room, which Jane liked to think of as her office.

It did not take long to establish the truth of what Mr Estaban had said and to hear the boys' account of their adventure. They had intended to go the nearest town just to look round, they said, but realised they had taken a wrong turn when the road ended in a vast expanse of water. In trying to turn round they had become stuck. The gentleman had helped them out.

'I explained to them the worry they would cause you,' Mr Estaban said. 'You are a woman alone in a household of women with only one elderly male servant. It is not good. You need a man.'

Jane looked at Mark and felt the colour flood her cheeks.

'Mr Estaban is right, you know,' he said. 'You do need a man.'

'But you come when you can.'

'Not often enough, I am afraid. There should be someone here all the time. Mr Estaban, I believe you applied for employment here? Do you still wish it?'

'Yes.'

'Tell me about yourself.'

'This is Lord Wyndham,' Jane explained. 'He is one of the Hadlea Children's Home trustees.'

Paolo told Mark the same story as he had told Jane. 'I can manage horses and I can manage children,' he ended.

'I thought of buying the pony and trap for the Home,' Jane put in. 'I think I am going to need it.'

'Good idea. I'll make an offer to Sir Edward on behalf of the trustees.' He turned back to Estaban. 'Where are you staying?'

'At an inn along the Lynn road.'

'Go and fetch your things. You can start straight away. And you boys, take these empty plates back to the kitchen and stay there until I decide what punishment to give you. You can start by grooming Bonny and my horse.'

They obeyed and Mark and Jane were alone. He shifted to sit beside her and put his hand over hers. 'Stop shaking, Jane, my love, it is all over. They are safe and Mr Estaban will be an asset, I am sure.'

'He cannot take your place.'

'I should hope not!'

It was an attempt at humour and she dutifully smiled. 'What have you been doing lately?'

'This and that. Asking questions, groping for a miracle.'

'Miracles almost never happen. We would be unwise to put our trust in miracles.'

'Oh, I don't know…' He could not go on. She had had enough upset for one day and he could not add to it. 'Would you like me to take you home?'

'No, thank you. The trap is here and I ought to wait for Mr Estaban to come back. Besides, I spend little time at Greystone these days. Lord Bolsover is always there, gloating.'

'Don't marry him, Jane, please don't. I could not bear it.'

'Mark, it is not up to you. You will be married to Isabel. And there are some who think I will be doing well for myself, finding a wealthy husband at my age and one with a title, too. I know many of the villagers think so.'

'Surely you don't.'

'It is something I have to bear in mind.'

'I do not believe it.'

She sighed. 'There is no point in going over the same ground again, it will not alter anything. Go home, Mark, please.'

Reluctantly he left her. Like an automaton he climbed into the curricle and picked up the reins. How, when he was married to Isabel, could he endure having Jane so close and yet so far out of his reach? Was she determined to accept Bolsover? He felt nothing but fury towards Sir Edward Cavenhurst and all his clan for bringing her to this pass. He felt fury at Drew, apparently ignoring his letter, probably because Isabel no longer stood high in his affections and he did not want to meet her again. Most of all he was furious with himself for his powerlessness.

The stage had gone from the Fox and Hounds and all was quiet as he turned the corner and set off for Greystone Manor. What he intended to say to everyone when he arrived, he had no idea, but he would burst if he did not tell them how he felt. He hoped it would make Isabel think again. He hardly heard the horse until it was almost on top of him.

'Mark! Hold up! Stop, will you?'

He turned to see Jonathan galloping after him and pulled the horse to a halt. 'How did you know where I was going?'

'Jeremy told me. Come back to Broadacres, Mark. Drew is there.'

'Drew?'

'Yes. He was all for rushing off to Greystone Manor as soon as he arrived, but I persuaded him he ought to talk to you first. It is as well I spotted you or I would have gone on to Witherington and missed you.'

Mark turned the curricle in a farm gate and was soon bowling back to Broadacres with Jonathan riding beside him. As soon as he arrived he sped indoors, leaving his friend to see to the horses. Drew was in the drawing room, enjoying hot chocolate and cake with his mother.

'Drew, where have you been?' he demanded.

'Mark, that is hardly a proper greeting,' his mother

said. 'Sit down and have something to eat and drink. I am sure you went out without breakfast this morning.'

He sat down and watched his mother pour him a dish of chocolate. He took it from her, but declined food. He was too tense to eat. He turned to Drew. 'Did you receive my letter?'

'I did.'

'And?'

'I could hardly believe what I was reading. Of course I left immediately.'

'But that was weeks ago.'

'Yes, hear me out, will you?'

'Go on.'

'When I consulted the timetables, it seemed easier to go to London and then out again to Norfolk and that is what I did. On the way I fell to thinking about what you had said in your letter and it seemed to me there was something havey-cavey about Hector Bolsover, something he would rather we did not know. Where did all his wealth come from when his estate is a modest one? Could it all have been acquired from gambling? Did he cheat on a grand scale? Why would he want to live in a rural place like Hadlea when he so obviously enjoyed the attractions of the city? He does not strike me as a man who would be particularly sensitive to past family history. Was he just using it as an excuse?'

'I thought of all that,' Mark put in. 'I went to London myself and made extensive enquiries of anyone who might have known him. All I could gather was that he had never served in the army though he had spent time in the Peninsula and that on his return his mother had given him an ultimatum to marry. It appears, whatever else he is, he is an obedient son.'

'Yes. He was born when his mother had given up all hope of having a child. His father died when he was a boy and he has looked to his mother for everything. Her word is law.'

'Go on.'

'I decided to find out what I could before I came on to Hadlea and started with Toby Moore. When I spoke to him before, I felt he was hiding something.'

'I looked for him myself but he was out of town. No one knew where.'

'He was back. No doubt he had run out of generous hosts. I decided to put the fear of God into him.' He smiled. 'He is not a valiant man, Mark.'

'No. Wellington had him drummed out for cowardice. He was lucky not to be shot.'

'It was at that time he met Bolsover, who was living in Lisbon. They teamed up to gamble, not always honestly. Bolsover was married to a Portuguese girl, the daughter of a wealthy count. She inherited a vast fortune on her father's demise and he was busy spending it. When it looked as though the authorities were catching up with them over their sharp practices, he and Toby fled the country and came back to England.'

'What happened to his wife?'

'I'm coming to that. You remember I said I was buying a ship? Well, I had one, a beautiful fast clipper, called the *Swallow*, and it was readying for a voyage to India. I sailed on her as far as Lisbon and found Lady Bolsover. He had beaten her to within an inch of her life and she had fled to her aunt and uncle and, as you can imagine, they are bent on revenge. They sent their son, Juanita's cousin, to England to track him down, but they have not heard from him for some time. I think Bolsover got wind of it and wanted somewhere to hide. Sir Edward's debts and the old family story of Colin Paget gave him the idea.'

'He's married,' Mark said, unable to keep the excitement from his voice. 'He's married already! He can't marry Jane.' He jumped up and wrung his friend's hand. 'Thank you, Drew, thank you.'

'What about Isabel?' Lady Wyndham put in. She had been listening intently, but had taken no part in the conversation. 'And there's Sir Edward's debts. You have solved only half the problem.'

Mark turned to Drew. 'What about Isabel?'

'I intend to go over to Greystone Manor just as soon as I have had a rest. I only returned to England yesterday and am devilish tired. My lady, if you could furnish me with a bed for an hour or two, I would be grateful. I need to be fresh and have my wits about me if I am to persuade Sir Edward to entertain my suit. If it takes money, then money he shall have. I have already told the skipper of the *Swallow* to find Teddy when he arrives in Calcutta and bring him home. That should sweeten Sir Edward up a bit, but, if not Sir Edward, then his lady wife.'

'I must go back to Jane,' Mark said.

'Not tonight, Mark,' Lady Wyndham said. 'You can go to Greystone together tomorrow.' She rang a bell at her side to summon a servant to conduct Drew to a bedroom. As soon as he had gone, she turned to Mark. 'Whichever way you look at it, this is going to cause a huge scandal.'

'I know, Mama, but nothing like the one that might have ensued had I run off with Jane, or if Drew had run off with Isabel.'

'I sincerely hope that you have not been entertaining that idea.'

'I could never have done it, even if Jane agreed, which I am sure she would not.'

'Then, let us hope Sir Edward is amenable.'

The next morning saw the two men, both of them nervous, set off for Greystone Manor. Mark was in a long-tailed coat in blue superfine and pantaloon trousers and Drew in a frockcoat and nankeen breeches buckled below the knee. Both had spent an unconscionable time tying their cravats and adjusting the sleeves of their shirts. For such a formal visit, they chose to ride in the Wyndham coach, driven by Jeremy.

'Shall we go and frighten Bolsover out of his bed?' Mark suggested as they approached the Fox and Hounds. 'I have a mind to make him crawl.'

'Nothing would give me greater pleasure.'

Mark called out to Jeremy to pull up at the inn and the two young men entered the inn and enquired for Lord Bolsover's room. Two minutes later they flung open the door to see the startled man sitting up in bed with a breakfast tray on his lap.

'What the devil—?' he began, but was cut short when Drew removed the tray and put it on a nearby table. 'Breakfast is over, my lord,' he said. 'It is time to say goodbye. The game is over and we hold all the trumps.'

'I do not know what you are talking about.'

'We are talking about a little matter of attempted bigamy,' Mark said. 'Very much against the law, that is. I know the Prince Regent got away with it, but you are not the Prince Regent.'

'You are talking rubbish.' He was clearly agitated, but with the two men standing over him, one each side of the bed, he could not move.

'The lady's name is Juanita,' Drew said. 'Juanita Estaban as was. I have a copy of the registry entry of the marriage made in the cathedral in Lisbon. Would you care to see it, to refresh your memory?'

'No.'

'No, of course not. You know exactly what it says. You left her for dead and fled back to this country. But are you safe? Did you know your wife's kin are searching for you? Yes, of course you do, that is why you are hiding here. I fancy they would like to know where you are. I would not like to be in your shoes if they find you.'

'You are talking rubbish.' He was clearly agitated.

'Is it bigamy or murder?' Mark queried, addressing Drew. 'Whichever it is, our man is in trouble.'

'He certainly is,' Drew agreed. 'Shall we lock him up until we can take him before the Justice?'

Mark laughed. 'I am the Justice.'

'I had forgot. Is there a lock-up in the village?'

'Yes, close by the church. He will be safe enough there while we send for his wife's relations. Or we could tell his mother. I wonder why he has never told her himself, since she wants him married.'

'Perhaps she does not like Portuguese ladies,' Drew said. 'Some of these old aristocrats are like that, they want good English blood in their line.'

'No, I beg you, no.' Bolsover was shaking with terror.

'Then you have only one course open to you,' Mark said. 'Leave Hadlea, abandon your torment of Miss Cavenhurst and take yourself off where the law cannot find you. I will not answer for the consequences, if you do not. Be on the afternoon stage.'

'If I do not?'

'It is up to you, of course,' Mark said. 'But I should not like to be in your shoes when Estaban finds you.' He turned to Drew. 'Shall we leave him to think about it?'

'You are too lenient, my friend, but as I am anxious to be on my way, let us give him the same chance we would give the fox. Run or suffer the consequences.'

Mark was thoughtful as they returned to the carriage. 'There is a man called Estaban working at Witherington House,' he said. 'It cannot be a coincidence, can it?'

'Unlikely, I should say.'

'He must know where Bolsover is or why would he be here?'

'Not our problem, my friend.' The carriage drew up at the Manor. 'I will leave you to tell Sir Edward the good news. I intend to spirit Isabel away somewhere where we can be alone.'

The door was opened by Sophie, who squealed at the sight of Drew and raced back to the drawing room. 'Papa, Mama, Issie. Lord Wyndham is here and he has Mr Ashton with him.'

Isabel rushed out to the hall and stopped to stare at Drew. 'Is it really you?'

He smiled. 'If it is not, I do not know who else it might be.' He took her hand and bowed over it. 'How are you, sweetheart?'

She looked from him to Mark. 'Mark?'

'Do not mind me,' he said. 'I will go and speak to your parents and Jane.'

'Jane is not here, she has gone to Witherington. She spends all her time there these days.'

He would have liked to have turned round and gone straight to her, but courtesy demanded he speak to Sir Edward and Lady Cavenhurst first. He went into the drawing room and bowed to them both. 'Good morning, Sir Edward. My lady. I hope you will forgive me for arriving so early, but I have good tidings and could not wait to tell you.'

'Sophie said Mr Ashton was with you.'

'So he is. He is talking to Isabel. No doubt they will join us shortly.'

Sir Edward rose angrily. 'You mean you have left them alone together?'

'Yes, but please allow them a few minutes while I explain.'

Sir Edward blustered, but subsided.

'The first thing I have to tell you is that you no longer have anything to fear from Lord Bolsover. His dastardly past has been uncovered and he has been discredited. He will not be bothering you again. You are out of debt and Greystone is safe.'

'Merciful Lord,' her ladyship said.

'That is indeed good news,' Sir Edward added. 'But how has that come about?'

'Through the good offices of my friend, Mr Ashton. It is he you have to thank.'

'Oh. You had better tell us the whole.'

'I will leave that to Drew, he knows the details. I intend to go to Witherington House to speak to Jane, if you will excuse me.'

'Yes, of course,' Lady Cavenhurst said. 'She will be much relieved.'

He bowed and left, passing Drew and Isabel in the hall. They had their arms round each other and were kissing. 'All yours,' he said, laughing, and went out to the carriage with a lighter heart than he had had for a very long time.

Paolo Estaban was proving an asset. He was young and strong and made himself useful in all manner of ways.

He had already identified what needed doing before Jane could ask him. Wobbly shelves, window catches, vegetables to brought in from the garden, Bonny to be groomed, all dealt with as if by magic. And the name Witherington House would soon be painted on the side of the trap. He had talked to Jane of his home and hinted of a terrible wrong, but most of the time he kept his thoughts to himself.

'Tell me about your family,' she asked him one day when they were working together in the garden. 'Do you miss them?'

'Yes, *senhora*, I do.'

'Tell me about them.'

'I have a father and mother and two sisters and a cousin who lives with us. She is married to an Englishman.'

'The officer who brought you to England?'

'No. This man is not an officer. He calls himself a gentleman, but he is no gentleman. He treated Juanita cruelly and when she confronted him about his gambling and his mistresses he beat her so badly she nearly died. I found her and took her home to my parents. When we went looking for him we discovered he had gone back to England, taking her fortune with him. Is it any wonder we want vengeance?'

'Do you know where he is?'

'Oh, yes, I know where he is. It will not be long now.'

'What do you mean to do?'

'I have not made up my mind. I might put a sword through his evil heart, or I might shoot him, but I have to have the money first.'

'You must not take the law into your own hands, Mr

Estaban,' she said, thoroughly alarmed. 'Tell the authorities. Have him tried.'

'And do you think they will believe me? They will say the man has a right to beat his wife and abscond with her money and jewels. Perhaps he will have an accident. Or perhaps I will challenge him to a duel.'

'Oh, no,' she exclaimed. 'Duels are illegal in this country and you could be killed. Your life is much too valuable to be thrown away like that. Tell Lord Wyndham your story. I am sure he will see justice done.'

He smiled slowly. 'No, *senhora*, I must do what I must do. Now I go and put these brambles on the bonfire.'

She watched him as he piled up the bonfire, took a tinder box from his coat pocket and set light to the heap. Some of it had been lying there for weeks and was dry and brittle. There was soon a good blaze going. She turned to go back to the house, wondering what to do for the best. She ought to try to stop him from doing whatever it was he had in mind. One or other of them would be wounded, if not killed, and though she had no sympathy for the Englishman, whoever he was, she could not stand by and let him be killed. Was this emergency enough to send for Mark? But Paolo had so far done nothing wrong and might even deny his conversation with her. She would just have to watch him and try to persuade him not to do anything rash.

She looked up to see Mrs Butler coming towards her. 'You have a visitor, Miss Cavenhurst. I left him in your parlour pacing about like a caged animal.'

'Did he say his name?'

'No. But I've seen him about Hadlea village a time or two.'

It could not be Mark, Mrs Butler knew Mark, nor her

father, for he would not have withheld his name. There was Mark's friend, Jonathan Smythe, but what would he want with her? Had something happened to Mark? She hurried indoors.

Chapter Thirteen

The last person she expected to see was Lord Bolsover, but that was who confronted her when she made her way to the parlour. 'What are you doing here?' she demanded.

'That is hardly a civil greeting.' He looked a little dishevelled, as if he had dressed in a hurry. His hair was not as carefully combed as it usually was and his cravat was askew.

'I am very busy,' she said. 'Please state your business and be on your way.'

'My business is with you.'

'You have no business with me until after my sister's wedding, and not then if I could think of a way out of it without ruining my family.'

'I am not disposed to wait that long. I must marry and the sooner the better if I am to please my mother. Pleasing my mother is paramount, you see. I do not think we can have the nuptials at Hadlea church, the reverend there is bound to want to call banns or have the bishop's blessing and we don't want all that nonsense delaying us, do we? A simple statement and a consummation will suffice.'

'If you think I will behave in that disgraceful manner, you may think again, my lord. You must wait until my sister is married. I made an undertaking to give you an answer then. Now, please go.'

'The trouble is,' he said, making no move to do as she asked, 'I do not think Lord Wyndham will marry your sister after all, which is a pity. It means I have had to change my plans.'

'What do you mean?'

'I think Miss Isabel has other ideas. I fear she is about to elope with Mr Ashton.'

'I do not believe you.'

He shrugged. 'That is up to you. There will be a terrible scandal, of course. As for Lord Wyndham…' He gave a cracked laugh. 'He will lose both bride and mistress.'

'Do not be ridiculous. You are drunk.' She was terrified, but trying not to show it. If she shouted for help, would someone come to her aid? She opened her mouth to scream, but he clapped his hand over her face, pushing her head hard against the wall.

'I told my mother I had found a suitable bride and she naturally wishes to meet you.' He grabbed her arm. 'My carriage is waiting.'

'Let me go.' Her head was spinning from the impact with the wall. 'I am not going anywhere with you.'

'Unfortunately, my dear, you have no choice.' He began dragging her towards the outer door. She opened her mouth to scream, but he had anticipated that and put one hand over her mouth and with the other thrust her arm up behind her back. She struggled, but he simply gave another tug on her arm. It was excruciatingly painful and forced her to move ahead of him. He propelled her out on to the garden path and round the side of the house towards his carriage. His driver was standing by it and opened the door. She felt herself being lifted bodily and dumped on the seat. Free of his hand over her mouth, she screamed and went on screaming. He lifted his hand to strike her. Then she saw another hand come up behind him, a hand brandishing a firebrand.

Bolsover abandoned her to deal with this new threat. The only weapon Paolo had was the burning stick and he was faced with two adversaries. He held them off with it, waving it from one to the other and shouting in Portuguese, poking it at them. They were all too close to the carriage for her to leave it. Then the hammer cloth caught fire. In the blinking of an eye, flames licked along the body work and caught the curtains.

The horses panicked and began rearing up, threatening to overtopple the carriage. Pandemonium ensued as other people arrived and tried to beat out the flames. Jane could not see them for the smoke, but she felt sure it was Mark's voice she heard giving instructions. Then someone reached in and pulled her out. She felt herself being carried away from the heat and gently put on the grass some distance away.

She coughed. 'Mark, is it you?'

He sat down beside her. 'Yes, my love. You are safe now,'

'Lord Bolsover?'

'Overcome by smoke. He will recover to stand trial.'

'And Paolo?'

'His hands are burned and his hair singed, but Mrs Butler is looking after him. Are you hurt?'

'No, only a little. I am thirsty.'

'A drink you shall have.'

He picked her up and carried her into the house. 'Bring Miss Cavenhurst a tisane and a drink,' he instructed Mrs Godfrey as he passed through the kitchen to the parlour.

He put his burden on the sofa and sat down beside her, putting his arm about her shoulders. 'I only just arrived in time. Estaban could not have held them off much longer and the coach was well alight.'

'He is a brave man. I think he knew Lord Bolsover. He had a score to settle and talked of revenge, but it wasn't revenge after all, he did it to save me.'

'He did indeed.'

Mrs Godfrey arrived with a cordial and a dose of tisane. He thanked her and helped Jane to drink.

'It was dreadful, Mark. Lord Bolsover said he was going to take me to meet his mother and we would not trouble with a church wedding.'

'It is all over, my love. Everything. He cannot harm you now.'

'He has a wife. Paolo told me about his cousin's English husband, but I didn't know he was talking about Lord Bolsover.'

'His lordship was under the impression he had killed her. He fled to England to escape Portuguese justice, but she recovered.'

'He said Issie was going to elope with Mr Ashton.'

He laughed. 'No, I do not think they will do that. Unless I miss my guess they will obtain the full consent of Sir Edward.' He paused to kiss the tip of her nose. 'We are free to marry, Jane, my darling. That is, if you will have me.'

'Of course I will, but the scandal…'

'There are to be no buts, Jane.'

'Oh, Mark.' Her head lolled on his shoulder as the tisane took effect. He smiled and kissed the top of her head and held her close. They would have plenty of time to talk when she woke. For the moment he was happy to sit with her sleeping body in his arms and contemplate a rosy future at home with the woman he loved.

* * *

Everything had been explained and mulled over at Greystone Manor as everyone gave their own version of events. Lord Bolsover, his face badly scarred by the fire, had retreated to live with his mother, hidden from society, and Paolo Estaban had gone back to Portugal satisfied with his vengeance. Even the scandal was reduced to a simple murmur. It had been made known that Lord Wyndham and Miss Isabel Cavenhurst had agreed to end their engagement by mutual consent and that was followed a few weeks later by an announcement of the betrothal of Miss Isabel Cavenhurst and Mr Andrew Ashton and that of Baron Wyndham of Broadacres to Miss Jane Cavenhurst, eldest daughter of Sir Edward and Lady Cavenhurst of Greystone Manor.

The announcement had been made at a musical recital given at Broadacres by Lady Wyndham. All her aristocratic friends had been invited and it was made clear to them that the evening was in aid of the Hadlea Children's Home and that they were expected to donate generously. It was a glittering affair, with everyone dressed in their finery to listen to the best musicians and soloists in the country. They had not been forewarned of the announcement and it was greeted with delighted surprise and congratulations all round. Several hundred pounds were raised for the orphans, who now numbered fifteen. The master and housekeeper had arrived at Witherington House, and so had a teacher, an enthusiastic young graduate Mark had found.

The villagers of Hadlea greeted the news of the double engagement with much relief and no surprise. As far as they were concerned, it was something they could all have predicted weeks before.

* * *

Two weddings took place on the same day at St Peter's church to which they were all invited. Isabel wore the wedding gown Jane had made for her and Jane made another for herself in a rich cream satin. The wedding breakfast, held at Greystone, was the splendid affair Isabel had hoped it would be. The house had been refurbished, not because Drew had paid for it, though he was willing to do so, but because Teddy had come back from India a rich man. On the voyage out to India he had had time to think about his life and where it would lead if he did not mend his ways and, remembering what Drew had said about making his fortune in trade, had turned his back on the card table and tried his hand at commerce. His arrival on the eve of the weddings had made the happy day even happier.

'Well, Jane, my love,' Mark said later that night. 'We had our miracle, didn't we?'

'Only because you and Drew made it happen.' She was sitting up in the four-poster bed at Broadacres, watching him undress. Dispensing with maid and valet, they had begun undressing each other, little by little, until she was naked and he was wearing only his trousers. It was then she became shy and he stood up to divest himself of the last stitch of his clothing. Then he tumbled on to the bed beside her.

'Are you happy with our miracle?' he asked.

'I could not be happier.'

'Oh, but I think you can and I shall show you how, my lovely wife.'

She laughed a little nervously as he reached out for her, but then forgot to be nervous as he pulled her to him and began kissing her and stroking her gently and tenderly until she was roused to ecstasies of delight, responding so naturally that he was enchanted. It was a long time before they spoke again and by then they were sated and drowsy and the words 'I love you', said by him and repeated by her, were said in a sleepy murmur.

* * * * *

THE HEMINGFORD
SCANDAL

To Sue Ballard

You light up a room with your smile and brighten my day with your cheerful optimism. Thank you for being the inspiration for my Faith and for me.

Chapter One

1811

Jane Hemingford was writing letters at her escritoire in the small parlour on the first floor of her London home, when her great aunt came bustling into the room in a fever of excitement. 'Jane, Mr Allworthy is here.'

'Mr Allworthy? You mean Mr Donald Allworthy?'

'To be sure. Who else should I mean?' Harriet Lane was a dumpy woman and the speed at which she had climbed the stairs had made her breathless. Her black lace cap had fallen over one ear and she straightened it as she spoke.

'But it is barely ten o'clock, too early for morning calls. I am not dressed to receive him.'

'Then you had better change at once. He has gone into the library to speak to your papa and then I have no doubt you will be sent for.'

'Speak to Papa? You surely do not mean he has come to offer for me?'

'That is precisely what I do mean. Now make haste and

pretty yourself up. I doubt he will be talking to your papa
for long, there is nothing to dispute. He is very eligible.'

Jane was thunderstruck. Aunt Lane, who had been widowed many years before and had ever since lived in se-
clusion in Bath, had suddenly taken it into her head to
pay a visit to her great-niece to 'take her in hand'. 'It is
time you got over that old nonsense and began to think
of finding a husband,' she had said.

'That old nonsense' was a previous engagement to her
second cousin, Harry Hemingford, which had ended in the
most dreadful scandal that she did not even want to think
about, much less discuss. It had been two and a half years
before and she had put it behind her, but that did not mean
she was ready to plunge into a new engagement, just because her aunt thought she should.

Since her aunt had arrived at the beginning of the Season, they had been out and about, going to routs, balls,
picnics and tea parties, it was at one of the latter that she
had met Donald Allworthy. She had seen him several
times since in company with other young people and
found him attractive and attentive, but never so attentive
as to suggest to her that he was seriously considering proposing marriage. 'But, Aunt, I hardly know him. I certainly had no idea he was thinking of offering.'

'Why should you? He is a perfect gentleman, he would
not have spoken to you without your father's permission.'

Not like Harry, in other words. Donald Allworthy was,
Jane conceded, quite a catch, so why had he chosen her?
She was not particularly beautiful, she decided, her nose
was a mite too large and her brows were too fair. She had
brown hair which in certain lights was almost auburn and
a pink complexion which became even pinker when she
was angry or embarrassed. She was not exactly angry

now, but certainly disconcerted. 'I do not have to receive him, do I?'

'Oh, Jane, do not be such a goose. You are not a simpering schoolgirl, you are twenty years of age and should have been married by now...'

So I would have, she told herself, if I had married Harry. Aloud, she said, 'I know, but that does not mean I should jump into the arms of the first man who offers.'

'He is not the first man to offer, is he?'

'Oh, Aunt, how could you speak of that, when I so much want to forget it?'

'I am sorry, dearest, but I must say what is in my mind. You did not choose very sensibly before, did you? Now you are a little older and wiser and, with me here to guide you, you are doing wonderfully well.'

Jane longed to tell her aunt she did not need that kind of guidance, but she was a tender-hearted, obedient girl and could not bear to hurt anyone's feelings. 'I am very sensible of your concern for me, Aunt Lane, but I had no idea Mr Allworthy wished to marry me. Are you sure that's what he has come to see Papa about?'

'Oh, I am sure. He spoke to me at Lady Pontefract's ball, asked me if I thought Mr Hemingford would agree to see him and naturally I said I was sure he would. But I gave no such assurance on your seeing him. That is your decision, of course.' She sounded hurt, as if Jane's refusal would be a personal slight on the efforts she had made to bring it all about.

Jane sighed. 'Then I suppose I must speak to him.'

'Good girl. Now go and change into something bright and cheerful.'

The house in Duke Street was in the middle of a tall narrow terrace. The ground floor was little more than a hall, dominated by a staircase and a small reception room with the library behind it, where her father spent much of the day writing a philosophical tome which he hoped would make his reputation as a man of letters. The kitchens were in the basement, the parlour, drawing room and dining room were on the first floor, and above those the bedrooms. Higher still were the servants' sleeping quarters. As the household consisted only of Jane and her father, there were few servants: a cook-housekeeper, Hannah, the housemaid, and Bromwell, who acted as butler and footman. They did not keep a carriage and so did not need outdoor servants. When Aunt Lane visited, her coach and horses were kept in a nearby mews and her coachman, Hoskins, boarded out.

Jane had never had a personal maid and relied on Hannah to help her with fastenings and pinning up her hair. 'At your age you should not be without a maid,' her aunt had said when she had been in residence a few days. 'I shall speak to your father about it.'

Jane had begged her not to. 'I do not need someone to wait on me,' she had said. 'My needs are simple and she would not have enough to do and we cannot afford to pay servants for doing nothing. Hannah does me very well.'

But she couldn't stop her aunt from sending Lucy, her own maid, to her when she considered the occasion important enough to warrant it. And it seemed today was important, because the young woman was already in her room when she went to change. She chose a muslin gown in palest green. Its skirt was gathered into a high waist and it had little puff sleeves over tight undersleeves. The neckline was filled with ruched lace edged with ribbon. 'I don't know that there's time to do much with your hair, Miss Jane,' Lucy said. 'I do wish the gentleman had given notice he was calling.'

'So do I, Lucy. Just brush it out and tie it back with a

green ribbon. He cannot expect a full coiffure at this early hour.' Would that put him off? That thought was followed by another. Did she want to put him off? It was a question she did not know how to answer. He was, as her aunt had pointed out, eligible, and though she was not quite at her last prayers, ought she to be particular? After all, her previous sortie into the matrimonial stakes had been disastrous. Left to herself, she had chosen very badly.

She was slipping on light kid shoes when her aunt knocked and entered. 'Are you ready, dear?' She stopped to appraise her. 'Very nice, a little colourless, but perhaps it is best to be modest, until you know your husband's tastes.'

'Husband, Aunt?' Jane queried. 'You are a little beforehand, don't you think? He has not asked me yet and I have not accepted.'

'No, but he will and I am sure you are not such a ninny as to turn him down flat.'

'I shall listen to him, that is all I can promise,' she said, following her aunt down to the beautifully proportioned drawing room which had been furnished in excellent taste by Jane herself when she and her father first moved to London. Her father and Donald Allworthy were standing by the hearth.

Donald was tall and lean. His impeccable coat in dark blue superfine and his biscuit-coloured pantaloons, tucked into brilliantly polished Hessians, denoted a man of some substance, though certainly not a dandy. He wore a diamond pin in his meticulously tied cravat, a fob and a quizzing glass across his figured brocade waistcoat. He smiled as he bowed to her. 'Miss Hemingford, your servant.'

'Mr Allworthy.' She dipped a curtsy, but she could feel her face growing hot and quickly turned to her father. He was a good head shorter than their visitor and was clearly not particular about his dress. It had been different when her mother was alive, but now he put on whatever came first to hand when he rose in the morning. On this occasion, he was wearing dark blue trousers and a brown coat with darker velvet revers. His white cravat was unstarched and tied anyhow; his grey hair, thin and wispy, stood out all over his head as if he had been running his hands through it. 'Papa, you sent for me?

'Indeed I did.' He was beaming at her. She felt a shiver of apprehension as she realised he was pleased with himself. At last he had managed to find someone to take his foolish daughter off his hands. She knew she had been a great trial to him, becoming engaged to Harry and then breaking it off. Not that it was the breaking off that had caused the scandal; that had come before and left her no choice in the matter. Papa had not blamed her; he had simply accepted the fact and left her to make what she could of her life. But he must have been worried. Poor dear, it was unfair of her to make difficulties for him.

'Mr Allworthy wishes to speak to you,' he said. 'I know you will listen carefully to what he has to say.'

'Of course, Papa.' She dare not look at the young man, but she could not but be aware of him; his presence seemed to fill the room. There was an air of expectancy, as if everyone was holding their breath, waiting for a pause in time before it resumed ticking away in a different rhythm.

'Then we will leave you.' He beckoned to Aunt Lane and they left the room.

The clock ticked louder than ever. Or was it her heart pumping in her throat? 'Mr Allworthy,' she said, sitting on the sofa and placing her hands in her lap. 'Won't you be seated?'

He came and sat beside her, perching himself on the edge of the seat, half-facing her, and doubling his long legs under him, so that she was afraid he might fall to the ground. 'Miss Hemingford, I trust you are well?'

'Very well, Mr Allworthy. And you?'

'I am in the best of health, thank you, but as to my mental state, that is not so sanguine. I have never done this before, you see.'

'Done what, Mr Allworthy?'

'Proposed marriage.' He paused, smiling. 'I have reached thirty years of age and never found a lady that I felt I wanted to marry, until now, that is…'

'Are your standards so exacting?' She was teasing him, which she knew was unkind and she had never knowingly been unkind. 'I am sorry, sir, I interrupted you.'

'Yes, you did, but I am not to be put off, you know.' He seized one of her hands in both his own. 'I have formed a deep attachment to you, very deep. In short, I admire you greatly and would be honoured and privileged if you would consent to be my wife.'

'Mr Allworthy!' She tried to retrieve her hand, but he held it too firmly. Rather than tussle with him, she let it lie.

'Do not tell me you did not expect it.'

'I did not, not before today. I do not know what to say.'

'Say yes and you will make me the happiest man in the world.'

'But we hardly know each other.'

'Oh, I think we do. I know you well enough to be sure that my future happiness lies in your hands. I believe I recognised that the first moment I saw you at Mrs Bradford's a month ago. You are so exactly my vision of a perfect wife, well bred, beautiful, intelligent and honest and yet you are no milksop. As for me, I am in possession of a small estate in north Norfolk. The house is not especially large, not what you might call a mansion, but it is well proportioned, and there is a small park and a farm. I am not, I confess, as rich as Golden Ball, but I am certainly not without funds and I have expectations—' He broke off as if he had said too much, and then continued. 'You would never want for comfort. I am persuaded we could be very happy together.'

It was a pretty speech and the fact that he could not command the wealth of Mr Edward Ball mattered not one jot, but she was sure he did not know as much about her as he claimed, for who would want to marry someone who had broken off a previous engagement? 'Oh, dear, this is difficult. Mr Allworthy, there are things you should know about me. I am not in my first Season. I am twenty years old and I must confess that I have been engaged before…'

'I know,' he said. 'Your papa told me of it, but he assures me it is all over and done with.'

'Indeed, it is.'

'Then it is not an impediment, not if you love me.'

'I cannot say that I do.'

'But you have no great aversion?'

'Oh, no, sir, no aversion at all.'

'Then I shall do everything in my power to make you love me.'

'Can one *make* someone do something like that? I mean, is it not something we cannot help, that is beyond our power to command or deny?'

'Perhaps, but perhaps the feeling is already there, hidden inside ourselves and simply needs bringing to the fore and acknowledging. Do you understand me?'

'Oh, perfectly, Mr Allworthy.'

'Then what do you say?'

'Sir, I cannot give you an answer today. Marriage is an

important step for anyone to take and I need to think about it.' She smiled. 'I was too young before, carried along on someone else's enthusiasm. I did not know what I was doing. I do not want to make the same mistake again and it has made me cautious.'

'I understand, indeed I do. I shall not press you for the present.' He lifted her hand to his lips and kissed the back of it. His lips were cold and dry on her skin. 'But allow me to hope. In your kindness, allow me that.'

She looked into his face. It was a handsome face, squarish, with a strong jaw and high cheekbones. His eyes were dark, unusual for someone with fair hair, and his brows were straight and thick. As far as she could tell, his expression was one of deep sincerity. 'I cannot forbid you to hope,' she said, rising to her feet to bring the interview to an end.

'Then that is what I shall do.' He rose too, many inches taller than she was. 'I should like to invite you and your papa to Coprise Manor for a short stay. I am sure when you see it, you will love it. And if you want to change anything, you have only to ask.'

'Mr Allworthy, you go too fast. I am quite breathless.'

He looked down at her; she was blushing prettily. 'I beg your pardon, Miss Hemingford, I am too impatient, I can see that. But perhaps I may have the pleasure of taking you and your aunt out in my carriage this afternoon? The weather is set fair and it will give us an opportunity to learn more about each other.'

'I am afraid I must plead a previous engagement,' she said, smiling to mitigate his disappointment. 'Tomorrow, perhaps?' She moved to the hearth and tugged at the bell-pull.

'Indeed, yes, I shall look forward to it. Will two o'clock suit?'

'I shall expect you at two,' she confirmed as Bromwell arrived to show him out. He bowed and was gone.

She sank back onto the sofa and let out her breath in a long sigh. It had all been very formal, very correct. There was nothing about his behaviour with which she could quarrel, nothing at all. And yet… She did not want to think about Harry, but this proposal had brought it all back. Harry, boisterous, jolly, teasing Harry, whom she had known almost all her life, had kissed her, a long bruising kiss that left her shaken and exhilarated, and then had said, 'You're the one for me, Jane, no use denying it. We were meant for each other, so shall we announce our engagement?' She had been so sure of herself and of him…

Her melancholy thoughts were interrupted by the return of Aunt Lane, rushing into the room, her small dark eyes alight. 'Well?' she demanded. 'Are we to felicitate you?'

'Not yet, Aunt. You did not expect me to agree on the first time of asking, did you?'

'Oh, you naughty puss, so he is to be kept dangling, is he?'

'He may dangle if he wishes, but I rather think he has more spine than that. Besides, I have told him he may hope.'

'Oh, that is as good as a yes! Now, we must make plans, organise a party—'

'Hold your horses, Aunt, I cannot see that letting Mr Allworthy hope is the same as saying yes, truly I cannot and there will be no announcement until I do. And you cannot go organising parties before the announcement, can you?' She smiled and bent to kiss her aunt's cheek. 'I'm sorry to spoil your fun.'

Aunt Lane wagged a black-mittened finger at her. 'You are a dreadful tease, Jane. It is to be hoped you will not roast him too, for I do not think he will stand for it.'

'He understands that I must have time to consider his proposal and is prepared to wait for an answer. Are you free tomorrow afternoon? He has asked us to take a carriage ride with him.'

'Even if I were not free I would make myself so.' She paused. 'Oh, Jane, I am so pleased for you. I was beginning to despair.'

'But why should you despair, Aunt?'

'I should have come before. I should have helped you to get over that disgraceful business sooner, but I thought no, let her come to it in her own time. I should have known you had no one to take you out and about and make sure you were seen. James always has his head in his books and hardly knows what day it is; I should not have left it to him.'

'Oh, do not blame Papa, Aunt, I told him I wanted to live quietly. I did not want to be seen out, it was too mortifying, and I have been able to help him with the copying. Everything he writes has to be copied, you know.'

'Yes, I do know, and I do not blame him, I blame myself. It was the Countess who pointed it out to me. ''That gel needs taking out of herself, or she will end up an old maid,'' she said. ''It is your duty to do something about it.'' And she was right.'

The Countess of Carringdale was one of the many aristocratic connections of whom her great-aunt boasted. She never tired of speaking of them. 'All on the distaff side,' she told anyone who would listen. 'My mother was the Countess's cousin, which makes her your cousin too, Jane, seeing as your mother was my niece, though I cannot work out how many times removed.'

Jane did not care a jot for aristocratic connections and she certainly did not like them interfering in her life. Her great-aunt she could tolerate because she was kind and affectionate and had comforted her when her mother died. Fourteen years old, she had been, bereft and bewildered, and Aunt Lane had wrapped her plump arms about her and let her cry on her shoulder. And when she had broken off her engagement to Harry, Aunt Lane had been on the doorstep as soon as the news broke, and told her cheerfully that she had done the right thing, no one could possibly expect her to stay engaged to that mountebank after what he had done.

Persuaded that Jane was not going into a decline, she had gone home and they had kept in touch by correspondence. Until this year, when the Countess had told her Jane was mouldering away in obscurity, though how her ladyship knew that neither Harriet nor Jane knew.

'Aunt Lane, you must not blame yourself; besides, two years is not so long to recover...'

'But you have recovered?' her aunt asked, looking closely into her face.

'Oh, yes, Aunt, I am quite myself. My hesitation has nothing to do with the past, that is dead and buried and I do not want to speak of it again. I simply want to be sure, to take time making up my mind. Mr Allworthy is fully in agreement with that.'

She was not sure that the gentleman was as complacent as he pretended, but she could not rush headlong into an engagement that might not be good for either of them. How could she be sure that old scandal would not touch him? How could he be so sure she would make him happy? She was no catch, she had no fortune and hardly any dowry because Papa had never earned a great deal with his writing and there was very little left of the money her mama had brought to their marriage. It came to her, then, that perhaps Papa might be low in the stirrups and needed to see her provided for. If that were the case, had she any right to prevaricate? If she said yes, she would make everyone happy.

'Then I suggest you go and acquaint your papa with your decision. He has gone back to the library.' Her aunt sighed heavily. 'I wonder he does not take his bed in there.'

Her father spent nearly all his waking hours in the library and only came out to eat and sleep and consult books and manuscripts in other libraries. Since her mother had died, his writing was all he cared for. Jane suspected that only while immersed in work could he forget the wife he had lost. As a fourteen-year-old and now as a fully grown woman, she had never been able to fill the gap in his life left by his wife. Oh, he was not unkind to her, far from it; he loved her in his way.

He had given her an education to rival that of many a young gentleman and an independent mind which those same young gentlemen might find an encumbrance rather than a virtue, but it was his great work, a huge treatise comparing the different religions of the world, which came first. She dreaded to think what would happen to him when it was finished. But she did not think it ever would be; the writing of it had become an end in itself. He did not want to finish it and therefore was constantly correcting and rewriting it, adding new information as he discovered it until it was now large enough to fill several volumes.

When she knocked and entered he was sitting at his desk, which was so covered with papers and open books the top of it was quite obliterated. He looked up at her over the steel rim of his spectacles. He looked tired. 'Well, child? Has he gone?'

'Yes, Papa.'

'And?'

'I am not sure how I feel about him, Papa. I told him I would think about it.'

'You are not still wearing the willow for that rakeshame cousin, are you?'

'No, Papa, of course not.'

'What have you got to think about then? Mr Allworthy comes of good stock and he is a scholar like myself and not a poseur, nor, for all he likes to live in the country, is he a mushroom. There is not a breath of scandal attached to him and he seems not to mind that you have no dowry to speak of.'

'That is something I cannot understand, Papa. Why offer for me when I have nothing to bring to the marriage? He does not seem the kind of man to fall headlong in love; he is too controlled. So what is behind it?'

'You are too modest, Jane. And what has falling in love done for you, except make you unhappy? Better make a good match and let the affection come later as you grow towards each other. That is what happened with me and your dear mama.'

'I know, Papa,' she said, smiling at him. 'I will give Mr Allworthy an answer soon.'

'See that you do, it is not fair to keep him dangling. Now, if you have no pressing engagement for the rest of this morning, I need some new pages copying.' He held out a handful of sheets covered with his untidy scrawl, much of which had been crossed out and altered between the lines and up and down the margins. He had once had a secretary, but the poor man had been unable to make head or tail of the way Mr Hemingford worked and did not stay long. Only Jane could understand it because she had taken the trouble to do so.

'Of course, Papa.' She took the sheets to a table on the

other side of the room and sat down to work, just as if she had not, only a few minutes before, received a proposal that could alter her whole life. Aunt Lane was busy making extravagant plans and her father had dismissed it as of little consequence. Both were wide of the mark. She needed to talk to Anne.

Anne was Harry's twin, but that made no difference; she was Jane's oldest and dearest friend. Anne had been overjoyed when Harry and Jane announced their engagement and bitterly disappointed when Jane called it off. Several times she had tried to plead on Harry's behalf. He had been foolish, she said, and it had cost him his reputation and his commission and caused an irreparable rift between him and their grandfather, the Earl of Bostock, whose heir he was, but it was unfair that it should also cost him Jane's love, especially when he had only been thinking of their future together. Jane's reaction was to quarrel with her friend so violently they had not spoken to each other for months.

They had been rigidly polite when they met in company and that had been unbearable until one day, finding themselves in the same room and no one else present to carry on a conversation, they had felt obliged to speak to each other. And talking eased the tension. Having few other friends and certainly none that was close, Jane had missed Anne, and it was not long before they had buried the hatchet, but only on Anne's promise never again to mention Harry and what had happened.

When she told Mr Allworthy that she had an engagement that afternoon, nothing had been arranged, but she must have known, in the back of her mind, that she would go to see Anne. News as stupendous as this needed sharing.

* * *

Although she could have borrowed her aunt's carriage the Earl of Bostock's London mansion was just off Cavendish Square, near enough for her to reach it on foot. The Earl was extremely old and rarely left Sutton Park, his country home in Lincolnshire, but Anne, who had made her home with him ever since both parents had been killed in a coaching accident when she and Harry were very young, had come up for the Season, as she did every year. The amusements on offer afforded her a little light relief from being at her grandfather's beck and call, gave her the opportunity to renew her wardrobe and spend some time with Jane. His lordship did not deem it necessary to surround her with retainers and so, apart from the usual household servants, she lived with her maid-companion, a middle-aged sycophant called Amelia Parker.

Jane had no qualms about coming across Harry while visiting her friend because he had left the country almost immediately after the scandal. If Anne knew where he was, she had never told Jane, perhaps because Jane had assured her she did not want to know and would not even speak of him.

She was admitted by a footman and conducted to the drawing room where Anne was dispensing tea to a bevy of matrons who seemed to think that just because she had no mother, it was their duty to call on her and give her the benefit of their advice, notwithstanding she was twenty-four years old and perfectly able to conduct her own affairs. 'Such a dutiful gel,' they murmured among themselves. 'She is devoted to that old man and stayed in the country to look after him when that scapegrace shamed him and ruined her own chances doing it. Now she is too old. We must go and bear her company.' Anne knew perfectly well what they said and often laughed about it to Jane, but there was a little hollowness in the laughter.

She came forward when Jane was announced and held out both her hands. 'Jane, my dear, how lovely to see you.' She reached forward to kiss her cheek and added in a whisper, 'Give me a few minutes to get rid of these antidotes and I shall be free to talk.' She drew Jane forward. 'Do you know everyone? Lady Grant, Lady Cowper, Mrs Archibald and her daughter, Fanny?'

'Indeed, yes.' Jane bent her knee to each of them and asked them how they did, but though they were polite and asked after her father, they had no real interest in her doings and the conversation ground to a halt. Not long after that, they gathered up parasols, gloves and reticules and departed.

'Now,' Anne said, as soon as the door had closed on them. 'I shall order more tea and we may sit down for a comfortable coze.' She turned to ring the bell for the maid, then took Jane's hand and drew her to sit beside her on the sofa. 'You look a trifle agitated, my dear, has something happened to upset you?'

'Not upset exactly. I have received an offer of marriage.'

'Oh.' There was a little silence after that, as if Anne was cogitating how to answer her. 'Who is the lucky man?'

'Mr Donald Allworthy.'

'Goodness, not that sti—' She stopped suddenly.

Jane laughed. 'That stiff-rump, is that what you were going to say?'

'Well, he is a little pompous.'

'Only if you count good manners and courtesy as pomposity. And I am sure he is very sincere when he says he has a high regard for me.'

'Oh, Jane, you are never thinking of accepting him?'

'I have said I will consider it.'

'But, my dear, you can't, you simply cannot.'

'Why not? I should like very much to be married.'

'But not to Donald Allworthy.'

'No one else has offered.'

'You know that is not true. You would have been married by now, if—'

'Please, Anne, do not speak of the past. It is dead and buried, along with my dreams. I must be practical. Papa is becoming tired and increasingly frail and I know I must be a great burden to him. Besides, Aunt Lane has taken so much trouble.'

'You surely would not agree to marry someone you do not love simply not to disappoint your aunt. That is the very worst reason I can think of for marrying anyone.'

'Of course it is not that, or not only that. I do not want to be an old maid, Anne.'

'You are four years younger than me, there is still time for you.'

'Oh, I am sorry, I did not mean—' Jane broke off in confusion.

Anne laughed. 'No, I know you did not, but it is true, isn't it? I am past my last prayers and resigned to it—more than resigned, I am happy. I do not think I would make anyone a good wife, I am too independent and outspoken and I value my freedom.'

'You think I should be like you?' They had had this conversation before, but then she had not just had a proposal and that made the argument so much more cogent.

'Not at all. I have never said that. You were born to be a wife and mother. I am only sorry—'

'Do not be,' Jane put in sharply. 'We are not talking of that, but what I should do about Donald Allworthy.'

'What do you want to do about him?'

'I do not know. I have asked him for time to think about it, but I cannot keep him waiting, can I? It would not be fair.'

If Anne was tempted to say Jane had not been fair to her brother, she resisted it. 'I cannot help you make up your mind, Jane. It is your decision. I wish you happy, whatever you decide.'

'Then I shall tell him to expect an answer at the end of the Season.'

'You might have a better offer by then.'

Jane laughed. 'And pigs might fly.'

'Jane, it is not the end, you know. It is not a case of Mr Allworthy or nobody.'

'Anne, if you are nursing the hope that you can bring Harry and me back together, you are wasting your time.'

The maid brought in the tea tray and Anne busied herself with the teapot and cups before speaking again. 'They have forgiven the Duke of York, you know. He has been restored as Commander-in-Chief of the Army. It was in the newspaper today.'

'What does that signify? The Prince of Wales was always close to him, closer than to any others of his family, so it is only natural that when he was made Regent, he would reinstate his brother. They are as bad as one another with their infidelities and their mistresses.'

'Harry wasn't like that, you know he wasn't.'

As she sipped the tea Anne had given her, the memories were crowding back, memories she had been pushing away from her for more than two years, memories resurrected by the day's events. The newly commissioned Lieutenant Harry Hemingford in the magnificent blue-and-gold uniform of the 10th Hussars was proud as a peacock, grateful to his grandfather for buying him the commission, sure that he would make his mark on history.

'Of course a lieutenant's pay is little enough,' he had told her. 'But I shall soon make my way. In wartime, promotion comes fast. We shall not have so long to wait and then, my darling Jane, you will be my wife.' And he had whirled her round and round until she was dizzy and begged him to stop.

But she had been so proud of him. He swore he had put his wild youth behind him and had eschewed the excesses of drinking and gambling that had led him into trouble and was the reason his grandfather had packed him off into the army. 'I have turned over a new leaf, Jane.' For a time it seemed he had; he worked hard and waited for the call to arms. The 10th Hussars, the Prince of Wales's Own Regiment, had been in the Peninsula at the time and he was expecting hourly to be sent out to join them.

'There will be no time to arrange a wedding before I go,' he had told her. 'And to tell the truth, I cannot afford it. You don't mind waiting, do you? When I come back I shall be a colonel.' He had laughed his boyish laugh and made her smile. 'Or even a general. Then you shall be able to lord it over all the other officers' wives.'

She had agreed it would be better to delay. Her father still needed her to help him with his work and she could start collecting her trousseau and thinking of her future home. But Harry's plans had been thwarted when, in 1809, the regiment was brought back to England after a series of setbacks that resulted in the army being withdrawn from Spain and, instead of seeing action, he was left kicking his heels. It was then that everything went wrong. Jane shuddered with shame even now.

Harry could not afford to marry her on a lieutenant's

pay and his grandfather, who had stood buff for his previous debts, would not increase his allowance. He needed
promotion and in London the chances of that were slim.
It was one of his fellow officers who told him that preferment could be gained through Mrs Mary Anne Clarke,
the Duke of York's mistress, and suggested he try that
avenue to promotion, offering to take him to one of the
many social gatherings that Mrs Clarke liked to organise.
As a mere lieutenant he would not normally have been
accepted in those circles, but the heir to the Earl of Bostock was a different matter. He was told to find four
hundred guineas and the lady would put his name on a
list she would give to the Duke, who would expedite the
promotion. She pretended she could give no guarantee,
though she intimated that the Duke never refused her anything.

Harry and Anne had both been left a little money by
their maternal grandfather, but Harry had very little of his
left, he had told Anne. Living the life of an army officer
was an expensive business and his pay and allowance
from their grandfather nowhere near covered it. And he
liked to give Jane little presents, and outings. Anne had
given him the money without a second's hesitation, something Jane found hard to forgive. 'If you hadn't let him
have it, he would not have got himself into such a scrape,'
she had told her friend when the scandal came to light. 'I
did not need or expect expensive presents and if he had
been honest with me I should have told him so. And I
was content to wait to be married. It is ungentlemanly of
him to lay the blame for his disgrace at my door.' But
Anne adored her twin and had never been able to refuse
him anything it was in her power to give him and she
defended not only her actions, but his as well.

His promotion never came. The Duke had tired of his

mistress and she had not taken it lying down. She had demanded a large sum of money to pay off debts she maintained had been incurred by having to live up to her position as a royal duke's mistress; the Duke had refused to pay it and she countered by threatening to make public the details of their love affair. The wrangle had come to the attention of Parliament and it all came out in an enquiry into the behaviour of the Duke in the House of Commons at which Mary Anne Clark was the chief witness.

Every member of that august body had listened with rapt attention to details of the love life of the King's second son, heard his love letters read aloud and learned the names of those officers who came and went to the lady's splendid home in Gloucester Place, among whom was a certain Lieutenant Harry Hemingford. At the end, the majority in favour of the Duke was so small he resigned as Commander-in-Chief and Harry felt obliged to follow his example. Jane was heartbroken and, encouraged by her father and Aunt Lane, had told him she could not love a man who got himself involved in such disgraceful goings on and broke off their engagement.

Hard though it had been, she had tried to put it behind her, but now everyone seemed bent on reminding her. She had to tell Mr Allworthy, of course; you couldn't deceive the man who hoped to marry you, but why did her aunt have to drag it up again? As for Anne, she felt very cross with her. She had promised she would not mention Harry again and it did not help to decide what to do about Mr Allworthy. Perhaps if she consented to marry him, it would put a period to the whole episode and everyone would stop prosing on about it.

'I know how much you love your brother,' Jane said. 'And I admire you for it, but let us say no more. Tomorrow Mr Allworthy is taking me and Aunt Lane for a carriage ride in the park and I shall perhaps learn more about him then.'

Anne sighed. 'I can see I will never influence you, so I shall give up, but promise me you will not rush into anything.'

Jane attempted a laugh. 'I have no intention of rushing into anything.'

They finished drinking their tea and Jane took her leave, wondering if she had been right to go and see Anne after all. She should have known that Anne could not be objective about Mr Allworthy, any more than her father and Aunt Lane were. She was on her own.

She had slept badly, then worked all morning for her father until her thumb and finger were stiff from holding a pen and her head ached from trying to decipher his script. She ate a light repast and afterwards went upstairs to her bedroom where Lucy had already been dispatched and was waiting to help her change for her carriage ride. 'What will you wear, Miss Jane? I have pressed your blue silk and your green taffeta, but it is such a warm day that I think the blue will be cooler.'

'Yes, the blue, if you please, and the white muslin pelisse.'

Half an hour later she presented herself to her aunt in the drawing room to await the arrival of her suitor. The blue suited her and its simple style showed off her slim figure. Her hair had been brushed until it shone like a ripe chestnut and was caught up into a knot on top of her head with two tortoiseshell combs. A few strands had escaped and formed ringlets about her face, softening the rather severe style.

'Very pretty,' her aunt commented. 'I am sure he will be quite entranced.'

They heard the door knocker at that moment, and a minute later Mr Allworthy was announced. He strode into the room, his hat beneath his arm, and bowed to them both. He was in grey, charcoal for his double-breasted coat, which had a high stand-up collar, dove-grey for his pantaloons. His waistcoat was lilac and his cravat tied in precise folds. His boots shone and his hair had recently had the attentions of a barber. 'My carriage is outside, ladies,' he said. 'The horses are a little restive, so if you are ready…'

He escorted them out to the carriage, helped them into their seats, climbed in facing them and ordered the coachman to drive to Hyde Park.

It was, as Lucy had intimated, a very warm day and the park was crowded as it had been all Season. Whenever anything out of the ordinary took place in the Royal family, the whole *haut monde* converged on London and this Season was no exception. The King's doctors had finally decided he would not recover from his madness sufficiently to rule and the previous February the Prince of Wales had at last become Regent. If those involved in the government of the country had expected sweeping changes, they were disappointed; the Regent carried on much as his father had before him, except that his love of pleasure meant there were even more balls and banquets.

Jane sat stiffly beside her aunt, facing Mr Allworthy, seeing and yet not seeing all the hubbub about her. Every sort of carriage, from high-perch phaetons to gigs, from grand town coaches to curricles, was there, getting in each other's way as they stopped for the occupants to exchange gossip and scandal. Aunt Lane was in her element and commented on everyone they saw. It was astonishing the number of people with whom she could claim a connection.

'There is the Countess,' she exclaimed. 'Mr Allworthy, please stop so that I may present Jane. Her ladyship has a particular interest, you know.'

Donald's coachman skillfully avoided a collision with an oncoming tilbury and drew up opposite the Countess of Carringdale's coach. 'Countess, we are well met,' Harriet called out. 'Allow me to present Miss Jane Hemingford. You remember, we spoke of her.'

'So this is the gel.' The Countess peered closely at Jane through her quizzing glass. Jane was annoyed enough to look her straight in the eye and saw a very old woman in a dark purple coat and a turban of the same colour, which had three tall plumes dyed to match waving from the top of it. Her deportment was regal, her pale blue eyes taking in every aspect of Jane's dress and demeanour.

'Very pretty,' she said at last. 'Too thin, though what can you expect from young gels nowadays, always rushing hither and thither, enjoying themselves?'

Jane thought that remark uncalled for and opened her mouth to protest, but her aunt quickly intervened. 'My lady, may I also present Mr Donald Allworthy.'

The Countess moved her examination to Donald. 'Mr Allworthy and I are already acquainted. Good day to you, young man.'

'Countess, your obedient.' He smiled and bowed stiffly from the waist.

'Harriet, I shall expect an accounting,' she said to Aunt Lane, and waved a peremptory hand to tell her coachman to proceed. 'I shall wish to be informed if an announcement is imminent.'

Jane was seething and her aunt knew it. 'Do not take

her remarks to heart, Jane, dear,' she said as they drove
on. 'She is only thinking of what is best for you.'

'I shall decide what is best for me, Aunt,' Jane said.
'And I hope you will tell her so, when you see her.'

'But should you be so adamant, Miss Hemingford?'
Donald said and, though his tone was mild, Jane detected
an undercurrent of concern, which surprised her and
added to her vexation. 'Her ladyship is surely worth cultivating? She is wealthy and your kinswoman and I have
always believed that family comes first.'

'There, Jane!' Mrs Lane said, triumphantly. 'Have I not
always said the same thing, times without number?'

'Yes, Aunt, so you have, but the relationship is so distant, I would not presume—'

'Fustian! If her ladyship chooses to take you up, then
you should be grateful. She has no children of her own,
you know, and approbation from her will ensure a place
in Society for you and your husband. You will have an
entrée to all the best drawing rooms.'

Jane had no intention of toadying to the Countess, even
if her aunt, and Mr Allworthy too, thought she should. He
was looking pensive, as if he would like to add his arguments to her aunt's, but she forestalled him. 'Mr Allworthy, do you think we could drive somewhere else? I
find the park too crowded for comfort.'

'As you wish, of course,' he said. 'We will leave by
the next gate and drive back up Kensington Road to Park
Lane.'

Jane was silent as they drove along; she was so put out
by the top-lofty behaviour of the Countess and Mr Allworthy's condoning of it that she could hardly speak. He
seemed to sense her displeasure and leaned forward to
murmur, 'Miss Hemingford, I beg your pardon, I was only
thinking of our...your interests. Lady Carringdale can

make or break...' He paused, as if realising he might make matters worse if he went on. 'Please do not let it make any difference to us.'

She looked up at him. 'Us, Mr Allworthy?'

'My hope. You did say I might hope, did you not?'

She smiled a little woodenly. 'How well do you know the Countess?'

'Only slightly. My goodness, you did not think I connived...? Oh, my dear Miss Hemingford, I can fight my own battles.'

'Is it a battle?'

'A battle, to win you? Yes, but it is one I take pleasure in fighting, hoping for a happy outcome.'

She did not know what to say to that and sat back in her seat and put up her parasol, to shield her from the sun. It was as they were passing Knightsbridge barracks that she caught a glimpse of a familiar figure, disappearing through the gates. The set of the shoulders, the dark curly hair, the jaunty way his arms swung as he walked, stopped her breath. With an effort, she managed to stop herself from crying out, glad that her parasol hid her face. As the carriage passed the gates, she leaned forward to look again, but whoever it was had gone.

It could not have been Harry. The man had a kind of lopsided gait that was not at all like Harry's quick stride, and he had looked older. Besides, Harry had resigned his commission and gone into exile; he was no longer a soldier. Her imagination was playing tricks on her. She had been reminded of him so many times in the last few days, she was seeing him everywhere.

'What is it?' her aunt asked her.

'Nothing, Aunt. I had something in my eye, but it has gone now.'

'Are you sure?'

'Oh, yes, Aunt, I am quite sure.'

The rest of the ride back to Duke Street, the smiles and gracious thanks to their escort, the promise to go to a musical rout somewhere or other the following evening, passed in a blur. Jane's head was full of memories, memories she could not erase, not even when she slept. She had said it was all in the past, dead and gone, and something had to be done to make sure it stayed that way.

Chapter Two

It was two weeks since Jane had seen the figure entering the barracks, two weeks in which she expected to come across him round every corner, two weeks with her heart in her mouth. She had not dared to visit Anne in case he was there, though she told herself a dozen times a day she had imagined him. And even if she had not, if he really had returned, did it matter? She had sent him away, told him she never wanted to see him again and had meant it.

And there was poor Mr Allworthy, still doing his best to win her, escorting her to functions, taking her out in his carriage, even walking with her to the library when she wanted to change a book and helping her to choose ribbons for her new bonnet. She did not think she needed a new bonnet, but Aunt Lane had insisted that if she was to be seen out and about with Mr Allworthy, who was always in prime rig, she must dress accordingly.

Often she had no chaperon apart from Hannah, dawdling several paces behind them, and when they were out in the carriage there was only Mr Allworthy's coachman to give lip service to propriety. No one could fail to see that the gentleman was seriously courting Jane and many of her friends had asked her when they could expect an announcement. She had been evasive, but was she being fair to him?

'Miss Hemingford, do you ride?' he asked her one day. They had been out in his carriage as far as Richmond and were coming back along the Kensington Road. She had not been that way since she had seen what she chose to call the apparition; as they approached the barracks, she could feel herself stiffening, holding her breath, half expecting to see it again. There were several officers about, but none that looked at all like Harry, and she let out an audible sigh.

'Is anything wrong?' he asked.

'Not at all.' She sat upright, inching away from him. 'What were you saying? I am afraid I was not paying attention. I have been doing some work for Papa and it suddenly came to me that I should have pointed out an error to him.'

'I believe he works you too hard. If you were to consent to be my wife, you would not have to do it.'

'Oh, but I love doing it. And Papa could not manage without me.'

'Is that why you have delayed giving me your answer?'

'I suppose in part it must be.'

'Then do not let it be a consideration. I can find him a good secretary.'

She laughed. 'No one but me can understand his hand.'

'Oh, I am sure someone could learn to decipher it, and perhaps he ought to try and make it easier to read.' He paused. 'You did not answer my question. Do you ride?'

He had a disconcerting way of abandoning the subject under discussion just when she was gathering herself up to answer him. Was it because he sensed her reluctance to delve deeper into her feelings and wanted to spare her or was he simply assuming she agreed with him? She smiled to show him she was not put out by it. 'I used to when I was a child and we lived in the country, but I have not done so since Mama died and we came to live in London. Perhaps I have forgotten how.'

'Then I think we should find out, don't you?'

'I have no mount or habit.'

'A hack can be hired and I will purchase a habit for you.'

'Certainly not!' she said sharply. 'I could not possibly accept gifts of clothing, they should only ever come from a husband.'

His smile was a little crooked. 'I wish that I were he.'

'I asked you for time to make up my mind, Mr All-worthy.'

'And while you do so, the whole *haut monde* waits with bated breath.'

'The *haut monde* is not the least interested in my affairs. I doubt more than half a dozen have even heard of me.'

'There you are wrong. Your fame goes before you.'

'Fame?' she faltered. 'Oh, you mean the tattlemongers have been at work.'

'With the help of your Aunt Lane and your relative, the Countess. The more your aunt sings your praises, the more people talk.'

'What do they say? No, you do not need to tell me, for I know already. I broke off one engagement for what many consider to be a trivial reason and any man who offers for me had better bear that in mind. I think I will never live it down and you were best to turn your back on me or some of the calumny will rub off on you.'

'I am not such a Jack Pudding as to turn tail at the first setback, and if anyone should say a word against you in my company you may be sure they will be sorry for it. But it was not that I meant. I was speaking of your goodness, your modesty and obedience, the way you have helped your papa.'

She tried to laugh. 'Oh, Mr Allworthy, how gallant you are, but it is all flummery and you know it.'

'Not at all. But you could put an end to the tattle at once, you know, if you were to consent to be my wife. I could carry you off to Coprise and they would soon find someone else to talk about.'

'Is that the answer? Would *you* find it so easy to forget?'

'I have your assurance it is all in the past, that you have no affection for the man in question and do not regret your decision to sever your ties with him, and that is enough for me.' He paused. 'Now, we have discoursed on the matter long enough. Shall we ride out together one morning? Friday, perhaps? Nine o'clock?'

Nine o'clock was early, but at that time there would not be so many people about to witness her clumsiness and so she agreed, knowing that the more invitations she accepted the more she was compounding her problem, if problem it was.

She purchased a ready-made habit in deep blue grosgrain. It had a tight-fitting military-style jacket decorated with silver braid and frogging. Her hat, like a man's top hat, was softened with a length of bright blue gauze tied about its narrow brim with the ends flowing freely behind. The skirt was full and plain. She decided if she did not take to riding again, it could be altered to make a walking dress and the money would not be wasted. Practising economy had become a habit with her since she had been in charge of her father's household and she could not break it, even though Aunt Lane had generously paid for many of her new clothes and told her to think nothing of it.

Donald arrived at her front door at the appointed time, with a magnificent black stallion and a small bay mare. 'She's called Blaze,' he told her as he escorted her out and helped her to mount. Having made sure she was comfortably seated, he mounted the stallion and they set out at a walk. She was aware of a groom, following them on a cob, but he was so far behind that as a chaperon he might just as well not have been there.

'Green Park, I think,' Donald said, watching her carefully to see how she was managing. 'It will be less crowded than Hyde Park.'

As soon as she was in the saddle, she knew she had not forgotten how to ride. It came back to her as something comfortable and familiar. She had ridden almost daily when she was young, mostly in the company of Anne and Harry, whose home had been less than a mile from hers. They had been three rather wild children, sometimes riding bareback, often bareheaded, frequently barefoot, chasing across the countryside, up hill and down dale, until they had been driven home by hunger. How happy they had been, how easy in each other's company, unaware of what lay ahead.

The first change had come when Harry went to university. It was not the same for the two girls after that. They were expected to grow into young ladies and were schooled with that end in mind. But they had remained good friends and when Harry came home in the vacations, he escorted them to dances in the assembly rooms and on picnics to local beauty spots, but there were always other people about; it was no longer just the three of them.

And then Mama had died and soon after that Papa,
eaten up with grief, had decided to sell the house and live
in London permanently. The decision seemed to compound Jane's own grief. The capital was dirty and noisy
and she missed everything that might have given her some
solace: the green fields, the pony rides, the people, Anne
and Harry most of all. It was from Anne's letters she
learned that Harry had fallen into bad company and had
incurred gambling debts of three hundred pounds. 'Grandfather stood buff for him,' she had written. 'And has
bought him a lieutenancy in the Prince of Wales's Own,
which he told him was more than he deserved, but I don't
think he meant it. From tales I have heard him tell when
I was a little girl, he sowed a few wild oats himself. Harry
is off to London any time now and no doubt he will call
on you.'

Harry, with his dark curls and laughing eyes, had arrived, splendid and proud in his uniform, and had capti-
vated her, won her heart and her hand, and then behaved
disgracefully and she ought not to repine over him. It was
not fair on the man who rode beside her now. Donald
Allworthy was everything that Harry was not: reliable,
thoughtful, truthful, correct to the last degree. Everyone
told her he was exactly right for her.

As they entered the park, she turned to smile at him. 'I
am so glad you persuaded me to come. I had forgotten
how much I enjoyed riding. It is such an age since I have
been on the back of a horse.'

'You could be on the back of one every day if you
became Mrs Allworthy. There are horses in the stables
and some good rides around Coprise.'

She smiled mischievously as they trotted past a herd of
cows being driven to the gate by milkmaids. 'Bribery, Mr
Allworthy?'

'No, a promise.' He paused. 'I collect you are fond of country pursuits.'

'Indeed, I am.'

'Then come to Coprise Manor for a visit. You should all come, Mr Hemingford, Mrs Lane and your maids. There is plenty of room. I have to go home soon, I have been away too long, but the prospect of being parted from you made me reluctant to return.'

'You are leaving London?' Why that should surprise her, she did not know. 'I did not know you were contemplating it.'

'I must be back for haymaking. I like to involve myself in the work of the farm; matters run more smoothly when I do. But I could make all ready for your reception. Say you will come.'

'I must consult with Papa and Aunt Lane. It might not be convenient for them.'

'But if it is, you will come?'

'I think I might like that.'

His little grin of triumph was not lost on her, but surely he had a right to be pleased? She dug her heel into her horse's flank and set it cantering across the grass, enjoying the feel of the mare's strong back beneath her, the sound of her hooves as she put her to gallop, laughing because she had taken her escort by surprise and left him behind.

And then she looked up and saw them, two riders outlined against the skyline, and she knew who they were by the way the young woman brushed a wayward curl from her face, the way the man sat in the saddle with his hands loosely on the reins. Her laughter faded and in that second, in mid-gallop, she thought of wheeling about to avoid them, but that would risk a fall and she would not subject herself to the indignity of being unseated in front of them. She managed to pull up and then stopped. They had surely seen her. Or was this another of her apparitions? What would it take to banish them? Marriage to someone else?

She looked round at Donald as he rode up beside her. 'That was good,' she said, making herself laugh again.

'Foolhardy, my dear, especially when you are so long out of practice. I should never have forgiven myself if you had taken a tumble.'

'Ah, but I did not.' She leaned forward to pat her horse's neck, aware that the other two riders were walking their horses towards them. 'Little Blaze is a goer.'

She found herself surreptitiously looking at Harry. It was indeed Harry, but so changed she hardly recognised him. In a brown stuff riding jacket and a tall beaver hat, he seemed older than she had expected. He had become broader, more muscled, his features more lined, almost weatherbeaten. And there was a tiny scar running from his mouth towards his cheek. She wondered where he had been in the last two years, but then told herself sternly she did not want to know.

But she had to acknowledge him for Anne's sake. 'Mr Hemingford,' she said, aware of Donald beside her. 'How do you do?' And then, before he could reply, turned to his companion. 'Anne, isn't it a lovely morning? I have not enjoyed a ride so much for ages.' And then she wished she had not spoken because she saw Harry's mouth twitch in a faint smile and knew he was thinking of days long gone. 'You are acquainted with Mr Donald Allworthy, I collect.'

'Yes, indeed.' Anne put on a bright smile, which only Jane knew was forced. 'Mr Allworthy, may I present my brother, Harry?'

The two men inclined their heads and bade each other good morning, but Jane could sense their animosity and decided to bring the encounter to an end. 'Do call on me, Anne,' she said, turning her mount. 'But do not make it too long. I am leaving town very soon to stay at Coprise Manor.' And then, as she drew away, 'Good-day to you, Mr Hemingford.'

Donald took a cool leave of the brother and sister and followed her. 'So that was the scapegrace,' he said. 'I thought he was out of the country.'

'So did I.'

'You had no idea he was back?'

'None at all. Why should I have? And it is of no consequence.'

'You are sure?'

'Yes. The man is a stranger to me now. I hardly recognised him.' She told herself that was true. Her so-called love had been nothing more than the infatuation of youth and youth had flown. 'Tell me about Coprise Manor.'

'You mean to come, then?'

She could feel two pairs of eyes boring into her back and sat ramrod straight. 'Of course, if Papa agrees.'

'Who is that fellow?' Harry demanded of his sister as they watched them ride away.

'A mushroom,' she said. 'A countryman up for the Season in search of a wife.'

'Jane?'

She nodded. 'They have been seen about town together every day for the last two weeks and I believe she is about to announce her engagement to him. She would not be going to Coprise otherwise. It is his country home in Norfolk.'

'Oh.'

'Harry, you should have come back sooner.'

He grimaced as they walked their horses forward, careful not to catch up with the two in front. 'I was not in a position to come and go as I pleased and what good would it have done? She has not forgiven me. You could see she hardly knew how to be civil, not even to you, and you are her friend. Besides, we have both moved on; there is nothing at all between us now.'

'Liar!'

'Childhood love rarely survives into adulthood, you know.' He chuckled. 'And I took rather longer than most to grow up.'

'But you have grown up, Harry. You are not the stripling that went away two years ago.'

'No, thank God.'

'What have you been doing?' He had turned up on the doorstep two weeks before, soon after Jane's last visit, bone weary, filthy and recovering from a wound to his thigh that had given him a limp. In that two weeks he had slept and slept, eaten like a hungry wolf, and slowly mended. Today had been his first outing. And they had to run into Jane, of all people.

He smiled, a crooked kind of smile because of the scar. 'I told you, fighting for King and Country. There is nothing like a few bullets and cannon balls flying around to make a boy into a man.'

'But you resigned your commission.'

'So I did. But there are other ways to serve. The army is not so particular about those they take into the ranks. I enlisted as a private soldier and was lucky enough to be taken into the 95th. It was a very salutary experience, I can tell you, but I made a good rifleman.'

'It must have been terrible. I cannot think why you did it.'

'I had something to prove, Sis. And it was not so bad. There was hardship, of course, and danger too, but there was also comradeship, a pulling together and sharing whatever you have with each other, rations, clothes, food, jests, even women.'

'Is it not like that among officers?'

'Not quite. They are too concerned about their position in the chain of command. A lieutenant's position as the lowest of the low is only surpassed by that of an ensign, who is truly a nobody. A major looks down on a captain and a colonel can have no friends, being at the top of the regimental pyramid, so to speak. His is a lonely life and I do not envy him.'

'I collect, when you first had your colours, you said you would come back a colonel.'

'That was the boy speaking, not the man.'

Looking back, he could not believe what a sousecrown he had been. The adoration of his sister and Jane had swelled his vanity to gigantic proportions. He had been hail-fellow-well-met at his college, had done very little work, learned to gamble and fallen into debt. But wasn't that the way of all young bloods? His grandfather had put down the dust, but there had been strings attached. The lieutenancy had been thrust under his nose and an ultimatum delivered. He had accepted it with gratitude.

Even then his good intentions had been trammelled underfoot as soon as he arrived in London. Living in the capital had been expensive, with regimentals to buy, a pair of horses to keep, his mess bills and a servant to maintain. It became even more so when he became engaged to Jane and there were parties almost every night, balls and routs to attend, presents to buy for her. He wanted to be the grand suitor, the generous lover, the husband and provider. He could not be that while he was a mere lieutenant, kicking his heels on home ground.

When Clarence Garfitt had told him about Mrs Clarke,

he had hesitated, but Clarence, who was a captain and always knew everything that was going on, had assured him that was how many men obtained preferment. Nothing was said against it because to do so would involve the Duke of York and of course no one would dare risk that. What a gull he had been! The whole scandal had come to light and his name became publicly known as one of those officers who had offered a bribe. Jane had been furious and he had compounded his villainy in her eyes by blustering and trying to excuse himself. 'Everyone does it,' he had said. 'I did it for us, so that we could marry. It is not the end of the world.'

But Jane was Jane. Seventeen years old, motherless and with a father who saw and heard nothing that did not relate to his work, she was far from worldly-wise and had been shocked to discover that such people as Mrs Clarke existed—not only existed, but were condoned so long as they never complained. Jane was appalled and outraged to think that her affianced husband had visited the house of such a one. To her everything must be either black or white; she would not admit to shades of grey. He had resigned his commission and taken himself out of her sight.

'But you did become an officer,' Anne said, breaking in on his thoughts. 'You are a captain.'

'Promoted in the field. My company commander received a mortal wound and there was no one else to take charge. Luckily for me, my conduct was noticed; I was mentioned in the colonel's report and the captaincy was confirmed. Later they were looking for someone who could speak French and I volunteered. I had to question French prisoners and deserters, and that led to using their information to obtain more.'

He had volunteered to go behind the enemy lines to

follow up a piece of information he had been given. It had been risky and exciting, but he had welcomed the danger, learned to survive, met some extraordinary people and emerged alive, but wounded. Making his way back to his own lines just outside Pombala, he had been skirting round a French bivouac when he was seen and challenged. He had been within half a mile of his own comrades and as he carried important intelligence, there was nothing to do but fight his way out of trouble. He had taken a ball in the thigh, but luckily for him they were in dense woodland and he was able to conceal himself in thick undergrowth until the bigger battle started. With pandemonium around him, he had managed to crawl to safety and deliver his intelligence. But the wound had put a painful end to his military career.

'What are you going to do now?' Anne asked him. 'You are not fit to return to duty.'

'No, more's the pity, I would have liked to see it to the end. I must find something to occupy myself.'

'Will you go to see Grandpapa?'

'Will he receive me?'

'Of course he will! When you tell him what you have done, that you have been wounded in the service of your country and been mentioned in dispatches, he will be as proud as a turkeycock. You have redeemed yourself and he will welcome you back into the family. You will be able to take up your proper position as his heir.'

'Not yet. I put my old life behind me when I enlisted. I cannot go back to it. I think I will go into business.'

'Business?' she repeated, shocked. 'You don't mean *trade*?'

He smiled, knowing she was only reflecting the attitude of their own social class. 'Why not? I have not quite made up my mind what, or how I can bring it about, but it must be something worthwhile.'

'Grandfather won't like that. You are a gentleman born and bred and one day you will be the Earl of Bostock and take over the estate.'

'That does not mean I cannot be some use in the world before that happens, does it? I have learned to stand on my own feet while I have been away and I found I liked it.'

'And Jane?' The pair ahead of them had disappeared through the gates on to Piccadilly, merging in with the traffic on that busy thoroughfare.

'Ah, Jane,' he said, thinking back to their encounter not five minutes before. She was no longer the hoyden of their childhood, not even the pretty young débutante to whom he had become engaged. She was another being entirely, a fully fledged woman. The new Jane had looked splendid in that riding habit, her womanly curves in all the right places, and that fetching hat had set off her thick hair to perfection. Sitting straight in the saddle, her gloved hands on her reins, perfectly composed, she had shown nothing of the Jane he had known and loved. She had outgrown him. 'I fear I am too late on that score, Sis.'

'Fustian! She still loves you.'

'I do not believe it. The Jane I knew would not encourage another man when her heart was elsewhere. She would be too honest.'

'Two years is a long time, Harry. I believe she has been coerced. You must do something.'

'Anne, even if I were to wish it, which I do not admit to, I could not step in now. What would that do to my reputation and hers too? I have done enough damage to the Hemingford name already. If I were to step into another man's engagement, all that other business would be dragged up again and I would be branded an unmitigated bounder.' He reached out and patted her hand. 'Thank you for trying, my dear, but I, too, have moved on.'

'Oh, Harry, I am so sorry. I love you both so much.'

'And you may still love us both. That has not changed. And I thank God for it. Now, do you think we can make a little more haste, I came out without my breakfast and I am gut-foundered.'

They rode home in silence but, for all his cheerful countenance, his heart was heavy. Had he really expected Jane to recognise the new man and be ready and willing to forgive and forget and take him back? It was the thought of redeeming himself in her eyes that had kept him going, been with him through the long watches of the night when he had been cold and wet; it had been with him on endless marches when he had been almost roasted alive. It had sustained him when he had been living among his country's enemies and helped him safely back to his comrades when his mission had been accomplished. The vision of her face had helped him to survive that long night hiding in a ditch with a bullet in his leg. When he had been praised for his daring by none other than Old Douro himself and mentioned in his dispatches, it was of Jane's good opinion he had been thinking. All for nothing!

They dismounted outside Bostock House and left the horses with a groom before going indoors. The house had been bought by the first Earl when Cavendish Square was an isolated residential area in the countryside north of London. He had chosen it for its proximity to the capital and its fresh air. Now it was part of the metropolis, an old house in the middle of new. It had not even been modernized, because the Earl had not visited London since his son, the twins' father, had died. Most of the year it remained empty and was only opened up when Anne came to town for the Season. If Harry had his way, it would be sold. The ground it stood on must surely be worth a fortune with the way London was spreading northwards and the Regent clamouring to have a new road built from his residence at Carlton House to Regent's Park.

'When are you going home to Sutton Park?' she asked him, as they entered.

He grinned. 'Do you want to be rid of me?'

'No, you know I do not. I have seen nothing of you for two years and there is no hurry, is there? I am going back myself in a week or two, we could go together.'

'You think I might need protection from Grandpapa?' He laughed as they climbed the stairs to their respective rooms. 'You are probably right at that. You could always turn him round your thumb.'

'Gammon!'

He stopped outside her room and put out a hand to stroke her cheek. 'Dear Sis, always looking after her wayward brother. I do appreciate it, you know.'

'I know. Will you take me to the theatre tonight? That is, if you are not too fatigued.'

'I will gladly take you, if my evening coat still fits me, but have you no beau dangling after you?'

'Oh, Harry, do not be so foolish, I am long past marriageable age.'

'Humbug! I think I will find you a husband while I am in town. In fact, it is my duty.'

'It is not! You look to your own affairs, Harry Hemingford.'

He knew she meant Jane, but that was entirely out of the question.

* * *

Not for a minute did he think that agreeing to take his sister to the theatre would have such a profound effect on his mind and heart. Jane was there with her new love, sitting in the box opposite theirs, accompanied by an elderly lady in a hideous mauve-and-lilac striped round gown, whom he recognised as her great-aunt. And he knew with a certainty that almost unmanned him that he had been lying when he said he had moved on.

Jane was in amber silk, almost the same colour as the highlights in her hair. It heightened the creaminess of her shoulders and neck, the softness of her complexion and the brilliance of her eyes. Looking through his opera glass, he could see her quite clearly. She appeared to be watching the stage, but he was sure she had also seen him and was looking away on purpose. Was she afraid he might see what was written in those eyes? He had known her since she was a small child, knew her every mood, had seen her eyes full of mischief, teasing, laughing, crying and furious with indignation. He had seen them sad and he had seen them happy. He could not make himself believe she was happy now. And he could do nothing to remedy it. He had forfeited the right.

Jane knew perfectly well she was being watched. She had seen Anne and her brother take their seats before the curtain rose and, though she had turned to talk to Donald while the rest of the audience filled the theatre and, when the performance began, had concentrated on watching the stage, she was aware of Harry's scrutiny. He had no right to look at her like that, no right to make her feel discomfited. She made herself angry; it was the only way she could go on.

She was still angry when the intermission brought the curtain down and everyone began moving about, waving to friends in other parts of the theatre, visiting other boxes. It made her a little sharp with Donald when he asked her if she would like some refreshment, but she immediately regretted it and smiled sweetly at him. 'A cordial would be very nice, please. It is warm in here, is it not?'

He left on his errand and Jane turned to talk to her aunt about the play. Aunt Lane, who had her opera glasses to her eyes and was surveying the other boxes, did not appear to be listening. 'Why, there is your cousin, Anne,' she said. 'And who is that with her, surely not a beau? My goodness, I do believe it is that rakeshame brother of hers. I wonder where he has popped up from.'

Jane had no answer, not having had the presence of mind to ask him that morning. 'I am sure I do not know,' she said.

'Did you know he was back in town?'

'We met him this morning while we were out riding.'

'You did not say.'

'I did not think anything of it. We exchanged greetings, no more.'

'He looks much changed.'

'I believe he is.'

'My dear, what will you do?'

'Do, Aunt? Why, nothing. If I meet him again, I shall be civil for Anne's sake, but that is all.'

'Very wise.' The old lady paused, still looking through her glass. 'But I admit to being curious. I wonder what he has been up to for the last two years? Not with the *beau monde* judging by his evening coat—it is at least three years out of date. Oh, my goodness, he has seen us and pointed us out to Anne. They are getting up. Do you suppose they are coming here?'

Anne and her brother arrived at the door of the box at the same moment as Donald returned with Jane's drink.

They greeted each other coolly and Aunt Lane, whose curiosity was overwhelming if she thought there might be a titbit of gossip worth passing on to her cronies, invited Anne and Harry into the box with something akin to cordiality.

Anne kissed Jane's cheek and sat down beside her, depriving Donald of the seat he had had. He gave Jane her glass of cordial and sat himself on the other side of Aunt Lane. Harry, smiling, pulled a chair round to face the ladies. Aunt Lane leaned forward and tapped him on the knee with her fan. 'Tell me, young man, where have you been hiding yourself these last two years?'

'He has not been hiding,' Anne said before he could reply himself. 'He has been serving his country in the Peninsula, and though he will not tell you so himself, for he is far too modest, he distinguished himself with great courage.'

'Is that so?' Mrs Lane queried, smiling.

'My sister was ever my champion,' he said, but though he was smiling at the old lady, his eyes were on Jane. She was looking a little taken aback. Did she find it so difficult to believe that the man she had known and professed to love could behave with merit? Or was she simply discomfited that he had had the effrontery to invade her box?

Given his way, he would not have come, but Anne had insisted. 'Jane is my friend,' she had said. 'If you were not here, I should go and have some discourse with her and I do not propose to change my habits because you are. It would be as good as cutting her and that would give the scandalmongers fresh ammunition and I will not give them the satisfaction. Besides, you have done no wrong and I will not have you ostracised. Better to let people think we are all friends together.'

He had smilingly given in, knowing she was right; politeness decreed they should acknowledge each other or have everyone talking about that two-year-old scandal all over again. Besides, although he could not and should not attempt to wrest Jane away from Allworthy, which would damn him all over again in the eyes of the world, he could not resist the temptation to speak to her again, if only for a few minutes. He might discover if Anne had been right when she said Jane had been coerced.

'I thought you resigned your commission,' Jane put in tentatively. She had noticed how tired he looked, and that, when he came in and took his seat, he limped. In spite of his smile, there was pain in his eyes and she wondered why she had not noticed it that morning. Her anger gave way to compassion.

'So I did, but that did not mean I had finished with the army or they with me. I enlisted.'

'Enlisted!' Aunt Lane was shocked. 'You mean you became a common soldier?'

'Yes, ma'am. I was not prepared to wallow in my disgrace or hang about waiting for someone to take pity on me. And as I did not have the blunt to buy a commission in another regiment, I decided to serve my country in the only other way open to me.'

'How brave of you,' murmured Jane. This was not the blustering rakeshame she had sent away, this was a man who had taken his courage in his hands and tried to redeem himself.

He laughed, not sure she wasn't roasting him. 'Not brave at all, but once I had done it, there was no undoing it and in the end I did not regret it.'

'He was soon promoted,' Anne put in, realising that Aunt Lane did not see the common soldier as a being to be admired, rather the reverse. 'He is Captain Harry Hemingford now.'

'Congratulations,' Jane said. 'I am very pleased for you.'

'But a private soldier!' Aunt Lane protested. 'How could you bring yourself to associate with the riffraff in the ranks?'

'Ma'am, they are not riffraff, they are the men standing between you and Bonaparte, keeping this country safe from his tyranny, and a finer bunch of comrades I never met. I am proud to have served with them.'

'I do not think Aunt Lane meant to denigrate them,' Jane said quietly. 'She was only thinking of your sensibilities.'

He turned towards her, looking directly into her eyes. 'I could not afford to have sensibilities, Jane.'

'Oh.' She squirmed inwardly with embarrassment, but she had, in the last two years, become adept at hiding it. 'I admire you for it.' She spoke quietly, but he was immensely comforted.

The orchestra had begun to play for the second act, calling everyone back to their seats. Donald, who had remained silent all through the encounter, rose as Anne got up to take her leave. Reluctantly Harry stood, bowed over Mrs Lane's hand, then Jane's and, murmuring, 'Good evening, Allworthy,' disappeared after his sister.

'What a strange fellow,' Donald said, resuming his seat beside Jane.

'I do not find him strange.'

'No gentleman ought to enlist as a private soldier. It is degrading. Their vulgar behaviour and speech are bound to rub off.'

'I saw no evidence of that.'

'No doubt he was being particular tonight.'

The curtain was rising, revealing the next scene in the play, and Jane turned towards the stage, glad to bring an end to the conversation. But she could not concentrate. Seeing Harry twice in the same day had unsettled her. And he was so changed, she could hardly believe he was the man she had sent away. She *had* been the one to send him away, not only from herself, but from his country, his family and his friends. He could have lived down the scandal over Mrs Clarke, everyone else concerned had soon done so; it was not necessary to exile himself for that. He had gone because she could not forgive him and railed at him that he had betrayed her trust, going behind her back and visiting that demi-rep. How top-lofty she had been!

And now he was back and she was likely to see more of him. She could not avoid him unless she cut Anne out of her life and she could not do that. She and Anne were as close as sisters and shared all their secrets; without Anne she would have only an increasingly preoccupied father and an eccentric great-aunt for company. And Mr Allworthy, of course, but she could not imagine herself giggling over the latest *on dit* with him.

The performance ended amid wild applause and they found themselves leaving the theatre alongside Anne and Harry. Jane realised, as they shuffled out in the crowd, that Harry looked pale and drawn and his limp was more pronounced. 'You have been wounded,' she whispered.

'Not worth mentioning, nothing but a scratch.' He grinned to prove it. 'A sympathy wound, you might call it. You'd be surprised how many expressions of compassion, how many offers of nursing, how many bowls of beef tea and posies of sweet-smelling herbs it has attracted. I put it all on, you know.'

She did not believe that. Not even the old Harry would have stooped so low and the pain she had seen in his eyes was real. 'But you will make a full recovery?'

'Oh, do not doubt it.'

They were outside in the street where rows of carriages and cabs waited. The two parties bade each other good night and parted: Jane, Donald and Aunt Lane made their way to the Allworthy carriage while Anne and Harry called up a hackney.

'Well, that was a surprise, I must say,' Aunt Lane said, as they were driven towards Duke Street. 'I doubt the Earl will take him back now.'

'Why not?' Jane demanded. 'I would expect him to be proud of his grandson. Anne said he was recommended for bravery in the field.'

'I think your aunt meant enlisting as a common soldier,' Donald put in. 'It is not the sort of thing a member of the *ton* ought to do. His family must see it as a shabby thing to do, almost as if he had denounced his heritage. But then he had already been disgraced, so perhaps it is not to be wondered at.'

'I hope he does not expect to introduce any of his rough friends to us,' Aunt Lane added. 'For if he does, I shall give them the cut direct and I hope you would do so too, Jane.'

'I cannot conceive of an occasion when I am likely to meet his friends,' Jane said sharply. 'We do not move in the same circles.'

'Quite,' Donald said. 'But you are his sister's friend.'

'Yes, Jane,' Aunt Lane said. 'I think, while he is staying with Anne, you would be wise not to call.'

Jane was about to retort angrily that unless her father specifically forbade it, she would see whom she liked, but thought better of it. She had already decided not to put herself in a position where she was likely to meet Harry, not because she frowned on what he had done since they last met, but because she did not want to be reminded of her heartache of two years before. It was over and done with and she wanted it to stay that way.

'I go home to Coprise tomorrow,' Donald said, changing the subject in his usual fashion.

'So soon?' Jane queried.

'Yes, I must. But I go in the expectation of a visit from you very soon.'

'In the circumstances, I think the sooner the better,' Aunt Lane said.

Jane knew very well what she meant; it did not take a genius to realise Aunt Lane intended to keep her apart from Harry. As if anything on earth would make her go back to him! She smiled. 'If Papa agrees, we could go a week from now.'

Her father had refused the invitation for himself, saying his work was at a critical stage and he could not leave it, but Jane could go if her aunt agreed to chaperon her, which, of course, the good lady was more than prepared to do. Jane could get his copying up to date before she left and he would save the rest for her when she returned two weeks later. He could not sanction a stay longer than that or he would be lost under the weight of paper on his desk. The suggestion that he should employ a secretary had been brushed aside as an unnecessary expense.

'But, James,' Aunt Lane had said, 'what will you do when Jane marries?'

'Oh, the work will be finished by then. I am near the end.'

Jane had smiled at that. The great work had been near the end for years. But he always found some alterations he wanted to make, some new information that must be included and, before Jane could take a breath, he had torn up pages and pages of her neat script and was busy scribbling again.

He had already retired when they reached home, and so it was arranged that Donald should call next morning before he left town, to learn exactly when he could expect his guests.

'I am quite looking forward to it,' Aunt Lane told him, as she left the carriage. 'We shall come post-chaise.'

This was a shocking expense and Jane said so, but was overridden. 'I am an old lady,' her aunt said. 'I need to be comfortable and I shall bear the cost.'

'Dear lady, allow me the privilege of paying,' Donald said. 'I would gladly expend more than the price of a post-chaise to have Miss Hemingford in my home.'

He turned up while they were breakfasting the following morning and, once all the arrangements had been made, begged to speak privately to Jane. They retired to a corner of the room where he picked up one of her hands. 'My dear, I shall be on hot coals until we meet again in one week's time. Pray, do not forget me.'

'Mr Allworthy, how can I possibly forget you in a week?'

'You know what I mean. There will be distractions, temptations, pressures…'

She knew perfectly well that he was referring to Harry, though she did not think he posed a threat. Her erstwhile fiancé had been polite the evening before, but cool, talking about the army as if nothing out of the ordinary had happened. If she were subjected to pressure, it was more likely to come from her aunt bidding her make haste and accept Donald. She smiled. 'Rest assured I shall ignore them all,' she said.

He lifted her hand to his lips. 'Then I bid you *au revoir*, dearest.' He released her hand and turned to her father and aunt, who had been listening to the exchange with satisfied amusement. 'Mr Hemingford, Mrs Lane, your obedient.' And then he was gone, leaving Jane feeling as though a whirlwind had taken her up and whisked her about hither and thither and set her down in a different and unfamiliar place.

'Well,' her aunt said, as they finished their breakfast, 'we have a week to kill.'

'It will pass soon enough,' Mr Hemingford said. 'I have a mountain of copying for Jane.'

'James Hemingford, you should be ashamed!' Aunt Lane protested. 'Working that poor girl as you do. She is young, she needs amusements; besides, we have shopping to do—she must be at her best for Coprise.'

'Oh, Aunt, there is nothing I need. I am sure Mr Allworthy will take me as I am.'

'Oh, so he might,' her aunt said airily. 'But he has a house full of servants and it is always wise to impress the servants, particularly if you expect to become their mistress one day. They must respect you, not look on you as someone's poor relation the master has been so foolish as to take pity on.'

Was that how her aunt really saw her? A poor relation whom it behoved her to pity? Was that why she had encouraged Mr Allworthy, because no one else would have her? Was she still shackled by the old scandal? But Mr Allworthy had said he admired her, that he paid no attention to gossip and he was a good man, if something of a sobersides. Perhaps that was what she needed.

'I won't have you saying Jane is a poor relation,' her father snapped.

Her aunt laughed. 'I did not say she was my poor relation, I only meant we did not want Mr Allworthy's servants to have grounds for criticism. You are a man, you cannot advise the dear girl on her dress, now can you?'

Jane smiled. 'Papa, I understood Aunt Lane very well, there is no need to refine upon it. I need very little, you know, just fripperies.'

'Which I can pay for,' he retorted. 'Go shopping, buy whatever you need, but never say Jane is to be pitied.'

And so they went shopping and returned in the early afternoon with Aunt Lane's carriage seat loaded with parcels and more to be delivered in the coming days, which her aunt had insisted on buying, leaving only a few small things to be set to her father's account.

She was sitting on her bed surrounded by them, wondering how she was going to cram all those new clothes into her trunk and if she really needed them, when Hannah came to tell her Anne had arrived.

Jane tidied her hair and straightened her skirt before going down to the drawing room. Anne was sitting on the sofa, glancing at the latest *Ladies' Magazine* when she entered. She was alone. If Jane had nurtured a hope that her friend would be accompanied by Harry, she refused even to acknowledge it, and smiled a welcome. 'Anne, I am so glad you have come. There is so much to tell you.' She rang the bell and, when Hannah came, asked her to bring refreshments. 'I have had an exhausting day.'

'Preparing for your visit to Coprise, I collect,' Anne said drily.

'Yes.' Jane chose to ignore her friend's tone. 'Aunt Lane has insisted on buying me a whole new wardrobe. I think she must have been thinking she was buying a wedding trousseau.'

'Perhaps she was.'

'No, indeed. I have made no promise. But come upstairs and I will show you.'

They went up to Jane's room where the purchases were

laid out for her inspection. 'I had such a job arguing with Aunt about colours and styles,' she said. 'But luckily the costumier agreed with me and so I have nothing too outrageous.'

'Jane, are you sure you are not being persuaded into something you do not truly wish for? Once you have been to Coprise Manor, it will be assumed that you will have him. It will be difficult to turn back.'

'I might not want to turn back.'

'But supposing you do? You know nothing about this man or his background.'

'That is what I am going to Coprise to discover. And if I find we do not suit, I shall simply say so.'

'Oh, Jane, surely you are not such a ninny as to think it will be as easy as that? You will never be able to extricate yourself without a dreadful scandal. I am afraid for you.'

'You have no need to be. Aunt Lane will take care of me.'

Anne felt like weeping. As far as she could see, her friend had been manipulated in the most disgraceful way and she could cheerfully have throttled both Mr Hemingford and Mrs Lane. 'I wish you happy, I really do, but forgive me if I do not stay to take tea. I think it would choke me.'

She got up and left Jane surrounded by her new finery, bewildered and tearful. She had only once before quarrelled with Anne and that had been over Harry. And so was this. Anne was like a dog with a bone, but was she right?

Chapter Three

Jane spent the next few days tormented by indecision. Anne's words had sunk deep and though she continually told herself that her friend had an axe to grind, she did not think that was the whole of it. But it was too late to say she would not go—her aunt talked about it endlessly, even so far as calling on the Countess, obeying that lady's instruction to keep her informed.

'Her ladyship tells me Mr Allworthy is related to Viscount Denderfield,' she told Jane on her return. 'He has a modest estate and an income of twenty thousand a year. The match has her blessing.'

Jane could not see how a modest estate could bring in that income, but she supposed he had inherited some of it. 'Aunt, how could you discuss my affairs so openly with someone I have only seen once in my life and that for no more than five minutes?'

'But, Jane dear, I have always done so; she is family, after all. And you must acknowledge Mr Allworthy is a great catch, better than I could have hoped for you.'

'Why? Am I monster? Do I have two heads? Do I eat with my fingers and never wash? Am I mad?' She was fiery with passion.

'My dear Jane, there is no need to fly into the boughs. You know I did not mean that you were not good enough for him. After all, you come from aristocratic stock on your dear mama's side and you have inherited her looks, nothing wrong there. It is only that you have left it so late and everyone of your age, including most of the eligibles, except widowers and old fogies, are suited. It is only because Mr Allworthy has spent most of his time buried in the country that he was overlooked.'

Jane laughed, but it was a hollow laugh. Mr Allworthy had been overlooked and forgotten in the country while she was being tainted by scandal and ostracised by the *haut monde* because she had dared to break off her engagement to one of their number. And now it looked very much as if it was all going to be raked up again. Harry was back and not only back, but had returned a hero. She was glad she was leaving town, very glad indeed.

But she was to see Harry once more before she left. Since she now had a fashionable habit and knew the stable from which Blaze had been hired, it was not difficult to go riding. The same groom whom Donald had employed was designated to ride behind her, to protect her from the villains with which London abounded and to act as an unofficial chaperon. Jane did not see the necessity for either role, but she consented to his presence to please her aunt. But it was not a sedate walk or trot she had in mind, but a full-blooded gallop, and once in the park she ordered her escort to wait for her by the gate and trotted off on her own.

Although it was early in the morning, it promised to be a warm day. The sun was a brilliant orange ball in a sky of cornflower blue, with not a cloud to be seen. Her problems were pushed to the back of her mind as she rode away from the usual bridleway where everyone was more concerned with how they looked, whom they might meet, the gossip they might hear and pass on, than with the business of exercising their mounts.

Gradually she became aware that she was not alone; there were other hoofbeats gaining on her and she was reminded that London was not a safe place for a lady on her own, not even Hyde Park in broad daylight. She spurred the little mare on, but the harder she rode, the nearer her pursuer came and she knew that Blaze was tiring. She was obliged to pull up or wind her horse completely. The other rider pulled up beside her.

'My God, Jane, you gave me a fright. I thought you were being carried away.'

She turned to confront Harry. He was wearing the same riding coat he had worn when she had encountered him in Green Park. It seemed too tight for him. She leaned forward to pat Blaze, who was blowing hard. 'Carried away, Captain Hemingford? It was you who taught me to ride, if you recall.'

'I also recall teaching you not to mistreat a horse,' he said with a twisted smile. She was breathless and her heightened colour was making her look even more desirable. It was all he could do to sound normal. 'That poor mare is blowing. Dismount and let her rest.' He jumped down from his own mount, a huge stallion that was hardly breathing above its normal rate, and held out his hand to help her down.

'I would not have had to gallop her so hard if you had not chased me,' she said, annoyed by his curt command. Her temper was not lessened by knowing he was right, though she took the offered hand and slid lightly down beside him.

'Chased you? Why should I do that? I am not so short

of female company that I have to chase after it, particularly yours. I have more pride than that. I thought your mount had bolted with you.'

'I did not know it was you.' He had not released her hand and the feel of his strong fingers about hers was having a strange effect on her. She had not felt such a fluttering of her heart since— She stopped herself asking when; it was too painful to remember. 'I thought it was some rogue and I was in danger.'

'You are in no danger from me.' He laughed and let go of her hand. 'But where is your escort? Surely he has more sense than to let you ride so far ahead of him…'

'There is a groom…'

'A groom! I meant the gentleman I met last week. What was his name?'

'Mr Allworthy.'

He laughed. 'How apt! And I am Mr Unworthy.'

'You are being silly.'

'So where is Mr Allworthy?'

'Gone to Norfolk.' She lifted her head defiantly. 'Aunt Lane and I go to join him tomorrow.'

He had known she was planning the visit because Anne had told him so. She had returned from visiting Jane in a fine old miff. 'I do not know what she can be thinking of,' she had said. 'She is not so green that she doesn't know that if she goes to Coprise there is no turning back, but she has convinced herself that she has only to say no and Mr Allworthy will meekly accept it. He doesn't seem the meek kind to me.'

'So?'

'Harry, she has got herself into a bumblebath or, more correctly, her aunt has tumbled her into it, and she cannot see she is being manoeuvred into an impossible situation.'

'Anne, please calm yourself. Jane is capable of making

up her own mind and perhaps it is what she wants. It is not our affair…'

'How can you say so? You love her and she still loves you, I know it.'

Looking at Jane now, her cheeks red with exertion and her eyes blazing angrily, she had never looked lovelier, but she showed no sign of softening towards him. And what good would it do if she did? 'Then I wish you a good journey and a pleasant stay.' He held his cupped hands to help her mount. 'Allow me to return you safely to your groom, who must be on hot coals wondering if he is to be punished for negligence.'

She opened her mouth to tell him she did not need his escort, nor was she going to punish her groom for obeying her orders, but he was looking at her in that old teasing way she remembered from her childhood and she felt the hard knot in her chest dissolve away. It was most disconcerting. It would have been a grand gesture to have galloped away from him, but Blaze was not rested enough for that and so she began to walk her sedately back towards the gate. He followed, riding slightly behind her.

They had almost reached the Row when they were met by Anne riding towards them. 'Jane, are you all right? Did you take a fall? Are you hurt?'

'No, of course not.' Then, seeing her friend's worried countenance, Jane smiled. 'I simply felt like a gallop. If that mad brother of yours had not come dashing after me, making me think I was being pursued, I would not have gone so fast.'

'He is not mad. And it was me who told him to go after you. He would not have done so on his own.'

'Then he has more sense than you,' Jane said, unaccountably disappointed that he had had to be urged to rescue her. 'Now, if you will excuse me, my groom is waiting for me and I must go home. There is much to do before I leave tomorrow.'

'You mean to go, then?'

'Of course I am going.'

'Then I hope you know what you are doing, that's all. Come on, Harry, let us leave the stubborn clunch to go her own way.' And she wheeled her horse round and trotted away.

Harry turned to Jane and smiled. He had a boyish smile that spread from his mouth to his eyes and crinkled the skin at either side. It seemed to encompass everyone about him. No one could be completely immune to it, certainly not Jane Hemingford, who had once loved him. 'Do not be hard on her, Jane, she loves us both and she cannot see that what she is asking is out of the question. I will try to reason with her and perhaps, when you return, she will be more her old self and accept that you must tread your own path. As I must mine.'

Jane did not answer, but watched him ride away through a mist of tears. She did not know why she was crying. Was it for a lost love, for a friendship broken or simply that she had been more frightened by that headlong gallop than she was ready to admit?

She set off for Norfolk the next day, determined to put Harry and Anne and all such distractions behind her and enjoy the visit; slowly, as the miles passed, she felt calmer. She sat beside her aunt with Lucy facing them, Aunt Lane's hatbox and jewellery case on the seat beside the maid and the boot filled with trunks and portmanteaux. Jane wondered why they needed so much baggage for a two-week stay, but her aunt insisted they must be prepared for every eventuality.

'Mr Allworthy will no doubt wish to take you out and

about and introduce you to his neighbours,' she had said. 'He might hold a ball or a formal dinner party or arrange a picnic and then there is riding and walking and carriage rides. We must always be appropriately dressed.' It sounded as if her aunt expected them to be paraded for everyone's inspection, and her heart sank.

Mr Allworthy had arranged the post horses when he passed that way the week before and everything worked smoothly. They rattled through Woodford and then took Epping Forest at a gallop for fear of highwaymen, before slowing down to enter Sawbridgeworth, where they stopped for a meal. After that, they passed through Bishop's Stortford and Great Chesterford and in the early evening arrived in Cambridge, where Mr Allworthy had arranged for them to stay overnight at the Blue Boar.

Once north of Ely and its majestic cathedral, which Jane insisted on stopping to visit, they found themselves travelling through a countryside so flat, there was nothing to see for miles but fields and dykes, interspersed with isolated farms. Above them and all round them was a huge sky, dark blue fading to a pale grey haze on the horizon, through which the morning sun tried to penetrate. After their next change of horses at Downham, they left the fens behind and were soon in a countryside that pleased Jane more. The sun came out and bathed the country in warmth.

Here were gentle hills, small woods and farms whose fields were surrounded by hedgerows and everywhere workers were bringing in the hay, loading it on to hay-wains. The hedgerows were festooned with wisps of it, which had been caught up as the carts passed along the narrow roads. Twenty minutes later they came to a tiny village, and just beyond that the gates of Coprise Manor.

The journey was over and Jane sat forward to catch her first glimpse of the house.

Built of red brick and surrounded by a narrow moat, it was squat and square, with a round tower in each corner. Its mullioned windows gleamed in the sun. There were formal gardens on two sides, a wood on a third and a great lake on the fourth that fed the moat. The coach rattled over the bridge and into a courtyard where Donald stood to greet them, wearing a brown riding coat and leather breeches tucked into riding boots. He was hatless.

He hurried to open the coach door and let down the step before Hoskins could do so, and extended his hand to Mrs Lane. 'Welcome, ladies, welcome.'

Aunt Lane stepped down, followed by Jane. Both stood looking about them. The courtyard was in the centre of the building, surrounded on four sides by the walls of the house. The main door, a vast oak affair that looked as though it might withstand a battering ram, faced the bridge over which they had entered; here were half a dozen servants standing in line. Their host offered each lady an arm and led them forward and proceeded to name all the servants and their duties. It made Jane think of a bride being introduced to her new domain and realised with dismay that was how Donald meant her to feel.

'You must be hungry,' he said as they entered the hall, which had a wide carved staircase right in front of them and a corridor leading off on either side. 'Martha will show you up to your rooms and help your maid unpack. There is hot water and everything you need to refresh yourselves, but if there is anything I have failed to provide, please tell me so and I will remedy the deficiency at once. It is my dearest wish that you should feel at home.' He handed them over to his housekeeper, who conducted them up the stairs to the rooms that had been allotted to them. 'When you are ready, we will have dinner.'

'He is determined to please,' Aunt Lane said, when they were alone in Jane's room. It was furnished with heavy oak furniture, including a four-poster bed. The sheets and bed coverings were new and everywhere gleamed with polish. 'I cannot fault the arrangements.'

They dined in country style. Aunt Lane had no criticism of his table or his manners, and afterwards Donald showed them all over the house, which was more ancient than Jane had expected. All its furniture was old and heavy, but it perfectly suited the house and everywhere gleamed with polish. 'My father bought the property with a wind-fall he had from dealings on the 'Change,' he told them. 'And the furniture came with it.'

'I had thought it was the old family home,' Aunt Lane said. 'You are related to Viscount Denderfield, are you not?'

He seemed a little disconcerted by the question, but quickly recovered. 'The relationship is a distant one,' he said. 'As I understand it, a hundred and seventy years ago the family became divided, two brothers fought on different sides in the war between king and parliament and neither branch has acknowledged the other since. My father always hoped for a reconciliation, but it was not to be—' He broke off, noticing that Jane had set her foot on the stairs to the tower. 'Miss Hemingford, I beg you not to go up there, it is unsafe. If you would like to see the view, I will conduct you there myself, but shall we leave it until tomorrow? It is growing dusk now and you will not be able to see much.'

This was obviously sensible and they returned to the drawing room on the ground floor and settled down to conversation over the tea cups, during which they discussed how he planned to entertain them in the following two weeks. At ten o'clock more refreshment was brought in and soon after that they retired to bed. 'Country hours,' her aunt commented as they made their way, candles in hand, to their rooms. 'I think I shall read in my room; if I go to bed now, I shall be awake at dawn.'

That suited Jane, who had asked if she might borrow a mount and ride out before breakfast.

She was awake at six and downstairs clad in her new habit by seven. Donald was waiting for her, dressed for riding. 'Good morning, my dear. Did you sleep well?'

'Like a log,' she said, not quite truthfully because she had had a lot to think about and the silence after London was as disturbing as the noise of night-time traffic passing along Duke Street, but the country air had won in the end. 'I am looking forward to my ride.'

He led her to a stable block, almost as pristine as the house, where two horses were already saddled for them. Five minutes later they were trotting across the bridge. If it occurred to Jane that she ought to have had a chaperon, she dismissed it. They were in the country and in the country there was no danger, either from ruffians or from the man who rode beside her.

The early morning air was clear and heady as wine and Donald was a perfect escort, pointing places out to her, stopping to comment on the wayside flowers, giving her their Latin names, talking about the farm, not in a condescending way, but as if he knew she would be interested. Which she was. And when they returned to the house he fulfilled his promise to take her to see the view from the north tower, conducting her up the narrow stair to a small room at the top.

She crossed the room to look out of the window over rolling countryside. 'Why, I do believe I can see the sea,' she said, catching sight of sparkling water. 'How far away is it?'

'Five or six miles as the crow flies,' he said. 'But it is The Wash, not the open sea.'

'And there is a ship out there, I can see its sails.'

He picked up a telescope from the table and trained it out to sea. 'It is early,' he murmured.

'Early?'

'It is a cargo ship. I have an interest in the freight it carries.'

'Oh, do let me see.'

He handed her the telescope and she trained it on the vessel. It looked small at that distance, its sails bowed out as it used the wind to sail westwards. 'Where will it put in?'

'King's Lynn. I expect it will dock tomorrow.'

'Shall you go to meet it?'

'Yes. Would you like to come?'

'Yes, if Aunt Lane agrees.'

The outing was a pleasant carriage ride and Jane enjoyed the sights and sounds of the busy port. There were hundreds of vessels, fishing boats, lighters and cargo boats in the harbour and seafaring men and dock workers scurried about their business. 'They export all manner of produce,' Mr Allworthy explained. 'Corn and wool principally, but also manufactured goods. And they import things like wine and tea.' He paused as one of the dockers came towards the carriage, obviously intent on speaking to him. 'Would you and your aunt care to wait in the carriage while I do my business? It will not take many minutes and then I shall be free to show you round.'

He left them and they watched as he had an animated conversation with the man, before leaving him to go aboard a vessel on whose side Jane noticed the name, *Fair Trader*. A few minutes later he rejoined them. 'All very satisfactory,' he said, smiling easily. 'Now, shall we take a stroll?'

He helped them from the carriage and offered an arm to each lady and they walked towards the town. The streets were narrow but well paved and there were a good number of shops and hotels. From the London road they turned on to an avenue lined with lime and chestnut trees and continued to the inner bank of the ancient town walls. Here they rested on a seat in the shade before returning to the carriage and the ride back to Coprise Manor. Mr Allworthy was a perfect guide and host and Jane's anxieties faded to nothing. London seemed a long, long way away.

Harry strode off towards Horse Guards. He could no longer fight in the field, but surely he could continue to serve his country in other ways? The problem had been taxing his brain ever since he returned home. When he wasn't thinking of Jane, that was. While he had been away he had almost convinced himself their parting was the best thing for both of them. They had been too young to know what they really wanted. In London in 1808, away from home for the first time, he had been glad to see someone he knew, someone safe and comfortable to be with, someone who was not for ever scolding him for his shortcomings, or looking down their noses because he was a mere lieutenant. Jane had looked up to him, hung on his every word, until the scandal broke and then she had angrily turned him away. He had dealt with it by enlisting and enthusiastically embracing the life of a soldier.

Since his return, seeing and talking to her again, he had known there could be no other woman for him. Oh, he might pretend he did not care that she had found someone else, might deny his feelings, might even assure Jane herself that he had no interest in her, but it was all a pose, his way of dealing with it. She was in his blood and in his bone, in the very essence of the man he was; she was not so easily dismissed. Anne knew that, but then Anne was his twin and they had always been close enough to read each other's minds. It made no difference. What had happened in the past could not be undone, harsh words could not be unsaid, and Jane's imminent engagement to Allworthy could not be refuted. That had been the final straw.

He squared his shoulders as he turned into Horse Guards, glad that he had decided to wear his uniform. The place was busy, with officers going hither and thither with sheafs of paper, others standing conferring in groups, still more standing about or sitting disconsolately waiting to be seen. There was a lieutenant sitting at a table, evidently there to ask everyone's business and direct them wherever they should go. Harry approached him, gave his name, asked to see Colonel Clarence Garfitt and was told to wait.

He paced the floor, if his limping gait could be called pacing, and tried to assemble his arguments, expecting a long wait, but it was only a few minutes before he heard his name. 'Harry Hemingford, by God! It's good to see you.'

Harry turned to face the officer who had dashed down the stairs to greet him. 'Colonel, your servant.' Clarence had done very well for himself and Harry wondered fleetingly if he had bought his colonelcy by the back door. He did not doubt there were other avenues besides dukes' mistresses; captain to colonel in the space of two years was a pretty sharp rise.

'I read your intelligence reports and first class they were, but nothing since you were reported lost. You must tell me all about it, but not now. There is a big panic on to get reinforcements out to Wellington; he is pushing forward again, you know.'

'Yes, I did know.'

'I will meet you at Boodle's. Three o'clock suit you?'

It left Harry kicking his heels for two hours, which he decided to spend sparring at Gentleman Jackson's; there was nothing like physical exercise to clear the brain. At five minutes to three o'clock he wandered into Boodle's and found an empty table in the corner of the dining room, ordered a bottle of claret and sat down to wait.

Clarence strolled in at five past and joined him. 'Have you ordered food?' he asked as he sat down.

'No, waiting for you. I'm told the beef pie and the pork chops are both good.'

They ordered and it was not until they were tucking into the pie that Clarence looked up and raised his glass. 'Your health, Hemingford. Tell me what you've been up to since we last met. Two years ago, it must be.'

'You know it was.'

'Yes, but it soon blew over. You did not have to resign, though on reflection I think the Prince of Wales was relieved, considering he imagines he is in command of the regiment. It reflected on him. It was why he did not step in to help his brother, though he has since reinstated him...'

'We don't need to go into that again, Colonel, all over and done with.'

'And now, I suppose, you want me to use my influence to get you a company?' he said, when Harry finished.

Harry smiled and tapped his wounded leg. 'Not possible, I am afraid, not active service, but I would like you to use your influence in another way. I want something to do, something useful. Anything. Intelligence, perhaps.'

Garfitt sipped his claret, looking thoughtful. 'There is something…'

'Go on.'

'Not abroad. Here in England. What do you know about guns?'

Harry laughed. 'As much as any rifleman, perhaps more than most.' He had been an excellent shot ever since the gamekeeper at Sutton Park decided he was old enough and strong enough to hold a sporting gun. When he could hit a target with consistent accuracy, he had been allowed to try his hand at something that moved, pigeons for the most part. Then he had been taught to stalk his prey—deer, rabbits, bigger birds—until he could beat his mentor. It was why he had made such a good rifleman, why he had often been chosen to lead small patrols, to creep silently on the enemy and take them unawares. He could stalk an enemy patrol unseen and unheard for miles, and he could pick off a lookout from a window or a tower at two hundred yards.

'There is someone running guns to the enemy. The navy recently intercepted a shipload of rifles intended for Calais. We don't know who is behind it nor where the weapons are being manufactured and bought. If you could discover that for us and bring the traitor to justice…'

'Glad to be of service,' Harry said, his heart quickening at the idea. 'Tell me all you know.'

'That is the trouble, we know very little. The cargo we intercepted was not shipped from London, it was probably one of the east-coast ports. The crates were labelled umbrellas. I do not know if we are looking for an umbrella manufacturer with a neat little sideline or an arms manufacturer who is making twice as many as he is licensed to do. Ezekiel Baker has the contract for the bulk of the army's supplies, but there are others. I can give you a list.'

'I need a cover, something to hide behind,' Harry said, thinking quickly as he warmed to his subject. 'An interest in the manufacture of an improved rifle, perhaps. I could make it known that I was interested in developing a superior gun, one that could be loaded from the breech...'

'There are people working on that idea already, it is a long way from being perfected.'

'I know. If I went to the War Department and asked them to fund such a development, what would they say?'

Clarence laughed. 'You know the department. They would not put up the blunt before they had seen the finished product and knew it worked.'

'Then I let it be known I am bitterly resentful. I do not have the wherewithal to finance myself and am looking for funding elsewhere. Nor am I particular as to who provides it. Do you think that would serve?'

'Probably, if the word went round. I will send you that list and leave you to do whatever you think fit.'

Harry returned home, his head spinning and his thigh aching. But he was more cheerful than he had been for some time. He found Anne sitting in the drawing room with her needlepoint on a frame in front of her, though the needle in her hand was idle. She looked up as he came wearily into the room and flung himself on a sofa.

'You are exhausted,' she said. He looked white and drawn and his eyes were full of pain. It was not simply physical tiredness that ailed him, she knew. She supposed it was seeing Jane again and knowing she had gone off with that mushroom, Allworthy, that was pulling him down, making it more difficult for him to regain his health and strength. 'I think you should go home and see Grandpapa. A rest in the country will do you good. It will give that wound time to heal properly.'

'I'd rather face a dozen Frenchmen armed with muskets than that old man,' he said, unable to tell her the real reason why he was not free to go.

'Don't be a ninny. He cannot eat you.'

He considered it. Sutton Park was in Lincolnshire, near enough to check on the busy ports of Wisbech and King's Lynn. It might not be such a bad idea, after all. He chuckled suddenly and for a moment he looked more like his old self. 'Very well, so long as you come too.'

'Of course I will. You need looking after. And I shall make sure you rest properly and then we will come back in time for the Regent's banquet at Carlton House.'

'Great heavens, you have never been invited to that, have you?' The Regent, fat and fifty, having decided that his father was never going to get over his madness and that he was king in all but name, had decided to hold a banquet to celebrate. Everyone among London's *ton* was waiting with breath bated for an invitation and for the last week the talk had been of nothing else.

'Not only me but you too, to represent Grandpapa. The invitation came while you were out.'

'I cannot believe it.'

'It is true. Look at this.' She produced a huge gilt-edged invitation card from the mantel where she had propped it against a porcelain figure of a milkmaid with a cow. 'It just goes to show you have been forgiven for your earlier indiscretion and are now the hero of the hour.'

He laughed. 'Hero, eh? I wonder how that will go down with those I hope to persuade to help fund my little scheme.'

'What little scheme?'

He had done enough intelligence missions in the past to know how vital it was to maintain secrecy; though he knew he could trust Anne, he decided, for safety's sake, not to tell her his real mission, but to stick with his cover story. He sat down opposite her and explained about his idea for a new gun and the need to find a backer. While he talked he grew animated; the tiredness seemed to leave him, and Anne marvelled. So this was his way of coping with Jane's betrayal, she decided, this was how he masked his hurt. There he was talking about guns, very little of which she understood, and there was Jane pretending to be in love with Donald Allworthy. If only she could get them in the same room, she would knock their heads together and make them see what was staring them in the face. 'You think the Regent might be interested?'

'In making rifles?' Harry laughed. 'You would have more chance of gaining an ear there if you were selling gold braid or field marshal's batons. No, I must look elsewhere.'

'Why don't you put the idea to Grandfather?' she suggested. 'He will be a better bet than bankers and money lenders.' She could not understand why he laughed.

It was surprising how swiftly two weeks passed. There was no grand ball, but her aunt had been right about the entertainments; they had ridden out almost every day, had walked the whole way round the lake, paid calls to Donald's near neighbours, gone for more than one picnic, been entertained at musical evenings and dinners, attended a botanical lecture in Holt, and had tea with an old general who fought the battles of thirty years before all over again and flirted outrageously with Aunt Lane.

'You must not mind him,' Donald said, when they left and were riding back to Coprise Manor in his carriage. 'He is harmless.'

Jane smiled and turned to look out of the carriage window at the landscape just fading into dusk, a dark purple kind of dusk which made her think it might rain. Their stay had been perfect, their host perfect, their every want satisfied and yet... What was missing?

She was still pondering as she went to bed on the last night of their stay. It was too perfect. Surely, the man had a little fault, something she could latch on to and say, 'That I cannot tolerate, for that I cannot marry you.' But there was nothing. She had no reason to refuse him. He had said he would make her love him. Had he succeeded? Even if she was not head over heels in love with him, she liked and respected him, and as her aunt had so succinctly pointed out, she could not afford to be particular.

She woke next morning to hear the rain lashing against the casement. It was as if the heavens had decided her idyll had gone on long enough and she must come back to earth and her humdrum life as her father's scribe. But it needn't be. She had only to say yes and she could live here permanently. She dressed and went down to breakfast.

Donald was already at the table, but he rose and kissed her hand and took her to her seat. 'Did you sleep? I was afraid the thunder would keep you awake.'

'I did not hear it.' She looked at his handsome but inscrutable face. 'I have loved being here. It is such a lovely house and everyone has been so agreeable.'

'Enough to make you wish to make it your home?'

'Mr Allworthy, I beg you to be patient a little longer.' She turned as her aunt bustled into the room. 'Good morning, Aunt. Did you hear the thunder?'

'Indeed I did. I barely slept a wink.'

'Perhaps you would prefer not to travel today?' Donald said. 'You are welcome to extend your stay.'

'Thank you, Mr Allworthy, but the post horses have all been arranged and the Countess is expecting me the day after tomorrow. She has invited a few friends to see her in her court dress before she goes to the Regent's banquet.'

'And Papa is expecting me,' Jane put in, smiling at the thought of the pretentious Countess showing off her finery. 'But you will come back to London soon, Mr Allworthy?'

'Not until after the harvest, I am afraid. But I shall come, you may depend upon it and, in the meantime, if you allow it, I shall write frequently.'

'Of course.'

'Expect me in the third week of August and by then I hope you will have arrived at a decision.' He rose, went to a side table and picked up a small box that he took over to her. 'A gift to be a remembrance of me until we meet again,' he said. 'It came in on the *Fair Trader*.'

She held it in her hands. 'But Mr Allworthy...'

'Please open it.'

She did so and found herself gazing at an exquisite necklace in silver and amethyst. 'Sir, I cannot accept this,' she said. 'It is too costly. It is the sort of gift—'

'The sort of gift a man in love might give to the woman he hopes to marry.'

'But I have not said I will marry you.'

'No, but you did say I might hope and you would not have come here if you had been intending to refuse me.'

He put his hands over hers, enclosing the box, and held them there, looking at her with an expression of such tenderness that she did not have the heart to thrust it back at him. She looked at Aunt Lane, hoping she might help her out, but her aunt was nodding and smiling.

'Thank you,' she said. 'It is beautiful.'

'Wear it while you travel home and think of me, waiting here in expectation of your answer.' He took it from its box and fastened it about her neck.

She touched it with her fingers. It was cold and hard and a small knot of hardness grew inside her chest and a voice in her head whispered, 'Traitor!'

'It's pelting with rain.'

'Do you think we should delay setting out?'

'If we don't, we'll miss the Regent's banquet.'

'I don't care a pin for the banquet, but with Grandfather being so obdurate, I really cannot stay a moment longer.'

The Earl of Bostock had received his errant grandson with a jaundiced eye, but he had not forbidden him the house. 'You are here now,' he had said ungraciously when Anne had produced him, like a rabbit popping up out of a burrow. 'Might as well stay.'

It was anything but welcoming, but Anne knew the old man was pleased to see the prodigal; he simply found it difficult to say so. She had spent the first meal they had taken together telling him of her brother's exploits; when she became too enthusiastic Harry broke in to correct her, making the old man smile. 'So, it made a man of you, did it?' he asked.

'I hope so, sir.'

'What now? Going to settle down, are you? Find yourself a wife and give me a great-grandchild. Now *that* would prove you are a man.' He had chuckled aloud and beckoned a servant to refill his wine glass. 'If I thought you would do that, I might restore your full allowance.'

The Earl had never stopped his allowance completely, though he had threatened to do so more than once. Harry had been managing on a much smaller amount and his captain's pay, now reduced to half, and though the extra money would be welcome, he would not be bribed. 'Not at the moment. I have other plans…'

'Oh?' The old man had put down his glass and eyed him warily.

'Harry has this wonderful idea for winning the war,' Anne said.

'Sis, that's coming it too brown,' Harry put in quickly.

'I will be the judge of that,' the old man said. 'Let me hear about it.'

Harry would rather not have involved him, but as Anne had mentioned it, he gave him the same outline of his plans he had given to Anne, at the end of which his grandfather laughed. 'So it's blunt you want, is it? I might have known you would not come back just to see an old man.'

'Grandfather, that's not true,' Anne said. 'Harry would have come anyway.'

'Be silent, miss, and let him speak for himself.'

'Yes, Anne,' Harry said. 'Let me explain.'

He had done his best, said he could not have come back before, being a soldier on active service, but that did not mean he did not wish them to be reconciled. He thought his grandfather would be glad to know he was going to do something useful.

'A tradesman, by God!' the old man had said. 'You are my heir, you should be here, taking up your responsibilities on the estate. I am getting old and shall soon stick my spoon in the wall—'

'Grandfather, no!' Anne cried.

He ignored her and continued to address Harry. 'Sutton Park is not entailed, you know. I can leave it elsewhere.' He meant Jane's father, who was his nephew and next in line after Harry, though what James Hemingford would make of it was uncertain.

'You must do as you think fit, sir. But if I have no expectations, then it is all the more important to have independent means, is it not?'

'And if you think that will make me change my mind, you are mistaken, young man. You are an aristocrat—if you cannot behave like one, then I wash my hands of you. And do not come to me when you swallow a spider.'

Harry was as stubborn as his grandfather and, to Anne's infinite sorrow, he had prepared to return to London.

They set off in the pouring rain, going back the way they had come, by stage, but when they reached Boston, instead of joining the main road to London, Harry announced he intended to visit King's Lynn. 'I know someone there who might help me,' he said and because she knew how important it was to him, Anne agreed. It meant taking a cross-country route, but he reckoned it would not add above a day to the journey. However, after they transferred to the local conveyance, she was not sure it was a good idea.

The coach was heavy and unsprung and its upholstery minimal and, to add to their discomforts, the rain continued unabated. Every time the coach door was opened for someone to enter or leave, the rain blew in and before long there was a puddle on the floor and Anne's skirt was sodden. By the time they reached King's Lynn and pulled into the yard of the King's Head, Anne was decidedly wet and grumpy.

Harry bespoke rooms for them and left her to change

her clothes and rest. 'If I am late back, don't wait for me. Go to bed, you look all in.'

She overslept and was woken by Harry hammering on her door. It was a minute before she could rouse herself. Her head ached, her eyes stung and her limbs felt heavy as lead and she knew she had caught a cold. By that time her brother was in the room and fretting round her, blaming himself. 'Oh, do stop fussing, Harry,' she said. 'I am not dying. Go down and have your breakfast, I will be down myself directly.'

It was more than an hour before she could force herself to get up and another half an hour before she finally entered the dining room to join her brother. She shrugged aside his concern and insisted on going on, but by the time they reached Cambridge she was done in. They went into the Blue Boar and he went off to see about a room for them, leaving her in the dining room. She had not been there more than two minutes when Mrs Lane and Jane came into the inn for refreshment, having set off from Coprise early that morning.

'Anne, what are you doing here?' Jane asked.

'We've been to visit Grandfather.' She nodded towards Harry returning from his errand. 'We are on our way back to London.'

If he was surprised to see them, he did not show it. 'Mrs Lane, Miss Hemingford, your obedient.'

'Captain Hemingford.' Jane knew if she attempted anything like a curtsy or a smile, she would come unstuck, fall to pieces, talk gibberish. How could she let herself down like that? He was nothing to her, not any more, and if it had not been for Anne, she might have been tempted to cut him. Her friend looked ill and she immediately forgot they had quarrelled. 'Anne, dear, you do not look at all the thing.'

'It is this confounded weather,' Harry put in, noticing Jane's heightened colour and the way she refused to look at him. Had his time as a soldier made him so uncouth, so odious? 'We do not keep a carriage in London, and if we had borrowed Grandfather's coach we would have had to arrange to send it back; it seemed easier to take the stage. It would not have mattered if the weather had been fine. Now Anne has taken cold and I do not know what to do for the best: go back to Grandfather, go on, or stay here.'

'Don't be a clunch,' Anne retorted thickly. 'I am certainly not staying here and it is just as far to go back as it is to go on. And we have an important engagement in London, you recall.'

'Oh, you poor dear,' Jane said. 'There is nothing worse than not feeling up to snuff when travelling.' Jane turned to her aunt. 'Could Anne not come with us? It would be much more comfortable and quicker than the stage.'

'I could not trouble you...' Anne looked from her to Harry and then to Mrs Lane.

'It is no trouble,' Mrs Lane agreed. 'We can easily make room for you, if you do not have much baggage.'

'Hardly any at all.'

'Then it is settled.' She paused and looked towards Harry. 'Captain Hemingford, you are welcome to ride up beside Hoskins. Your sister will undoubtedly be glad of your presence when we arrive in London.' And having thus disposed of everyone, like a commander on a battlefield, she ordered refreshment.

Half an hour later, with the boot full of luggage, more strapped to the roof and Lucy with the jewel case on her lap and Anne beside her in its place, Harry cheerfully climbed up to share the driving seat with their driver and they set off again. There was nothing Jane could say against it. It seemed days ago, not hours, since she had left Coprise and Mr Allworthy. Only by touching the necklace was she able to bring him back to mind.

Chapter Four

Jane was worried about Anne; she looked so ill and it was obvious that every jolt of the carriage was making her head hurt. Whenever they stopped, Harry went into the inn to fetch a hot drink for her and hot bricks for her feet. 'It's my fault,' he told Jane at one stop, while they were waiting for water to be heated. 'I should not have taken her to King's Lynn, not in that weather.'

'No, you should not,' she said sharply, wondering what he had been doing in that town. 'But it is done now. Let us hope it is nothing more than a catch-cold.'

'Amen to that,' he said fervently. 'You know, Jane, she was the only one to stand by me over that scandal, the only one. She had faith in me, you see. Without her I should not have come through.'

Jane knew his words were aimed at her. She had not stood by him; she had shouted and wept and sent him away. If she had really loved him, she would not have done that, she would have ignored all her well-meaning friends and relations who advised her to break off the engagement. Should she feel guilty? No, she told herself over and over again; he had deceived her by visiting that woman secretly, then tried to deny it and that had been his crime, not what had gone before, and she had done the right and proper thing. 'She is your twin,' she said now. 'I should have been very surprised if she had not.'

The flannel-wrapped bricks were brought to them and he carried them out to the coach, put them carefully under Anne's feet and they resumed their journey.

They arrived in Bishop's Stortford hours later than they should have been. The innkeeper told them gruffly he couldn't keep post horses standing idle and they had all gone out—they must either wait for fresh ones or go on with what they had. Jane was anxious about Anne and thought the sooner she was home and in her own bed with her own servants round her, the better. Besides, Harry unsettled her and it was all she could do to remember that she was all but engaged to Donald Allworthy.

It was Anne herself who decided the matter. 'I long for a bed,' she said in a husky voice. 'If I could only sleep for a few hours, I would feel better in the morning. If we go on and the poor horses collapse in some out-of-the-way place, we shall be in worse straits.'

'She is right,' Aunt Lane put in. 'Do go and bespeak beds for us all, Captain. If we set out early in the morning, we should be home by ten. I am not expected at the Countess's until the afternoon.'

Jane helped Anne to bed as soon as the rooms were prepared, dosed her with a tisane and then settled down to sit with her until she fell asleep. 'You do not need to stay with me,' Anne said thickly. 'Go down and eat with your aunt and Harry,' and, when Jane demurred, 'I shall be perfectly all right. All I need is a good night's rest. And if you do not rescue Harry, your aunt will talk him to death.'

'Oh, I am sure he can hold his own.'

'Are you afraid?'

'Afraid?' Jane repeated. 'What have I to be afraid of?'

'Of yourself, your own feelings, of being thought soft, of relenting by the smallest degree.'

'You must be more ill than I realised, you are rambling.'

'So, I am rambling. Then leave me to ramble alone and go down to the dining room and have some supper. You must be hungry.'

Jane was hungry, and it was true she was also afraid, which was very foolish of her. She had nothing to be afraid of. It would have been different if she still loved Harry and had been waiting for him to come back to her, ready to throw herself into his arms as soon as he appeared, which of course was unthinkable. There was no reason at all why she should not join him and her aunt. 'Very well,' she said slowly. 'I'll go to please you. If you need anything, call Lucy, she is in the room next door and she will fetch me.'

After going back to her own room to change out of the dusty gown she had been wearing all day, brush her hair and tie it back with a mauve ribbon, she made her way down to the dining room, ignoring the quick fluttering of her heart that made her slightly breathless. The room was crowded with people either staying or simply waiting for coaches to arrive or horses to be changed. There were well-dressed families, gentlemen on their own, women who could not be exactly described as ladies and working men in moleskin trousers and fustian coats, some of whom looked very rough. It was a moment or two before she spotted her aunt and Harry, seated at a corner table.

He had his back to the door and had not seen Jane arrive, but some sixth sense told him she was there and he turned to watch her approach. Her gown was in a pale shade of lilac, trimmed with coffee-coloured lace. It set off a glorious body, a body that had matured in the two years since he had last seen her. From being a girl just out of the schoolroom, she had blossomed into a woman he could sigh for. Did sigh for. He moved his glance upwards. Her hair was just prevented from being unruly by a couple of combs and a length of ribbon, but some of it had escaped and was framing her oval face. There was a soft blush on her cheeks and her expressive green eyes were fringed with dark lashes and in the poorly lit dining room seemed to have a light of their own. It was a moment or two before he remembered his manners and rose to pull out a chair for her. 'Miss Hemingford. I am glad you could join us. How is Anne?'

She accepted his ministrations with a smile, apparently in total control of herself. The control was almost lost when he sat next to her and his pantaloon-clad thigh brushed against her skirts. 'The tisane is making her drowsy,' she said, recovering quickly. 'I think she will sleep and that will do her more good than any medicine.'

'I have been telling Mrs Lane how grateful I am to you both—'

'Nonsense! Anne is my dear friend. I would do anything I could for her.' She nearly added, 'Even to having supper with her brother', but decided that would be unkind.

But he knew what was in her mind, for he laughed. 'Even to sharing a meal with her reprobate brother!'

A waiter came to take their order. Jane asked for a little roast chicken and vegetables, her aunt plumped for the lamb and Harry asked for beef and oyster pie. After consulting the ladies, he ordered a bottle of hock for himself and ratafia for them.

'And how did you find your grandfather, the Earl?' Mrs Lane asked, when they had been served.

'As cantankerous as ever,' he said, laughing. 'If Anne had not been there to soften him, I doubt I would have been allowed over the doorstep.'

'You are still disinherited, then?'

'Am I?' he queried, half-mockingly. 'Do you know, I had not realised it?'

'You sound as if you do not care,' Jane said.

'I do not. If my grandfather wishes to leave the estate elsewhere, who am I to quarrel with his decision?'

'What will you do, then?'

'No doubt I shall find something to pass my time.' He paused. He did not want to talk about himself or what he had undertaken to do, he wanted to hear about her. 'What about you?'

'I have been helping Papa with his work. It is a comparison of the different religions of the world and how in many ways they are similar. I do not pretend to understand half the arguments, but what I do comprehend is very enlightening.'

'And do you go out and about in Society?'

'Of course she does,' Aunt Lane put in before Jane could reply. 'She is very popular, you know. The number of eligibles we have had to fight off is prodigious.'

'But now the right man has come along.' He smiled, though it was an effort. 'I collect a betrothal is imminent.'

Jane did not know what to say. If she said yes, she would definitely commit herself, but if she said no, he would think... She stopped her foolish thoughts; he did not want her, any more than she wanted him, not now. 'It is not imminent,' she said. 'We have decided to wait until the end of the Season.'

'Oh, I see.' Instead of eating her supper she was fiddling with the necklace she was wearing, he noticed, as if she wanted to gain strength from it. It would not have been out of place in a ballroom, enhancing her creamy throat, but here, in a posting inn, it was incongruous and a temptation to thieves. Some of the occupants of this room were quite capable of taking it from her. He felt an almost overwhelming desire to snatch her hand from it and rip it from her neck. 'How was your stay in Norfolk?'

'Delightful,' she said. 'We went out and about everywhere, paying calls on Mr Allworthy's friends, who were all very welcoming. We attended a botanical lecture which was very interesting, made a visit to King's Lynn where Mr Allworthy has an interest in one of the cargo ships, and we went walking and riding. The countryside around Coprise is very pleasant and luckily the weather was beautiful until yesterday—' She stopped suddenly, realising she had been babbling.

'It has made up for it since,' Mrs Lane put in. 'I do not believe it has stopped raining for twenty-four hours. The roads will be awash.'

'Yes, but perhaps it will have stopped by tomorrow. I do not know what I shall do if Anne is not well enough to travel.'

'If she is not, then I shall stay with her,' Jane said. 'If you are in a hurry to return to London, Captain Hemingford, you may go on alone.'

'I am not in such haste that I would abandon my sister,' he snapped. 'No one is more important to me. Now, if you will excuse me, I shall go and see how she is.' And with that, he stood up, bowed to them and hurried away.

'Living with common soldiers has not improved his manners,' Aunt Lane said.

'He is worried about Anne,' Jane said mildly. 'And I did provoke him.'

* * *

Harry was angry with himself for allowing her to goad him into being rude. She had managed to upset his hard-won equilibrium. Enemy gunfire, hunger and cold had not upset him half as much. Not even the ostracism he had received immediately after the scandal broke had affected him in the same way as one angry word from her. Two years of battling, not only with the French but also with his emotions, had been for nothing. But it had. In one thing his grandfather had been right, it had made a man out of the boy. He had come back determined to put his past life behind him. The lazy life of one of Society's favourites, the conviction that he could enjoy himself without the need to work, the fanaticism about fashion and the snobbery of it all, would no longer satisfy him. If Jane and others like her could not stomach the change, then bad cess to them.

He went to Anne's room, but, though she was hot, she was sleeping, so he retired to his own bed and lay there, thinking of his visit to King's Lynn. Funny that Jane and Allworthy should be there too. If he had gone a day or two earlier he might have run into them. In the event it had been a wasted journey, and he wished he had never made it because it had resulted in Anne taking cold.

He could spread the word of his disappointment that no one would back him and hope it would bring the rats out of their holes, but the odds were very long. On the other hand, pretending to be bitter and resentful would not help his restitution in Society, which had apparently begun with that invitation to the Regent's banquet. It would only take one tattler of a courtier to remind his Highness that this was the man who had brought disgrace on the regiment he had graced with his name, and it would be over before it had properly begun. He did not care for his own sake, but for Anne and his grandfather. In any case, it looked as though Anne would not be fit to travel, let alone go to a banquet, and he could not and would not leave her, for all Jane Hemingford had implied that he might.

Anne was slightly better the next morning and insisted on continuing the journey. As soon as they had breakfasted, more hot bricks and warm blankets were acquired and they set off in glorious sunshine, though the roads were full of puddles and the trees dripped water.

Aunt Lane was her usual talkative self and did not seem to notice the silence of the other three. Lucy, of course, would not speak unless addressed, Anne was feeling too ill to bother and Jane was thinking of Donald. He had sent her home in the sure knowledge that she would eventually accept his proposal. And why should she not? Surely not because of the man who was sitting on the box of the coach in which they travelled, talking to Hoskins as if they had always been lifelong friends. She could hear his voice, though not what he said, and the occasional laugh. Harry was easily moved to laughter and just as easily roused to anger, unlike Donald, who was always calm and courteous; Mr Allworthy would never dream of raising his voice, either in anger or merriment. He was always so reasonable. And he had said he loved her.

Then why was she not happy? Why was she prevaricating? She refused to entertain the idea it had anything to do with Captain Harry Hemingford, who had come back from the wars an embittered man. He might deny it, but she knew it was true. The past still haunted him. It was why he had all but ignored her at breakfast and wished himself anywhere but sharing a journey with her. Well, she did not wish it any more than he did!

They stopped for the usual changes of horses, though the arrangements that had been so carefully made no longer worked because of their change of schedule, but Harry, who had become used to being obeyed, soon had the innkeepers and ostlers running about after him. 'I am on my way to see the Regent; if I am detained he will want to know the reason why,' he said in an imperious voice. 'Find fresh horses at once. I don't care where you get them from, just get them.' And thus it was a gentleman going north who was obliged to wait for his horses so that Aunt Lane's carriage could continue its journey.

'What did he mean about the Regent?' Aunt Lane mused, voicing the question that had been in Jane's mind too.

Anne smiled wanly. 'We were supposed to be going to the banquet at Carlton House.'

'Good heavens! Do you mean to say you have been invited?'

'We would hardly go without an invitation.'

'But that must mean the Regent has forgiven your brother.'

'Why should he not? He has forgiven his own brother, so why not mine? I know which of the two was most at fault.'

'And you were looking forward to it,' Jane put in, when she realised her aunt was so thunderstruck she had flopped back in her seat and was applying her fan vigorously to her hot face.

'Yes, of course. It is not every day one is invited to dine with royalty.'

Jane did not think Anne would be well enough to go, but she was not given the chance to say so. Everything happened at once. They had been travelling through woods and had arrived at a very dense part where the trees almost met overhead, when they heard the sound of riders coming up behind them. Their driver slowed and pulled in to allow them to pass on the narrow road, but instead of passing, they rode alongside, their black riding cloaks flying out behind them and eyes covered by masks. 'Highwaymen,' Lucy shrieked. 'We'll all be murdered!'

One of them men, apparently their leader, waved a pistol at Hoskins and commanded him to stop. The four women in the coach stared at each other when, instead of obeying, he whipped the horses into a gallop that flung them about like rag dolls and had them clinging to each other in terror. But a laden coach could not outrun galloping horsemen and a pistol shot and the yelled command, 'Pull up, if you want to live!' brought the coach to a shuddering halt.

Jane risked a look out of the window. There were three robbers; one was reloading his pistol, the second was training his gun on Hoskins and the third was pointing his gun at Harry. 'Get down,' he commanded.

The coachman hurriedly obeyed, but Harry hesitated; it was not in his nature to give way to threats and his mind was working fast. He was no match for three men, two of whom had loaded pistols, and he had to consider the women. He risked a glance down at the coach. Jane had her head out of the door and that cursed necklace was dangling from her neck like an open invitation!

The robber noticed the direction of Harry's glance and his eyes gleamed with avarice. Still training his gun on Harry, he moved forward to rip the pendant from Jane's neck. His inattention, though only momentary, was long enough for Harry to launch himself on top of him and bring him down. They rolled together on the ground, trading blows, first one on top and then the other. The man who had fired his pistol was busy reloading it, while the other dare not shoot for fear of hitting the wrong man.

Aunt Lane was screaming fit to burst out of her stays, Lucy was hugging herself and moaning and Anne's already pale face had lost the last vestige of its colour.

Only Jane retained her wits and she could see the man's gun had been knocked from his grasp and was lying just under the carriage. Making sure the other two would-be robbers were busy watching the scuffle, she opened the door, sprang down and seized the weapon. But having picked it up, she did not know what to do with it. She stood pointing it at one of the men, her hand shaking visibly. She hadn't intended to fire it, but there was a flash and a bang that sent her reeling and the man yelled and fell from his horse. His own gun went flying from his hand and was grabbed by Hoskins, who had obeyed instructions to sit on the ground with his hands on his head.

Horrified at what she had done, Jane dropped the smoking pistol and stood transfixed. The man with the half-loaded gun, seeing the tables had been turned, put spurs to his horse and disappeared into the trees.

Harry finally overcame the leader of the gang with a blow to his chin, which would have felled an ox, and stood up, 'Tie them up,' he commanded Hoskins before going over to Jane, dabbing at a cut on his cheek with his handkerchief. There was a bruise on his mouth and another on his forehead, his jacket was torn and there were more red marks on his hands and arms where he had parried blows. 'Are you hurt?' he asked.

'No.' She was shaking violently. 'Thank you.'

'That was a fool thing to do,' he said, shocked by the enormity of what she had done. 'You could have been shot yourself.'

'So could you. You threw yourself at that man and I could not sit by and do nothing to help.' She wanted to fling herself into his arms and sob her heart out. She had injured another human being and she felt overwhelmed with guilt. 'I did not mean to hit anyone.'

'Then let us be thankful your aim was poor; if you had not floored the rogue and if the other had not run away…' He wished he dare take her in his arms, cradle her head against his chest until she stopped trembling, but he knew she would rebuff him. 'Now, we must decide what to do about those two,' he added, indicating the robbers. The leader was trussed up with a rope that was kept in the boot to tie luggage on the roof and Hoskins was about to start on the other one.

'Will he be all right?' she asked, indicating the wounded man.

'Right enough to stand trial. It is only a flesh wound in his leg.' He could hear Lucy sobbing and Mrs Lane's sharp voice telling the girl to pull herself together, just as if she had not been shrieking herself not five minutes before. 'I assume everyone else is all right?'

'Frightened.'

He grinned. 'And you were not?'

'I was terrified. But I think I had better see what I can do to help that poor man.'

'That poor man, as you call him, was bent on robbing you and he would not have hesitated to shoot anyone who got in his way.'

'All the same, I must see to him.'

'Then for goodness' sake take that necklace off and put it somewhere safe. If you had not been flaunting it—'

'I was not flaunting it,' she retorted. 'Mr Allworthy asked me to wear it in remembrance of him.'

'Then he is a fool!'

'I won't have you speaking of him like that. He is a kind and generous man.'

'Who nearly got us all killed.'

'Oh, there is no talking to you,' she snapped. Taking off the necklace, she took it to the coach and handed it silently to Aunt Lane before going to bend over the wounded man to see what she could do to help him. He had pulled off his mask and was revealed as a young man of about twenty, with a mop of fair hair and pale blue eyes clouded with pain. 'I am sorry,' she said, bending to examine his leg. The bullet appeared to have gone clean through the flesh of his calf and torn the muscle, but it did not look as though it had touched bone, although there was a great deal of blood and it was obviously painful. 'I did not mean to hurt you.'

He grinned. 'Then I should hate to be in your sights if you did mean it.'

'You should not have tried to rob us, you know. The ladies in the coach are in great distress. But I will do what I can to make you more comfortable' She went back to Harry, who was reassuring himself that Anne and the others were not hurt. 'Captain, will you be so good as to fetch my portmanteau from the boot? I have a cambric petticoat in there which I can use for bandages and there are scissors in my workbox.'

'You are never going to doctor him?' Aunt Lane was horrified at the idea.

'I must help him. I wounded him and he'll bleed to death if something is not done. I could not bear to have his death on my conscience.'

'He would have killed you and thought nothing of it.'

'I do not think so. He was as frightened as I was. No doubt he was coerced by that other ruffian.' She left them and went round to the back of the coach where Harry had her portmanteau on the ground. 'I have seen the older man before,' she told him. 'It was in King's Lynn. On the docks near the *Fair Trader*. But if he was, what is he doing here?'

'Jumped ship, perhaps,' he said laconically.

'Perhaps.' She picked a petticoat out of her case, tore a large strip off it and took the rest of it and the scissors to Lucy and instructed her to cut it into bandages. Then she went back to her patient and made a pad of the cloth to staunch the flow of blood.

The man submitted stoically as she pressed the pad on the wound. 'You are more than a pretty little thing, ain't you?' he grunted. 'It is almost worth being shot to have such an angel of mercy to tend my wounds.'

'That's enough of your impertinence,' Harry growled, watching her at work. 'Think yourself fortunate you are being looked after, for if I had my way I'd leave you where you fell.'

Jane took the bandages from Lucy and finished binding up the wounded leg. 'There,' she said. 'That will do until you can be seen by a doctor.'

She looked up at Harry to find him grinning broadly. 'Oh, Jane, my sweet girl, you are too good to be true. The man is a criminal. He does not deserve your compassion.'

She stood up beside him. 'He is a human being and he has been hurt. *I* hurt him.'

'I am a human being and I was hurt,' he said softly. 'I do not remember you being so gentle with me.'

She turned to look at him and was unable to make up her mind whether he was roasting her or making a serious point. Whichever it was, it reminded her of something she had tried hard to forget and had failed miserably in doing. She did not answer him, but put her head in the air and climbed back into the coach. Now the danger was past, the hysterics forgotten, they were all telling each other how exciting it had been and how brave Captain Hemingford was. Mrs Lane, in particular, was inclined to amend her previous poor opinion of him. 'We would have been robbed of everything we possessed if it had not been for your brother,' she told Anne, who was sitting quietly in the corner wishing for her bed. 'He was brave as a lion.'

'Naturally he was,' Anne said. 'I never expected anything else from him.'

Harry and the coachman had caught the robbers' horses, but though the older one was able to ride, even with his hands tied, it was plainly too much for the wounded man and the climb on to the driving seat of the coach was impossible. 'We might squeeze five into the carriage if everyone was fit and healthy,' Jane said. 'But Anne is ill and the young man's leg needs to be kept up or he will bleed again.'

Harry realised the truth of this. 'If you would consent to ride up beside Hoskins,' he said. 'I will ride the other horse.'

'Oh, then he shall teach me to tool a coach,' she said irrepressibly.

A few minutes later, everyone was organised. The wounded man sat beside Lucy with Mrs Lane opposite him, determined not to take her eyes off him for a single second, while Anne was bundled in rugs in the opposite corner. Jane climbed up beside Hoskins.

Their coachman was a thickset man in his early forties, but he was happy as a lark to have a pretty girl beside him and, as soon as they left the forest behind, gave way to her entreaties to be allowed to take the ribbons. She had driven her father's gig in the country and once Harry had allowed her to drive his curricle on the estate roads, but neither experience was anything like driving a coach and four. She listened to his instructions carefully and allowed him to put a gnarled hand over hers to guide her, but she loved the sensation of being in control. It allowed her to put to the back of her mind her lack of control where Harry Hemingford was concerned. She was sorry when Hoskins took over again to take them into Epping.

The leader of the robbers, who could not guide his horse with his hands tied behind his back, was being led by Harry who questioned him as they rode. He learned the man was not a seaman but a docker, and had been engaged on loading the *Fair Trader* and its cargo. 'Wine and tea and precious jewels,' he told Harry. 'Not all of it on the manifest.'

So, it was a smuggler's ship. 'What do they take out?'

He shrugged. 'Manufactured goods: woollen cloth, ornaments, mirrors, umbrellas and walking sticks.'

'Umbrellas and walking sticks?'

'That's what we were told. The nabobs and Indians like them.'

'You're a long way from port. What made you change your lay?'

The man shrugged. 'Had a disagreement with the ship's owner. We took the risks and he reaped the benefit. That ain't right, now, is it?'

This was very interesting information and Harry studied the man for several seconds before speaking again. 'Supposing I let you go, would you do something for me?'

'Depends what it is. And what about my mate? Can't leave 'im to go to rumbo on 'is own, now, can I?'

'He can go too. All I want is information.'

'Then let's 'ear it.'

Harry explained what he wanted and how much he would pay for it, at the end of which the man, who said his name was Jerry Thoms, nodded agreement. 'Smugglin's one thing,' he said. 'A keg or two of brandy and a few cases o' tea comin' in is one thing, but we don't hold with sendin' no guns to the Frenchies, not nohow. I'm your man and Dick will be too when I tells 'im.'

'Do you have anywhere you can stay while his wound mends?'

'Yes. There's a certain wench at the Hungry Horse, if you would be so good as to take us there.'

Instead of going to the town gaol, Harry directed Hoskins to take the coach to the Hungry Horse, where the two men were left. 'They did not manage to steal anything,' he explained to the ladies. 'I had not the heart to send them to gaol and almost certain hanging.'

Jane was glad; she did not like the idea of the young man going to prison, especially after she had wounded him. Aunt Lane was not so sure, but she knew if they handed the men over to the law, they would probably have to give evidence to a magistrate and that would delay them even further. And she was anxious to call on the Countess as arranged.

They changed the horses and set off again, this time with Jane in the carriage and Harry tooling the coach. He was a good whipster and the miles passed pleasantly. At the last change of horses before London, Harry returned to the ladies in the coach. 'If you do not object,' he said, speaking to Mrs Lane, 'we will go to Bostock House first and leave Anne with Miss Parker and then see you safely home.'

'Oh, no, Anne is coming home with me,' Jane said. 'She needs someone to look after her and, admirable as Miss Parker is, I do not think she can manage on her own. Ask Hoskins to take us straight home. You can send Miss Parker to us later.'

'Jane, please do not put yourself to the trouble…' Anne began, but was quickly silenced.

'It is no trouble, and if I cannot help a friend then I am a poor thing.'

'Mrs Lane?' Harry queried.

'Of course your sister must come to us, I never thought otherwise,' the good lady said.

'But, Harry, what about the banquet?' Anne asked, though it was evident to everyone she was not fit to be out at all, let alone at a banquet. Her nose was blocked and her eyes were streaming.

'To hell with the banquet,' he said, not even bothering to apologise for his language. 'Come on, the sooner we get you to bed and a doctor called, the better.'

As soon as they arrived, Anne was put to bed in Jane's room, while another was prepared for her; the footman was dispatched to bring a doctor; Lucy supervised the unloading of the luggage and Mr Hemingford, emerging from his study, demanded to know why they were a whole day late and what was that rakeshame doing in his house and in no fit state to be seen in civilised society?

'I shall be out of it directly,' Harry said. 'As soon as a doctor has seen my sister.'

It was left to Aunt Lane to explain what had happened and Mr Hemingford returned to his study slightly mollified, telling them to do what they must as long as he was disturbed no more until dinner was ready.

'Is he always like that?' Harry asked Jane.

'Like what?'

'Self-absorbed, indifferent to other people.'

'He is not indifferent. I expect he is in the middle of a difficult piece of work and needs to concentrate.'

Harry did not think so. He began to feel sorry for Jane if that was the way her father normally behaved. No wonder she wanted to be married. But would Allworthy be any less of a petty tyrant than her father?

Doctor Harrison was young, hardly older than his patient. He was also a handsome man, scrupulously clean and with a twinkle of humour in his eye. 'A severe chill,' he said when he returned to the drawing room where Harry waited impatiently for his verdict. 'Keep her in bed and keep her warm. I will leave something to alleviate the symptoms, but rest and good nursing are the best cure.'

'She shall have that,' Jane told him.

'Jane, are you sure you want to do this?' Harry asked, after the physician had gone. 'I can arrange for good nursing at Bostock House.'

'Of course I am sure. The doctor has said she should not be moved, and do you not think she has had enough jolting for one day?'

'Then, may I call and see her?'

'Good heavens, naturally you may, what a silly question. Papa is not an ogre, you know.'

'I was not thinking of your father's lack of a welcome, I have become used to that kind of thing, but of you.'

'Me? Do you think that I would stop you coming? You must have a very poor opinion of me, if you do.'

'Not at all, but we will inevitably meet. And if it is distressful to you, then I will endeavour to come at a time when you are out or busy elsewhere.'

'It is not distressful to me, why should it be?' She was aware, even as she spoke, that she was not being wholly truthful. 'And I do not plan to be out while Anne needs me.'

'I am glad,' he said softly, noticing the colour flare in her cheeks. 'Does that mean you have forgiven me?'

'For what? For your rudeness to me? You have just

saved all our lives, and if not our lives, then our valuables. If you had not been with us, I do not know what we would have done. In the circumstances it would be churlish to hold a few hot words against you.'

'So, I have my uses, after all?'

'What are you trying to make me say?' she demanded, made uncomfortable by his steady gaze. 'You wish for compliments? You would like me to grovel?'

'No, but perhaps that is what you expect of me, but I have to tell you grovelling is something that is not in my nature.'

'I already know that,' she snapped.

'Then if I ask you again if you have forgiven me, will you accept that as the nearest I am likely to come to a good grovel?' He was smiling down into her face, winding her round his thumb, and even knowing that, she could not maintain her animosity. She found herself smiling back at him.

'Oh, do stop acting the fool, Harry. If you are referring to your behaviour when I broke off our engagement, then of course I forgive you. It was a long time ago and we have both grown up since then.'

'So we can be friends again?'

'We can be friends. It will not help Anne's recovery if we are constantly at odds with one another.'

'Thank you.' He bent and brushed his lips lightly against her cheek.

It was only a featherlight pressure, but it sent a surge of heat flowing right through her to her very toes. She felt her insides tighten like a coiled spring that would fly all over the place if she did not keep a tight hold on it. Her breath came out in a gasp and her hands lifted and then fell uselessly to her side. She stepped back from him, away from whatever it was that held her in thrall. 'That does not mean you may take liberties, Captain.'

'A little kiss for old time's sake, you surely do not object to that?'

'Yes, I do. You forget that I am all but promised to another man.'

'I do not forget.' He stood gazing down at her, no longer smiling. 'Are you sure he is the man for you, Jane?'

'Of course. He is kind, considerate, courteous at all times, and generous too.'

'A paragon, then.'

'I have yet to find a fault in him.'

Harry broke the tension by laughing. 'How very boring, my dear.'

'But safe.'

'Ah, you wish to feel safe?'

'Why not?'

'Is this the woman who confronts highwaymen with a pistol? Is this the woman who rides hell for leather across country? Is this the woman who tools a coach and four as if she had been born with ribbons in her hands? That woman did not think of safety. She was fearless.'

'That was different. And I was not fearless. When those highwaymen stopped us I was never so frightened in my life. What I cannot understand is why they chose us. It wasn't as if we had a cache of valuables with us.'

'They did not know that. They saw the necklace you were wearing when we stopped at the inn and supposed we were all plummy. That's what the older one told me.'

'Oh, then you were right. I thought…'

He smiled wryly. 'You thought I was jealous.'

'I did not!'

'Jane, there is no need to fly into the boughs. I was

thinking of your safety, and as safety seems so important to you…'

'I am sorry,' she said, then smiled. 'We are not making a very good hand at being friends, are we?'

'Oh, I think we are doing very well. Friends may be open with each other, may disagree without making a Cheltenham tragedy of it, and still be friends. I was thinking of something Oliver Goldsmith wrote: "Friendship is a disinterested commerce between equals: love an abject intercourse between tyrants and slaves." It is better to be friends, don't you think?'

'Yes.'

'Now, if you will excuse me, I shall go and see Anne before I take my leave, and as soon as I reach home I will send Miss Parker to help you look after her. Where is your aunt? I should bid her farewell.'

'I don't know.' Aunt Lane should have been chaperoning her, but she had disappeared almost as soon as she had spoken to her father. 'Oh, she must have gone to see the Countess of Carringdale in her court dress before she sets out for the banquet. It was why she was so determined to be back in town today.'

'The banquet. I had forgot it. If I hurry, I might not be too late.' And with that he rushed from the room and up the stairs two at a time to see his sister. Jane followed at a more leisurely pace.

Harry was reassuring himself his sister was comfortable when Mrs Lane bustled in, her eyes bright with excitement. 'How is the patient?'

'A little better, thank you,' Anne said.

'I am glad to hear it,' she said, sitting in the chair Harry had just vacated by the bedside. 'Now, I am come to cheer you up by telling you all about the Countess's court gown. It is magnificent. The skirt is at least two yards wide, net over silk, embroidered all over with pearls and silver thread. The bodice has a deep point at the front and the décolletage is so low it is almost indecent, but she assured me it is nothing out of the way. And she has had her hair done up monstrous high, powdered and finished off with three long feathers. She told me they had been obliged to take the seats out of the carriage and put in a little stool, so that they would not hit the roof. And the Earl is in white breeches with a dark blue coat, with yards of gold braid and white silk stockings and high-heeled shoes—'

'My goodness, how old-fashioned!' Jane said. 'Anne, you were never going to dress like that, surely?'

'It is *de rigeur* for court functions,' Mrs Lane said, slightly miffed.

'So it may be for the old ones,' Anne said. 'I could not wear anything so outrageous. But I did have a beautiful gown…' She paused. 'Harry, I will not be denied. Do you go home and send Miss Parker back here with it. Jane shall try it on. It will compensate me a little for not being able to go.' And, as Harry hesitated, looking from her to Jane, she added in a croaky voice, 'Go on, you have no time to dally. Make yourself ready, then come back. I want to see you and make sure you pass muster before you go. I should not like to think of you meeting the Regent with your cravat all awry.'

He opened his mouth to protest, but decided against it. If she was crossed, she might take a turn for the worse and he would never forgive himself.

'Anne, you will make him late,' Jane protested. 'And you have exhausted yourself. You must rest.'

'I will, but promise to let me know immediately Amelia arrives with that gown.'

'Can it not wait until tomorrow?'

'No.' She grabbed Jane's arm in a grip that was surprisingly strong. 'Promise me.'

Jane made the promise and they left her to rest.

Half an hour later, Amelia Parker arrived in a cab, carrying a small valise and the gown wrapped in tissue. She was a thin, middle-aged woman dressed in brown. 'Where is she?' she demanded almost before she was through the front door. 'Where is my lamb?'

Jane took her up to Anne, hoping they might find her asleep, but Anne had heard the door knocker and was sitting up in bed.

'Oh, you poor dear,' Amelia said, hurrying over to her. 'You do not look the thing at all.'

'I am better than I was.'

'You cannot possibly go to that banquet and it is unkind of the Captain to expect it.'

'He does not, Amelia. I want Jane to see my gown.' She sighed. 'I want to look at it and dream of what might have been. Jane, put it on to please me. Pretend you are me.'

Jane knew that to argue would exhaust her friend, so she smiled and gave in. Besides, the temptation to wear the gown that Amelia had unwrapped and laid across a chair was overwhelming. The underdress was made of shining cream satin, the overdress of fine gauze. There were dozens of silk roses sewn in a double line down the front from the high waist and three rows round the hem, the stems and leaves of each one embroidered with silk floss. The train, falling separately from the high waist, was similarly embroidered. The round neckline and the little puffed sleeves were decorated with rows of cream satin ribbon, studded with pearls.

It had looked rich, lying on the chair, but on Jane it

was magnificent. It fitted so well it could have been made for her. She lifted the train over her arm and moved about the room, turning this way and that. 'Oh, Anne, it is lovely. But it must have cost a great deal.'

'I do not know how much it cost. Grandfather paid for it.'

'You will wear it one day for another occasion.' Jane began to struggle with the back fastenings to take it off.

'Don't take it off,' Anne said. 'Put the shoes on too. And let Amelia do your hair. There are some matching roses for that.'

Jane was completely arrayed in everything Anne had intended to wear, including a necklace of pearls, when Harry returned. So absorbed were the two girls they had not heard the door knocker and were taken by surprise when Aunt Lane brought him up to them. 'Here is Captain Hemingford, all ready to—' She stopped suddenly. 'Oh, Jane!'

Harry silently echoed her exclamation. Jane had never looked lovelier. The soft folds of the dress draped themselves bewitchingly over her slim figure. Her eyes were brilliant, her cheeks a soft rose, her pink lips slightly parted as if she was going to speak but had suddenly stopped. Her hair, thick and shining and interlaced with cream silk roses, had been wound into a chignon behind her head, with soft curls in front, one of which lay on her forehead. He simply stood and stared at her.

'Does she not look lovely?' Anne asked her brother.

'Indeed she does.'

He was looking very grand himself in dress uniform. Tight-fitting breeches and stockings did nothing to disguise muscular calves and thighs. The epaulettes on his jacket made his broad shoulders seem even broader. Rows of black braid decorated the jacket and sleeves. It was finished with an orange sash, black buckled shoes and a sword. He had looked good in his lieutenant's uniform two years before and Jane had been proud of him, but this magnificent specimen took her breath away.

'She must go to the banquet in my place.'

'Anne, have you run mad?' It was Jane who uttered what they were all thinking.

'Jane, it is important to Harry and he ought not to go without a partner. It will throw all the Prince's arrangements out and you know how particular he is.'

'Too particular to entertain a cuckoo in the nest.'

'Why should he know? Pretend to be me. His Highness will never know the difference. There will be hundreds of people there, he won't be able to see and speak to everyone, will he?' She was seized with a fit of coughing and had to wait until Jane had helped her drink a little of the cordial placed by her bed before she could go on. 'You will go, won't you?'

'Certainly not! How could you even suggest it?'

'But you are dressed now and it would be a terrible waste to take it off. Harry, you persuade her.'

Jane, realising her friend had manoeuvred her into a corner, turned to Harry, who was laughing. The magnificent upright soldier had turned into the mischievous boy Jane had always known. 'It is all very well for you to laugh…'

'Shall we humour her, Jane?' he asked. 'I fear she will go into a decline if we do not.'

'Jane!' Aunt Lane exclaimed. 'You cannot. You have no invitation.'

'Oh, but I have,' Harry said, producing the card from inside the cocked hat he held under his arm and pretending to scrutinise it. 'Captain Harry Hemingford and Miss

Hemingford, it says. It does not specify which Miss Hemingford.'

'What will Mr Allworthy say?' her aunt asked.

By reminding her of Donald, Aunt Lane could not have said anything more calculated to spark off the contrary quirk in Jane's nature. 'He cannot possibly object, can he? An invitation from the Regent is a command. I shall write and tell him all about it tomorrow.' And with that, she bent and kissed Anne's cheek, curtsied to her aunt and sailed from the room, the magnificent train over her arm. Harry, grinning broadly, followed her.

Chapter Five

Harry had hired a tilbury as soon as he had received the invitation and it was as well he had, for there was not a carriage, cab or chair to be had in the whole of London. Long before they reached the corner of St James's Street and Pall Mall the traffic was building up, all moving slowly in the direction of Carlton House. There were carriages in front and carriages behind and it took over an hour to cover the last fifty yards. Both sides of the street were packed with onlookers, all waiting for a glimpse of the guests arriving, hoping to catch sight of some visiting royal, debating among themselves whether the Regent's estranged wife would appear, or his mistress, Mrs Fitzherbert, or even both!

Neither Harry nor Jane had spoken since he had given the driver their destination. Both were unwilling to begin a conversation that might end in recrimination or dissension, but both knew that they could not spend the whole evening in silence. He was the one to speak first, as the carriage came to a complete halt. 'We shall be lucky if we arrive before they serve the first course,' he said. 'I hope we shall not be refused admission on that count.'

'If we are, there will be hundreds of others in the same

predicament,' she pointed out. 'They can hardly turn so many away.'

'No, you are right. I have no doubt they have allowed ample time for everyone to arrive.'

'I believe it happens every time his Highness entertains, so I expect they are prepared.'

They were talking to each other like strangers, stiff, awkwardly, uncertain how the other would react.

'Why is this banquet so important to you?' she asked. 'Do you hope that it will set the seal on your acceptance back into Society?'

'If, by Society, you are referring to the *ton*, then no, I care little for it. Most of its members are shallow and selfish and think of nothing but fashion and gossip.'

'You used not to think that; you were once very careful of your dress and manners. I collect it was because you cared so much for the opinion of Society you went away.'

'Perhaps.' He had cared, oh, how he had cared! But it was not Society's condemnation that had driven him to enlist, but hers and his determination to prove himself worthy of her. How foolish he had been! She had moved on, found another love, and dragging her off to this banquet was unlikely to alter that.

They began to move forward very slowly, then stopped again, indicating that someone at the head of the queue had left their carriage and it had rattled away. 'So, you do hope to be reinstated in Society?'

'I believe I have already achieved that, except where it matters most to me.'

'Oh.' She paused, wondering what he meant. 'And you hope tonight will remedy that?'

'I have little expectation of it.' He knew they were talking at cross purposes, but he could not tell her that without destroying every gain he had made. Their fragile truce would not survive an altercation about the mistakes of the past. He had repented his folly, but she had been foolish too; she had listened to the stiff-necked, sanctimonious people who told her what to think and feel, instead of listening to her own heart. The trouble was, she was still listening to them.

'I am sorry for that, Harry, truly I am.'

He turned in his seat to look at her. There were street lamps at intervals and lights from windows that spilled across the road; they were not in complete darkness. Her eyes and the gossamer embroidery on her gown seemed to pick up what little light there was. He could see the creaminess of her throat and the outline of her dear face and all he wanted to do was take her in his arms, crush her to him and kiss her until she was breathless. For a brief moment he imagined it, felt her lips on his, her small body pliant in his arms, but then he pulled himself together and smiled slowly. 'It is of no consequence.'

'Then why come at all? What do you hope to gain?'

'Your company for an evening. Is that not enough? I shall have a beautiful woman on my arm, the envy of every man present, even if it is only for one night...'

She was unsure whether to be flattered or annoyed that he was going to use her in that way, to make a point among the *haut monde*. 'But I am not the right woman, Harry. I am the one who made your shame worse and everyone knows it.' Another jolt forward, another stop. There were only two carriages in front of them now and they had reached the end wall of Carlton House. Light was blazing from every window and spilling from the front door on to the carriage at the head of the queue as it disgorged its occupants. 'And they also know Mr Allworthy has offered for me. I am afraid it was very unwise of me to allow you and Anne to inveigle me into coming.'

'You are afraid Mr Allworthy will disapprove?'

'No.' As the carriage immediately in front of them drew up at the door, she began to shake with apprehension. 'Harry, it is not too late. Are you sure you need me?'

'Oh, my dear Jane, be assured, I do need you.' He turned to look at her, smiling. Again she felt there was more behind his words than the words themselves. What was he planning to do? And why drag her into it?

The carriage in front of them, empty now, was driven away and they drew up at the entrance. A magnificently liveried footman came forward to open the door of the carriage and she knew it was too late. Harry stepped down and turned to hold out his hand to help her alight. Together they entered the Regent's residence. The servant who looked at Harry's invitation simply waved them on; he had enough to do to keep people moving forward without questioning their identity.

With Jane endeavouring to keep her train from being trampled on, they found themselves being hustled along with the other guests, every one of them clad in colourful silks and satins and loaded with jewels and feathers. Anne's estimate that there would be hundreds of them fell way below the mark; there were thousands. Only the most favoured were received by the Regent in a room hung with blue silk and decorated with white fleur-de-lys. 'In honour of the French royalty,' Jane heard someone say.

Harry edged forward, taking Jane with him, until they could see the Prince, who was dressed in the highly decorative blue and gold uniform of a field marshal. Fat and foolish though he looked, there was a certain charisma about him, which had nothing to do with the fact that he was the King's heir. He talked animatedly to those nearest to him and seemed in no hurry to begin the banquet, while everyone stood about exchanging the latest *on dit*, wondering if they would be favoured with a word from the Prince. Jane's feet ached and Harry's leg was reminding him that his wound was still new enough to hurt when he had to stand for long periods.

'There is Colonel Garfitt,' he said, indicating a man with bushy side whiskers, standing close to the Regent. 'I need to speak to him, if I can.'

The last thing Jane wanted was to be brought forward and presented to the Regent. It would be dreadful if it came to his notice that she was not the Miss Hemingford he had invited. 'Then I shall stay here and wait for you.'

He disappeared in the crush and Jane found a spot by a pillar where she could remain unnoticed and watch everyone else. There were several reception rooms leading from one another and they were all crammed with people and she amused herself trying to guess who they were. So engrossed was she that she jumped when a voice at her elbow said, 'Jane Hemingford, I declare!' Jane swivelled round to face the Countess of Carringdale, who had lifted her quizzing glass to her eye and was inspecting Jane through it as if she could not believe what she saw.

'Countess.' Jane managed to bend one knee and was nearly overbalanced by someone pushing from behind. Aunt Lane had not exaggerated the Countess's appearance, but since arriving the crush of people had ruined the stately effect; the padding under her skirt had slipped and the construction that held her hair up looked squashed. Taking out the seats from her coach seemed not to have worked.

'What are you doing here?' the Countess went on. 'How did you get in?'

'In the usual way,' Jane answered, piqued by the note of disapproval she detected in the strident voice. 'Through the door.'

'I shall have to speak to Harriet Lane about this. What is the world coming to when almost anyone can push their way into the Royal presence?'

'I am not the one doing the pushing,' Jane said, wondering what her aunt had to do with who did and did not receive invitations from the heir to the throne. 'It is everyone else pushing me. I am endeavouring to stand still.'

'Impertinent, miss. Where is your escort? I assume you have an escort?'

'Oh, indeed, yes, he is with the Regent as we speak.'

The Countess's eyes looked as though they would pop out of her head. 'I did not know Mr Allworthy was on intimate terms with the Prince.'

'Neither did I.' With every word she uttered she was digging herself into a deeper pit and yet she could not help herself. The words were out before she could stop them.

Harry compounded her iniquity by returning at that moment and taking Jane's arm. 'Sorry to be so long,' he said.

'Oh, I have been well entertained. You are not acquainted with the Countess of Carringdale, are you?' She turned to her inquisitor. 'Countess, may I present my cousin, Captain Harry Hemingford?'

The quizzing glass was raised again. 'Bostock's grandson?'

'Countess, your obedient,' he said, making her as elegant a leg as was possible in the confined space.

'Come to grovel, have you?'

As they remembered their earlier conversation, her words were enough to make both Jane and Harry splutter. 'To whom should I grovel, my lady?' he asked, controlling his mirth with an effort.

'His Highness, of course.'

'I bowed. He seemed to think that was enough.'

Jane looked sharply at him. Had he really been received or was he bamming her, or more likely the Countess?

'It is coming to a sad pass when a common soldier is granted an audience with the Regent. He cannot have known who you were.'

'There is nothing common about the British soldier, my lady. His Highness and I are in accord on that point.'

Defeated, she turned to Jane. 'Where is Mr Allworthy?'

'I do believe he is at home in Norfolk.'

'Then I think someone should appraise him of this night's doings. It is not becoming for a gel who is all but engaged to one man to attend functions with another. And without a chaperon.'

'The invitation did not include a chaperon,' Jane said. 'And Harry is my cousin.'

'Second cousin, if I know my peerage.'

Jane gave her a little curtsy. 'I stand corrected, my lady.'

'You should not have accepted the invitation. You must have known it was a mistake.'

'I cannot think the Prince's advisers would make a mistake,' Jane said. 'They are too careful. And I do believe that is the Earl of Carringdale over there and he is looking for you.'

The Countess left them to go to her husband and they breathed a sigh of relief. 'She makes me so angry I do and say outrageous things,' Jane said. 'And Mr Allworthy will hear of it.'

Harry laughed. 'Does that worry you?'

Jane considered the question. 'No. He is not the keeper of my conscience, but I shall write to him tomorrow and tell him all about tonight's banquet. No doubt it will amuse him.'

'Oh, no doubt of it,' he said laconically.

'Did you really speak to the Regent?'

'No, I was gulling the Countess, but I spoke to Colonel Garfitt.'

'What about?'

'Nothing of consequence,' he said airily. There had been no opportunity to talk to the Colonel at any length, but he had arranged to meet him the following day in order to report progress so far, but there was no need for her to know about that. He trusted Jane as he trusted his sister, but he did not want her involved. 'I hoped he might find work for me.'

'I see.' So he wanted to return to active service. She did not know why that idea dismayed her, but it did. 'And did he say he would?'

'He made no promises.'

'I shall be sorry to see you go,' she said softly. 'You have done your duty and should not be expected to return to the field. I am sure there are other things you can do.'

He turned and looked down at her. 'Why, Jane, I do believe you care what happens to me.'

'Of course I care,' she said, feeling herself colouring under his gaze. 'You are my cousin and brother to my dearest friend.'

'Second cousin,' he corrected her and they both laughed, easing the tension.

It was half past two in the morning before they sat down to dine, nearer breakfast time than supper time. Jane was astonished when she saw the table. It had a canal of pure water running down the whole length of it, fed from a silver fountain at its head. Its banks were covered in moss and flowers. Colourful fish swam in its bubbling current. The top table at which the Regent and his special guests sat was behind the head of the fountain and those at the lower end could not see him. News of what he was doing was filtered down from person to person.

'The Princess of Wales is not here,' someone said.

'Did you expect she would be? He hates her.'

'What of Mrs Fitzherbert?'

'She isn't here either.'

'What of the Queen?'

'No. She'd stay with the poor mad King, wouldn't she?'

The extravagance of it all took Jane's breath away and she fell to wondering how much everything had cost and who had paid for it. The silver-gilt plate alone must have cost a fortune and that was before any food had been put on it. If it were public money, and she guessed it might be, it would be better spent on the poor. It made her angry.

It was six in the morning before they rose from the table and eight by the time their carriage arrived at the head of the queue to take them home. 'I was never so tired in my life,' Jane said.

'But it was an experience not to be missed, don't you think? It is not everyone who can say they dined with the Regent. We shall have something to tell Anne and your aunt.'

'I hope Anne is feeling better.'

'Oh, so do I. Do you mind if I come in and see how she is?'

'No, of course not, but I expect she will be asleep.'

Anne had moved to a guest room in their absence, but she was not asleep. She had heard them arriving and was sitting up in bed with a shawl about her shoulders when Jane tapped at the door and put her head round it. 'Come in and tell me all about it,' she said.

'Harry is here.'

'I should hope he is.' And then to Miss Parker, who had been sitting in a chair beside the bed and had evidently been there all night, 'Amelia, go to bed, I am perfectly comfortable.'

Her companion left and Jane sat on the edge of the bed. 'How are you now?'

'Better. But never mind me. Was it a big success?'

Harry had slumped into the chair Miss Parker had vacated. 'It was noisy and extravagant, but Jane was a hit—'

'I was not. No one even noticed me.'

'Gammon! I was the envy of every man there.'

'Well, who was there?'

'Stow the quizzing until tomorrow, Sis. I am dashed tired, only came in to see how you did.' He stood up and ran his hand through his hair, reminding Jane of Harry as a boy, returning home after a day in the fields, grubby, tousled and tired, but happy. They had all three been happy. He bent to kiss Anne's cheek and then turned to take Jane's hand and raise it to his lips. 'Thank you, my dear, you made a tedious evening more than tolerable.' With that, he bowed and was gone.

'So?' Anne asked. 'What was it like? Did you speak to the Regent? Who was there? What did you have to eat? How did you deal with Harry?'

Jane laughed. 'Anne, dear, I am also very tired; we were standing about for hours. Can you bear to wait until I have rested?'

'Oh, how selfish of me. Go to bed, Jane dear, I will be patient.'

Jane knew perfectly well the last of Anne's questions was the one she really wanted answering, but nothing had changed. She and Harry had called a truce, enjoyed each other's company, had been able to laugh at the ancient court clothes of some of the other guests, and express their disgust at the manners of others and agree that it was too lavish by far, when there were people starving to death in some parts of the kingdom. But that was friendship, 'the disinterested commerce between equals', as Harry had said, and could never be anything more. Too much water had flowed under the bridge and could not be made to go backwards.

She went to her own room and, with Lucy's help, took off the borrowed finery and was soon asleep.

It was the middle of the afternoon when Hannah woke her with washing water and hot chocolate. 'It is a lovely day, Miss Jane,' she said, pulling back the heavy curtains. 'Lady Carringdale is downstairs talking to Mrs Lane and Captain Hemingford has come to see his sister.'

Jane completed her toilette in record time and made her way along the corridor to Anne's room. Harry was sitting in the chair beside the bed. He rose when Jane entered. 'Good afternoon, Jane.'

Jane greeted him politely, and then went to stand over Anne. 'How are you, my dear?'

'Better, I think, but so very tired. I cannot think why, when I have done nothing but sleep for the past twenty-four hours.' Her voice was still very husky and when Jane put a hand on her forehead it felt hot and clammy.

'Shall I have the doctor come again?'

'No. I shall be well directly.' She patted the bed beside her. 'Sit down and tell me all about the banquet.'

'Has Harry not told you?'

'Oh, he has said very little. He ate a meal, but he cannot tell me what it consisted of, and he sat between two ladies but he does not know who they were or what they were wearing. And something about a river full of fish…'

Harry laughed. 'I had eyes only for my partner. And by the time we sat down to eat I was so gut-foundered, I did not care what I ate.'

Jane sat down and filled in the detail of the evening, making it sound comical, and they were soon all three laughing.

'But on a more solemn note, we did come face to face with the Countess of Carringdale,' Jane said. 'And she let us know in no uncertain terms what she thought of us. According to her, his Highness has run mad, inviting common soldiers to eat with him. By which, I collect, she meant with her.'

'Oh, dear,' Anne said. 'I forgot about her.'

'I believe she is even now filling my aunt's ears with it,' Jane said. 'And she is determined Mr Allworthy shall hear of it.'

'I know, for we arrived at the front door together,' Harry said. 'I bade her good afternoon, but she did not deign to answer.'

'Worse and worse,' Jane said. 'She will tell Mr Allworthy you are never off the front step.'

'But surely your aunt will explain?'

'She will not listen.'

'If Mr Allworthy believes ill of you, then he is not worthy of you,' Anne put in.

'Anne, please do not refine upon it,' Jane said quickly. 'I shall write to Mr Allworthy this very day. And you must rest. We are tiring you.'

Harry took his cue from Jane and they left the sickroom together, though after he had thanked her for looking after his sister they parted on the landing, and he went down to the drawing room where Mrs Lane and the Countess were gossiping over the teacups. He bowed to both, declined tea, and took his leave.

Tired as he had been after being up all night, he had slept very little. He felt as if he was losing control of a situation that was confused enough to start with. He had come back to England with a firm resolve to do something useful to help his country and try to forget what had sent him abroad in the first place. Jane was in the past, part of his childhood and adolescence, with no place in the life of the man he had become. And yet, as soon as he had set eyes on her again, he had known that was not true.

She was as much in his heart and mind as ever she had been and she was managing to push his good intentions right out of his head. He had never expected to be sent back into service, and this instruction to find a traitor was causing more problems than it solved. Anne and his grandfather thought he was going into manufacturing and Jane thought he was longing to escape from her and go back on active service. And now there was the Countess, on her high horse because he had taken Jane to the banquet. He had wanted to give her a treat, a break from her endless copying and looking after her father, but if he were honest with himself, he had used it as an excuse to spend time with her, and in that he had been ably assisted by Anne. But what had he gained by it, except more calumny heaped upon his head and hers? Jane herself was obviously anxious to allay any doubts Allworthy might have about the outing. If she did not intend to accept him, she would not care what he thought.

He turned into Boodle's, found himself a seat in the library, ordered a bottle of wine and picked up a broadsheet to read the latest news from the Peninsula. Wellington had won a victory at Fuentes d'Onoro and the French had been checked at Albuera. The tide of war was turning in the allies' direction and he half wished he could still be out there with them.

He set aside the paper when Clarence Garfitt joined him, slumping heavily into the next chair. 'Hemingford, sorry I am late. I had endless dispatches to read. Wellesley wants more guns and ammunition and we are losing ship-loads to the enemy. It makes my blood boil.'

Harry beckoned to a waiter to bring another glass and, when it arrived, filled it from the bottle. 'Your health, Colonel.'

Garfitt raised his glass and drank deeply before speak-ing. 'Now tell me what progress you have made.'

Harry told him about the highway robbery and the fact that he had recruited the robbers. 'They are going back to King's Lynn to keep watch for suspicious cargo. I have my eye on one vessel in particular. It looks hopeful.'

'Glad to hear that. What is happening about your cover story? Has anyone taken the bait?'

'Not yet. I need to spread the word that I am bitterly disappointed by the government's failure to recognise the potential of what I am offering.'

'I will do what I can, but it will mean the disapproval of the *ton*.'

'It can hardly be worse than it is.'

'Then I wish you luck, my friend.' He finished his wine and stood up. 'I am going to play a hand of whist. Would you like to make a four?'

He ought to go home and go to bed. He was dog-tired and not at his best, but what was there to go home to? An empty house, not even Anne to welcome him. He might as well try his luck. He drained his glass. 'Very well, but I am not playing deep. I have seen too many ruined by that.' At the back of his mind was a tiny voice of caution that sounded unbelievably like Jane's, telling him that gambling was evil and he could not afford another scandal should he ruin himself. Jane, dear, lovable Jane, who always tried to do the right thing, who was so concerned about doing what was proper, she forgot that sometimes you needed to compromise.

In the early hours, two hundred pounds richer, he sent out for a link boy and a chair to take him home; it was unsafe to walk the streets alone at night, especially with money in one's pockets. But it might help to fuel the rumour that he was low in the stirrups and needed cash.

Once in his bed, he fell asleep almost instantly and slept until noon, when he set off for Duke Street, smiling to himself. The tattlers might very well say he was never off the doorstep, but Anne had furnished him with an excuse. Was she as ill as she pretended? He shook the thought from him; she had certainly been very unwell travelling back to London and he had been very worried. Yesterday she had said she was better, so perhaps in a few days she would return home. He did not know if he would be glad or sorry—not about her sickness, of course he was sorry about that, but about her leaving Duke Street.

Jane had avoided meeting the Countess the day before by going to her own room to write to Mr Allworthy. It had been difficult to strike just the right balance between relating the story of the banquet in detail and glossing over it as if it were of little note. She did not want it to sound as if she were making excuses for going, when as far as she could see she did not need excuses. She did not have to account to him where she went. On the other hand, she did not want him to think she had behaved improperly.

And there was the attempted robbery on the way home

from Coprise. How much of that should she tell him? Should she mention the fact that she had recognised one of the robbers as the man he had been talking to on the docks at King's Lynn? In the end she decided to make little of the attempted robbery, assuring him it had come to nothing because of Captain Hemingford's exemplary courage, and then went on to tell him about the banquet, making it as amusing as possible. Once the letter had been sent to the post, she relaxed. Let the Countess do her worst. It was not until the next day that she realised just what the lady had in mind.

'The Countess is very worried for you,' Aunt Lane told her. 'She is afraid you will be led astray by your cousins and become the subject of gossip.'

'And no doubt she will make sure of it,' Jane said. She had spent the morning copying for her father and now he had gone to the public library to consult a reference and she had a little spare time. Most of it she had spent with Anne, but now that Anne was asleep she had come down to join her aunt for tea. 'Aunt, I hope you set her to rights.'

'How could I? I know she is right to be worried. I am myself. I should never have allowed you to go to that banquet last night. It was foolish of me.'

'Why?' She forbore to point out that her aunt could not have stopped her. Only her father could do that and he had shown little interest, believing that at twenty she was old enough to know right from wrong.

'I knew the Countess would be there.'

'Aunt, I do believe you are afraid of her.'

'Afraid of her? Why should I be? I listen to her because she has the ear of Society and people take note of what she says. She can make or break a reputation, you know.'

'Fustian! What I cannot understand is why she is taking such an interest in me? I am nothing to her.'

'Jane, how can you say so? You are kin and she has always believed in the importance of blood ties; she knows them all going back hundreds of years.'

'And is she afraid I am about to taint her precious bloodlines?'

'Jane, please do not climb on your high ropes; it is a terrible failing you have, though where you learned it, I do not know.' She sighed heavily. 'When I told her I was concerned that you seem to be mouldering away at your father's musty books, when you should be married and having children, naturally she took an interest. She is rich as Golden Ball and generous to a fault.'

Jane was not sure where the conversation was leading, but it was definitely leading somewhere. Her aunt was behaving oddly, agitated to the point of not being able to sit still, and yet her small eyes were bright with excitement. What had being rich and generous to do with tattling to Mr Allworthy? She waited.

'Her ladyship has offered to give a ball for you,' her aunt said breathlessly. 'There! What do you think of that?'

Jane was so taken aback she could not speak for a moment and then all she said was, 'A ball?'

'Yes, a dance, with an orchestra and supper and everyone dressed in their finery.'

'You must have misunderstood.'

'No, dear, she was quite explicit. You are to have a ball and everyone will be there. Your engagement to Mr Allworthy will be announced and silence the tattlers.'

'Never. If she thinks she can ride roughshod over me like that…' Jane could not find the words to express her anger and dismay, but neither could she remain silent, which would indicate acquiescence. 'I will not be the object of her condescension. And Mr Allworthy will not have it either. He will not allow me to be browbeaten by that dried-up old goat.'

'Jane!' Aunt Lane was horrified. 'How can you say so? The Countess has offered you nothing but kindness. But she is right when she says you have been allowed too much of your own way. And such language too! No doubt you learned it from that scapegrace cousin Harry.'

'He is not a scapegrace. He is—' She stopped suddenly, asking herself just what Harry was. Her friend, her childhood playmate, her confidant, her cousin. 'He is my friend's brother and therefore my friend too.' She paused and gave a hollow laugh. 'I'll wager he will not be on the guest list.'

'Oh, Jane, please do not be difficult. The Countess can be very waspish if she is crossed. She has already called me weak and indecisive.'

Jane moved over and kissed her aunt's cheek. 'I love you just as you are, Aunt. And she is a dragon to terrorise you so. Take no notice of her.'

'Then accept this ball and thank her ladyship prettily when she comes.'

'What does Papa say?'

'He is in favour. He is as anxious to see you settled as I am. And I believe Mr Allworthy has given him certain undertakings and waived a dowry.'

'Why?'

'Because the young man admires you, Jane. Has he not said so?'

'Yes, he has, but I cannot believe that is all there is to it. What is he hoping for?'

'Jane, why are you so obdurate? It is very generous of the Countess to give a ball for you and it would be the ideal opportunity to make an announcement.'

'But I want to make up my own mind, can you not understand that? There can surely be nothing worse than being locked in an unhappy marriage.'

'What reason have you for supposing that it might be unhappy?'

Jane looked at her aunt and burst into tears. They had been building up for weeks, ever since Mr Allworthy had proposed, building up while she was at Coprise and on the journey home, building up to a crescendo when she found herself at the Regent's banquet and had come face to face with the Countess. She was being torn in two, pushed one way by Anne and another by her aunt, while her father, who might have offered wise counsel, sat on the fence and disappeared to the library when her whole future was being mapped out for her by a stranger. And she could not banish the idea that it was not love which guided her suitor.

Aunt Lane looked startled and then sought to comfort her, putting her arms round her and stroking her hair, but nothing she said could stem the flow. 'Jane, Jane, do not take on so. But you know, this proves you are not happy now. Do you not think that once you have made the decision to accept Mr Allworthy, you will be all smiles again?'

'I do not know.'

'You were not so undecided before Captain Hemingford came back.'

'He has nothing to do with it, nothing at all.' She was very adamant about that.

Mrs Lane breathed a sigh of relief. 'Then shall we wait and see what Mr Allworthy thinks of the plan? The Countess is writing to him today.'

It was too much for Jane. She scrambled to her feet and fled upstairs, to lay sobbing on her bed until there were no more tears to be shed. Then she splashed her face with cold water, tidied her hair and went along the corridor to see Anne.

'You are never going to agree?' Anne said, after Jane had poured out the whole story.

'I don't know. Everyone tells me I should accept Mr Allworthy. Aunt Lane seems to think it is because I have not given him a proper answer that I am all at sixes and sevens and once I have made up my mind—'

'Then make it up. Say you will not have him.'

'If I do that, I shall never marry.'

'There are worse things than being single,' Anne said flatly. 'We will be old maids together. We will dabble in politics and campaign for women's rights and terrorise those men who have the effrontery to disagree with us. We will keep animals and ride to hounds, let our hair grow wild and wear breeches.'

Jane was laughing in spite of the tears which threatened to break out afresh. 'That would set the cat among the pigeons.'

'Be strong, Jane,' Anne said softly. 'It's your life, no one can live it but you, and giving in to everyone will not make you happy.'

'It is all very well for you, Anne, but you do not have to face the Countess. She is a dragon. And I am not at all sure that Aunt Lane is not right and I ought to agree to the marriage.'

'If you do, I shall never speak to you again.' She paused. 'What you need is a breathing space, to get right away.'

'I have only just returned from Coprise.'

'That only made matters worse. I meant right away, where you can have a little peace.'

'Where?'

'I need to regain my strength in the country. Come with me.'

'To Sutton Park?'

'No, to my aunt. She lives on the banks of Lake Windermere and is always asking me to visit her. We could spend our days doing nothing but take long walks and go boating on the lakes.'

The prospect was appealing. 'But how can we bring it about? How can I persuade Papa and Aunt Lane to allow it?'

'I think I need the doctor again, Jane. Will you have him sent for?'

'Oh, I am so sorry, Anne, I have made you ill again, piling all my woes onto you. Why did you not say?'

Anne smiled. 'I am not ill. In fact, I am fully recovered. But I think you are about to catch my cold.'

'Am I?'

'Oh, yes. Just look at you, all red eyed and stuffed up. Take to your bed, Jane dear. I am going to get dressed and give your aunt the sad news.'

Whether it was because Anne had put the idea into her head or that she was truly already sickening, but Jane did develop the cold and this was confirmed by Doctor Harrison, who afterwards spent some time with his previous patient. When the Countess arrived to go over details of the ball, she was met by a very worried Harriet Lane who told her that Anne's illness had been more serious than was at first thought and that Jane had also fallen victim to it. It was apparently very contagious. The news was enough to send the Countess scuttling to safety, all thought of a ball put to one side until the danger was passed.

* * *

'When Jane is sufficiently recovered, I am going to persuade the doctor that she needs country air,' Anne told her brother. He had called to see his sister and was surprised to find her up and about and full of energy and it was Jane who was ill. He was all concern for her and would have gone to her sickbed if such a thing had been allowed, but as it was not, he had to make do with Anne's report delivered in the hall. 'We will go to Aunt Bartrum. Once she is away from London, Lady Carringdale will forget about her and, with luck, she will forget all about Donald Allworthy.'

'Anne,' he admonished. 'Ought you to interfere?'

'Why not? Everyone else is. And she needs a true friend. I am not going to try and persuade her to anything except to consider her own happiness. The calm air of Windermere will do the work for me.'

'How will you travel?'

'Post-chaise, of course. I never spend all my pin money and I can afford it. And to keep us safe from highwaymen, you will be our escort.'

He laughed. 'And Allworthy?'

'I shall write to him as a friend and tell him how the Countess has been pushing Jane so hard she has become ill through it and is in a terrible mull, not knowing which way to turn. I shall suggest that, left in peace for a few weeks, she will undoubtedly come to the right decision. I shall ask him to give her that time. All in his best interests, of course.'

He laughed. 'May you be forgiven.'

'Oh, I am sure I will be,' she said complacently. 'And I have sent Amelia home for a little holiday. She hates Westmorland anyway. There will just be the three of us.'

Nothing was happening in the capital, so perhaps he was best out of it, but he would have to make arrangements for Jerry Thoms to contact him at his aunt's address if he turned anything up. He had also written to one or two armaments manufacturers, asking if he might look over their operations, but their replies would be forwarded to him as a matter of course.

Anne accompanied him to the drawing room where he spent a few minutes with Mrs Lane, thanking her for the good care taken of his sister and hoping Jane would soon be well again, and then he took his leave. An hour later he returned and left a bouquet of flowers for Jane, but he did not stop. He had letters to write, one to Colonel Garfitt to keep him abreast of developments; another to Jerry Thoms at a secret address they had arranged, and a third to his grandfather, requesting the loan of the family travelling coach to take them to Westmorland. He would not allow Anne to use her pin money to pay for post horses and was thankful for the two hundred pounds he had won.

Jane was so worn out she was almost glad to lie in bed and let others do the worrying. 'I am staying to nurse you,' Anne said. 'After all, I have had the fever and am safe from the contagion.'

'I thought it was just a catch-cold. I do not feel as ill as all that.'

Anne grinned. 'A contagious fever sounds better and keeps the Countess away. Even your aunt has been persuaded not to come too close and stands outside your door to ask how you are.'

'Anne, it is not fair to deceive her. She is an old lady.'

'I know and I am sorry, but we cannot have her running to the Countess every five minutes. By the time you are well again, Harry will have made all the arrangements for our journey to Westmorland.'

'Sometimes, Anne, I think you are as bad as the Countess.'

Anne came and sat on the side of her bed and took her hand. 'No, I am not, for I shall not bullock you into marrying against your will. I shall not mention marriage at all, that is a promise. But if you do not want to come with me to Windermere, say so now.'

'Oh, you know I would like to go, but Papa—'

'Oh, he will take the advice of Doctor Harrison, that's what he pays him for.'

'And how did you persuade the doctor to comply?'

'Oh, it was easy,' Anne said loftily, but there was a slight rosiness to her cheeks that made Jane look hard at her, but she decided not to comment. 'He is a great believer in the efficacy of country air and you have no country retreat, have you?'

'No.'

'Harry has sent for the Bostock travelling coach, it is comfortable and roomy and as soon as you are well again we will go. Of course, Grandfather will not let us take it without an escort.'

'Harry?' Jane's heart began to thump. Was she simply jumping out of the frying pan into the fire and taking her problems with her?

'Who else is there? I think he needs a rest too; he is not completely over that wound and it will do him good.'

Who else was there? Jane asked herself. And if being a friend to Harry was the price of Anne's friendship, then it was a price worth paying. They had already proved they could be friends. But would her aunt agree? And her father? Ever since her mother had died, Papa had been afraid of illness of any kind and, like her aunt, had not come into the sickroom. She did not blame him; if he were ill he could not carry on with his important work. And who would do his copying while she was away?

What Anne said to Mr Hemingford she did not divulge, but she was with him at least half an hour, and, in the face of his agreement, Aunt Lane could not object and she was wise enough to realise that mentioning the Countess again would not serve. But she did demur on behalf of Mr Allworthy. 'What will he think of you going off like that?' she asked Jane, as soon as she was allowed in to see the recovering invalid.

'He knows Jane has been very ill,' Anne put in before Jane herself could answer. 'I wrote and told him so. He wanted to come to London, but it is the middle of harvest and he could not get away. I said the doctor had advised country air, and as I was going to the Lakes anyway I proposed to take Jane with me.'

'And he agreed?'

'He wrote to me,' Jane said. 'It was a very loving letter, hoping I would soon be well and saying he would come to London again when I return. He said he would try to be patient.'

'And what did he say about Captain Hemingford accompanying you?'

'Why should that bother him? The Captain is Anne's brother, it is only natural he should escort her. He knows what happened in the past, but he knows it is in the past.'

'I would come with you,' Aunt Lane said. 'But I think I should return to Bath. I have been away too long.'

It sounded as if she were hurt and washing her hands of her recalcitrant niece and Jane was struck with guilt. She reached over to take her aunt's hand. 'Oh, Aunt Lane, you have been so good to me. I shall miss you dreadfully.'

'Indeed, I shall miss you, my child. But you know, all I ever wanted was your happiness.'

'I know.'

The deed was done, the arrangements made and the day dawned for their departure. The Bostock travelling carriage, the last word in comfort, arrived outside the house at Duke Street. The luggage was strapped on, goodbyes said and Jane and Anne, both looking surprisingly healthy, were helped into the coach by Harry, who climbed in with them; with final goodbyes and waved handkerchiefs, they were off. Jane leaned back against the padded seat, to find Harry's smiling eyes on her. Friendship, she told herself, friendship. It was what she needed most.

'Are you fully recovered?' he asked her, taking off his hat and putting it on the seat beside him. It was the first time he had seen her since she had been taken ill and, though it had been little over a week, he had missed her. It was strange how that week seemed to have been longer than the whole two years before. But two years before he had been bolstered by anger and resentment, now there was nothing but tenderness and longing, a longing he had to suppress.

'Oh, yes, thank you. I am looking forward to seeing the Lakes. I believe they are very beautiful.'

'Yes, however, we will take our time getting there, so that you are not jolted too much but please say if you want to stop and rest. Simmonds has ridden ahead to secure post horses and accommodation, but the arrangements can easily be changed.'

She laughed suddenly. It was a joyful sound and lifted his spirits. 'I am quite well and strong,' she said and meant it. She felt stronger than she had for weeks, strong enough to be herself, to make decisions for herself and the first one was to enjoy her holiday.

Chapter Six

Mrs Georgiana Bartrum, younger sister to Anne and Harry's mother, was as unlike Aunt Lane as it was possible to be. She was only thirty-five and still a very handsome woman, with straight dark hair, drawn into a coil at her neck, humorous brown eyes and a ready smile. She was tiny, but what she lacked in height she made up for in energy. As soon as the carriage pulled up at the gate of Lakeshead House, she bustled out to make them welcome.

'So you are come at last,' she said, taking Anne into her arms as she stepped down. 'I thought I would never persuade you.' She turned to Jane as she followed Anne from the coach. 'And you must be Jane. You do not mind me calling you Jane, do you?'

'Not at all, I would prefer it.'

'Anne has written so much about you, I feel we are already good friends. Welcome, welcome to Ambleside. And where is that young shaver of a nephew of mine?'

'Here, Aunt Georgie.' Harry joined them on the gravel and kissed his aunt's cheek. 'I trust I find you well?'

'Of course. I am never ill. Now come inside and tell me all your news over a little refreshment. Todd shall unload your boxes and show your coachman to the stables. Your footman is already here, there is adequate accommodation for them both in the rooms above.' All the time she was talking she was leading them up granite steps towards the door of a square stone-built house. 'You have not brought a maid, I see.'

'No, I did not think we would need one,' Anne said. 'I collect everything used to be informal and we dressed for comfort. If we need help, we can maid each other.'

'Good. I want you to feel entirely at ease while you are here.'

Jane smiled, remembering all the clothes they had taken to Coprise and how she and her aunt were for ever changing their dress for one occasion or another. They had needed Lucy. The next week or two would be very different. Already she was feeling more relaxed.

They were led into a small hall. It gleamed with polish and the scent of the flowers placed in a vase on a side table. There was a staircase straight ahead of them, a door on either side and a corridor presumably leading to more rooms at the back of the house. 'We will have tea and cakes while your luggage is taken up to your rooms,' Mrs Bartrum went on, leading the way into the drawing room and indicating they should be seated. 'Then I will take you up and show you round. Not that there is a great deal to see, the house is little more than a cottage, but it suits Bartrum and me.' This was addressed to Jane. 'He is out, but he will be back directly to make you welcome.'

Harry smiled at her as she seated herself on one of the sofas next to Anne. 'You will have noticed that Aunt Georgie never stops to take breath,' he said. 'I do not know how she manages it.'

'And you are an impudent young rascal,' his aunt admonished him. 'I should have thought being in the army might have taught you some manners.'

He laughed and, flinging up his coat-tails, subsided into a chair. 'That was the last thing it taught me. How to fight, perhaps. And rigorous discipline.'

His aunt laughed. 'And no doubt that came hard to one used to having his own way.'

'It is necessary. Disobedience cannot be tolerated when each man's life depends on his comrades when it comes to a fight.'

'And you were wounded. My poor, dear boy. Are you quite well again?'

'As well as I will ever be.'

'Harry is left with a slight limp,' Anne said. 'But it seems not to discommode him. He can still run after me.'

The refreshments arrived and Jane, who had been enjoying the exchange between her friends and their aunt, accepted a cup of tea and a delicious little honey cake and felt the tiredness drain from her. Here she felt safe. Even Harry had ceased to be a threat to her peace of mind.

He had been a perfect escort on the journey, looking after their welfare, making sure their rooms in the inns where they stayed were clean and the bedding aired, ordering delicious meals and instructing Giles, their coachman, whom he had naturally known since he was boy, to avoid the potholes as far as he was able and not go too fast. On some stretches where he considered there was extra danger from highwaymen or discontented mobs, he had sat on the box beside Giles with a shotgun on his knee.

When he was sharing the carriage with them, he had been a splendid companion, pointing out places of interest, telling them its history, or beguiling them with stories of his time in the army, always careful not to frighten them with gruesome details. It made Jane realise just how much he had changed and how little she had understood him in the few months of their engagement. She had been an immature seventeen and he only one and twenty, much too young to know the difference between real love, the kind that lasted a lifetime, and their childish conception of romance. Did she know it even now? Would she be making the same mistake again if she accepted Donald Allworthy?

'Now, Jane, tell us what you would like to do while you are here,' Mrs Bartrum said, making her put aside her troubled thoughts. 'Do you like to walk? Are you interested in natural science?'

'Yes, indeed.'

'We are going to walk the feet off her,' Harry said. 'And take a boat on the lake.'

'Then do be careful,' his aunt put in. 'Remember Jane has been ill. You must not overtire her. Nor Anne either.'

'I will guard them both with my life, you may depend upon it.'

'You are to stay with us, then?' Jane asked, wondering why she had not thought of it before.

'Of course,' Anne said. 'There is no point in Harry going back to London and then having to return to fetch us home; it is too far. Besides, I think he needs a holiday as much as we do.'

'You do not mind, do you?' Harry asked, cocking his head on one side and smiling at Jane.

'No, of course not.' What else could she say? Harry could be very good company and with his protection they would be able to explore further afield.

'Good,' Mrs Bartrum said. 'Now, here is Bartrum to greet you.'

Mr Bartrum, who had just entered the room, was only

an inch or two taller than his wife. He was dressed in country jacket and leather breeches, but his cravat was pristine and his riding boots highly polished. He had straight grey hair and grey eyes and his smile was gentle. 'Welcome, Miss Hemingford,' he said, taking her hand as she dropped him a small curtsy. 'I trust the journey was not too trying.'

'Not at all, I was well looked after.'

He turned and shook Harry's hand and kissed Anne's cheek. 'Good to see you both. Well, are you?' Without waiting for a reply he went on, addressing his wife, 'That fool, Posset, has been poaching again. He never seems to learn. I had to give him a month in the Bridewell, couldn't let him off with another caution.'

'Oh, dear, I had better go and see what I can do for Mrs Posset. She has eight children,' she added to inform her guests. 'He only poaches to feed them, but Bartrum has to sit in judgement when he is caught. Poaching is a crime, when all's said and done, and the landowners are right to expect him to be punished.'

So Mr Bartrum was a magistrate, Jane realised, and a very lenient one too. She warmed to him as well as to his hospitable wife.

'I will go after dinner,' Mrs Bartrum said as a maid came in to tell them the luggage had been conveyed to their rooms and hot water had been taken up for them. 'Come, girls, I will take you to your room. You do not mind sharing do you?'

'Not at all,' they said together, and followed Mrs Bartrum out of the room and up the stairs.

'Harry can have the smaller room opposite. We naturally keep country hours, so dinner is at three. I will leave you to unpack and change. Come down when you are ready.' And with that she flung open the door of a bedroom and ushered them inside before leaving them to settle in.

'Oh, she is so agreeable,' Jane said, wandering over to the window. 'I never felt so welcome anywhere in my life. And what a view!' The house stood on a slight hill at the northern end of Lake Windermere. She could see almost down its whole glittering length. Small craft bobbed about on its smooth water and beyond it, almost near enough to touch, the hills rose invitingly. She turned back to look at her friend. 'Oh, I am so glad you persuaded me to come.'

Anne came forward and kissed her. 'Good. Now you are not to worry about a thing. And if you do not feel like walking, then please say so and we will find something else to do.'

'Oh, but I want to.'

'Then tomorrow we will make a start. Harry knows all the paths and where the best views are. We can safely leave everything in his hands.'

Harry, in the room across the corridor, was also looking out of the window. It was a view he knew well, but now he was seeing it with new eyes. If he could not live at Sutton Park, he could settle here, among the lakes and craggy fells. He did not need to be in London. But that was the future and before he could settle on that he had to tread a tightrope. Jane must find her own way and he prayed constantly that it would lead to him.

'I thought it always rained in the Lakes,' Jane said, when she woke next morning to find the sun streaming in the window and Anne already up and dressed.

'Not for us,' Anne said. 'For us the weather will be perfect, I have decreed it. Now out of bed with you and dress in something practical for walking and let us go down to breakfast. I heard Harry go down ages ago.'

The Bartums had a little one-horse gig and Harry, dressed in a light wool tailcoat, calfskin breeches and top-boots, borrowed it to take them to Grasmere, where they left it at a local inn and set off on foot, to walk round the lake and up the fells that surrounded it, carrying a small picnic hamper with them.

Occasionally the path was uneven and Harry stopped to take Jane's elbow to help her along. His touch was still capable of making her tremble, but she did not try to shake it off. To do so would be churlish. She smiled and thanked him.

'You are looking better already,' he said. 'I had begun to think you would fade away before my eyes.'

She laughed. 'Oh, I was never as ill as that.'

'But you were so pale, even before that, and your eyes had a haunted look, except when you were riding, of course. Then you came alive again.'

She was reminded of that ride with Donald, but quickly put it from her. She had promised herself she would not think of him until she had been here at least a week, by which time she hoped she would know whether she wanted to marry him or not. 'Is it possible to ride while we are here?' she asked.

'No reason why not. There are sturdy little hill ponies capable of plodding up and down these hills all day. I will ask Aunt Georgie where I can hire some.'

They reached the top of the rise and stood to look at the scene around them. The ground was a mixture of rocky scree and heather-covered grass, scattered with boulders. Below them the shimmer of the lake reflected the sky and the trees that spread along the water's edge. Along the road could be seen a few small cottages, some with paths leading down to the water and little moored craft. They could see people, as small as dolls, moving about their business and, on the lower slopes, walkers like themselves and the white shapes of sheep. The sun was warm on their backs and it was difficult to believe that these hills could be dangerous in bad weather.

'Food,' Harry said, breaking in on their silent contemplation. 'I am hungry as a hunter.' He took off his coat and spread it on the ground for the ladies to sit on, then knelt and opened the basket. From it he took chicken legs, ham pie, crusty bread and butter and a bag of sweet plums from the trees in the Bartrums' garden. 'Fit for the gods,' he said, fitting a corkscrew into a bottle of wine.

In the last few weeks Jane had had little appetite, not only because she was ill but because she was so oppressed. Now she ate hungrily, enjoying the taste of the food and sipping the wine. It was warmer than it should have been, but that did not matter. Afterwards, replete and somnolent, she lay back against a cushion of heather and dozed.

Harry sat and watched her. She was achingly lovely. Her blue muslin dress was absolutely plain, decorated only with a band of ribbon about the high waist, but its very simplicity made it perfect. Her bonnet had fallen off and lay upside down beside her and her hair, escaping from its combs, was spread out on the heather, thick and coppery. Her eyelashes, the same deep colour, lay on sun-kissed cheeks. Fearing she might burn, he opened her parasol and propped it up between two rocks so that it shaded her face.

She felt the shade move across her and opened her eyes. He was kneeling beside her, looking down at her, his eyes dark and soft with tenderness. His lips were slightly parted, his breath a little ragged and a nerve twitched in his cheek. She lay looking back at him, searching his face, too startled to move, too confused to speak.

'The sun is stronger than you think,' he said, breaking the moment in a voice so matter of fact, so down to earth, she thought she must have been dreaming. 'Can't have you burning.'

'Thank you.' She closed her eyes again; it was the only way to avoid that look of his. She knew its meaning and she knew there had been an answering flutter in her own heart, deny it though she might. But up here, away from Society, almost away from civilisation itself, she felt cocooned in a different world, where dreams and reality were intertwined, where being practical and sensible had no place and fantasy reigned. Here she could dream.

He stood up and walked a little way off to where Anne sat leaning against a boulder, surveying the scenery, a slight breeze lifting a tendril of her hair. 'She is very tired,' he murmured, dropping down beside her.

'I am not surprised. She has been put through so much, pulled this way and that, trying to please everyone and quite forgetting her own needs. You have no idea what it is like to be a young unmarried lady, Harry, always trying to be good and obedient, always believing that other people know best because that is what they are constantly telling you.'

'I thought she was stronger than that. She was certainly not weak when it came to sending me away.'

'She had been convinced by others it was the right thing to do and it took courage. Do not blame her.'

'I don't, not now. I did then. I was angry.'

'Angry because you cared so much.'

'And still do.'

'But you are not to upset her, Harry. I promised her we would not speak of it.'

'The last thing I want to do is worry her or hurt her, but it is damned difficult to stand by...'

'But you will, won't you? You will give her time to realise what she truly wants?'

'And if it is Allworthy, after all?'

'It won't be. He is not for her. I know it and she will come to know it too.'

'I hope you are right, but even if she rejects him, I still have a mountain to climb.'

'Patience, brother, patience. Now, I think we should start for home, don't you?'

He rose and collected up the picnic things and repacked the basket, then he gathered a posy of heather and went to wake Jane. 'Wake up, sleeping beauty, time to go home.' His voice was deliberately teasing.

She stirred and smiled sleepily at him. 'I think I must have dozed.'

'It has been good for you.' He held out his hand to help her to rise and then presented her with the posy. 'For luck,' he said.

'Thank you.' She was still not sure what had been dream and what reality, but she was too indolent to care.

They walked slowly back to the village, climbed into the gig and returned to Lakeshead House, pausing on the way to stop and look at Wordsworth's cottage, wondering if they might catch a glimpse of the great poet, but he was not to be seen. They spoke very little, but Mrs Barrum made up for that when they arrived, asking them where they had gone, how far they had walked, when and where they had eaten their picnic. Taking it for granted they would be ravenous, she had ordered a huge supper and they did justice to it before settling in the drawing room to drink tea and listen to Anne playing the old harpsichord which stood in the corner. It was the end of a perfect day.

* * *

The next day was just as good. As soon as breakfast was over, Jane wrote to her father, her aunt and Mr Allworthy to tell them they had arrived safely. Once the letters had been sent to the post, Harry took the girls to Bowness in the gig and hired a little sailing boat. 'I will make sailors of you before the day is out,' he said, helping them aboard.

It was hard work, but they set to with a will and were soon skimming over the water in a light breeze with Harry at the tiller. They put in to a little secluded bay, where they disembarked to eat their picnic. Afterwards, they leaned back and watched a few fluffy white clouds sailing past above their heads, laughed at a family of ducks waddling by and held their breaths as a group of rabbits ventured out on the bank beside them, their fears allayed by the stillness of the watchers.

'If Posset were here, he would take his shotgun to them,' Harry whispered.

'Then I am glad he is not,' Jane whispered back.

The rabbits disappeared as quickly as they had arrived, alerted by the sound of oars and voices as a group of young men rowed past. Almost reluctantly, they returned to the boat and had another sailing lesson, this time on how to tack into the wind, making their slow way back to the landing stage.

Jane was exhausted, every muscle ached, but it was a happy tiredness. She could not fault Harry's behaviour. He had not coddled her or Anne, neither had he expected too much of them. He had praised them when they did well and chaffed them when they made a mistake. Once when Jane let the boom go and it swung out of control almost turning the boat over, he had caught it with commendable swiftness and averted disaster. She had no idea how much effort he was putting into being a disinterested friend when all he wanted to be was a lover.

It was the same every day, and each day Jane felt the tension ease from her until she could join them in reminiscing about their childhood, recalling adventures they had all three enjoyed: the day he had fallen out of a tree chasing a squirrel and broken his arm; the day Jane fell in the river and Harry had pulled her out dripping wet and covered with slimy weed; the day Anne was thrown from her horse after making a wager with Harry that she could jump a particularly high hedge. Neither set of parents had learned of these escapades because they always covered up for each other.

'What dreadful children we were,' Anne said. 'We could have killed ourselves a dozen times over.'

They were returning from a longer jaunt to the coast in the growing dusk and were winding their way across the moors on a very narrow track which was only just wide enough for the gig. Harry had to drive very carefully. 'It is a pity we had to grow up,' he said.

'But we did, and we are still friends,' Anne said. 'Is that not wonderful?'

'Yes,' Jane said, thoughtfully. 'Real friendship endures.'

Every day Jane slipped more and more into a kind of lethargic complacence. She hardly thought of Donald and when she did, thrust the image from her mind, telling herself that there was plenty of time, but time was running out and they could not stay hidden away forever.

The day before they were due to go home, Harry fulfilled his promise to hire ponies. Anne did not care for riding and elected to go shopping in Bowness with her aunt, leaving Jane and Harry to ride alone. It was not galloping terrain and their small round ponies were not suited to it, so they ambled round the head of the lake and into the small wood the other side.

It was cool among the trees and the light, filtering through the overhead branches, had a golden, greenish tinge. There was a smell of mould and slight scuffling sounds she could not identify. 'It is like being in a great green underworld,' she said. 'We could easily become lost.'

'Not while we stay on the path,' he said. 'And there are landmarks.' He pointed to a huge oak tree, its branches making an umbrella many feet wide. 'There are not many as big as that. And a little further on there is a little stone hut, home of a hermit. He will tell your fortune if you provide him with food.'

The hut stood in a small clearing. It had no windows, and a doorway but no door. A wizened old man sat on the ground in the opening. His hair and beard were so long that only his large nose and dark, bright eyes were visible. He wore a ragged cloth coat, which was tied about his middle with a rope, and his feet were bare. He held out a bony hand to them as they approached and dismounted.

'Shall we give him some of our picnic?' Jane asked, filled with compassion for the poor man.

He grabbed the bread and chicken leg as soon as it was offered and ate it greedily. 'Good lady,' he said, waving the bread in Jane's direction.

'I know that,' Harry said.

The old man ignored him and continued to speak to

Jane. 'Sit down by me and I shall tell you what is coming to you.'

Jane glanced at Harry questioningly, but he simply shrugged. She smiled and sat down on the ground in front of the hermit, who put his bony hand out and laid it on top of her head. 'Your head aches,' he said. 'You have a problem to solve.'

'It does not take a special gift to tell that,' Harry said. 'Most people have problems of one sort or another.'

The man was not put off. 'This is a problem of what is right and what is wrong and there is more than one interpretation of it. Right in the eyes of others might not be right in your heart. I have learned that in the years I have been sitting here in solitary contemplation. You are a good woman, you know what is right, but choosing it will not please everyone.'

She had known all that, of course, but it was uncanny how he had managed to put it into words. 'Thank you,' she said, scrambling to her feet and rejoining Harry, who had been watching with tolerant amusement.

'Beware of accidents and meddlers,' the hermit called after her, as she remounted.

'I hope you thought that was worth half your picnic,' Harry said, as they rode away. 'You do not need to be a fortune teller to think up that nonsense.'

'I know, but I suppose he felt he had to give us something in exchange for the food. And really it wasn't nonsense, not about knowing right from wrong.'

'That is something we all have to face. But accidents and meddlers?'

She laughed. 'As soon as he spoke, I was reminded of the Countess of Carringdale.'

'She is certainly a meddler. But you have escaped her clutches, haven't you?'

'I hope so.'

'Why has she got such a hold over your great-aunt?'

'I do not know, except Aunt Lane has always been very attached to her aristocratic connections. They seem to be important to her, perhaps because her husband had no title and she was disappointed by it. And the Countess is such a strong character.'

'But not stronger than you.'

'How can you say so? I ran away rather than face her and it has only postponed a confrontation, not eliminated it.'

'And your heart is doing battle with what other people expect of you. My poor Jane, I feel for you.'

'Let us speak of other things,' she said, unsure whether he was roasting her. 'I promised myself I would not think of Mr Allworthy while I am here.'

'I am in full agreement with that,' he said, then laughed. 'You know I wish we could stay here among the Lakes. I have always been happy visiting my aunt and I could easily make my home here as well as anywhere.'

'What about your grand plan? Anne told me that you had a splendid scheme to develop a new kind of gun.'

He smiled wryly. There was no need to involve her in his scheming, especially as she had been the one to point out that the highwaymen were really disgruntled dockers and that he had put them to work. It could be dangerous for her. On the other hand, Anne had evidently told her about his fictitious plan to start a business and he could not refuse to speak of it. 'My grand plan, as you call it, has been postponed,' he said. 'It needs capital and I have none.'

'You could take your idea to a banker, surely.'

'Bankers demand collateral and I have none.'

'Then you had better marry an heiress.'

He looked at her sharply, wondering if it was meant to be a serious suggestion. 'I could,' he said, deciding to humour her. 'Can you suggest one that might take on an impoverished captain of infantry on half pay?'

'You have the prospect of a title.'

'Would you marry for a title?'

'No. I am not an heiress, but there are many who would.'

'Sorry, Jane, that won't serve. I will not live under the cat's paw because my wife holds the purse strings.'

'How cynical. And how proud...'

'My pride is all I have left.'

'Oh, Harry, I am sorry for that, indeed I am. But you are home again now and should be back to normal.'

'What is normal?'

'You know what I mean. Finding a loving wife, having children, passing your days in interesting ways, helping others less fortunate, looking after your grandfather's estate. He is old, I am sure it would please him.'

'Do you know, you sound just like Anne.'

She laughed. 'I shall take that as a compliment.'

They had been climbing as they rode and now came out of the trees in strong sunlight. It was so bright that for a moment Jane could not focus, but her vision cleared and she realised they had been riding uphill and had come out quite high and before them was a hill of rough brown grass and heather, interspersed with yellow gorse bushes. Above them a kestrel hovered and she reined in to watch it swoop on its tiny prey and fly off with it.

'You think my grand plan is nothing but empty air, then?' he said, as they continued up towards the summit.

'I cannot tell for I do not understand it, but if it gives you something to do...' She paused. 'When Mama died,

Papa was lost, he was alive but not alive, if you know what I mean.'

'Oh, I do,' he said fervently.

'But then he had this idea for his book and his enthusiasm for it carried him through and now he is content in his own way.'

Thinking of Mr Hemingford and his unequivocal preoccupation with his manuscript made him smile, but he did not like the idea that making a better rifle was no more than a pastime to help him overcome his disappointment. 'You think I should write a book?'

'No,' she teased. 'You could never sit still long enough to put a whole sentence together. And you cannot spell.'

'Then it has to be a new gun.'

'Tell me about it.'

He tried to explain the technicalities in plain language, though she did not understand half of it. 'It could save lives,' he finished. 'Shorten the war.'

'It is an implement of death. And after the war, it would still be made and it would finish in the hands of robbers and highwaymen and murderers.'

'So would any guns, improved or not. You cannot get away from that. And there will still be sporting guns. You cannot eliminate guns, Jane.'

'No, I suppose not.' She paused. 'Do you think these animals could be made to trot?'

'Try it and see.'

The pony was surprisingly agreeable and from a trot was persuaded into a short canter, and then Jane dropped back to a walk to negotiate a particularly steep rise. At the top she stopped to look around her. The whole country seemed spread before her, craggy hills, winding roads, flat sheets of water, a little village, isolated cottages, the wood through which they had passed. 'It's magnificent,' she said, dismounting to rest the little pony. 'I wish I could put it into words, or paint it.'

'Can you?' He had dismounted and was standing beside her.

'No, I have no talent for either. I shall have to rely on memory.'

'Then may you always remember it as a happy time.'

'Oh, I shall.' She turned to face him. 'I am so grateful for this, Harry.'

'The pleasure is mine,' he said, reaching out to tuck a strand of hair behind her ear. 'All I want, have ever wanted, is your happiness…'

His eyes, as he looked down at her, had taken on that deep, soft brown that she had seen before and which had so disturbed her, speaking to her more eloquently than words. It was always the same. Whenever she thought they had established a bond of friendship, he said something and did something that spoiled it, made her realise that it could never be that disinterested commerce he had spoken of, but something so different it could not be borne. She was, and always had been, under thrall to him, slave to his tyrant.

'Look how the clouds fly across the landscape and change its colour,' she said, turning away to look at the view again. 'Bright here, dull there, and a moment later they have moved on and it is all different again.' That was how she felt, ever changing under the clouds that hung over her.

He stood beside her, watching the landscape, idly thinking of what she had said. The shadows were scudding at great speed, and then, alerted by a cool wind that had suddenly sprung up from nowhere, he turned and surveyed the horizon behind them. The clouds were massing in grey, purple and magenta, deep and heavy, rolling in over the hills towards them. 'There is a storm coming,' he said. 'We can't stay here.'

He had hardly spoken before a flash of lightning split the clouds, and a moment later a rumble of thunder startled her. The once bright landscape became dark and forbidding; she could see the rain coming, sweeping across the landscape as the shadow of the clouds had done earlier. She reached for her bridle to mount, but the pony was restless and disinclined to cooperate.

'Lead her,' Harry said, raising his voice to make himself heard above the wind. 'Stay close to her head and talk calmly. We'll make for those boulders over there.' He pointed at an outcrop 'They might give us shelter.'

The rain swept across them long before they reached their destination, driving into their faces, running down their necks, soaking them in no time. They ran in between two huge boulders that had a slight overhang, bringing the ponies in as far as they could so they had their backs to the oncoming storm. The thunder and lightning was almost continuous and frightening in its intensity. Jane found herself shivering uncontrollably.

'Oh, my poor darling,' he said, taking off his coat and draping it round her shoulders, holding it there with his arms round her. 'You look like a drowned rat.'

'So do you.' His shirt was wet and flattened against his skin, moulding itself to his shape. He had a strong neck, she noticed, and broad shoulders and his arms were comforting. An extra loud rumble made her jump and bury her head into his chest, where she could hear his heartbeat. It was strong and steady, though a little quick, as hers was. He held her close, stroking his chin over her wet hair and wishing the storm could go on forever.

She turned in his arms and looked up into his face. 'Harry.'

'Yes, my love?'

'There is nothing to be afraid of, is there?'

'No, nothing in the world,' he said. Was she talking about the storm or something else altogether? He tilted her chin up with his forefinger and slowly bent his head to kiss her lips very gently, a butterfly's touch. She did not resist, did not want to resist. She allowed his mouth to move over hers, slowly, adding just a little more pressure, delicately, tenderly, loving her, wanting her to know and understand his love for her, to know that it could not be killed by two and a half years of war, nor under the pressure of outside influence, nor the appearance of a rival. It was eternal. A mere storm could not wash it away.

He had kissed her before, when they had been engaged, before the scandal erupted, lightly, affectionately, but it had been nothing like this explosion of emotion, this fire burning inside her, this melting of everything until she thought her whole body was turning to liquid. Her legs would not support her. She put her arms round his back, feeling the strength of him holding her safe, keeping her upright and whole, and knew she could never love anyone else.

He lifted his head at last, to look into her eyes. They were filled with tears. 'I have made you cry,' he said. 'Forgive me.'

'It's the rain.'

'Of course, the rain.' He smiled. She was not indifferent to him, she loved him still, but would she admit it, would she tell him she still wanted him? 'Jane?'

She pulled herself from his arms, angry with him, angry with herself. 'I think the rain has stopped.' She gave him back his coat, picked up the reins of her pony and, using one of the smaller boulders as a mounting block, pulled herself into the saddle and set off down the hill.

He stood a moment, the sodden coat in his hand, and watched her. Her back was straight, though her hair hung on her shoulders in soaked tresses. Everything was wet, her clothes, the pony, the saddle and the ground beneath its feet. The path, which had been dry loose scree when they came up, was now a rivulet of water rushing down the hill, making the stones wet and slippery. It was too dangerous to ride. He went after her and seized her bridle. 'Get off and walk.'

'Let go.' She tried to wrest the rein from his hand and the pony's hooves began to slip. He grabbed her from the saddle and set her on the ground. The pony cantered off out of harm's way and stood still, facing them, defying them to catch her.

'You little fool!'

'Let me go!' She pummelled at his chest with her fists, but he rode the blows easily. 'I want to go home. Anne will be worried.'

He grabbed her wrists and held them away from him. 'She would be even more worried if you were to break your neck.'

'I'm sorry. I didn't think…' The words were punctuated by sobs.

He took her in his arms again. 'Jane, Jane, what am I to do with you?'

'Take me home. I am cold and wet and—'

'Confused?'

'No.' She refused to admit it. 'What a silly thing to say.'

'Yes, wasn't it?' he said, smiling grimly. 'Now, let us lead these animals until we reach more stable ground.' He caught both mounts and handed over her reins. 'Go behind me and watch where you are putting your feet.'

He set off and she followed. His back was straight, his

steps sure, but she could tell by the tilt of his head and the slope of his shoulders that he was angry. She supposed he had every right to be; she should never have tried to ride on that slippery slope. All she had been thinking about was to get away from him, away from temptation, away from the bittersweet slavery of loving him. He had cast a spell on her, made her forget herself, and she would not forgive him for it. Would never forgive herself for her weakness. The time had come to think of Donald and what she meant to do about him; it could be put off no longer.

They stopped at the hermit's hut. He had retreated a little further into the interior, but he still sat cross-legged on the ground. Jane handed over the uneaten picnic, re-mounted and rode on silently, following Harry out of the trees, round the top of the lake to Lakeshead House, plodding wearily, shivering with cold and misery, though neither would admit to the latter.

They were greeted with cries of relief from Anne and Mrs Bartrum. 'Hot water, up to Miss Hemingford's bed-room,' the lady commanded her servant, ushering Jane upstairs as she spoke, leaving Harry to look after himself. Anne followed and helped Jane strip off and climb into a bath set on the rug. Only when she was clad in a warm undress gown and had been given a medicinal tot of brandy did Anne ask her what had happened.

'We were caught in the storm while we were on the summit. There was no shelter.' She tried to laugh. 'And the ground was so wet after the rain had passed we had to walk our horses and my riding boots are no good for walking.'

'Didn't you see it coming?'

'No. We had stopped to rest our mounts and were looking at the scenery. It came on so swiftly, one minute the sun was shining, the next we were in the middle of it.'

'What were you doing?'

'Doing? Why, nothing. Anne, I did not expect to be roasted as if I had brought the storm on purpose.'

'No, of course not. But you are not telling me everything, are you? When you arrived, I could tell by your expression something had happened. And Harry looked as though he would like to murder someone.'

Jane gave a weak laugh. 'Me, probably.'

'Why? Did you quarrel?'

'Not exactly. I was wet and he put his coat round me and...' She paused and swallowed. 'Anne, he kissed me.'

'The varmint!' Anne laughed.

'It is not a laughing matter.'

Anne became serious. 'No, not if you say it was not. I shall have words to say to my brother on the subject.'

'No!' The word was spoken sharply. 'I do not want him to think I considered it of enough import to report it to you.'

'I see. But it evidently was.'

'It has made me realise that your brother does not know how to behave like a gentleman and I was right to break off the engagement.'

'Of all the reasons you could have dreamed up, that is surely the most illogical.'

'It is very logical.'

'Did you tell him that?'

'No, I did not speak to him on the subject. Nor do I want to. Please, Anne, say no more about it.'

'Very well. Are you going to come down for supper?'

'No, if you do not mind, I'll go straight to bed.'

Anne left her, crossed the landing and knocked lightly on the door of her brother's room. When he bade her enter, she found him sitting in fresh pantaloons and shirt, staring out of the window. 'How are you?' she asked.

'Me? I am perfectly well. I've been wet many times before,' he said. 'And with no means to get dry either. How is Jane?'

'She has come to no harm from the soaking, I think.' She paused. 'But what have you done to her?'

'What has she said?'

'You kissed her.'

'She told you, did she? I couldn't help it, Sis. There she was standing in my arms, wet and shivering, her face tilted up to mine, all shining and, I thought, inviting.'

'You are a fool, you know. I promised her—'

'That we would not mention Allworthy. I didn't. His name never passed my lips, and she spoke it only once and that was to say she didn't want to think about him. She did not object, not to begin with. Then suddenly she was angry and jumped on that pony and set off at a trot. She could have killed herself and I told her so, too.'

'I told you to be patient.'

'Yes, but how long must I stand by and do nothing? say nothing. I want her now.'

'What do you propose to do about it?'

'Apologise, I suppose. Grovel.' She did not understand why he suddenly burst into laughter.

'The apology will have to wait until tomorrow,' she said, ignoring the laughter; he was obviously as distraught as Jane. 'She has retired.'

'Tomorrow, we go home. You said the air of the Lakes would do its work.'

'I believe it has,' she said softly.

He wished she could be right, but he was sure he had cooked his goose. How could a woman of twenty years take offence at something so innocent as a kiss and a kiss given with love, real love, the kind that led to marriage? Was she so artless, so innocent that she thought a kiss condemned her? Or was she reacting as she thought Society expected her to? If she had, then the atmosphere of the Lakes had failed. He had been so sure she was softening towards him. They had laughed a great deal in the last two weeks, teased each other, reminisced, quoted poetry learned at school, smiled at each other, but he had misread all the signs.

'Finish dressing and come down to supper,' she said, interrupting his reverie. 'It is our last night and Aunt and Uncle want to hear all about your adventures.' She laughed. 'Leave out the kissing, though.' She left him.

Slowly he dressed, then left his room. He crossed the landing and stood outside Jane's door, his hand lifted ready to knock, but then he changed his mind and went downstairs to join the company, masking his hurt and confusion with joviality.

Jane lay staring at the ceiling until sleep claimed her at last. But the sleep was full of dreams, dreams of Harry, of ponies and storms and fear. The fear was not of the storm, not of falling from her mount, not of a man with a long tangled beard, though he was there too. And so was Donald Allworthy, holding out a glittering necklace, beckoning to her to come and take it from him. And behind her Harry laughed.

She woke in a cold sweat, but her mind had been made up. She would not marry Mr Allworthy; it was not fair to him. She could not promise to love him, cleave to him and no other, live her life with him, have his children when she was bound to someone else, even if it was impossible to turn to that someone else.

It *was* impossible. She had broken off her engagement to Harry for what she considered good and sufficient reason, and both she and he had been the subject of gossip because of it. Some, including Anne, said he had done nothing bad enough to be punished so harshly, others maintained he had been a rakeshame of the worst order; the men who frequented Mary Anne Clarke's establishment were not respectable. Some people, including her father and Aunt Lane and, she supposed, the Countess of Carringdale through her aunt, had said she should cut him out of her life, he was not worthy of her and she, hurt beyond reason by his conduct, had believed them and sent him away.

Whatever the truth of it, she had made her decision and she would not change it. To do so would bring it all back into the public eye and they would have to live it all over again, just when he was being accepted back into Society and she had the offer of marriage from a good man who loved her. Most important of all, Harry had not said he wanted her back, he had only asked for forgiveness and taken advantage of her when she was wet and cold. He thought she was weak, would succumb to kisses without any commitment, and she could not allow that. She was perfectly aware that her mind was trying to justify her behaviour, running from the truth like a hunted fox runs from the hunters.

The bed beside hers was empty. Anne was already up and dressed. Her box and portmanteau were on the floor, packed and ready to go. Jane rose stiffly, almost reluctantly, washed and dressed, tied her hair back with a ribbon and made her way downstairs. She was not looking forward to that long journey back to London, back to reality. Harry had been so good coming up here, looking after them both, laughing a lot, arguing with his sister, throwing his orders about to innkeepers and ostlers, and no doubt he would be equally solicitous going back, but now it had been spoiled. What would they find to talk about? Would they manage to laugh?

They were gathered in the breakfast parlour waiting for her. She fixed her face in a bright smile. 'I am sorry, I overslept. But my things are all packed, ready to go.' She sat down and accepted a cup of coffee from her hostess, who presided over the pot. 'Thank you for having me, Mrs Bartrum. It has been a…a wonderful experience and quite restored my health.'

'I am so glad, though after yesterday I began to have my doubts. You were so wet and bedraggled.'

She managed a light laugh, though she dare not look at Harry, who was stirring his own coffee absent-mindedly. 'I was well looked after.'

'Yes and I hope he will continue to look after you,' Mr Bartrum said. 'But be careful, Harry, my boy, there is a lot of unrest in Lancashire. The handloom weavers have been breaking machinery again. Avoid the trouble, if you can.'

'I will. It's only a few hotheads, after all. And Simmonds has gone on ahead to arrange the horses; he will alert us if it becomes necessary to change our route.'

Half an hour later, the carriage was brought to the door, their boxes and bags stowed and Mrs Bartrum was hugging them one by one and begging them to come again.

'We will,' Anne said.

Harry fastened a bunch of heather on to the bracket that held the carriage lamp and grinned. 'I want to take a little bit of Westmorland back with us.' Then he handed them in and climbed in with them. A small jolt and cries of goodbye all round and they were on their way.

Chapter Seven

They travelled in silence until they reached their first stop at Kendal. Anne had made a half-hearted attempt at conversation, but had met with so little response she had given up. Jane sat and looked out of the window, while Harry, with his beaver hat on his knee, stared straight ahead, as if he could see something written on the velvet squabs above her head.

It was when he got out to inspect the fresh horses that Anne tackled Jane. 'Are you going to sulk the whole way back to London, Jane?'

'I am not sulking.'

'You are not talking.'

'There is nothing to say.'

'Jane, my brother loves you to distraction. Can you blame him for wanting to kiss you?'

'He does not love me, he said we would be friends, a disinterested commerce between equals, he called it. And he spoiled it all. Friends do not kiss like that.'

'Oh, so you know that, do you?'

'Of course I do. It was…it was…' She stopped in confusion.

'A lover's kiss?'

'Yes.'

'And you hated it?'

She smiled wanly. She had not hated it. She had welcomed it, wanted it to go on, wanted more, much more, and therein lay her dilemma. How could she have been so brazen, so capricious? After telling him as forcefully as she knew how that she would never marry him, how could she have been so weak? Lover's kiss, was how Anne described it, but Harry was not her lover; she had rejected him. 'It was wrong.'

'Why? Because you are engaged to Mr Allworthy?'

'I am not engaged to him.'

'As good as.'

'No.'

'Then be honest, Jane. Did you hate Harry's touch? Did you struggle to free yourself? Did it make you want to be sick?'

'No, of course not.' Her face was fiery red. 'I wish you would not refine upon it so.'

'You have hurt him, Jane.'

'Hurt him? He was not hurt, he was laughing about it. You both were. I heard you.'

Anne looked puzzled. 'When?'

'Last night, after I had gone to bed. You went to his room and enjoyed a joke at my expense.'

'Jane, I am sure we were not laughing at you.' She paused. 'Oh, I remember now. He said he was going to grovel to you. It seemed to touch a nerve and he laughed, but it was not hilarity, not a happy laugh. Oh, Jane he was certainly not in a laughing mood.'

Grovel. She managed a wan smile. 'He does not like to grovel, he told me so.'

'But he was going to do it for you.'

'Why didn't he, then?'

'When has he had the opportunity? You were late down to breakfast and there was no time afterwards when we were in a flurry of leaving and bidding my aunt and uncle goodbye. And you have hardly been encouraging since.'

'It won't change anything.'

Anne smiled. 'It might make the atmosphere in this carriage a great deal more comfortable.'

'I am sorry, Anne.'

'Say that to Harry when he comes back.'

'I meant sorry for not conversing, not for anything else.'

'Are you being deliberately provoking, Jane? You are as bad as he is. I could happily knock your heads together. Now, I am going into the inn for a few minutes; when I return, I expect to continue this journey in a pleasant atmosphere.' And with that she opened the door, stepped down and walked across the inn yard. Jane saw her stop and speak briefly to her brother before disappearing inside. She thought about following her, but found herself unable to move; her limbs would not obey her.

She choked back tears as Harry opened the door and climbed in opposite her. It was a roomy coach, but his knees were almost touching hers and his face, as he leaned forward, was only inches from hers. She turned and gazed out of the window, unwilling to look at him.

'Jane.' He reached out to take her hand, but changed his mind. 'Please do not be angry with me.'

'I am not angry.' It was not anger so much as hurt and confusion, a feeling that she had lost control of a situation she should have been able to manage.

'It looks like anger to me. I am sorry, Jane. I took advantage of the situation in which we found ourselves and that was unforgivable, but I am not sorry I kissed you.'

She turned to face him, eyes blazing. 'You call that an apology?'

'Yes, an abject apology for upsetting you, which I never intended. What more do you want?'

She smiled suddenly. 'You could try grovelling.'

He laughed aloud and slipped on to one knee on the dirty floor of the coach, taking one of her hands in both of his. 'See, I am grovelling. I cannot bear your displeasure. I—' About to say 'love you', he stopped. 'I want us to be friends again. As we were.'

'Oh, do get up, Harry, you look quite foolish down there and you will dirty your clothes.'

'Not until you say you forgive me.'

'I forgive you.'

He risked putting his lips to the back of her hand before releasing it and resuming his seat. 'Thank you.'

'I am sorry too. Anne says I have been sulking and making everyone uncomfortable with my silence.'

'I collect you have much to think about.'

She looked at him sharply and decided not to comment, and then Anne returned to the coach and there was no need. 'In the inn they are talking about rebellion and insurrection and how dangerous it is to travel alone,' she said, as they set off again. 'Do you think we shall be safe?'

'Oh, I think so,' Harry told her. 'We are not mill owners, after all, and it is the mills they are attacking. I am sure travellers going about their lawful business will not be harmed.'

'They tried it before,' Anne said. 'If you and Jane had not acted so swiftly, we could all have been murdered.'

'That was the high toby, not discontented homeworkers afraid to lose their livelihood to machines.'

'What is the difference?' Jane asked. 'They are still

lawless ruffians, bent on destruction, threatening people. I cannot see how offering violence will help to keep them in work.'

'They feel driven to it,' he said. 'The machines are of necessity housed in the mills and they require fewer hands to operate them. The handworkers have been accustomed to labouring at home so that everyone in the family can take part and they are proud of what they produce. Their whole way of life is being threatened and they are afraid. Frightened people are bound to react against whatever it is that is frightening them. It is human nature.'

Jane was thoughtful, not only because she realised Harry was deeply sincere, but because he was right about frightened people reacting to their fear. That was why she had run from him when he kissed her. She had been frightened, frightened of something she did not understand, frightened of her own feelings, frightened of the condemnation of family and friends, because well brought-up young ladies, unmarried young ladies, did not allow themselves to be held tightly in a man's arms to be kissed.

If Mr Allworthy had kissed her like that, would her reaction have been the same? She did not know. She sat looking out of the window and tried very hard to imagine him taking her in his arms and kissing her until she was breathless and crying for more, but the image would not come, the warmth refused to flare. He remained a cold and distant figure.

'Is it true that tiny children work in the mills?' Anne asked her brother.

'Yes, but you see, when they all worked at home, the children joined in the labour; they were used to it. So those parents who have been given work in the mills take their offspring with them. Unfortunately the work is nothing like so congenial as when it was done in the cottages; the children are expected to grub around under the machinery and that is dangerous. There are enlightened mill owners who look after their workers, children included, but they are few. There ought to be legislation.'

'Against the machinery?'

'No, we cannot halt progress. I meant against the employment of children. If the adults were paid properly, there would be no need for children to work.'

'How fortunate we are,' Anne said. 'We have everything we need, clothes, food, houses. I have never had to do a day's work in my life.'

Harry laughed. 'Let us hope you never need to.'

'But Jane works. She spends hours copying her father's manuscript for him.'

'Oh, that is nothing to the point,' Jane said. 'I enjoy it and like to help him. If I did not, I would hardly see him from one week's end to the next.'

'How is he managing without you now?' Harry asked.

'He has taken on a clerk. Mr Allworthy found him. I believe he was once employed by Mr Allworthy's man of business.'

Jane had spoken Donald's name easily, but now she was aware of a quietness in the coach, as if the name was like a pebble thrown into a pond, spreading its ripples over the whole surface, clouding the water. She stole a look at Harry. He was sitting tight-lipped, his eyes half-closed.

Anne's light laugh broke the tension. 'Then your papa *can* manage without you, Jane, and you were so sure you were indispensable.'

'I never said that! I said anyone else might find it difficult to understand his hand, but as Mr Allworthy pointed out, I cannot work for Papa when I am married and he must learn to make his writing more legible...'

'So you do mean to marry, then?' Anne leaned forward to emphasise her point.

'One day, perhaps. I am not at all certain that I would not do better to remain single.'

'Why?'

Jane had no answer. Everyone, including Mr Allworthy himself, assumed she was going to accept him. She had allowed it to happen, had listened to Aunt Lane and her father, and the obnoxious Countess of Carringdale and let herself be carried along by the tide, knowing she would disappoint them if she did not. How weak she had been! And how much weaker to allow Harry to kiss her, to let him see how much she craved his love. Well, from now on, she would be strong. She would have a will of iron; she would allow no one to influence her. She did not want to marry Donald, but she knew if—no, when she rejected him, the old gossip would be resurrected and added to; she was the woman who could not be trusted to be faithful to a promise, and she would not have Harry and Anne drawn into the tittle-tattle again.

Harry covertly watched the expressions flit across her face, the troubled eyes, the softness of her sweet mouth, the determination manifested in the slight uplifting of her chin and knew, as if she had said her thoughts aloud, what she was thinking. And although he was as interested in her reply as Anne was, he also knew that pressing her would drive her in the opposite direction from the one he wanted. He had already acted too precipitously and had to apologise for it. It had been a hard lesson to learn. But something had come out of it. He had discovered Jane to be a warm, passionate woman who only needed to have that passion awakened. He did not think Allworthy could do it. He hoped no one but himself would be given the opportunity, but he must be patient.

'Anne, I collect you said I was not to quiz Jane, and you are doing it yourself.'

'Yes, I am sorry,' Anne said, touching Jane's hand.

Jane suddenly laughed. 'Now that everyone has taken a turn to say sorry, do you think we could talk of something else?'

'Well, I am famished,' Harry said. 'I vote we have something to eat when we stop at Sedgewick for a change of horses. It seems ages since breakfast.'

They all agreed and the uncomfortable quizzing was abandoned, to Jane's great relief. They had an adequate but indifferent meal and were soon on their way again, but this time, Harry elected to ride on the box beside their driver. He did not say he thought there was danger, but they would be travelling through Lancashire where a great deal of the unrest was taking place and he wanted to be where he could keep a sharp lookout, leaving Giles to concentrate on driving. He had his shotgun across his knee.

'You know he had that gun in pieces last week,' Anne said. 'Every tiny screw. I hope he put it together again properly.'

'Why did he take it to pieces? Was it broken?'

'No, he wanted to see how it all fitted together. Until he explained it, I had not realised how much precision goes into making a gun and how many people are involved. The designer, stockmaker, barrelsmith and locksmith all have a role to play. The gunsmith needs to know all about iron, how to purify it, soften it, shape it and polish it like glass and keep it from going rusty. Some of it is beautifully chased too. And there is the bore and the rifling which must be exact to the last degree. And the stockmaker must understand the wood he is using, how to shape it so that the whole is perfectly balanced and fits comfortably in the hand. To hear Harry you would think it was a work of art, not something meant for killing.'

'I wish he had found something less warlike to occupy him. I hate guns.'

Anne smiled. 'The remedy is in your hands, Jane. You could easily persuade him out of it.'

'How?'

'You know how.'

'I do not.'

'He'll do anything for you, settle down and live the life of a country gentleman, looking after the estate for Grandfather, if you tell him you will marry him.'

'I cannot do that. For one thing, he has not asked me and I do not think he will. He has lived down the scandal and so have I; it is dead, cold ashes, and it would be too mortifying to rekindle it. And that will surely happen if Harry were to start paying his addresses to me again. We all know that. I beg you, do not mention it again.' She stopped suddenly, realising they were slowing down to a walking pace, and put her heads out of the window. The road ahead of them was filled with people, old and young, marching determinedly, blocking the way. Giles was having difficulty with the horses, who were disinclined to force a way through. 'There is a great crowd walking in the road.'

They were travelling so slowly, Harry was easily able to jump down and walk alongside them. 'They do not look threatening,' he told Jane and Anne. 'But I am going to ride postilion until we are safely past. If the horses are panicked, they could gallop off with the carriage and injure dozens of people, not to mention throwing you and Anne about. I will guide us through.'

He left them and mounted the leader. There was no saddle, but that hardly worried him, he was more concerned with persuading the walkers to stand aside. One of them, a big strong man carrying an ancient blunderbuss which, in Harry's opinion, would do more harm to him than whoever he was aiming at if he were to fire it, turned and grabbed the horse's bridle and they were forced to stop or run him down. 'Not so fast,' he commanded. 'Who are you? Where are you going?'

Harry decided it would be prudent to answer politely. 'I am Captain Harry Hemingford of the 95th Rifles and I have with me my sister and cousin. We are on our way to London from Windermere, passing through, no more.'

'Been fighting in Spain, have you?'

'Yes. Wounded. Came home to recover.' Normally he would not speak of his wound, but in this instance, he thought it might help to gain them safe passage.

'You have chosen a bad day to travel, my friend. We are not the only ones on the road today, all going to the rally. You will find your way blocked more than once before you reach Stockport. I advise you to find another route unless you want to stop and answer questions at every mile. Some of the men are so fired up, they will assume a good travelling coach must be carrying one of the hated mill owners, and will deal none too gently with you.'

'Thank you. We will go another way.' Harry took out his purse and selected a guinea and some smaller change. 'Here, put this in your fund and I wish you well.'

The man accepted it, touched his hat in a kind of salute and resumed his place in the march. Harry signalled to Giles to pull up and then took a map from his valise and climbed into the carriage to talk to Jane and Anne.

'Their leader—I assume he is the leader—has advised

us to find another route. The road from here to Stockport is likely to be crammed with people on the march. And if the magistrates try to put a stop to it and bring in the militia, it could become dangerous.'

'What about Simmonds?' Anne queried. Their groom had gone on ahead to arrange post horses and would not know they had stopped.

'If he has seen all these people, he will know we cannot get through.' He opened the map and studied it for a moment. 'We could go via Skipton to Leeds and across to Nottinghamshire and make our way south from there.' It must be fate, he decided, that Leeds should be on the new route. He had received a letter from Jerry Thoms, telling him of a manufactory near Leeds run by an Austrian called Franz Stoller, which might be worth a look. He could leave the girls sightseeing and go and investigate. 'It means going over Ilkley Moor,' he added. 'But the weather is good, we should have no trouble.' He got out to consult Giles and quickly returned. 'He says he would rather chance the coach on the hills than have the horses bolt because of the mob.'

Anne and Jane, who had been made as nervous as the horses by the noisy crowds, were happy to agree. They continued slowly behind the marchers until they reached a small hamlet where a fork in the road went off to the left and they turned down it.

'We might not be able to find a change of horses until we reach Skipton, so we will need to go slowly,' Harry said, as a farm cart pulled over to let them pass. 'But it is a lovely day and the views are quite superb.'

'I shall look upon it as an adventure,' Jane said.

The road wound on and up, between heather-covered moors dotted with sheep. There was an occasional lonely farmstead, a cottage, a river, snaking its way down to the valley, and above the peaks a wide expanse of blue sky. A shepherd and his dog were driving a flock of sheep along the side of a ridge. To their right a kestrel hovered, so intent on its prey it was oblivious to the vehicle on the road. Jane watched it swoop and then climb, a small animal in its sharp beak.

It was getting late when they reached the little hamlet of Giggleswick, where they stopped to rest the horses and Harry went into a tiny tavern to see if there was food to be had. 'They can give us food,' he said, when he returned. 'And they have a room. It is very small and not very clean, but if we go on, we might not find anything else before dark, so what do you think?'

'Only one room?' Anne queried.

'Yes, for you and Jane. Giles and I can sleep in the coach. There's a paddock where we can let the horses graze and rest.'

'Then we had better take it,' Anne said.

They went inside, ducking their heads below the low lintel. It was no more than a hedge tavern, one ill-lit, ill-ventilated room and a lean-to at the back. It was kept by a bony old man, bent almost double, and a younger woman who was as fat as he was thin. 'M'wife,' he told them, waving an arm in her direction. 'She be a good cook, so she be. Be an hour, if ye likes to wait.'

'We'll take a stroll, until our meal is ready,' Harry said, and ushered the girls out into the fresh air, where they took an arm each and walked across the road towards a promontory where a huge boulder stood against the skyline. 'I am not at all sure I have done the right thing bringing you here,' he said. 'Perhaps we should have turned back to Ambleside and set out another day.'

'I would not have missed it for worlds,' Jane said.

'What a story I shall have to tell when I return home. I do thank you both for inviting me.'

'Have you truly enjoyed it, Jane?' Anne asked.

'Oh, yes.' She could be strong, she told herself, and she was succeeding.

'All of it? Getting wet and…' she paused '…everything?'

For a moment, Jane thought about what had happened in the storm. How foolish she had been to be so angry over a kiss! It had been nothing to fall into a quake about. It was, she told herself firmly, all part of the adventure. 'Everything,' she confirmed as they continued to the top of the hill and stood looking about them. It was wild moorland, almost uninhabited, except for the two or three houses in the village and a distant farm. 'I would not have missed a minute.'

'Good,' Harry said and she felt his arm tighten her hand against his side. 'I am glad.'

They saw the old man come out of the tavern and wave to them. 'Supper is served,' Anne said. 'I hope it is edible.'

It was more than edible, it was a delicious lamb stew. How the woman managed it in those primitive conditions, Jane could not think, but all three did justice to it, then Jane and Anne made their way up what was little more than a ladder to the room above.

Harry had been right to call the room small. It was no more than a tiny box under the thatch. It contained a bed, a chair and a cupboard and there was only just enough room to move between them. The cupboard, when they opened it, contained a pair of men's breeches, a shirt, a lady's skirt, two blouses and an old pair of boots. 'It's their own bedroom,' Jane said. 'I wonder where they are sleeping.'

'On the floor downstairs,' Anne suggested. 'And I am not sure I would not prefer it. There are no sheets and the blankets are filthy. I propose we sleep in our clothes.'

Even the thought of bedbugs could not keep them awake.

They both slept soundly, to be awakened by a cock crowing as daylight filtered through the tiny window. They rose, tried to tidy their clothes and comb their hair, then went down to breakfast. Half an hour later, they were on their way again.

Harry was laughing, as he sat back in the coach. 'My goodness, they know their worth, those two. They charged as much as a good London hotel. I was on the point of complaining, but then I decided they had earned it.'

The day continued much as the one before, but nowhere had spare horses and so they were obliged to continue with those they had, walking them at an easy pace and resting them frequently. Their second night was spent in a similar way to the first and the girls were beginning to feel decidedly grubby. 'Oh, for a bath,' Jane said when they were shown up to a musty room with only a bowl to wash in.

In the middle of the next day, hot and sticky, they stopped beside a stream to eat the food the last innkeeper had provided. The water looked inviting and Jane longed to immerse herself and wash the grime of travel from her body. 'Do you remember when we were children, how we used to swim in the brook at Sutton Park?' she said to Anne.

Anne laughed. 'We went in in our petticoats and Harry went in in his drawers. And then we had to put our dry clothes on top of wet ones to go home.' She sighed. 'How innocent we were and how happy. I wonder what our parents would have said, if they had known.'

'You both looked like drowned rats,' Harry said. 'I cannot believe it was not noted by nurses and governesses. It was as well they did not know I had been with you.'

'I recall on one occasion when Mama noticed, I told her I fell in and you rescued me,' Jane said. 'She was very grateful to you.'

Harry laughed. 'There's no one about. We could take a bath now.'

'Harry!' His sister was shocked. 'I do hope you are joking.'

'Giles and I could take a walk, while you bathed and then you could sit in the carriage while I took a dip. I promise not to look.'

Anne looked at Jane, one eyebrow raised. 'Yes, why not?' Jane said. 'I feel so grubby. If Giles brought the carriage a little nearer, we could undress in it.'

And this is what they did. When the men had disappeared from view, the girls stripped off their outer garments and lowered themselves gingerly into the fast-flowing stream, shrieking because it was icy cold. They were sitting on the pebbles at the bottom, splashing each other like children when they heard the sound of horses' hooves.

'Someone's coming.' Jane tried to scramble to her feet, but there was no time to regain the coach. She was standing knee deep in water with her petticoat plastered to her body, showing every contour, when two riders came into view.

'Sit down!' Anne commanded, immersing all but her head and shoulders. Jane did likewise.

The riders pulled up. Both were young men, dressed in riding coats of good Bath cloth and leather breeches.

'Now who'd expect to find mermaids on the moors?' one said, doffing his hat. 'Good afternoon, ladies.'

Jane and Anne glared at him, their cheeks pink with warmth for all they were shivering in the icy water.

'If they are mermaids, then I should like to take a look at their tails,' the other said, dismounting.

'Don't you dare!' Anne shouted. Shouting was all they could do. They were not going to stand up while the men were ogling them.

'My, they do talk after all.'

A gunshot spattered the ground at the feet of the one who had dismounted. Startled, he looked round to see Harry standing on a rock a few yards away, holding his smoking shotgun. 'On your way,' he said. 'Or the next one will be aimed at your heart.'

'We thought the young ladies needed assistance.'

'They don't and I shan't tell you again.' Harry lifted the gun to his shoulder again. The man scrambled back into the saddle and they both disappeared over the brow of the next hill at a gallop. Harry let the gun down. 'You had better come out or you'll freeze to death,' he said laconically.

Anne rose, but Jane hesitated. She knew she might as well be naked for all the cover her underclothes afforded her. Harry smiled and turned his back on her. He had seen her trying to get out when the men arrived, had noted the curve of her breast, belly and thighs beneath the softly clinging cambric and his desire had welled up and was likely to be an embarrassment to him. He needed a cold bath himself to cool his ardour. But, oh, how lovely she was!

He heard the carriage door shut with a bang and risked a look. The girls were safely inside. He smiled and waited patiently until the rocking and swaying stopped and he knew they had finished dressing themselves in dry clothes. 'Giles, take the coach back on to the road and wait for me,' he said. 'I am not going to forgo my dip.'

'I never felt so mortified,' Jane said, smoothing down her skirt and bundling the wet clothes under the seat. Somehow they would have to be dried. 'We haven't seen another traveller all day and then those two had to come along just at the wrong moment.'

Anne laughed. 'Your petticoat didn't hide much.'

'Oh, no!' Harry must have seen her and somehow that seemed a worse embarrassment than being ogled at by those two young men. She was unlikely to see them again, but Harry would be joining them again in two or three minutes and how could she look him in the eye?

She turned in her seat to look out of the window just as Harry emerged from the water. He didn't have a stitch on! Hurriedly she looked away, her face on fire. She had never seen a naked man before, not unless you counted marble statues, and she had not seen many of those. Pink and white flesh was another matter altogether. And though she tried to banish the picture from her mind, she could not forget his lithe body, the strong shoulders, narrow hips and his masculinity on show for all to see. Even as she was dragging her gaze away, he climbed the bank to pick up a towel and her mind registered that one leg was strong and well shaped, the other badly scarred. And it came to her, as if she had only then thought of it, that this man, this slightly less than perfect man, was the one she loved above all other. But it could not be; she had made that quite clear.

He joined them in the coach, rubbing his head with the towel to dry his hair. 'Clean and fit for the company of ladies again,' he said, with no trace of embarrassment but then, she decided, he had probably been unaware that she had seen anything.

They reached Skipton in the middle of the next day, where they were able to change the horses and eat a meal while they waited. They were glad they had fresh horses for the next long pull up to Ilkley Moor, where they arrived just as dusk was obscuring the landscape. And here they could find no welcoming tavern and were obliged to sleep in the coach. Harry offered to drive while Giles rested, but the old coachman would have none of it. ''Tis my job, Captain,' he said stiffly. 'And if anything were to happen to the two young ladies...'

Harry laughed. 'You do not trust me.'

'I didn't say that, Master Harry. Didn't I teach you to drive myself? But it's dark an' these roads ain't like Lincolnshire roads, now are they? You settle down and have a good sleep and tomorrow you may spell me if you've a mind to.'

Harry gave in and climbed into the coach to sit beside Jane and the coach rumbled on through the darkness at no more than walking pace. Anne, in the opposite corner, shut her eyes and was soon dreaming, but Jane, acutely aware of Harry's leg, clad in clean pantaloons, brushing against her muslin skirt, was wide awake. It was, she noted, his good leg and that brought on memories of his nakedness and even in the dark she felt the heat flare in her face.

'It is a strange feeling,' he whispered so as not to wake his sister, 'sitting here with you like this. It is like being wrapped in a warm cocoon. There is no one else in the whole world, no outside influences, no thought for tomorrow, no memories of the past. It is as if time is standing still.'

'But the sun will come up, day must surely follow night and we must emerge into the light.' Her voice, too, was a whisper.

'Ah, but by then we will have undergone a change. We will emerge as butterflies, more beautiful than the creatures who inhabited the cocoon.'

'You do say some foolish things, Harry Hemingford.'

'But don't you feel it too, this change that is taking place between us?'

'No.' She would be strong. She must be strong. 'Nothing has changed, except you grow more fanciful.'

He laughed softly. 'But that is part of it. This strong fancy I have to spread my wings and fly.'

'Where to?'

'Straight into your heart. I want to see inside it. Is it a living, throbbing thing, or a stone? Passionate or cold? Can it love? Does it hate?' His voice dropped to a thread of sound as he put his lips close to her ear. 'Can it be governed?'

She shivered and she knew he had noticed it. 'Harry, please…'

'Please what?'

'Please do not roast me.'

'Is that what I am doing? Now, I thought I was beguiling you, flirting a little, trying to make you smile, no harm in that, is there?' Feelings he could not declare were hidden beneath flippancy.

She did not answer, but turned to look out of the window. The sky was too overcast for moon and stars and there was nothing to see but black shapes and one spindly tree standing out on the distant horizon where it met the lighter sky.

'Jane, you do know you cannot marry Allworthy, don't you?' he murmured in her ear.

She turned to face him. 'Why not?'

'He will stifle you. You will not be able to breathe.' He gave a grunt of wry humour. 'Can you imagine him letting you bathe in your underwear in the river?'

She allowed herself a small smile, but that was quickly overtaken by a feeling of acute embarrassment. 'He would not take me to wild inaccessible country where there was no place to bathe or sleep.'

'No.' He gave a melodramatic sigh. 'You would have no more exciting adventures. Everything would be pristine and tidy, everything exactly arranged for your—no, his convenience and comfort. Does that not fill you with sadness?'

It did, but she would not admit it. 'He is a careful man. I admire him for it.'

'Admire him? Oh, dear, that is damning with faint praise, don't you think? Where is love? Where is passion?'

'It will come.'

'Jane, my dear, forgive me, but I hate to see you throw yourself away…'

'I am not throwing myself away and it is not your business.' Her voice was rising and she noticed Anne stirring in her sleep.

'Oh, but it is. I am your friend.' He bent his head so that she could feel his warm breath on her cheek and it was turning her insides to fiery liquid. 'You agreed we should be friends, did you not?'

'Yes…' Oh, he could be so maddening sometimes. Did he mean he only wanted to be her friend? Was that all she was to him? Then why had he kissed her in that all-too-telling way, making her forget herself? Did he glory in his power over her? Was he punishing her for sending him away, making her suffer as he had suffered?

'Then, take a friend's advice. Do not marry Allworthy.'

'I shall marry whom I please, or not at all, as I please,' she said, doing her best to sound severe, though this conversation was becoming so fraught, she did not know how she could bear it. She never knew from one moment to the next whether he was teasing or not, nor what he truly felt. If Anne was to be believed, he loved her, but he had not said so and she could not think that he had forgiven her for sending him away, condemning him to the life of a common soldier, putting him in the forefront of the battle so that he had been wounded. That lovely masculine body was scarred for life. She could not forgive herself, so how could he be expected to?

'Where are we?' It was Anne who spoke, her words cutting through the tension in the air, severing the invisible chain that had connected them, bringing them back to reality.

'Going over Ilkley Moor,' Harry said in his normal voice. 'Very, very slowly.'

'Oh. What were you two talking about?'

'Butterflies,' Jane said.

'And having adventures,' her brother put in. 'Jane likes adventures, don't you, Jane?'

'Yes, as long as they are not too dangerous. I should not like to be in fear of my life.'

Anne smiled. 'You were not quarrelling, then?'

'Not at all.' Jane could not see his face, but she could imagine him grinning in the darkness. 'We are the best of friends.'

'Good.'

The carriage rumbled on. The steady clop of the horses' hooves, the crunch of the wheels and the jingle of harness were soporific and, as the conversation died, Jane's eyes closed and she slept.

Harry knew she had fallen asleep because her breathing, which had been ragged when they were talking, became a gentle flutter and her head lolled against his shoulder. Gently he eased his arm round her and made her more comfortable against him. He was dozing himself, savouring the faint scent of her hair beneath his chin, so he had no warning that anything was amiss. There was a jolt that woke all three, but before they could ask each other what it was, they heard the horses shriek and Giles give a great shout and then a rending sound and the coach rolled over. And then it began to slide, faster and faster, with the three people inside, flying about like dolls.

It came to rest at last, with a final grinding and tearing, and then there was an awful silence. It seemed to last a long time, but could only have been seconds, before Harry came to his senses with Anne straddled across him and Jane beneath him. Both were unconscious. There were bits of wood and torn upholstery piled up around them. He pushed away as much debris as he could and carefully lifted Anne off him, then turned to kneel beside Jane. It was too dark to see anything; the only light came from a flickering flame, which he realised was caused by the oil from the broken coach lights catching fire to the undergrowth. He could hear Giles yelling as he tried to reach them. 'Master Harry! Oh, God, Miss Anne.'

'I'm all right,' he told Giles, though his injured thigh was hurting badly. 'What about you?'

'Bruises, nothing to speak of. What about the young ladies?'

'Out cold. Can you wrench the door open and I'll hand my sister out to you.'

Giles's big hand pulled at the door until it came off and then his head was outlined against the lighter sky. There was blood running down his face. Incongruously

Harry noticed it would soon be dawn. 'Here, take her from me,' he said, extricating himself from Anne's inert body. She moaned and came to her senses at that point. 'Anne, dearest, can you move?'

She sat up and rubbed her elbows. 'Yes, I think so.'

'Giles is out there, he will help you out, while I see to Jane.'

'Is she hurt?'

'I don't know. She hasn't moved.'

'And you?'

'Bruises, no more.' He attempted a smile. 'I was stuck between the pair of you, cushioned my fall at your expense.'

Helped by Giles, Anne scrambled out and over the wreckage and sat on the grass a little way off, too dazed to do anything. Harry dare not manhandle Jane until he knew what her injuries were. He flung out all the loose cushions, bonnets and broken seats and then climbed out. Feverishly he began pulling at the splintered wood at the side of the coach. Giles was beside himself, moaning that it was his fault, that he hadn't seen the subsidence in the road until the horse stumbled into it. He should never have agreed to drive over the moors, he should have seen the trouble…

Harry, shaken himself, told him to pull himself together and do something useful. 'We've got to make room to get at her,' he said, stamping out the flickering flames before they could spread. 'Have you any tools?'

'A few things in the boot.'

'Fetch them.'

The man was hobbling painfully as he went to obey. With the help of the tools, they dismantled one side of the coach and were able to lift Jane out and lay her on the grass. Harry knelt beside her. 'Is she bad?' Anne asked.

'I can't tell.' He was busy feeling the back of Jane's head. It had a lump on it the size of a hen's egg. Her leg was twisted and swollen and was almost certainly broken, and she had cuts and bruises everywhere. Because she had been underneath as they fell she had sustained more injury than Anne, more than he had. How was he going to get her to safety?

Giles, who had been scouting around, limped back to them. 'One of the horses is dead, one has run off, the third will have to be put out of its misery, but the leader seems unhurt, though very skittish. Shall I ride him to fetch help?'

'You're hurt yourself, man.'

'Oh, 'tis nothing. I can ride. We can't be that far from the outskirts of Leeds.'

Harry considered going himself, but he did not want to leave the girls. His medical skills were confined to knowing how to dress wounds sustained in battle, but that was better than nothing. Giles was hurt, for all he said he wasn't and he needed help too. It was best if he went. 'Then go. Find someone to bring a flat cart and a doctor. I'll do what I can here.'

Giles scrambled up the slope on his hands and knees and a minute or two later they heard the horse's hooves clattering on the road and then fading into the distance. Harry found a flat piece of wood, part of the coach's side panel and took it back to where Jane was lying with Anne kneeling beside her, crying. 'She won't come round,' she sobbed. 'Oh, I wish we had never come. Adventure she wanted, but not this. If she…' She could not say the word. 'Why won't she come to her senses?'

'I am glad she has not. I want to straighten that leg out

and tie it to this piece of wood and it is going to hurt. She is better out of it.' He turned to her. 'Are you all right?'

'Yes. Don't worry about me.'

'Then do you think you can you make some bandages with petticoats? The luggage is somewhere about. And I heard the sound of a stream. We'll need water. There is a flask in my valise, use that.'

Glad to be busy, she went to obey and he began very gingerly and very gently to feel along Jane's leg, afraid to move it for fear of making the break worse. By the time Anne returned, he had straightened the knee and slipped the board under it and, with the bandages she had brought, strapped the leg to it carefully but firmly. That done, he bathed her bruises and covered her with his coat, then sat back on his heels to look up at the road. How long would Giles be? He could do nothing about hauling Jane back to the road without help. He could hear the injured horse neighing.

'Look after her,' he told Anne, getting to his feet. 'Don't let her move.'

She was alarmed. 'Where are you going?'

'To see to the horse. I won't be long.'

It took a search to find his gun, but he spotted it under a bush and went to the horse. It was halfway down the slope, trying vainly to get to its feet, though one leg was obviously broken. A single shot and it lay still.

When he returned to the girls, he found Jane was beginning to regain consciousness. At first it was a mere whisper and then a moan and then a cry of pain. He fell on his knees beside her and stroked her brow. 'Lie still, my love, lie very still. You have been hurt. Help is on its way.'

'What happened?'

'The coach turned over.'

'You? And Anne?'

'Right as rain.'

She looked up towards the road, thirty feet above them. It was an impossibly steep slope, scraped and littered with debris. 'Did we come down there?'

'Yes.'

'Then it is a miracle we weren't all killed.'

'Yes.' He said nothing about his own feelings when he saw her lying so crumpled and still beneath him. For a brief second he had thought she was dead and he had wished for death too. She was the breath of life to him, and without her, he did not want to survive. Only minutes before they had been talking, railing at each other, bantering, pretending to misunderstand each other, when each knew perfectly well what was in the other's heart. And all in a flash, they had ended up at the bottom of a ravine and she was in pain. He wished with all his heart he could suffer it for her. 'Thank God we were not.'

He had wrung a clean handkerchief out in water and he bathed her face and parched lips. She tried to move her head and winced with pain. 'My head hurts.'

'I know it does, my darling, and I would do anything to have it otherwise, but lie still, please lie still. Giles has gone for help.'

He sat and held her hand, willing his strength into her, willing her to live, while Anne, too distraught to sit still, wandered about picking up their belongings and making a little heap of them. It was fully daylight now and they could easily see the extent of the accident. The coach had gouged a long slit from the road to the bottom of the slope, breaking down small trees and bushes in its path until its remains came to rest not far from the banks of a small stream. Anne fetched more water from it and Harry dribbled a little of it into Jane's mouth.

She slipped in and out of consciousness as the hours passed. Sometimes she muttered in delirium, sometimes she moaned quietly, and sometimes, which to Harry was almost worse, she was so silent he had to keep checking she was still breathing. 'God keep her safe,' he murmured, lifting her hand to his cheek. It was so cold, it frightened him.

'How long will they be?' Anne asked him. 'Suppose something has happened to Giles? He was hurt, he might have passed out or fallen off the horse, or lost his way.'

He didn't want to think of that possibility. Without help, he could not get Jane to the top of that slope. 'Can you climb up there?' he asked.

'I think so.'

'Then go and see if anyone is coming.'

He watched her struggling to find her footing, but she managed it in the end and disappeared from his sight. He looked down at Jane. Her face was deathly pale. 'I am sorry, so very, very sorry, my love,' he murmured. 'It is all my fault, all of it. I should not have brought you here. I should have left you with your comfortable, cosy life, left you to a man who has everything to give you…' He grimaced. 'I was right when I said I was unworthy, wasn't I?'

'Did you say that?' she murmured. 'I don't remember.'

'Jane, oh, Jane.'

They heard the sound of wheels and the clop of horses' hooves and then Anne was outlined against the sky at the top of the slope. 'They're here. Help is here, my love.'

She was joined by a little man carrying a small black bag and three others. Harry, holding Jane's hand, watched them scrambling down the slope to reach them and was surprised to find his cheeks were wet.

Chapter Eight

The doctor, a tubby little man, with a round cheerful face, decided not to undo the strapping on Jane's leg. 'You've made a good hand of it,' he told Harry, before moving on to feel around the bruise on her head, making her wince. 'No sense in making the poor child more uncomfortable. I'll take a look at it when we have her safely back in an infirmary bed.' He looked up at the road from which he had just come. 'Your man said it would be a good climb, so we have come prepared with a stout door and some strong rope.' He opened his bag and produced a bottle of brownish liquid from which he measured a good spoonful. 'This will dull the pain, my dear, so take it down.'

Jane obeyed and soon her head lolled. 'Now, while she's out, let us move quickly.'

She did not remember anything of the struggle to haul the makeshift stretcher up to the cart, and very little of the journey afterwards. It all went by in a haze of pain and drug-induced sleep. But every now and again she woke to find herself lying on straw in the bottom of a flat cart, her head in Harry's lap, where he was carefully cushioning it against the jolting of the cart. He was stroking her forehead and murmuring endearments and encouragement. 'Not long now, my darling.'

When had he started to call her darling? Since this terrible pain had started or before? She could not remember, could remember nothing of what had happened, not where they had been, nor where they had been going, nor for that matter, why. Her mind was a fog that lifted every now and then to a brighter image: sunlight on water, and laughter, hers and Anne's and Harry's. They were running through the woods, Harry had seized her overskirt and was flying along waving it like a banner and she was running after him, shrieking at him to give it back. But Harry was only a boy and she was small, very small, and very angry.

And then she was standing in her father's library and Harry was facing her. He was in the blue and gold uniform of the Prince of Wales's Own Regiment, stiff and silent, his hat beneath his arm. She was the one doing the talking, but she could not hear herself, could not understand what she was saying. When she stopped, he bowed formally, put his hat on and left. And then she was weeping.

'Jane, please do not cry.' It was Harry's voice in the present and he was gently wiping the tears from her cheeks with his handkerchief. 'I know it hurts...'

'Can't feel anything,' she murmured. 'Tired, so very tired. Did we quarrel?'

'When?'

'I don't know. Can't remember. Can't remember anything.'

He was momentarily shocked, then smiled. 'You do remember me, though?'

'Don't be silly, Harry, of course I do.'

'And me?' Anne's anxious face appeared above her.

'Anne, are you here too?'

'Yes. We have all three been to the Lakes to visit my Aunt Bartrum, you remember that, don't you?'

'No.'

'Oh, dear,' Anne said, looking towards her brother with a worried frown.

'The memory will almost certainly return,' the doctor put in. He was perched on a pile of sacks on the other side of the cart. 'Do not fret about it.' He gave her another dose of laudanum and she fell asleep again, with her hand in Harry's.

When she came to her senses she was in a bed and the doctor and a nurse were standing over her. 'Good,' the doctor was saying. 'She is back in the land of the living.'

'Where am I?'

'In Leeds infirmary, a private room. You have been here a week, hovering between life and death, but now I think we can safely say you will live.'

'I have been ill?' Her leg felt stiff and heavy and her head ached.

'You were injured in an accident when the coach you were travelling in rolled down a bank. Severe bruising to the brain and a broken leg, which I have strapped to a splint to immobilise it. You have some cuts and bruises too, but they will heal.' And, as she struggled to sit up, he put out a hand to restrain her. 'No, do not move, you are still very weak and likely to feel faint.'

'Papa. My friends…'

'Captain Hemingford has kept your father informed.' He paused to smile at her. 'The Captain has been here the whole time, pacing up and down and sitting with you night and day. He did a grand job on your leg and it will mend, though you might be left with a slight limp.' He smiled. 'Better than losing the limb, eh? Or your life, and it might have come to that if he had not kept his head.'

'Where is the Captain now?'

'Waiting outside the door. Shall I call him in?'

'Yes, please.'

He and the nurse disappeared from her line of vision, and though she tried to turn her head it sent waves of dizziness over her and she decided not to attempt it again. A moment later Harry was standing over her. He was unshaven and looking grey and drawn, but he was smiling. 'So, you have decided to wake up, have you?' His cheerful tone belied the strained look in his eyes.

'Yes. I have been a terrible trouble to you, haven't I?'

'Terrible,' he agreed.

'The doctor says I owe you my life.'

He sat on the edge of her bed. 'The good doctor exaggerates. Your own courage brought about a miracle. And the prayers of your friends.'

'Then I thank them. And you. Where is Anne? Was she hurt too?'

'She is resting at our hotel. She had a few bruises, which are healing well, nothing broken, thank the Lord. Giles had a badly twisted knee, but he is also recovering.'

'Giles?'

'Our coachman. He was thrown off the box when the coach went over. Do you still not remember?'

'No. Though I think it was dark and we were talking…'

'Do you remember what we were talking about?'

She frowned, tried to bring it back and failed. 'No. But I have no doubt it was some nonsense. You always had an aptitude for that.'

'Yes, it was nonsense,' he said.

'Tell me about it, tell me everything—where we had

been and where we were going, how the coach came to turn over.'

And so he did, beginning with Anne being ill, of the Regent's banquet, of Jane's own illness and her need to recuperate, their happy time at Ambleside, the walking and boating and the storm. 'It was the day before we left to come home,' he said. 'We had hired ponies to go for a ride and it came upon us suddenly. We were soaked. Do you not remember it?'

'No.'

She had not remembered him kissing her, had not remembered her own anger. He did not know whether to be relieved or sorry. 'Do you remember the workers marching in the middle of road and holding us up when we were coming home?'

She tried, she tried very hard, but nothing came to her. 'No.'

'We were advised there might be trouble and changed our route to avoid them, but the rain had washed part of the road away. Giles did not see it until the horses stumbled and then it was too late... Oh, Jane, we thought we had lost you. And it was my fault. I should have known better than suggest taking a road we none of us knew.' And because part of his decision had been the opportunity to visit a gun manufacturer made it worse.

'I am sure you are being too hard on yourself.' She paused. 'There is such a blankness in my mind, like a black hole, but there is something there, clouding everything, something I ought to remember, something important, but I can't grasp it.'

'It will come back to you in time,' he said. He had deliberately not mentioned Allworthy, but he supposed she would remember him in due course, perhaps when the man himself appeared, if not before. He ought to say something like, 'By the way, you are in the way of being engaged to a worthy gentleman from Norfolk and Anne and I have been doing our best to persuade you against it.' But he didn't want to spoil her recovery by introducing a jarring note. Allworthy was definitely a jarring note. He would be pleased if she never remembered the man at all.

'I hope you are right. It is dreadful having this awful blank, not knowing what you have done, what you have said. I might have done something very silly, for which I should be sorry.'

She reached out a hand and he grasped it and sank on his knees beside the bed, putting the tips of her fingers to his lips. 'If you have, and I beg leave to doubt it, it is best forgotten.'

'Thank you for taking such good care of me,' she said, looking at his dear face. He looked exhausted and no wonder if he had been keeping vigil by her bed.

'It was my privilege. I will not say pleasure because seeing you so white and still and in such pain was dreadful. I should never have put you in jeopardy at all. Can you ever forgive me?'

Was she right in thinking that he had asked her that before, quite recently? Why? What had he done to need that reassurance? Why could she not remember? He was keeping something from her, she was sure. Was it so bad it could not be spoken of? 'There is nothing to forgive. You could not have known about the hole in the road.' She paused. 'Does Papa know what happened?'

'I sent word as soon as we arrived in Leeds and you had been made comfortable and he has written back. Now you are awake you can read it yourself.' He reached out to the table beside her bed and handed her a letter in her father's untidy hand.

Her vision was blurred and she found reading a strain, so she let it drop. 'Tell me what it says.'

'He trusts me to take good care of you and asks me to keep him fully informed of your progress. He says his work is going very well and you are not to worry about the copying.' He wondered at the insensitivity of the man who could write about his work when his daughter was injured, miles from home. If she had been a child of his, he would have arrived post haste at her bedside. 'He hopes you will recover quickly and looks forward to hearing from you as soon as you are able to write, and seeing you safely home again as soon as the doctor says you are fit to travel.'

He decided to skip the paragraph asking what he was doing, taking his daughter on roads that were evidently unsafe, also the mention of Donald Allworthy and the fact that he had informed him of what had happened. He hoped the man would not take it into his head to rush up to Leeds to see her. It reminded him he had not yet seen Franz Stoller.

The nurse returned and straightened the covers over Jane. 'Time you went, Captain. We must not tire our patient. She needs to rest.'

Reluctantly he rose, bent to kiss Jane's cheek and left. He was dog-tired and his thigh was giving him hell, the bruises round the area of his wound seemed reluctant to subside and he knew he was limping more than usual. He went back to the hotel, a modest one because he had very little left of the money he had brought with him. Most of it had gone on a private room at the infirmary, doctor's fees, day and night nurses, treatment for Anne and Giles and paying the men who had brought the cart. The expense was increasing day by day, but he would pay it gladly to have Jane well again.

Anne was sitting in a chair by the window of their sitting room, endeavouring to read, when he joined her. She looked up anxiously. 'How is she?'

'Awake at last. The doctor is very hopeful, but he says she might always limp.' He sprawled in a chair opposite her, exhausted and worried. 'I cannot bear it, Anne. I did this to her. If she is left permanently lame, how will she ever forgive me? I cannot forgive myself.'

'How can you say so? It was an accident and accidents happen. Mother and Father…' She did not need to go on. Their parents had been killed when a coach lost a wheel and overturned, their mother immediately; their father had lingered a few weeks before succumbing to his injuries.

'I know. I have been thinking of that ever since it happened. I thank God you were not badly hurt, but Jane…'

'She is recovering. Hopeful, you said, didn't you?'

'But not to be able to walk properly again…'

'It might not come to that. We should be thankful she is alive and recovering.' She paused. 'She doesn't blame you, does she?'

'No, but then she still does not remember what happened. Not a thing. I had to tell her why we were in Westmorland and why we were going home over the Pennines. She could remember nothing of our stay at Aunt Georgie's.'

'Nothing?'

'Nothing. I do not think she can remember Allworthy either. She did not mention him and neither did I.'

Anne smiled. 'That's good, isn't it?'

'The memory will return and then she will ask us why we did not tell her.'

'We'll worry about that when it happens. How soon will it be before she can be moved?'

'I do not know.' He paused. 'It is a long journey to

London and it will exhaust her if we attempt it all at once. Sutton Park is about halfway. I thought of writing to Grandfather to ask him if we might bring her to stay there until she is fully recovered.'

'What a good idea! She has not been there for years. The happy memories will surely help her recovery.'

'Grandfather might be more amenable if you were to ask him. She is your friend.'

She laughed. 'Not yours?'

'You know it is more than that, always will be, but I can say nothing of that now, not until she is well again and then there are other impediments.'

'Mr Donald Allworthy.'

'Yes.'

'Forget him. She has.'

'Not for long, I'll be bound.'

'She will take weeks, perhaps months, to recover and by that time he will have grown impatient and found someone else.'

He brightened. 'Do you think so?' Then he became morose again. 'No man with any sense or any tenacity would forget Jane, and, say what you like, Donald Allworthy is not lacking in either.'

'Then the sooner we can get her to Sutton Park, the better.'

Although her memory remained obstinately blank Jane's physical improvement continued and Harry took the opportunity while Anne was sitting with her to visit Stoller's manufactory. The man was stiff and unwelcoming and Harry had to act the part of the resentful inventor for all he was worth in order to be shown round the premises 'Are they all being bought by the War Department?' he asked, looking at the racks of weapons. He was sure he was only being shown a small part of the operation, the legal side of it.

'Of course.' Stoller spoke excellent English with a strong Germanic accent 'Who else would purchase dem?'

'Are you interested in making a superior gun, one that can be loaded from the breech?'

'De French are ahead of you. Have you seen any of Jean Pauly's weapons?'

'Yes, when I was in France last year, I saw an early model.' No need to tell the man he had been on an intelligence mission at the time. 'It gave me the idea.'

'And you t'ink you can improve on de Pauly model?'

'Yes. All I need to make a start is a small workshop and enough blunt to buy tools and equipment. Unfortunately, the War Department is too short-sighted to see the potential.' He paused, then added, 'My grandfather has cut me off, disinherited me, my regiment has dispensed with my services and I am deep in dun territory. I need to make money and I am not particular as to who pays me.'

The man looked thoughtful, but he was also wary. 'I need to make some enquiries before deciding. Leave everyt'ing wid me and I will contact you again.'

Harry told him where he could reach him and left. He knew there was more to be seen. He decided not to wait until Stoller accepted him as a fellow conspirator, but to return after dark and look round on his own. What he saw, after feeding the watchdogs with meat and picking the lock of a small door at the rear of the building, convinced him he was on the right track. He went back to the hotel and wrote to Jerry Thoms.

A letter arrived for Jane from Donald Allworthy later that week. She read it with a puzzled frown. Its style was a mixture of correctness and familiarity, but she evidently knew the writer well. He was sorry to hear of her accident and hoped she would make a full recovery. As soon as she was well enough to travel, he would come himself to fetch her home. He had known the expedition was not a good idea, especially after she had been so ill, and wished now he had objected to it. He signed himself 'Your devoted Donald Allworthy'.

Who was he? Try as she might, she could not remember him. Was he the dark memory she had been groping for? But why had she forgotten him? What did he look like? Did she like him? Had he the right to object to anything she wanted to do, expecting her compliance? Or sign himself in that way? She decided to ask Anne when she came to visit her. She was allowed visitors now the headaches had gone and it was only her broken leg that was keeping her immobile.

'I have had a strange letter from someone called Donald Allworthy,' she told her friend. 'Who is he? He writes…' she paused '…like someone with whom I am familiar, but though I have racked my brain, I cannot recall him at all.'

'You are sure you cannot remember him?'

'Yes. I have repeated the name over and over in my mind but, though it seems familiar, I do not remember its owner. Here, you had better read the letter yourself.'

'But it is a private letter. He would not be pleased to have it read by others.'

'Oh, so you do know him.'

'Not well. All I can tell you is that he proposed marriage to you.'

'Proposed!' She was taken aback. How could she forget a thing like that? 'And did I agree?'

'No, he is waiting for your answer.'

'While I went on holiday with you and Harry?'

'Yes. He lives in the country and was busy with the

harvest. You and your Aunt Lane visited him there before you fell ill.'

'Did we?' Visiting him surely meant she intended to accept? 'Why can't I remember?'

Anne shrugged. 'I do not know. The bump on your head affected your memory.'

'But I can remember you and Harry and Papa and Aunt Lane.' She stopped. 'Did Mr Allworthy ask Papa if he could propose to me?'

'Yes, I am sure he did. He is excessively correct in everything he does.'

'How could I forget him? Is he tall or short, fat or thin? Is he handsome? Is he rich? Why, why, will it not come back to me?' The questions went on and on with Anne endeavouring to answer them without bias, but Jane soon realised how reluctant her friend was. 'Is there something wrong with him?'

Anne gave a bitter laugh. 'Nothing at all, he is handsome, wealthy and in every way eligible, except he is not right for you and you must have realised that yourself or you would not have run away from him.'

'Is that what I was doing?'

'I think so.'

'Why? Why didn't I simply say no?'

Anne shrugged. 'Only you know that.'

'You do not like Mr Allworthy, do you?'

'What has my liking or not liking him got to do with your loss of memory?'

'What does Harry say about it all?'

'You had better ask him.'

'Perhaps I will. But how am I to answer this letter?'

Anne smiled. 'Leave it until you feel stronger. Your memory may return soon and then you will know what to say.'

Jane tired very easily and the effort of thinking about it exhausted her. And Anne was probably right; her memory would come back and she would have the answer to all her questions. But if she had received Mr Allworthy's proposal with pleasure, had spent some time as his guest, how could she erase him from her mind so completely? Her headache returned as she puzzled over it and the only relief she had was in a kind of apathy, putting it aside until she felt able to deal with it.

It was September before the doctor pronounced Jane fit enough to travel. He decided to leave the splint on for the journey, but advised them to call in a doctor as soon as they arrived at Sutton Park who would take it off; then she could build up her strength and slowly learn to walk again. The cuts and bruises had all healed, though there was a small scar on her forearm and another down the side of her face, which she covered by bringing her hair forward over her brow.

'It is nothing, nothing at all,' Harry had assured her when she had called for a looking glass and seen herself for the first time. 'You are no less beautiful.'

He hired the most comfortable carriage he could find, one wide enough for her to lie with her leg stretched out. It had to be paid for with a promissory note, but he would worry about the money later. Giles had gone home on the stage as soon as his knee healed and so they hired a driver and postilion as well as the coach and horses; Harry was not going to take any more risks with his precious burden.

On the morning of their departure, he carried her out to the coach and put her carefully on the seat with her broken leg lying along it and her back and head supported by soft cushions. He climbed in beside Anne on the facing seat, the step was put up and the door shut and the driver given strict instructions to go slowly, especially where the ground was uneven or the potholes more than usually deep. Luckily the weather was warm and dry. Jane was so pleased to be feeling better and away from the unpleasant smell of the hospital, that her spirits revived almost at once.

The road from Leeds to Doncaster was a good one and they bowled along smoothly, taking three hours over a journey which the mail did in half the time. When they stopped for refreshment, Harry picked Jane up and carried her tenderly to a table in the dining room. His own injury seemed not to inconvenience him and when she asked him if she was perhaps too heavy for him to carry, he laughingly said she was as light as thistledown.

'Do you want to stay and rest?' he asked her when they had finished their meal. 'If you are too tired to go on, we could rack up here...'

'No, I am perfectly comfortable in the coach.'

And so they went on: Doncaster to Worksop, then to Ollerton and Newark and on to Sleaford, which they reached in the early evening. Jane was very tired by then and her leg was aching in spite of Harry's care, but, because they were so near their destination and there were several hours of daylight still left, she would not countenance stopping. They rolled through the gates of Sutton Park at nine o'clock.

By now Jane was nearly fainting with pain and exhaustion and she was put straight to bed by the old nurse who had looked after Harry and Anne from the time they were born until they no longer needed her. Now pensioned off, she remained in the house passing her time reading, sewing and reminiscing. Her name was Elizabeth Harris, but no one ever called her by it. She was known to one and all as Nurse. 'I will look after her,' she told Harry and Anne. 'You need to rest yourselves. You look done up, both of you.'

It was the true beginning of Jane's recovery. She slept most of the following day, but the day after that she was alert and impatient to be up and about. The local doctor came and examined her, removing the splint from her leg, saying she should try a little gentle exercise before attempting to walk on it, but there was no reason to stay in bed.

Looking down at her leg after the doctor had gone, she was shocked; it looked so thin and wasted. Would she ever walk again? Run or dance? Would she ride? The thought that she might never enjoy her favourite pastime ever again made her unbearably miserable. Harry and Anne had been wonderful to her and she was very grateful, but they had been friends a long time and would not desert her in time of need. But surely they would soon lose patience with her?

And there was Mr Allworthy, whom she still could not remember. Before they left Leeds, she had received another letter from him, which she asked Anne to acknowledge on her behalf, saying she was not yet well enough to write herself. She did not know what to say to him. She did not remember what he looked like, had no recollection of him proposing to her, but how could she tell him that? Anne and Harry both told her not to worry about it; it would all come back to her in time. In the meantime, she must concentrate on getting well.

She still needed to be carried about, a task Harry did willingly. Nurse washed and dressed her and one of the maids brought her breakfast, then Harry was allowed in to take her to the morning room, a sunny room at the back of the house with long windows that looked out on to the garden. He sat her down carefully, putting a cushion at her back and wrapping a blanket about her legs. He did it tenderly and unselfconsciously, though they both knew he ought not to be touching her in that intimate way. They were, after all, unmarried and not even promised to each other. He wished it were otherwise.

'Harry, you do not have to stay by me,' she said when he drew up a chair to sit beside her. 'You must have something else to do, walking or riding or attending to the estate.'

'I can walk or ride at any time and Grandfather has not yet entrusted me with the running of the estate. Besides, I prefer to be with you.'

'But I believe we quarrelled.'

He looked sharply at her, wondering if her memory was returning. 'Quarrel with you, my dear? Never!'

'But something happened, I know it did. I have a mental picture. It is hazy, but I see you in uniform and we are both angry...'

'It was a long time ago. Over two years. Done and dusted. Do not refine upon it.'

'I thought it could not have been recent, because in my mind we were so young.'

'We were. Too young. But one can mature a great deal in two years, do you not think?'

'Oh, indeed I do. So, are you going to tell me what it was all about?'

'Must I? It is not an episode of which I am proud and you did say you forgave me.'

'I wish I could remember, Harry. I have an idea that I was feeling very muddled. Or is it simply that I am muddled now? I feel like a stranger in my own body.'

'It will pass and no doubt you will recall everything.'

'I do remember some things, mostly incidents from my childhood. Mama and Papa when we lived near here, you and Anne when we were children and into dreadful mischief, Mama's death and moving to London. But nothing recent, nothing of the last few weeks, and in that time I am supposed to have met a man called Donald Allworthy. Anne tells me I have even visited his home. How can I have forgotten that?'

'The mind is a funny thing. Perhaps you do not want to remember.'

'Why not?'

He shrugged. 'I do not know.'

'Anne said I was running away.'

'Were you?'

'I do not remember.' She paused. 'Tell me what it is I have forgotten, please. I asked Anne, but she seemed reluctant to say more than I had received an offer of marriage and was considering it.'

'That is my understanding too.'

'But you and I were engaged, Harry.'

'Yes, but we decided we should not suit.'

'Did we?' She remembered something of the sort; it must have been that quarrel. It was coming back to her slowly. 'What have you been doing since then?'

He told her about enlisting and being wounded and that brought another image flashing into her brain, one which brought the colour rushing to her cheeks: a picture of him naked, his muscular body glistening with drops of water, one leg strong and supple, the other badly scarred. When had she seen that?

He noticed her heightened colour and wondered what had caused it. 'I can no longer fight, so I had an idea to build an improved rifle, safer and more reliable. I postponed doing anything about it because Anne wanted me to accompany you both to Ambleside.' He paused, then added quickly, 'Do not think I did not want to, I did, very much.'

'And Mr Allworthy? When did I meet him?'

'Earlier this year, I believe. Before I returned from the Peninsula.'

'Have you met him?'

'Briefly.'

'What did you think of him?'

'You surely do not expect me to answer that,' he said sharply. 'I could not give you an unbiased opinion.'

'Why not?'

'Jane, my dearest girl, you must know I still love you, never stopped loving you.'

'Oh.' She looked sideways at him, her eyes showing a glint of the humour she had always had before the accident. 'Even when we quarrelled?'

'Oh, yes.'

'I do not understand. Are you saying it was my fault?'

'No, it was entirely mine. But, as you said, a great deal can happen in two years and in that time we both went our separate ways.'

Did that mean she no longer loved him? Had she ever truly loved him? But she knew she had and knew she still did. 'But we are together now.'

'Yes. Fate. The accident.'

'Oh, I see.' She was not sure she did see. Harry and Anne were looking after her at their home, tending her with loving care, and yet she had entertained a proposal of marriage from a stranger. Until she remembered him, knew what he looked like, the kind of man he was, he would remain a stranger. It was all such a muddle and worrying about it, gnawing at it like a dog with a bone, was making her head ache.

She could see Anne and her grandfather walking towards them up the garden path. Anne was carrying a trug full of late roses that she had just cut. The Earl was using a stick, but he was still sprightly for his age. When he saw Jane he raised the hand holding the stick, then spoke to Anne and a minute or two later they came into the room.

'Jane, it has been a long time,' the old man greeted her. 'How are you?'

'Recovering, my lord. I thank you for allowing me to come here to recuperate. I always loved Sutton Park.'

'You are very welcome.' He sank into a chair, his hands on the knob of his cane, while Anne kissed Jane's cheek and sat on a nearby sofa. 'I hope that rakeshame of a grandson of mine is looking after you.'

'Indeed, he is.'

'Anne tells me you have lost all remembrance of the accident.'

'Yes.'

'Sometimes it happens, you know—when something is too terrible to remember, the mind hides it away. Best forgotten. Cannot give you nightmares then, can it?'

'No, my lord.'

He stood up again. 'Stay as long as you need to,' he said gruffly. 'You might keep that renegade here a little longer. It's about time he learned how to be a gentleman.'

He stumped away. Anne smiled at Jane. 'He is secretly very pleased to have us all here, you know. I think he hopes you will help to change Harry's mind about going into the gunmaking business.'

'I would not dream of doing that, even if I could. It is plainly very important to him.'

Anne looked closely at her. 'How are you today?'

'Tired. I seem always to be tired, though I have done nothing. But I must bestir myself and try a little exercise.'

'Not today,' Harry said firmly. 'I think I should take you back to your room to rest. Tomorrow, if all goes well, I shall let you try and take a few steps.'

It was a frightening prospect. The leg might have mended, but it still looked a little misshapen and it was so thin, the muscles wasted to nothing. But she was determined to walk again, and not only walk, but ride. Oh, for the joy of feeling a horse beneath her and the wind on her face; for that, she would make herself strong again.

The next morning, she took six steps across the drawing room floor, supported by Harry. With his arm about her waist she felt safe, able to do as he asked and put one foot in front of the other, but as soon as he showed signs of letting her go, she cried out and clung to him. He had endless patience and gradually she became more adventurous. At first it was only about the house: the morning room, the drawing room, the library to look for something to read, but a week later, she was walking with the aid of a stick, even going up and down the steps that led from the terrace to the garden. But she limped.

'A pair of lame ducks, we are,' Harry teased, when she commented on it, angry with herself for not doing better. 'Matching jugs.'

'But you have mastered the art of walking with a limp. It hardly shows. And you can ride as well as you ever did.'

'And you will too. Be patient. In any case, your lopsided gait adds to your charm.'

She laughed. 'Why are you so good to me, Harry?'

'Because I love you,' he said simply.

She sat down on a garden bench to rest. The leaves on

the trees of the park were turning colour, red, gold and yellow; some of them had been blown down and were piled in little heaps, but the air was still warm enough to enjoy the sunshine out of doors. 'It was me who broke off our engagement, wasn't it?' she said slowly. 'I sent you away.'

He sat down beside her. 'I came back.'

'But too late, I think.'

'It is never too late.' He took her hand and raised it to his lips.

She smiled wanly. She had had several more letters from Mr Allworthy, all more or less in the same vein as the first, and wanting to know when he could come and fetch her home. She had begun answering them herself, but he did not seem to understand about her impaired memory, convinced that she would know him and love him again as soon as she saw him. 'There is unfinished business…'

'You mean Allworthy?'

'I must see him. As soon as I am strong enough, I must continue my journey home.' What would she make of him? What would he make of her? She was not the same girl who had left him two months before. She was scarred, and who would want to marry her with one leg shorter than the other? And did she even know if the battering her body had received had impaired her ability to have children? But she did not have to wait to return to London.

Donald arrived a week later, presenting himself to the Earl very correctly before asking if he might speak to Jane.

She was resting in her room when Anne came to tell her he was in the drawing room with the Earl. 'You do not have to see him,' she said when she saw the alarm in

Jane's eyes. 'He gave no warning of his arrival, it would be easy to send him away.'

'But that would be impolite and cowardly. Please tell him I shall join him directly, then do you think you could come back and help me to tidy myself?'

'Of course.' She looked at Jane's blue sarcenet gown, with its trimming of plum-coloured braid and smiled. 'But you look perfectly presentable to me.'

She disappeared and Jane hobbled over to sit before the mirror to brush her hair. But her hands were shaking and she could hardly breathe for the rapid thumping of her heart. She had to go down to meet a man to whom she was as good as promised in marriage, his letters had implied that, and yet she could not even remember what he looked like. The days of arranged marriages were no longer as prevalent as they had been, but they still happened, especially among the aristocracy. Girls were still being dragged unwillingly up the aisle to make their marriage vows to virtual strangers. They must feel as she did now, frightened and apprehensive, worse, she supposed, because they had no choice and she did; no one was forcing her. But if there had been no pressure, no coercion, then surely it meant it was something she wanted? If only, if only, she could remember.

When Anne returned she was sitting perfectly still, staring at her reflection, the brush idle in her hand. Anne took it from her and began stroking it down her chestnut tresses, being very careful to avoid the spot where the egg-sized lump had been. The doctor had had to cut some of the hair away and though it had started to grow again, it was short and spiky. 'If you wear it loose and just tie it back with a ribbon, it will hide where it has been cut,' Anne said.

'Do what you can,' Jane said. 'He will have to take me as I am, won't he?'

Anne carefully brushed it to the back of her neck and secured it with a ribbon, then pulled a curl or two out to cover the scar on her face. 'There! Will that do?'

'Yes, thank you.' As she finished speaking there was a knock on the door, which made her jump. Her instant thought was that she had taken so long her visitor had come to find her and she began to shake uncontrollably.

'It's only Harry come to carry you down,' Anne said, opening the door to admit her brother.

He strode into the room and then stopped to look at Jane. She was pale and very fragile, and very young with her hair hanging down her back like a schoolgirl's. Her green eyes were wide, almost fearful, and his heart went out to her. It was his task to carry her downstairs and set her before that man. It would be like offering her up to a hungry lion. Allworthy was waiting for her in the drawing room, immaculately attired, his cravat tied in a mathematical knot, his hair cut and curled within an inch of its life, making polite conversation with the Earl, perfectly at ease. How he hated him!

'Jane, are you sure you feel strong enough for this?' he asked gently.

'Yes. I must meet him. He has come a long way.'

'Very well, but if you find it is too much, you must send him away and I will bring you back to your room.' He scooped her up in his arms and turned towards the door.

He had carried her like that many times in the last few weeks and it was a burden he relished. The feel of her leaning against his body, her arms about his neck, her head close to his shoulder, was so intimate, so wonderfully gratifying that he hated putting her down. Recently she had been a little more determined to be independent and had insisted on walking, but he still held her arm to steady her.

At the bottom of the stairs, she began to struggle. 'Put me down,' she said sharply. 'I can manage now.'

'Are you sure?'

She had to be sure. She could not meet Mr Allworthy in the arms of another man. She had to stand alone. 'Yes.'

'Then take this.' He grabbed a cane from a stand by the door and handed it to her. 'Call me if you need me.'

'Yes, thank you.'

She was glad of the walking stick as she made her way slowly to the drawing room, watched by Harry and Anne who had followed them down. It was not so much that she needed it to walk, but it hid the fact that she was shaking violently. She stopped outside the door, took a deep breath and pushed it open.

He rose from a chair by the fireside as she entered. He was tall and broad and seemed to fill her vision so that she was aware of nothing else. He was very handsome, classically beautiful even; his features, nose, mouth, forehead were perfectly proportioned. His hair curled about his ears with two or three locks carefully arranged over his forehead. There was intelligence in his dark eyes and an arrogant tilt to his head. Her first reaction was that he was supremely self-assured as he came forward to greet her, her second was that she did not recognise him. He was a stranger.

'Miss Hemingford, your obedient,' he said, bowing over her hand.

'Mr Allworthy?' She put the question in her voice, to indicate she did not know him. When he did not comment on that, she indicated a chair. 'Do sit down.'

He seated himself, throwing up the tails of his coat and

arranging his long legs in elegant fashion. She laid aside her cane and perched awkwardly on a sofa, her leg stiffly out in front of her. He saw it and winced a little. 'How are you, my dear?'

He was confident enough to risk the endearment, she noted. 'I am improving a little day by day, thank you, sir.'

'Good. You will make a full recovery, I trust.'

'I am hopeful, though I might always walk with a slight limp.'

'Oh.' He paused, as if this information needed some thought. 'But with the proper treatment that can be cured, I am sure. How soon can you be ready to leave?'

She was taken aback by his bluntness. 'You mean with you?'

'Of course I mean with me. Who else?'

'But I cannot go now, Mr Allworthy. His lordship has been kind enough to say I may stay as long as is necessary for a full recovery and I have not yet reached that happy stage.'

'But surely you wish to be home among your own people? Your father is particularly anxious to be reunited with you. As I am.'

'My father has been invited to come and visit me and he has chosen not to do so.'

'He is busy at his work. It is at a critical stage. I have arranged with Murray to have it published.'

She was surprised. She paid lip service to her father's genius, had agreed with him that it was a defining and scholarly work, but she was not blind to its faults. It was far too weighty and repetitive to earn critical acclaim and Mr Murray must know that. 'You mean you have paid for it to be published?'

'Sometimes great works need a helping hand and it was

my pleasure. If I am to become part of his family…' He let the sentence hang in the air, waiting for her reaction.

He was buying her, surely her father understood that. 'Sir, I do not know you.' She was aware, as she spoke, of a deep chuckle coming from a winged chair by the hearth and realised that the Earl was acting as chaperon and he was finding the conversation deeply entertaining. 'I explained when I wrote to you that I had lost all memory of the last few months of my life and I cannot recall ever having met you before.'

He looked startled. 'But that was only a temporary condition brought about by a bang on your head.'

'So I have been told, but unfortunately, however hard I try, I cannot remember you.'

'But we are engaged.'

'Oh, dear.' She was dismayed. 'Do you mean that it has been announced formally?'

'No, not exactly,' he admitted. 'But it was anticipated by everyone, agreed that we should announce it this autumn, after the harvest was finished and I was free to return to London. You spent two weeks at my home and I presented you with a parting gift when you left. It was not a tawdry gift.'

'Oh, what was it?' Had she really entertained a proposal from him, even considered accepting him? She did not even like him.

'A necklace in silver and amethyst. You accepted it as a token of my regard and a promise of intent. You expressed yourself delighted with it. I cannot believe you have wiped all that from your mind.'

She had seen that necklace among her other trinkets and assumed her father had given it to her. 'I have not wiped it, the accident did that.'

'But you remember other things, other people, your father and your cousins.'

'My cousins were with me when it happened. They saved my life.'

'Then I am grateful to them, but it is time they relinquished you to me and to your father. While you shut yourself away here, you will never recover your memory, there is nothing to stimulate it. I have a very roomy and comfortable coach, we shall be home in no time. And I have engaged an eminent physician to attend you. He is particularly good with...' he paused before adding '...nether limbs.'

'You mean legs.' She laughed, shocking him. 'My leg is twisted and no amount of money will change that.' She lifted her skirt slightly. 'See.' He averted his gaze, but not before he had caught a glimpse of her calf, with its slightly crooked look and wasted muscle. She could see he was repulsed by it. And it came to her that he delighted in having everything perfect; that imperfection could not be tolerated. 'And I have other scars, too. One here.' She lifted her hair so that he could see the one on her face. 'I believe it will fade in time, but it will not go away completely. Luckily I can hide it under my hair.'

He stood up. 'Miss Hemingford, it is clear to me you have been led into mischief. I put it no more strongly than that, but the young lady I once knew would never be so brazen as to— No, I cannot say it. But it is clear to me the sooner you are removed from here the better.'

'Removed!' She was furious. 'I am not a piece of furniture or a parcel.'

'I am sorry, that was badly put. I should have made more allowances for your state of health and spoken more gently. But you must know your father will be brokenhearted if I return without you.'

'I say, Allworthy, that's an unfair tactic,' said the voice from the winged chair. 'Playing on Jane's love and respect for her father. If he wants to keep his heart intact, he can come here and see her. He would soon see she is not yet ready for the journey or the bustle of life in the capital. We will send her home the moment she expresses a desire to go.'

'And what shall I say to the Countess of Carringdale?'

'And who is the Countess of Carringdale?' she asked innocently. 'Do I know the lady?'

'I cannot believe you have forgotten her as well.' He was obviously miffed. 'Why, she is your kinswoman and sponsor. She has given her approval of our betrothal and that counts for a great deal in Society.'

'Mr Allworthy, you are giving me a headache. I truly cannot take it all in.'

'Then I will withdraw until your head is better.'

'Yes, please do that. In fact, go back to Norfolk.' She smiled, sugar sweet. 'That is where you live, is it not?'

'Yes, but I shall stay at the inn tonight and return tomorrow.'

'That will not serve, sir,' she said stiffly. 'I am conscious of the honour you do me, but I do not think we should suit.'

He bowed, more angry than hurt; he had expended time, money and energy on his pursuit of her and he did not like having it thrown in his face when so much depended on it. 'I will see you when you return home, perhaps you will have come to your senses by then.'

The next moment he had gone and a slow handclap came from the chair by the hearth and the Earl poked his head round to look at her. 'Well done, my dear.'

Suddenly another memory slotted into place and it had nothing to do with Donald Allworthy. She had recalled why she had broken her engagement to Harry, the conversation which had so eluded her in her half-memory. Every word. The hurtful accusations, the anger and the gossip. It was a painful recollection. No wonder Harry had been reluctant to tell her about it. And now she had as good as broken off another. What would the tattlers make of that?

She could hear them in her head. 'Sent him about his business once, when all the poor lad did was try to better himself. Oh, it was not the best way of going about it, to be sure, but it did no one any harm. And then she ensnared that handsome Mr Allworthy and made a fool of him. Led him along, took his gifts, visited his home and was treated like a duchess, then dropped him like a hot brick when the prodigal returned a hero. Heir to an earldom is better than a squire with no title.'

Any hope she might have had of finding happiness with Harry died within her. She could not subject him to that.

Chapter Nine

If Anne and Harry were delighted with her decision, they wisely hid it. Jane was still too emotional, too confused, to think clearly. Instead they set out to amuse her. Each day she grew a little stronger, each day she walked a little farther, each day a little of her memory returned. That was the part of her recovery hardest to deal with. Her memories were almost as confusing as struggling with the loss of them had been.

'Don't worry about it,' Harry said. They were strolling through the park surrounding the estate. She had one hand tucked into his arm, the other held a cane and in that way she was managing very well. 'Let it come when it will, do not force it. Anne and I will be your memory.'

'Dear Anne. She has been a good friend to me. And I have not always appreciated that. She is loyal, too.' She paused, as they sat down on a fallen tree trunk side by side. 'You know, I have remembered why I broke off our engagement.'

'Oh.' He waited for her to continue, wondering if it was the end of their idyll. Since Allworthy's visit, they had become so close he had begun to hope, but if she still thought she had been right to end their engagement, they would be back to estrangement and bickering and he did not know how he was going to cope with that.

'I was young, influenced by others. I did not understand about Mrs Clarke. Papa and Aunt Lane said she was not at all respectable and if you had visited her, then it could only mean you were as bad as she was. And there were all those horrid details in the newspaper. I didn't understand half of it, but it was plain she entertained lovers, took money and presents from them. The Duke of York was not the only one and if the Duke could be stripped of his command, then it must be very dreadful. I was very hurt that you, who professed to love me, had resorted to visiting a…' She paused, unwilling to voice the word a carefully raised young lady should not know. 'I am sorry.'

He reached out a hand and laid it over hers. 'I am sorry too,' he said. 'I should have realised how much you had been manipulated.' He wanted to say, let us start again, but decided it was too soon, she was still too vulnerable 'Please do not think about it any more.'

'Now we have forgiven each other, we can be friends, you and Anne and I.'

Friends! That was not what he wanted, at least not all he wanted, but he did not correct her. 'You are not unhappy about Allworthy?'

'No. Do you know, he recoiled when he saw my leg, recoiled as if it would harm him? When I said we should not suit, he seemed relieved.'

'Then he is an arrogant fool.'

'You are kind, Harry, because you have been through it yourself, but I doubt your limp will be an impediment to marriage.'

He laughed. 'I should hope not!'

'But it will be to me. Mr Allworthy showed me that. I

have no dowry to speak of and I had only a healthy body and good sense to recommend me.'

'Good sense!' He laughed, teasing her. 'You are the most capricious woman I know.'

'I am being serious, Harry. An empty head, a broken body, a scarred face is no advertisement for a husband.'

'You are being silly. I know of at least one—'

She stood up suddenly. 'Let us talk of it no more. It will not help me strengthen my muscles sitting here. I want to learn to dance and ride again. How long will it be before I can do that, do you think?'

He smiled wryly and joined her to resume their walk. 'It is up to you. If you will it, then it will happen.'

She gave a little skip, surprised that she did not fall over. 'Then I shall set myself a target. I shall run a few yards by the end of the week and ride next week.'

'End of the week? Why not now?' He seized her hand. 'Come on, run.'

Her first attempt was ungainly. Her leg felt so weak she was afraid it would snap in two if she put too much pressure on it. 'It won't break,' he assured her. 'It is probably stronger than the other one now.'

Thirty yards later, she collapsed into his arms, triumphant. 'I did it!' She looked up into his face, her cheeks glowing, her eyes bright. 'I ran.'

'Yes, my love, you did.' He held her, studying her uptilted face, line by line, feature by feature, even the thin scar, fading more each day. There was nothing imperfect about her. He wanted to kiss her but, remembering her reaction when he had kissed her in the storm, dare not spoil the moment and contented himself with raising a hand to brush away a stray curl, looking into her eyes, trying to convey without words his love, his desire, his determination to protect her.

'Harry,' she said. 'Thank you.' Then she reached up and kissed his cheek. 'I owe you so much and can never repay you.'

He rubbed the spot, bemused, then gave a wry grin. 'You will repay me best by getting well again.'

'Yes, I must have been a great trial to you and you have been so patient. But you do not have to stay, Harry, I can do it on my own now. You must be worrying about the delay to your gun project. The war will be over before it comes to fruition.'

It was almost like being dismissed and it maddened and frustrated him. He sighed, tucking her arm beneath his elbow for the short walk back to the house. 'So, my usefulness is done.'

She heard the hurt in his voice. 'I did not mean that, Harry, and you know it. I was thinking of you. I have been holding you back. And truly now that I am better, we ought not to be out without a chaperon.'

He laughed loudly, scaring a crow pecking on the ground nearby. 'That would be shutting the stable door after the horse has bolted, don't you think?'

'I suppose so, but I do not want your name tarnished by impropriety. You have lived down the old scandal, it would be foolish to set the tongues wagging again.' She paused. 'Harry, you must get on with your life.'

'Without you?'

'No. I shall always be your friend.' She attempted a laugh but it had a hollow sound. 'I shall be outspoken, critical even, praise you and harangue you, but I shall try not to judge you. Isn't that what friends do?' She paused, smiling. 'I remember something else you said. A disinterested commerce between equals, that's what you called friendship.'

'That was Oliver Goldsmith, not me. Supposing I preferred the other option, the abject intercourse between tyrant and slave?'

'But you don't, do you? You are no one's slave, least of all mine. And I am not yours, and neither of us is a tyrant, so it will not work. Harry, we have to put the past behind us.'

'I am all in favour of that.'

'Then look forward.'

'To what?'

'Oh, do not be so downpin! You have spent weeks buoying me up, trying to keep me cheerful and optimistic, and you succeeded. Now is not the time to submit to the blue devils yourself. Make your gun. Be clever and famous and before long you will be the toast of London, next Season's most eligible bachelor.'

'And you?' He was beginning to wish he had never taken on that assignment, never invented that gun story and put himself in a position where he could hurt her again. While she needed him he had been happy, more than that, he had been delighted, to stay, but if she insisted on managing without him, he must do something else. His grandfather, who was tolerant of him but no more, refused to countenance anything except that he should find himself a wife and hang about waiting to inherit. He did not wish the old man dead; in spite of everything he was still very fond of him and he hoped he had many more years of life in him, but the last two years had taught him idle hands found the devil's work and he preferred to be busy. But not with guns.

They had come on to the mown grass in front of the house. It was a large rambling old building, beautiful in the late autumn sunshine with its ivy clad walls, shining windows and strange turrets, which she supposed had been built as lookout posts when England was at war with

itself. Jane had always loved visiting it and this occasion
had been more enjoyable than most, even though she had
been in pain some of the time and struggling against
weakness and infirmity the rest. She had learned to forgive
and love again, to treasure life because she had so nearly
lost it. And though she did not think she would ever
marry, she would learn to accept that and, like Harry, find
something useful to do.

'I shall return home, go on helping Papa. I wonder if
Mr Allworthy will withdraw his patronage now I have
turned him down?'

'Oh, Jane, Jane, what am I to do with you? Why do
you always think of everyone else instead of listening to
your own heart?'

She did not answer. Did he know what was in her heart,
did he know how much she loved him, that she would
forever regret her part in his downfall and that, now he
had pulled himself up again by his own efforts, she would
never subject him to gossip and rejection again?

'Well, I shall not let you go until you have danced with
me and ridden out into the country on the back of a dear
little mare I have picked out for you,' he said. 'Only then
will I be convinced you are truly recovered.'

'I shall like that.'

'Next week,' he said, as they mounted the steps to the
front door, going carefully one step at a time. 'It will give
you time for your leg to become a little stronger.'

The week passed much the same as those preceding it,
except that there was a kind of restraint in their dealings
with each other, a quietness. The laughing and teasing,
though still evident, seemed a little forced. She found herself asking Anne to accompany them more often on their
outings but on the day Harry had chosen to take her riding

for the first time, Anne had arranged to visit a friend and so she and Harry went alone.

It was strange to be in the saddle again. Harry lifted her up and carefully put her feet in the stirrups, handed her the reins and stood back to see how she felt. She felt wonderful. As long as she had enough strength in her thighs to guide the animal, her damaged leg, hidden beneath the wide skirt of her habit, seemed not to matter. She sat tall, eager to be on the move.

'Good?' he queried.

'Amazing.'

He turned and mounted himself and together they left the stable yard and walked the horses across the park. He watched her carefully. She had a great deal of courage and it was that courage which had pulled her through. Oh, how he ached to hold her in his arms, to make love to her, to marry her, but she had made it clear that she wanted no more than friendship. But could he endure that? When she needed him no longer, would it not be better to turn away, go somewhere where he would not have to see her day by day, tortured by her presence?

Gaining confidence, she broke into a trot and then a canter. He measured his own mount's stride to hers and stayed alongside. 'Oh, this is freedom,' she called to him. 'I am not a cripple while I am on the back of a horse.'

'You are not a cripple at all, Jane. Having a slightly one-sided gait is not being a cripple, or I would be one too. And I deny that most vigorously.'

'Yes, but you are so strong, so in command. No one dare look down on you because you are disabled.'

He cursed Allworthy for not hiding his feelings. 'And you will be strong too. Very soon.'

'Now,' she said. 'Now. I will prove my strength.' And she dug her heels in and urged the mare into a gallop.

He smiled and followed. She had always been at ease on a horse, ever since she had learned to ride with him and Anne as children. She had been the one ready to try anything, jumping a hedge or a wall, or even a brook. Thundering along the common, hair flying, scattering rabbits and birds as she went. 'Take care!' he called after her.

'Come on, I'll race you to that fallen elm,' she shouted, pointing with her crop.

He let her go a little ahead, preferring to stay just behind her, to make sure she came to no harm. His heart was in his mouth as she leaped a ditch, but she landed safely on the other side and a minute later pulled up at the tree and slid from the saddle. Only then did she remember her weakness as her leg buckled under her. He jumped down to steady her, but she laughed. 'Forgot,' she said. 'Lost my balance for a moment.'

He smiled. 'It is good to forget.'

They let the horses graze while they sat on the tree trunk. She was breathing heavily, but there was a glow about her as if she had suddenly come awake after a long sleep. Her eyes shone; her hat had come off and her heavy hair was all over the place. 'Oh, Harry, that was good.'

'Glad to be of service,' he said laconically, then added, 'If you were not in such a hurry to return home, you could ride here every day.'

Mr Allworthy had said something very similar, when she visited Coprise. She startled herself remembering the name of the place. She remembered its neat perfection, the manicured park and the beautiful horses. She had accused him of bribing her to marry him. But Donald Allworthy and Harry Hemingford were not alike in any way.

'How can you say I am in a hurry?' she said. 'I have been away from home three months now. Papa will have forgotten what I look like. And I can always hire a hack and ride in the park.'

'It's not the same, though, is it?'

'Harry, you are very wicked to tempt me so. I must go home, you know that.'

'You could marry me instead.' He spoke quietly, throwing the suggestion into the air, waiting for her reaction.

It was tempting, so very tempting, but he had spoken so casually, not as if he truly meant it, might even have mentioned it because he thought she was expecting it. But whether he meant it or not, she could not entertain the idea. Her refusal of Donald Allworthy would soon become common knowledge, if it hadn't already done so, and everyone would blame her. It would be worse if it appeared she had turned him away in order to become a future countess. And worse even than that, Harry would be condemned as a man who enticed another's intended bride away from him. She could not allow that to happen, even if it meant denying the love she felt for him.

'Oh, you will have your little jest, Harry,' she said, giving herself no more time to think. 'But you would run like a hare if you thought I would take you seriously.'

'Yes, a merry jest,' he said, laughing to hide his hurt. After all, what had he to offer but a broken body, a tarnished reputation and empty pockets? 'I am glad you know me so well or I would be halfway to Lincoln by now.'

'I do not know about Lincoln, but I think we should go back or we will be late for dinner.'

Dismissed, he stood up and held out his hand to help her to her feet. He did not speak again until they were both mounted and walking their horses slowly back to the stables. 'You still have not danced,' he said.

'No.'

'Then we shall have to remedy that before we leave.'

'We leave?' she queried.

'Yes, naturally I shall escort you. And as the family travelling coach is still lying in fragments at the bottom of a Yorkshire ravine, we shall have to go by stage or the Mail.'

'Was your grandfather very angry about the carriage?'

'He was thankful none of us was killed. I have been entrusted with the task of ordering a new carriage from Robinson and Cook.'

The holiday was at an end. Her broken body had mended, she had turned down two proposals of marriage and now she had to pick up the pieces of her life again, go back to being the dutiful daughter, back to her copying and housekeeping for her father. It would not be easy, but there was no help for it.

They parted on the landing to go to their respective rooms to change for dinner. Nurse, hearing her come in, arrived to help her dress. The old lady was more used to looking after children than grown women, but she was a wise and gentle soul and this was what Jane needed. She did not want to be laced into a corset, nor sit for hours to have her hair put up in some fashionable style. She had neither the strength nor the inclination for it.

Having helped her into a peach-coloured silk gown with a high waist and leg o' mutton sleeves, which covered the fading scar on her arm, Nurse set about her hair, trying to untangle the knots. 'Like curly wire, it is,' she told her and then laughed. 'Rusty wire at that.'

'I know. I think I might have it cut short, like a man's. The windswept style might suit me.'

'Windswept!' The old lady laughed. 'You are halfway there already. Did your horse take you through a bush?'

'No, but I lost my hat. Harry sent the stable boy back to look for it.'

Nurse finished tying a ribbon in a large bow to one side and stood back to survey her handiwork. 'That's the best I can do.'

Jane thanked her and made her way down to the drawing room, to find Anne and the Earl already there. She curtsied to the old man and sat down beside her friend. 'I have been riding,' she announced. 'And it was wonderful.'

'Good for you,' Anne said.

'I think it means my recovery is complete. I am so grateful to you, to Harry and to his lordship, for everything you have done for me...'

'My goodness,' Anne said with a light laugh. 'What has brought this on?'

'It is time I went home.'

'Oh. You have not quarrelled with Harry, have you?'

'No, of course not. He has been my saviour, but I must stand on my own feet now. Papa needs me...'

'And we do not, I suppose.' Anne's voice was sharp.

'Need me?' Jane laughed. 'I have been a millstone round your neck, an invalid stopping you from doing what you want to do, someone who has to be carried and coddled.'

'Jane, that is not true...'

'Leave her be, Sis.' Harry had entered the room unobserved. He moved over to bow to the ladies. He was in a black evening suit, with a pale blue waistcoat and a white muslin cravat. 'Jane has said she wants to go home, so I will take her home. There is no more to be said.'

Anne subsided into silence, though Jane knew she would return to the subject when they were alone and she must be firm. It would be so easy to give in, to say she would marry Harry, to allow herself to be persuaded, but she had done with being biddable, of subjugating herself to the will of others. From now on her decisions must be her own and Anne must be made to see that.

The butler came to announce dinner was served and they moved into the dining room, the Earl leading the way with Anne, and Harry and Jane bringing up the rear. 'Thank you,' she whispered to him. 'I do not think I could survive a quizzing tonight.'

'Then no one shall quiz you.'

The food was good and plentiful, but in spite of the exercise of riding, Jane had no appetite. She was still with Harry in the woods, feeling his warm dry hand holding hers, listening to him suggesting they should marry. It had not been a proper proposal, couched as a formal question, any more than it had been when they had become engaged before. Perhaps that was why she had been so quick to reject it, to suggest he had been joking, although did it matter how it was delivered if that was what they both wanted? But even if he had been serious, she could not have agreed, knowing he would be hurt by it.

'You are quiet, Jane,' Anne commented.

'A little tired,' she said. 'I have had more exercise to-day than I have had for a long time.'

Harry chuckled. 'She even managed to gallop.'

'Was that wise?' Anne asked.

'My infirmity disappears when I am on horseback.' She paused. 'You should have come with us.' If Anne had been there, Harry would not have spoken as he had and she would have been saved a painful conversation. 'I mean to ride again tomorrow, why don't you come too?'

'Oh, you are not dashing off to the Smoke first thing, then?'

Jane ignored the slight acerbity. 'Not unless you wish to be rid of me.'

'Oh, Jane, you know nothing would please me more than you should stay here forever.'

'And you know that is not possible,' she said quietly.

'Anne!' Harry admonished. 'I am taking Jane back to her father on Friday, that's three days from now. You may come or not, as you wish.'

'Of course I am coming.'

'But, Anne,' Jane protested, 'it's late in the year. The place will be dead.'

'I have things to do. And you must be chaperoned.' She looked from one to the other in puzzlement when they burst out laughing. 'London is not like Lincolnshire,' she added lamely. 'Arriving back in the capital unchaperoned would cause the tongues to wag.'

'So, I am to lose all three of you at once, am I?' the Earl said. 'And when shall you be back? Will it be before I stick my spoon to the wall, or only for the funeral?'

'Grandfather,' Anne cried, 'please do not speak of such a thing. You are not dying and it is unfair of you to pretend that you are. I shall be back.'

'And Harry?'

Harry, who thought he was only there on sufferance, did not know what to say. 'If you want me to, then naturally I shall return.'

The old man shrugged. 'Do as you please. I expect it is too much to expect you to give up this mad idea of going into manufacturing? You would do better to find yourself a wife and settle down.'

'I am doing my best, sir,' he said and then winked at Jane. She blushed scarlet and looked down at the portion of raised mutton pie on her plate. 'The trouble is, she will not have me.'

The old man chuckled. 'Try harder.'

He knew exactly what had been going on, Jane was sure, and he delighted in goading his grandson, but that did not mean he did not love him. She was sure he did, but he was used to having his own way and he could not bear to be crossed. And Harry did not like to be beaten either. They were as stubborn as each other. She wondered how she would feel if Harry did find himself a wife. Horribly, horribly jealous, she was sure.

Anne brought up the subject when the meal ended and they left the men to their brandy and went into the withdrawing room for tea. 'Harry asked you to marry him, didn't he?'

She managed a smile. 'It was not so much a question as a statement of what I could do if I chose.'

'Same thing. And you turned him down. Why?'

'Oh, for many reasons. It would not do. We had our chance two years ago and we both ruined it. I admit it was as much my fault as his, but we cannot turn the clock back. And I have just given Mr Allworthy his *congé* and no doubt the tongues are already wagging over it. I must go on quietly if I am to live that down and not embarrass Papa and Aunt Lane.'

'I cannot believe Harry accepted that.'

'He did. He is no more anxious to rake up old wounds than I am. He is set upon developing his gun, and it will not help if there is a cloud hanging over him, though I am sorry his lordship cannot find it in him to be more encouraging.'

'He is stubborn,' Anne said, confirming Jane's own opinion. 'He laid down the conditions for Harry's return to grace some time ago and he is finding it difficult to change them. He thinks it will make him look weak.'

'What conditions?'

'He says he will reinstate Harry's full allowance, and even add to it, if he marries and settles down to running the estate like a proper aristocrat. I thought you knew that.'

'Oh, was that why Harry asked me to marry him?'

'No, it was not!' Anne snapped. 'He loves you and you know it.'

'Do I? I don't think I can be sure of anything any more. His love may be as ephemeral as Mr Allworthy's. I am sure he was relieved when I sent him away.'

'Who? Mr Allworthy or Harry?'

'I meant Mr Allworthy, but the same may be true of Harry. He may have mentioned marriage just to please you because you have been pushing him. After all, he wants to go into business, but I cannot help him do that.'

'He would give up that idea for you.'

'Anne, please stop. You are trying to bully me and I have decided I will no longer be influenced by what other people think.'

Anne gave a hollow laugh. 'But you are! You are worrying about gossip.'

'Not for myself.' She was near to tears. She had so wanted to accept Harry, had worried about the effect of gossip on the Hemingford family name and how it would spoil Harry's reinstatement in Society and his stature as a hero, not to mention returning into favour with his grandfather; then to be told the Earl was trying to bribe him to marry her was the outside of enough. 'And I collect it was you who mentioned gossip at dinner, so you cannot be impervious to it.'

'That was different. I only want to protect you both.'

'I know, dearest Anne, I know. But you would do it best by accepting what cannot be changed.'

'Then if you have quite made up your mind, I shall have to help Harry make his gun.'

'How?'

'I still have the money my grandmother left me. It is not a fortune, but I mean to give it to him for his project.'

'But, Anne, is that wise? You might need it yourself.'

'I do not think so. As neither of us expects to marry, we might as well live together. I will be his housekeeper and his helpmate. With my money and his half-pay and what Grandfather allows him, we shall do very well and he shall have his ordnance manufactory.'

This turn to the conversation was worrying Jane. It was as if Anne had known all along that she would not agree to marry Harry, or that Harry himself was not convinced that was what he wanted. 'Anne, are you sure you should? The war might end before he could produce his gun and you would lose everything.'

'He said when the war ended he would turn to making the perfect sporting gun. I know he will be a great success and everyone will have to acknowledge it.'

'But it is tantamount to gambling.'

'Jane, dear, I have faith in Harry, even if you do not. And I beg you not to refine upon it or we shall have a falling out.'

Jane turned away as the men came into the room and sat down. Anne poured tea for them and they began a desultory conversation, polite but meaningless, until the Earl decided to retire. After he had gone, leaving the three young people to amuse themselves, Harry suddenly jumped up. 'Jane wants to dance,' he said, holding out his hand to her. 'You will play for us, won't you, Sis?'

'No, no,' Jane said quickly. 'I am too tired. It has been a long day...'

'Just a few steps,' he pleaded, as Anne went to the

piano. 'Prove you can do it. You said you would not go home until you had learned to ride and dance again. If you do not, we cannot leave on Friday.'

She took his hand and allowed herself to be led into the middle of the room. They danced a minuet, slow and stately, which caused no problem at all. 'There,' he said when they finished. 'All your accomplishments back in working order. Shall we try a gavotte now?'

That was more energetic, but she managed to complete it without stumbling. At the end she was breathless, but the rapid beating of her heart had little to do with the energy she had put into it. It was far more complex than that. 'Thank you,' she said quietly.

'Now, I'll teach you a new dance,' he said. 'I learned it while I was abroad, but it is coming to London and will soon be all the rage. You must be able to waltz.'

She had heard of it, but she knew many people considered it too *risqué* for polite society. The man was expected to hold his partner round the waist! 'Oh, no, I could not,' she protested. 'I have heard it is immodest.'

'Jane, I have been carrying you about for weeks, supporting you, catching you when you stumbled, so how can my hand held lightly on your back matter?' He turned her to face him, took her right hand in his left and put his other hand about her waist, holding her a foot from him. 'See, there is nothing improper about this. Put your hand on my shoulder. Now, move backwards and follow my steps.' He moved forward taking her with him. 'One, two, three, one, two, three.'

She faltered once or twice and he turned to his sister, watching them from the piano stool. 'Have you any suitable music, Anne? It is much easier with music.'

Anne sorted through the music on the top of the piano and found something in the right tempo and they began

again. In no time at all, Jane had mastered the steps and
caught the rhythm. She allowed herself to relax, to enjoy
being held in this daring way, to be near him, knowing it
might be the last time they were so close. 'Perfect,' he
murmured, looking down into her upturned face.

'I have a good teacher. Do you really think the waltz
will become the rage?'

'No doubt of it, and you will be one step ahead when
it is danced in the ballrooms of the *haut monde*.'

'I doubt I shall be invited to the ballrooms of the *haut
monde*, and even if I am I will not be so daring as to stand
up for a waltz.'

'You will, if I ask you, surely?'

'Will you ask me?'

'Oh, undoubtedly.' He smiled and drew her closer so
that their bodies were touching and a strange sensation
coursed through her, making her falter. She would have
fallen if he had not been holding her so firmly. Did he
enjoy tormenting her, teasing her, testing her? She risked
glancing up at him, and found his eyes searching hers.
The pupils were dark, fathomless, asking questions she
could not answer, making statements she found uncomfortable. It was as if they were repeating everything he
had ever said to her, reducing it to its essence. Love, forgiveness, repentance, hope, all rolled into one searching
look.

She was beautiful, he decided, with that puzzled look
on her face, her lips slightly parted. Why could she not
see that he would do anything, make any sacrifice, for
her? For her he would be what his grandfather wanted
him to be and take pleasure in it. He could see her in his
mind's eye, living at Sutton Park, gracing it with her presence, making a real home of it. And in the spring, they
would go to Bostock House and enjoy the Season in their

own way. The gossip would die down. Gossip was only good if it was new; as soon as something fresh came along, the tattlers would spring on it like a cat on a mouse and forget Jane and Harry Hemingford and Donald Allworthy. Why could she not see that?

'Jane,' he murmured softly, as the music came to an end and they stood facing each other. 'Change your mind.'

'What about?'

'Marrying me.'

'So that you can enjoy your inheritance? No, thank you, Harry.' She broke away from him and ran from the room.

He looked perplexed. 'What did she mean by that?' he asked his sister.

'She thinks you want to marry her to please Grandfather and have your allowance reinstated.'

'Whatever gave her that idea?'

'I am afraid I did. I did not mean to, we were talking about something else.'

'Then you had better disabuse her of that idea at once.' For the first time since they were squabbling children he was seriously displeased with his twin.

'I tried. She refuses to listen to me and has hardened her heart.'

'Sis, I warned you not to interfere. Jane needs time to get over Allworthy, to realise for herself what is in her heart. And it is not hard, it is soft and malleable, too malleable sometimes. It was you who told me how she had been coerced and you should have known better than to try the same thing yourself.'

'I am sorry.'

'Then accept her decision, because I have.' Only by speaking firmly could he convince her of that, especially when it was far from true. Not until Jane married someone else would he give up hope, but another lesson he had learned in war was patience. If only other people would leave them alone! He smiled to mitigate his anger. 'I am taking her home on Friday and we shall accept your offer to be chaperon, with gratitude.'

'Then I suppose it will have to be your gun.'

'What do you mean by that?'

'Harry, I have been thinking about it.'

'I wish you would not.'

'Why not? It is the least I can do when you have been so disappointed by everyone else.'

'If you mean Jane, I am not disappointed.'

'Fustian! And I did not mean only Jane. Grandfather was unhelpful…'

'Oh, Anne, what else did you expect? I am still an incorrigible bantling to him.'

She ignored him. 'And Colonel Garfitt. He was your friend, but he has not acted your friend over this.'

'Anne, do leave off.'

'Harry, do listen. We could continue to live at Bostock House and you could have your manufactory in the rooms above the stables.' Because the Earl never came to the capital, they did not keep a town carriage and had only one groom to look after the riding horses. 'The groom can move into the house. There are a dozen attic bedrooms and only a handful of servants to occupy them. It would save expense.'

He smiled at her enthusiasm. 'I cannot fire guns in the stables, Anne. It is too dangerous and would frighten the horses. And Grandfather would never sanction it.'

'Then we do not ask him. He need never know. You can find somewhere to fire them. Manton's would be convenient, and we could manage the tools and materials, whatever else you needed, with my money.'

'Your money?' he repeated, astonished. 'A fine brother I would be to take your nest egg from you to further my own ends.'

'I do not need it.'

'Nothing would induce to me accept it.'

'What will you do then?'

'I thought of settling in Westmorland and breeding sheep.'

She sat back and laughed. 'You, a sheep farmer, that's doing it too brown! What about your gun?'

'Be damned to my gun! Now, if you will excuse me, I have things to do.'

He left her and went to the stable to speak to Giles, who had long since returned to his duties. 'Go to the Nag's Head tomorrow and book four seats on the London stage for Friday,' he told him. 'You will be coming with us. I have to buy a new coach and horses and you will be needed to drive them back.'

That done, he went up to his room, to sit at the window looking out upon the quiet landscape of his childhood, slumbering under a full moon. It had been his home and one day it would be again, but in the meantime he must make a life for himself. He had been home from the war for several months now and in that time he had done nothing, though he might he halfway to uncovering a traitor. Had it been worthwhile? Looking after Jane had been worthwhile, of course, and he would treasure the time they had spent together, but he had known from the start it could not last. He sighed. The day after tomorrow, they would go back to London.

They had one last ride the next day, all three roaming all over the estate, taking their leave of it, and then they returned to the house to pack for the journey. They would have to be up at six to be sure of catching the stage at seven-thirty. The Earl would not be up at that time and they said goodbye to him the evening before. Jane thanked him for having her to stay and he surprised her by taking both her hands in his and kissing her cheek, murmuring, 'Take care of that grandson of mine, Jane.'

She had hesitated, not knowing what to say. 'My lord, I cannot influence him,' she said.

'Oh, I think you can.' He smiled and released her. 'Come back and visit an old man, won't you?'

She said she would be happy to do so and then watched as he walked stiffly from the room. What did his lordship expect her to do? She could not, would not, try to persuade Harry to marry. That was a decision for him alone.

Early next morning the three young people and Giles, together with their luggage, were taken to the Nag's Head in a large, old-fashioned barouche that had not been used for years. Giles had ordered the stable boy to sweep out the cobwebs and give it a good clean. It was serviceable enough for a journey of four miles, but Harry would not risk it any further. 'Besides, I would not be seen dead in it in town,' he said, an opinion shared by Giles.

The stage was on time as it usually was. Their luggage was loaded, Harry helped Jane and Anne in before climbing in himself, while Giles climbed up beside the coachman who was an old friend of his. The other seats were soon filled and they were on their way.

They took breakfast at the Angel in Grantham, passed through Stilton and three hours later were in Baldock, where they ate a meal before going on. After stops at Welwyn and Barnet they rolled into the Bull and Mouth in London at half past five. The girls rested in the inn while Harry set about finding them a conveyance to take them home and a carrier to shift their luggage.

Now they were back, Jane was filled with trepidation. Most of her memory had returned, but not all of it, and she was worried that she might make some awful *faux pas* by cutting someone she was supposed to know or being ignorant of a fact like a death or a new baby, which she ought to mention. She was also anxious to know if Mr Allworthy had returned to London or gone straight from Sutton Park to Coprise Manor. She hoped, more than anything, it was the latter.

But her hopes were dashed. When she arrived at Duke Street, she was greeted, not by her father, but by her Aunt Lane, who bustled out to the hall as soon as she heard her arrive. 'Jane, my dearest,' she cried, taking Jane's hands in her own and holding her at arm's length while Harry stood watching. 'How glad I am to see you. Let me look at you. Why, you look well.' She stopped suddenly and peered into Jane's face. 'You do remember me, do you not?'

Jane laughed. 'Of course, I do, Aunt Lane. But I did not think to see you here.'

'I came back as soon as I heard what had happened.' She sent the maid who stood by the door scurrying for refreshments.

'I have made a full recovery, thanks to Anne and Harry.' She turned to him. 'Harry saved my life.'

'Then I must thank him.' She offered her hand to Harry, who took it and raised it briefly to his lips.

'Your obedient, Mrs Lane.' He could feel the hostility in the air and decided to take himself off. 'I will leave Jane in your hands, madam.' He bowed and left them.

'Where is Papa?' Jane asked, as she followed her great aunt into the drawing room.

'He is in the library, working on his book. He will join us directly.'

'Oh. Mr Allworthy did not withdraw his patronage, then?'

'Yes, I am afraid he did.' She paused, watching Jane walking across the room, as if assessing the limp. 'When I heard that you had given him the right about when he had been so kind as to offer to fetch you home, I had to come and see for myself what was going on. Jane, I cannot believe you have been so foolish.'

'Aunt, I am sorry for Papa, indeed I am. But when Mr Allworthy came to Sutton Park, I did not even remember him. He was a stranger.'

'So he told us. But he also said you remembered your cousins and you had no difficulty in finding your way around Sutton Park.'

'But, Aunt, Harry and Anne were with me when the accident happened. How could I not know them? My loss of memory was strange. I remembered my childhood, when Mama was alive and we lived near Sutton Park, but nothing of recent events. I did not know I had been ill, nor why we went to Westmorland, nor anything of the journey up to the point of the accident.'

'Not even Mr Allworthy, who loves you?'

'Does he? I think not.'

'But he offered for you and welcomed us at Coprise Manor. We were planning to announce your engagement to him. How could you forget that?'

'But I did. I tried to remember, gave myself headaches trying, but it would not come to me.'

'If you had come home with him, you might have remembered everything.'

'I was not well enough.'

'Mr Allworthy was of the opinion that you were well on the way to recovery; if you had come home with him, the physician he had employed would have straightened out your leg and you would not have been left lame.'

'I had a very good doctor, Aunt, I do not think anyone could have done better. And Mr Allworthy was so pompous and overbearing, as if I was being deliberately provoking. I was not, I assure you, it was as if I had just met him for the first time and I found I did not like him.'

'You were influenced by those cousins of yours, Harry in particular. I do not know what went on while you were in Westmorland, but I fear it was nothing to your credit. I did not want you to go, but of course you would take no notice of me, who has always had your welfare at heart.'

'I am sorry, Aunt, but nothing went on.'

'You said you could not remember.'

Oh dear, this was becoming very difficult. 'I have remembered since. We had a pleasant holiday, all three of us together. I am sure I wrote to you at the time.'

'I do not know how we are going to live it down. Mr Allworthy was intent on calling Captain Hemingford out for enticing you from him, but luckily he was dissuaded.'

'By you and Papa?'

'No, the Countess. She is most displeased that you did not consider her sensibilities when she had been so kind as to offer to hold a ball for you to announce your engagement.'

The Countess! Jane would have laughed aloud if she had not been so distressed and so tired. 'I am sorry about that, but I do not wish to marry Mr Allworthy and I have told him so.'

'You intend to marry Captain Hemingford?'

'Not him either.'

Her father came into the room at that point, kissed his daughter, and sat down beside her. He looked pale and his eyes looked strained, which was hardly surprising considering the time he spent poring over manuscripts. 'Well, Jane, how are you?'

'Almost as good as new, Papa. I am sorry Mr Allworthy has withdrawn his patronage. I think it was very unkind of him. You deserve recognition for all your hard work.'

'Perhaps it would not have been the kind of recognition I need, Jane,' he said with a sigh 'There would have been strings attached.'

'You mean Mr Allworthy made it a condition that I accept him?'

'No, for he assumed you would until he went to Sutton Park. He believes you have been spoiled—'

'He did not say *despoiled*?' she put in quickly.

'Good gracious no!' he exclaimed. 'He did not go so far as to say that.'

'No.' She managed to laugh then. 'By spoiled he meant lame, scarred, imperfect, not fit to be his wife.'

'Jane!' Her aunt sounded horrified. 'I am sure you are wrong.'

'Then what strings are you talking about?'

'I meant the gossip, Jane. This is the second time our name has been linked with gossip. It would not help to sell my book. It is a serious work of scholarship and I wanted and expected it to be recognised as such. If it were published now, it would be "that book written by the father of that notorious tease".'

If she had not been so tired she might have found a reply to that, but it had been a long day, and she could argue no more. She wanted her bed. 'I am very sorry, Papa,' she said. 'I hope you will be proved wrong. And now, do you think I might retire? I am still not fully recovered.'

She kissed him and climbed the stairs where Hannah helped her into bed. In spite of her exhaustion, or perhaps because of it, she could not sleep. She had been right about the gossip; if her aunt and father were not exaggerating, it was not going to be pleasant going out and about and she was glad the Season was over and only the year-round residents were in town. But what angered her most of all was the thought that Donald Allworthy had fuelled it. He could have stayed in Norfolk and kept quiet and it might have come to nothing. And though Papa was putting a brave face on it, she knew he was bitterly disappointed.

She missed Harry already, missed his quiet humour, his understanding, his strength. She turned into her pillow and cried herself to sleep.

Chapter Ten

Harry called at Duke Street at noon the following day and was received by Mrs Lane, who told him Jane was not at home, a euphemism for telling him she did not wish to see him. He was unsure whether it was Jane herself who did not want to meet him or whether her aunt had advised her not to do so, but whichever it was, he was perplexed and annoyed. He had come to enquire that she was well and suffering no ill effects from her journey and unless she was indisposed, it would have been polite to receive him.

'Is she not well?' he asked. 'I know the journey was a tiring one.'

'She is exhausted, Captain. After all, she is not completely recovered from the accident, but now she is home, she will be well looked after, you may be sure of that.'

'Then please convey my good wishes,' he said, bowing and taking his leave.

Jane, who had heard the door knocker and voices in the hall from her bedroom, heard the front door shut and went to the window to look out on the street. Harry was striding away, his uneven gait hardly noticeable, his long unbuttoned greatcoat swirling out behind him, his top hat clamped firmly on his head. At the corner, he turned to look back at the house and even at that distance she could see the strong set of his jaw, the tension in every muscle of his body, and she wished with all her heart she could call him back. But she had told her aunt to send him away. She could not entertain him, even briefly, and maintain her resolve to scotch the rumours, not so much for her sake but for his and her father's. But, oh, how her heart ached for him. She turned as Aunt Lane came into the room.

'I sent him away, as you asked.'

'I know.' She sank on to the bed and put her hands over her face. 'What have I done, Aunt?' she cried. 'What have I done?'

Her aunt sat beside her and put an arm about her shoulders. 'Bear up, child. It is for the best.'

'Is it?' she asked dully.

'You know it is. You have to live down the scandal of your treatment of Mr Allworthy and it will be sooner done if Captain Hemingford is not seen as a frequent caller.'

'I know. But I promised to be his friend. How can I be that if I turn my back on him?'

'My dear child, refusing to see him will be the act of a friend. You are not the only one who has to live down scandal. He must distance himself from that accusation of enticement too.'

'Poor Harry, it is so unjust.' She paused. 'Why do people take so much notice of gossip? It is always the same—if the tattlemongers can blacken someone's name, they are triumphant.'

'While they are gossiping about someone else, no one is looking at what they are doing themselves. It is a kind of defence.'

'That may be, but why choose me? Why pick on Harry?

He has been kindness itself. I would have died but for him and I cannot even publicly acknowledge that. I blame Mr Allworthy. He did not have to come back to London and spread malicious rumours. I cannot imagine what he hopes to gain.'

'I think he is trying to save face. Everyone knew he had offered for you, and he is a proud man.'

'He is also a hypocrite. He is repelled by my infirmity. He cannot abide anything that is not perfect, and I am now imperfect, damaged. You remember what he was like at Coprise, always setting things to rights, moving an ornament two inches, grumbling at the gardener because there was a weed in the flower bed, insisting on meals being on time to the minute. And so formal. I think I began to know then that I did not want to marry him.'

'You remember all that?'

'I do now. I had not done so when he came to Sutton Park. When he saw me there, he recoiled from me, his distaste was obvious, and I believe he was relieved when I told him I would not marry him, which makes it so much more difficult to understand why he is so vindictive towards Harry. And Papa, too—it was not his fault.'

'I know. Your papa was very disappointed.'

'Where is he now?'

'In the library, where else would he be at this time of day? When you have dressed and had your breakfast, go down to him. He is expecting you.'

Her father was at his desk surrounded by mountains of paper when she joined him. He looked exhausted. 'Papa, you work too hard,' she said, going over to kiss his papery cheek. 'You will make yourself ill.'

He ran his fingers through his spiky hair. 'I am perfectly well, simply tired. You have been away so long and I have missed your help.'

'I thought the book was finished.'

'I would have drawn it to a close, if...' He shrugged. 'But no matter, it may have been a blessing after all. I need to make some changes. It is not right yet.'

It was always the same, always more changes, more improvements, more research. She was becoming convinced he did not want to finish it and, if he ever did, he would be at such a loss to know how to fill his time that he would fade away and die. She smiled encouragingly. 'I am here now, Papa. Tell me what you wish me to do.'

He gave her a pile of handwritten pages to copy and she took it to her desk and began work. It was as if she had never been away.

They had been working in silence for some time when her aunt knocked and came in to tell them she had had the tea things taken to the drawing room and it was time they took a rest. 'I am too busy,' Mr Hemingford said. 'Ask Hannah to bring mine here.'

'Very well, but Jane must take a rest. There might be callers and it would be agreeable to have her with me.'

Jane, whose eyes were aching from the close work, was glad to put down her pen and follow her aunt to the drawing room. 'Are you expecting calls, Aunt?'

'When your friends know you are home again, naturally they will want to know that you have made a full recovery.'

Jane could not think who might be interested enough in her welfare to call, except perhaps Anne, but she joined her aunt in the drawing room. They had hardly settled themselves in their seats when the Countess of Carringdale was announced. She was the last person Jane wanted to see and she would have liked to plead a headache or business to attend to, or another engagement away from the house, but she was given no opportunity. The lady was in the room, looking about her, appraising the decor and the furnishings, shaking her head, making the plumes on her pink turban nod.

'Afternoon, Harriet,' she said, addressing Mrs Lane who murmured a greeting, fluttering her hands uselessly.

Jane rose and made a small curtsy. 'Countess, good afternoon. Please be seated. I am afraid Papa cannot be with us. He is much occupied with his work, you know.'

'Yes, I did know,' her ladyship said, seating herself on the edge of a chair and putting both her hands on the top of her parasol, as if she mean to beat the ground with it. 'But he should not shut himself away as he does, it cannot be good for him. Nor can he keep up with the latest *on dit* if he neglects to be in company.'

'I think he is not much interested in gossip, my lady.'

'Then he should be. How is one to avoid it, if one does not know what is being said?'

'I think if people are determined to prattle, then there is no avoiding it,' Jane said, as her aunt dispensed tea. 'One can only hope the tattlers will tire of it and turn to something else.'

'Oh, indeed, but they can do prodigious damage before that happens.'

Jane was not sure where the conversation was leading, but it seemed to be loaded with innuendo and she was sure it was directed at her. She had this confirmed when her ladyship, having accepted a cup of tea, went on. 'I will speak plainly, Jane. You are distant kin and so I must declare an interest in what you do. And I have been shocked by what I have been hearing.'

'Oh, what have you been hearing?' Jane asked, smiling sweetly, though inside she was boiling with fury. If it were not for her aunt, who set so much store by the good opinion of the lady, she would have shown her the door.

'That you have been cavorting in the Lake District with that rakeshame of a cousin and his hoyden of a sister, and getting into all manner of scrapes.'

'I cannot accept cavorting,' Jane said. 'Anne and I went on holiday together to recuperate from illness and Captain Hemingford escorted us. Unfortunately we had a very bad accident on the return journey. We were lucky we were not all killed. I owe my life to Captain Hemingford and I do not like to hear him described as a rakeshame. He is a gentleman I am proud to call my friend.'

'Well!' her ladyship exclaimed. 'If that isn't the outside of enough! Impertinence added to impropriety will hardly mend matters.'

'I am sorry, my lady, but I must defend my friends.'

'Then I have no more to say to you. I had hoped that you might repent of your folly and accept Mr Allworthy, but I see I have been wasting my time.' She put down her cup and turned to Mrs Lane. 'Harriet, I am leaving.' And with that she rose and sailed out of the room.

As soon as she had gone Aunt Lane burst into noisy tears; though Jane tried to comfort her, she was inconsolable. 'She will never speak to me again, I know it.'

'Does it matter so much?'

The old lady dabbed at her eyes with a lace-edged handkerchief. 'Of course it matters! She has so much influence in Society. One word from her, and we shall be given the cut direct by everyone.'

'But, Aunt, the Season is long over and there is hardly anyone in town. I am surprised the Countess is here.'

'The Earl came to attend the House of Lords and though she does not often travel with him out of Season, she decided to come this time.'

'To see for herself what I have been up to?'

'I suppose so. She has taken a great liking to Mr All-worthy and was determined to encourage the match with you.'

'Why?'

'She is wealthy in her own right, you know, but she has no children of her own, no one to leave her fortune to. She told me in confidence she had been looking about her for a worthy recipient and had decided you would be the one. She meant to raise you up in Society and leave you a substantial inheritance if you shaped up.'

Jane could not help laughing. 'And I did not shape up! How disappointed she must be!'

'It is not a laughing matter, Jane. She is in a strong position to ruin your reputation.'

'I thought I had managed to do that very well on my own.'

'It will be worse. She is a great letter writer and knows everybody.'

Jane was not sure how it could be worse, but when she ventured out to the shops or the library, or took a stroll in the park, she noticed people turning away and becoming engrossed in something their companions were saying when she approached. Some even crossed the road to avoid her.

Once, when she and Aunt Lane were taking a carriage ride in Hyde Park, they met the Countess in her carriage, accompanied by Donald Allworthy. He was immaculately attired in a double-breasted tailcoat of snuff-coloured superfine with a high stand-up collar. His cravat was tied in an intricate froth of muslin and lace, spilling over the top of a striped marcella waistcoat. Both carriages were obliged to come almost to a standstill to pass each other.

The Countess looked straight ahead, her nose in the air, but Mr Allworthy, being on the side nearest the Lane carriage, doffed his tall hat and smiled without speaking. Jane did not like that smile; it was wolf-like, as if he were saying he had not done with her yet.

As the carriages moved apart, Jane could hear the Countess berating him for acknowledging them, but she did not hear his reply. Jane did not care for herself, but it upset her aunt so much, they decided not to risk going to the park again.

No one called and no one sent invitations. 'It is not at all surprising,' Jane said, one afternoon as they sat together in the drawing room. 'It is because the knockers are off all the doors, not because we have been ostracised.'

'All the same, I think I shall go home to Bath. There is plenty to do there. You could come with me, away from all this. Stay until after Christmas.'

'It is very kind of you, Aunt, but I have been away from home so much this year, I cannot leave Papa again.' Mr Hemingford was working in the library as usual. He had always been of a retiring disposition, but just recently he was becoming more and more of a recluse. He had even waved away her offers of help, preferring to be alone. Apart from his disappointment over the publication of his book, the gossip had not touched him.

'He should come too. The change will be beneficial. If he stays in that gloomy library much longer, he will shrivel and die.'

Jane was of the same opinion. Her father was becoming thinner and more haggard and his sight was getting very poor. And he always seemed to be in a far-off place and hardly heard her when she spoke. 'Perhaps I should try and persuade him.'

But he would not hear of it and Jane would not leave him. Mrs Lane returned to Bath alone. After she had gone, Jane was left without company or advice. She came down to breakfast each morning in order to see her father before he shut himself away, but after that there was nothing to do. She read book after book, did a little needlepoint and kept house, but that barely filled her time. Sometimes, when Hannah was not too busy to accompany her, she went for a walk, taking a cane to help her along. She would not admit that she hoped she might meet Harry, but it must have been in the back of her mind because she found herself looking for his broad frame, his dark curly hair, the ungainly gait, so like her own, and was disappointed when he failed to appear.

The disappointment was acute. She could not banish him from her thoughts. He was there, in her head, whatever she did. In the middle of reading a book, his face would appear on the page, smiling at her. When she was sewing, she could hardly see where to put her needle for the tears that welled up at some memory of something he had said. Her memory had returned completely; it was all there, everything they had ever said and done, and most particularly the way he had kissed her when they were caught in the storm and the intensity of her response. He loved her, she knew it, and she loved him, but it was that love which prevented her from seeking him out. If they were seen together, his newly won good reputation would be gone and no one would finance his gun project.

Harry, together with Giles whose opinion he valued, left Robinson and Cook in Mount Street, well satisfied with the carriage they had chosen. It would be delivered the following day after the Bostock coat of arms had been painted on its doors. Their next stop was Tattersall's, where they spent some time choosing four horses to draw it, two chestnuts for leaders and two bays that he decided would work well together. Leaving Giles to arrange for their delivery, he returned home.

He found Anne in the conservatory, one of Cook's big aprons over her gown, painting a watercolour of an exotic plant that grew there. 'All alone?' he queried.

'As you see.' She put her brush in a pot of water and turned to him. 'Did you buy the coach?'

'Yes, the horses too. I venture to think his lordship will be pleased with the bargain I made.' He gave her a wry smile. 'As far as he is pleased with anything I do.'

'Oh, Harry, I wish you could deal better with each other. If you are not going ahead with making your new gun, just what are you going to do?'

'I am waiting.' It was October now, July when he had first visited Clarence Garfitt, and in that time he had made some small progress, but not enough. He had no proof of treachery and he would have to have that before anyone in authority would move. Thoms was on the trail, watching the Leeds manufactory, ordered to follow the carts that left it. He was as sure as he could be they would end up in King's Lynn aboard the *Fair Trader*, and even then the owner of the vessel could easily blame the captain and say it was all being done without his knowledge. He needed to be caught red-handed.

'She will not come here, not now. You must go to her.'

She had misunderstood him, but he knew perfectly well what had been in her mind. 'Anne, she has said she does not want to see me and I must accept that. There is already gossip and I do not wish to add to it.'

'For her sake?'

'Yes.'

'And she is estranging herself from you for your sake. What a pair of ninnies you are!'

He sighed heavily. 'What would you have me do? Batter down her door?'

'I am sure it is not beyond your ingenuity to think of something. She has to go out sometimes.'

'You would have me waylay her in the street like a thieving footpad?'

'If it is the only way...'

'Oh, leave off refining on it, Anne, you make my head spin.'

He knew he had hurt her and quickly apologised, but being reminded of Jane unsettled him and he could not sit still. He sent for his horse to be saddled; he needed some exercise.

He rode for hours, covering ground on Hyde Park and Green Park, where he was reminded again of Jane. She had been riding there with Allworthy when he had seen her for the first time since returning to England and realised what he supposed he had known all along, that he still loved her. He wished that confounded fellow, Allworthy, would take himself back to Norfolk. While he remained in London, going about with the Countess of Carringdale, the gossip would never end. Nor could he complete his mission for Colonel Garfitt. He returned his tired horse to the stable and went indoors, where he found an ill-spelled letter from Jerry Thoms waiting for him. It sent him scurrying to Horse Guards.

'I heard you were back in town,' Garfitt said when Harry was shown into his office after kicking his heels in an anteroom for over an hour. 'Some mushroom from

Norfolk threatening to call you out for enticing his lady love from him.'

Harry was as sure as he could be that Allworthy no longer wanted Jane, but if he had realised how close on the trail Harry was, he would want to bring him down, discredit him in the eyes of the world. What better way to do it than by pretending to be aggrieved by Jane's rejection and calling him out? But surely a duel would be too risky? 'Strange, isn't it?' he said. 'Everyone seems to know about this but me. I have seen neither hide nor hair of the man myself.'

'It's not true what he is saying, then?'

'Whatever he has been saying, he has not said it to me.'

'So you have not been diverted from your purpose over a lady?'

Harry was glad the colonel did not know how very nearly true that accusation was. 'No, though I think that is what our man has in mind.'

'Oh? Enlighten me.'

'I visited the manufactory of Franz Stoller in Leeds. He is the one making the traitor's guns, I am sure of it. I set my man watching the premises and he has today sent me word the cargo is on the move, heading for King's Lynn. According to him, the crates are labelled umbrellas.'

'Umbrellas?'

'Yes.' Harry smiled grimly. 'Long narrow boxes. The wagon is heavily laden and will take several days to reach the port, by which time the *Fair Trader* is expected to dock. I will have ample time to be there ahead of it and catch the culprit red-handed when the boxes are taken on board, but I will need to enlist the help of the Excise men to examine the manifest and the cargo. They can make the arrest.'

Clarence rubbed his hands together, smiling wolfishly.

'I'll give you a letter to take to the local Excise, asking them to give you whatever assistance you require. But what has that to do with Allworthy?'

'I discovered he owns the *Fair Trader*.' He had to be doubly sure of his ground or the tattlers would have a field day. 'We have to make sure he is there himself or he might well wriggle off the hook.'

'Where is he now?'

'Here, in London.'

'Then you have to entice him to Norfolk.'

Harry smiled. 'As soon as he learns that is where I am heading, he will not be able to resist coming after me.'

'I hope you are right.'

'So do I.'

He waited while the colonel wrote the letter to the Excise, then went to Boodle's, intent on letting it be known he was going out of town to Norfolk, before setting off for Bostock House.

He was striding up Bond Street, deep in thought, when he found himself face to face with Jane. They stopped two yards apart and looked at each other. She was wearing a wool cloak with a deep hood that had fallen back from her head, revealing startled green eyes in a pale face. He doffed his hat, but did not speak. Instead he raked her with his eyes, waiting for her to acknowledge him as politeness demanded.

She could not find her voice and simply looked up into his face. It was the dearest face in the world to her; she knew every mark, every tiny scar, the way he smiled, the way he frowned. 'Captain Hemingford. How do you do?' she managed at last.

'My health is excellent. And yours?'

'I am perfectly recovered.'

She did not look it. She looked very pale, as if she had not been sleeping, and her green eyes had lost their customary sparkle. But she held her head high. He knew she had been troubled by the gossip; if he had had his way, he would have stuck by her side and defied them together. But she would not have it. And he had to abide by that. 'I am glad to hear it,' he said. 'Will you allow me to escort you home?'

She looked about her like a frightened rabbit. 'I do not think so, it will undo all the good.'

'To hell with that! And I will not apologise for my language. I want to talk to you.'

'No, Harry, no.'

'If you cannot bear to be seen in my company, then we must meet secretly.'

'It is impossible to keep a secret in London. I do not go out unaccompanied, even now Hannah is only a few paces behind me, waiting for me to go on.'

'Then come and visit Anne. She misses you.'

'I miss her too, but you know it would not do, not yet, not until—' She stopped. 'She told me she was going to devote her life to you.'

'Did she?' She was trying to look fierce and it made him smile. 'Dear, faithful Anne.'

'Yes, she is. I cannot comprehend how you can bear to take her money.'

'Take her money! Whatever are you talking about?'

'She told me she would give you all her inheritance to set up your manufactory and live with you as your housekeeper.'

He laughed. 'And you believed I would accept it? I am very disappointed that you do not know me better than that.'

'But the project was so important to you. It was becoming an obsession.'

'No, my love, it was the means to an end. I have done with it now.'

'Oh.' She did not understand—what end? And if he could not tell her so, why could he not have confided in Anne, who was as close to him as any sister could be? 'Does Anne know that?'

'She will, very soon.'

'What will you do instead?'

'What would you have me do?'

'It is not for me to say, but perhaps you should listen to your grandfather.'

'Settle down in domesticity, you mean?'

'Yes. It would scotch the rumours once and for all.'

'Then perhaps I will.'

She felt a cold wind whirl about her though there was not a breath of it in the street. How would she endure it, if he took a wife? 'I must go. Tell Anne I will write.' And with that she turned and beckoned to Hannah, who hurried to join her mistress.

He watched them until they had turned the corner and then hailed a cab to take him home. Anne had suggested accosting Jane in the street, and though he had not deliberately done that, it had made no difference. She was still too worried about the gossip. Well, the gabble grinders would soon have something else to talk about. What would Jane say when she learned he had been instrumental in her erstwhile suitor's downfall? It might look like spite; though she had rejected the man, it did not mean she would take pleasure in his disgrace. It would be better if his part in the affair was never made public.

He was completely taken aback when he arrived home and the footman who admitted him, and took his coat and hat, told him the Earl of Bostock had arrived and was in the drawing room with Miss Hemingford. The Earl had not been to the capital in years, saying he hated the place, and this unexpected change of heart was puzzling and, coming so soon after Jane had mentioned him, was ironic. 'How did he get here?'

'He came in the old barouche, Captain. It has not improved his temper.'

Harry thanked the servant for the warning, went up to his room, changed out of his riding clothes and donned a blue kerseymere tailcoat and matching pantaloon trousers, yellow-and-white striped waistcoat and a modest cravat. Feeling a little more ready to face whatever was coming, he ran lightly down the stairs, stopped to tweak his cravat and put a cheerful smile on his face, and entered the drawing room.

His grandfather was sitting in a wing chair by the hearth, a glass of brandy on a small table at his elbow. Anne sat opposite him, her hands resting lightly in the lap of her amber silk gown. 'My lord, this is an unexpected pleasure,' Harry said, acknowledging him with a bow. 'Anne, good evening.'

'Grandfather is come to join us for a few days,' she told her brother.

'Oh, then I wish you had forewarned us, my lord, for I am obliged to leave for the country tomorrow morning.'

'Running away?' the old man queried. The journey had evidently taken its toll, for he seemed more frail than he had been when they had left him at Sutton Park.

'My lord, I protest. I have never run away from anything in my life. And why should I need to?'

'Not from me, you clunch, I am too old and near my

end to be a threat to you. I was referring to that mushroom who turned up at Sutton Park to carry Jane off.'

'I am certainly not running away from him.'

'No? I heard he had called you out and you had refused to meet him.'

Harry laughed. He had been telling the truth when he told Clarence he had not seen Allworthy and he saw no point in seeking him out in order to quarrel with him. It would have been different if Jane had not made it perfectly clear she did not want to see him again. He would fight for her, die for her, but not to satisfy the vanity of a rejected man. 'Is it not wonderful how these rumours spread and grow? I have not refused to meet him because I have not been given the opportunity to do so.'

'That is just what I said,' Anne put in. 'Mr Allworthy is making a great deal of noise, but that is all it is, empty noise.'

'Then you must call him out,' the Earl told his grandson. 'You cannot, in honour bound, ignore what he is saying.'

'Oh, I do not intend to,' Harry said grimly.

'Oh, Harry!' Anne cried. 'You surely do not mean to meet him. It will be as good as admitting you have done what he accuses you of.'

'And what is that?' the old man demanded.

'I believe he is saying that I persuaded Jane to refuse him, that I enticed her away.'

'We know that is not true,' the Earl said. 'I was there. He must be made to eat his words.'

'Is that why you are come to the Smoke?' Harry asked him. 'To see me fight a duel?'

'If that is what it takes to defend the family honour, then you must do it. I have it on the best authority he is no swordsman, nor marksman either.'

'And what do you think Jane will say to that?'

'Jane?' he queried, as if surprised that Jane came into the matter at all. 'She will be proud of you.'

'No, sir, she will be angry. She is doing her best to live down the scandal, as I am. If I kill Allworthy or he kills me, there will be no end to it. He is not worth it.'

'I never thought to hear kin of mine refuse to demand satisfaction when he has been wronged.'

'I shall have my satisfaction, never fear, but not in a duel and not in a way that reflects badly on Jane or the Hemingford family name.'

'Harry is trying his best to protect us all, Grandfather,' Anne put in.

'Then I want to hear how he is going to do it.'

Harry sighed. He told them what he suspected and why he had to leave for King's Lynn the following morning. 'If all goes well, he will be arrested by the Excise men,' he told them, 'and I shall be as surprised as the rest of the *haut monde* when the arrest is reported.'

'I knew there was something havey-cavey about the fellow,' the old man cackled. 'Oh, I'd give a deal to see his face…' He paused. 'But what did you mean, you will have no hand in it?'

'I do not want the world to know. Jane might not understand.'

'I cannot believe she is wearing the willow for him.'

'I hope she is not.'

'Why did he offer for her?'

'Why would he not?' Harry demanded. 'Any man would be proud and pleased to have her for a wife.'

'And she is a Hemingford,' the Earl murmured. 'Marriage to her would have set the seal on his acceptance in Society.'

'But he is related to the Earl of Denderfield,' Anne put in.

'So he might be, but Denderfield don't recognise him. His father was a second cousin, born on the wrong side of the blanket.'

'I did not know that,' Anne said. 'I wonder if the Countess of Carringdale knows it?'

The old man sipped his wine. 'Why should she? It ain't something he's likely to noise abroad, is it?'

It was news to Harry, too, but it explained a great deal about the man's character: his correctness, his fanaticism about having everything just so, his need for recognition, his open display of his wealth, come not through inheritance but by treachery. He was a nobody who liked to behave as if he were a somebody. His grandfather was right—Jane would have set the seal on his rise in Society, especially if the Countess of Carringdale had a hand in it.

'Poor Jane,' Anne said. 'What an escape she has had.'

'It is not over yet,' he said. 'I have to go to King's Lynn in the morning.'

'Do take care,' Anne said. 'He will not give himself up willingly.'

'I know.' He paused. 'Will you go and see Jane? I know she sent the man away and as far as I know is not pining for him, but she must have had some feeling for him in the beginning. She will be shaken by the news of his arrest.'

'You can tell her yourself, when you come back.'

'No, she must come to me.'

'I never heard such a farrago,' the Earl said. 'Swallow your pride for once, boy.'

'Pride!' He gave a bark of a laugh. 'I digested that two years ago when I enlisted. It is not pride, but reticence.

She must come to me, so that I know she has accepted Allworthy's downfall and does not blame me.'

'Of course she will not blame you,' Anne said. 'If she has any sense, she will be relieved.'

'Take the new carriage,' his grandfather said. 'I collect you have done as I asked and purchased it?'

'Yes, it is to be delivered in the morning, a well-sprung travelling coach, upholstered in red velvet and drawn by as fine a quartet of cattle as you'll find anywhere.'

'Then take it, but be warned, if that finishes up at the bottom of a ravine, you shall pay for it yourself.'

Harry smiled. 'Then I had best decline, for I could not find the blunt to have a simple scratch repaired, let alone buy a whole carriage.'

'Does the War Department not pay you?'

'I have a captain's pay, sir. And the allowance you are pleased to give me.'

'What about this gun you are going to invent?'

'There is no gun, sir. It was a ploy.'

Anne gasped. 'Harry, how could you? How could you let us think you really wanted it? And you had me feeling sorry for you because no one would back you.'

'Sorry, Sis. I had to maintain secrecy, should not have told you now, but...' He shrugged.

The old man laughed. 'Take the carriage, my boy, it's as good as yours anyway. Giles will drive you.'

'But you will need it yourself to go back to Sutton Park. You can't use that barouche, it is falling to pieces.'

'I know that, but if you think I am going home before this fracas is resolved, you are mistaken. I shall stay here until you return, and then we will talk of the future.' He drained his glass and reached for the bell on the table at his side. 'Where's my dinner? I haven't had a bite since an indifferent meal at the Swan in Stevenage.'

The meal was served almost immediately, during which they chatted amiably. Harry was surprised and pleased that they were dealing so well together. Now, all he needed was his errand to King's Lynn to pass off successfully and for Jane to realise they belonged together and he would be the happiest man alive.

Jane had been exceedingly disturbed by her meeting with Harry. She had been telling herself that once the gossips had tired of talking about her, then she could resume visiting Anne and slowly she and Harry could mend whatever had gone wrong between them, that they would come to realise they loved each other. But he was still keeping things from her, as he had two years before. She could tell by the cagey way he said the gun project was no more, which not even Anne knew, and the way he had readily agreed that he would marry and settle down. Surely, if he loved her, he would have protested that nothing was further from his thoughts?

She spent the rest of the day copying some work for her father, noticing that his words were jumbled and did not make grammatical sense; it was almost as if he had been rambling when he wrote them. 'Papa,' she said, at last, 'it is nearly dinner time. Shall we stop?'

'Are you not well?'

She was about to say it was him she was concerned about, but decided he would take no notice of that. 'I am a little tired.'

'Then stop, my dear. We can catch up tomorrow.'

Worried about her father, worried about Harry and Anne and what Mr Allworthy intended, she spent a restless night, full of dreams in which she relived the terror of being tossed about in a carriage tumbling down a steep incline. But in her dream Harry lay white-faced and still

and she could not bring him round. The Countess of Carringdale was there too, picking her way over the debris,
telling her it was God's retribution and unless she married
Donald Allworthy, she would never know another moment's peace. And there was Mr Allworthy, wiping blood
from his sword. She woke in terror, the tears wet on her
face. Surely, surely it was not an omen?

She dressed quickly and went downstairs. There was
no one about; the house was silent. Slipping out of the
side door, she walked round to the mews and asked for a
hack to be saddled. Ten minutes later she was making for
the park. But today, not even a gallop could dispel the
heavy feeling gripping her heart and she turned back.

As soon as she entered the house, she knew something
was wrong. The door stood wide open and the first thing
she noticed was Dr Harrison's black hat on the hall table
beside the vase of chrysanthemums she had put there the
previous day. 'Papa!' she cried, and ran swiftly upstairs,
followed by Hannah, who had been watching out for her.

They were met on the landing by the doctor coming
from her father's bedroom. She stopped, afraid to ask.
'Papa?' The word was a whisper.

'Miss Hemingford,' he said. 'I am afraid your father
has had a seizure.'

'How bad is it? Can I go to him?'

He stepped in front of her, barring her way. 'Miss Hemingford, I regret to have to inform you that Mr Hemingford is no more.'

'Dead?' she shrieked. 'Oh, no, it cannot be.'

He put his hand on her shoulder. 'It was very quick,
my dear, he did not suffer.'

She put her face in her hands and would have fallen if
he had not caught her. 'Sit down, Miss Hemingford, sit

down,' he said, drawing her towards a chair. Then, to Hannah, 'Fetch your mistress a glass of brandy.'

Once the fiery liquid had burned its way down her throat, she looked up at the kindly doctor. 'When did it happen? I have been gone little over an hour.'

'In the night. The footman found him when he went to wake him.'

He was already dead when she left the house. She could not believe she had not known, had not sensed something about the silent house that should have alerted her. Guilt flooded over her in great waves, impossible to bear. 'I should not have gone out.'

'You could have done nothing for him, my dear, do not distress yourself on that account.'

'Can I see him?'

'Of course. When you are ready.'

She stood up, took a deep breath and went into her father's room. He lay in the big bed he had brought from their country home, the one he had shared with her mother, looking tiny and hollow-cheeked. There was a single sheet draped over him and turned back so that his crossed hands lay above it. She noted absently that the fingers were still stained with ink. Poor Papa! That book had killed him, that book and his disappointment that it had not been published and he had never been recognised as an authority on his subject.

She drew a chair up by the bed and sat beside him, contemplating what his life had been like for him the last few years. Always, always working, often late into the night by candlelight. Why had she not stopped him? Why had she not persuaded him that his health was more important? 'I knew he wasn't well,' she whispered, as the tears trickled unchecked down her cheeks. 'I should have stopped him working so hard.'

'Now, now, Miss Jane,' Hannah soothed. 'You know you couldn't stop 'im, you tried, you know you did. It was his life.'

'And now it is his death.' She mopped her eyes and turned to look up at the doctor, standing at the foot of the bed. 'There will be things to do, arrangements to be made...'

'Yes, do not trouble yourself about them now. Is there anyone you should send for?'

'Aunt Lane. She lives in Bath. I will write to her. And Anne, my cousin Anne.' The person she most wanted at her side, the person she did not mention, was Harry.

'I'll go and fetch her,' Hannah volunteered.

'Good,' the doctor said. 'But you should have a man to call on, someone to see to the funeral.'

'There is no one, except Mr Redmayne, my father's lawyer.'

'Then he must be sent for. A young woman should not have to deal with funerals.'

'There's the Captain,' Hannah put in. 'He would come, you may depend upon it.'

Jane did not argue. In the face of this tragedy, what did all the petty reasons, the quarrels and jealousies, the power of gossip, matter?

But it was not Harry who came with Anne, but the Earl of Bostock. He took charge at once, arranging everything, leaving Anne to comfort her friend. 'Harry would have come, I am sure,' Anne said. 'But he is gone out of town.'

'Out of town?' Jane queried, though the tone of her voice betokened no great interest in the reply. She was numb. She could not think of anything except that her beloved papa was gone and what would she do without him?

'Yes. An errand for...' she paused '...for someone of importance.'

The pause alerted Jane enough to bring her out of her lethargy. 'No. He is going to fight Mr Allworthy.'

'Whatever gave you that idea?'

'Mr Allworthy said he was going to call Harry out. And I had a dream. He was wiping blood from his sword.'

'Harry?'

'No, Donald Allworthy. Harry was dead.'

Anne gasped and turned pale. 'No, it was a nightmare, nothing to the purpose. I promise you Harry has not gone to fight a duel.'

Jane relaxed. 'I cannot think straight, Anne. What am I to do? Papa was all I had, except Aunt Lane.'

'And me and Harry and Grandfather. We are kin, after all.'

Jane hugged her cousin. 'I do not know what I would do without you.'

Aunt Lane arrived in a flutter of black silk three days later. She crushed Jane to her ample bosom and said tearfully she was not to worry about a thing. Once the funeral was over she would take her to Bath to live. They would do very well there. Jane was too bereft to argue.

The day of the funeral, Aunt Lane, Jane and Anne sat in the darkened house and waited for the men to return from the committal service. There were few of them: the Earl of Bostock, Dr Harrison, Mr Redmayne, several of her father's literary friends and the Earl of Carringdale, sent by his nosy wife, who would not come herself. All would require refreshment. Hannah had laid it out in the dining room, sniffing back tears. The maid cried because she had respected Mr Hemingford and because she was worried about her job. Jane could not go on living in the house alone.

'I wish Harry would come back,' Anne said, breaking a long silence.

She did not wish it any more than Jane herself. She could not shake that nightmare from her, and Anne's reaction when told of it had not been reassuring. Harry was in danger, she was sure of it. 'You are worried about him?'

'Yes.'

'Where has he gone and why?'

'I cannot tell you.'

'Is he in a scrape?'

Anne gave a hollow laugh. 'You could say so, though not of his choosing.'

'And I am to be content with that?'

'I am afraid so.'

She was about to continue quizzing her friend, but the black carriages returned at that point and the men trooped into the house. Jane was kept busy dispensing refreshment. It was while she was offering Lord Carringdale a glass of wine from a tray that she overheard his conversation with the man standing beside him. 'Heard it myself from the Home Secretary. Arrested for treason the day before yesterday, caught for running guns to the French. They are bringing him to London to stand trial.'

'That's a turn about for the gossips and no mistake. He was supposed to be the wronged one and Hemingford the villain. Are you sure there's no mistake?'

'No mistake. The whole cargo was seized. He put up a good fight, so I heard. It will be in all the papers by morning.'

Jane only just managed to not to drop the tray and, putting it down safely on a table, rushed to find Anne, where she related what she had heard. 'Anne, what did he mean? Was that the scrape Harry was in?'

'Yes.'

'So, are you going to tell me now?'

'I do not know any more than you do. He was sent to arrest a traitor. If Lord Carringdale is right, he was successful and for that I am prodigiously thankful.'

'But they said the man put up a fight. Harry might have been hurt.'

'Let us pray he was not.'

'Amen to that.' She did not know how she was going survive the night. Already sad and tearful about her father, she had to put on a brave face, act the hostess, listen to Mr Redmayne, who would undoubtedly tell her that, unless she could find a way of earning a living, she was now to be a burden on her relatives. How could she bear that? And all the time there was that knot of fear in her gut about Harry. Where was he?

Chapter Eleven

Jane sent Hannah out to buy a newspaper as soon as she heard the cry on the streets. Taking it to her room, she sat down on her bed to read it. It was all there, including the identity of the traitor. It shocked her to the core. Why, Mr Allworthy had even taken her to see the *Fair Trader* and told her he had an interest in her cargo. Guns! So that was why Harry had professed an interest in them! And though Harry's name was not mentioned in the report, Anne had known he was involved. Had he known all along that Mr Allworthy was a traitor?

She was not sure how this changed her feelings for Harry, or even if it did, but she had to know the truth, the whole truth, or they could not deal together. But perhaps he did not want to deal with her, perhaps he had been using her to reach Mr Allworthy. He had quizzed her about her visit to Coprise and King's Lynn, or had she volunteered the information? She could not remember. And he and Anne had suddenly turned up in Cambridge, on their way back to London from Sutton Park, they said, but Cambridge was not on the usual route. Harry must have been spying on Mr Allworthy even then. Was that

why he was so against her marrying the man? Why had
he not confided in her? Did he not trust her?

Harry was driven back to London by Giles, well satisfied with the way things had gone, glad that Allworthy
was now where he belonged—in custody. And it had
nothing to do with Jane, or very little. He hated treachery
of any kind, but that a man could sell weapons to an
enemy, knowing they might be used against his own
countrymen, was more than he could stomach. War was
bad enough when it was conducted in an honourable way;
men were killed and maimed in the name of patriotism,
but when they were being shot at by weapons that should
have been in their own hands, he raged.

As the new coach rolled smoothly towards the capital,
he went over what had happened. Having alerted the Excise officers to be ready, he had disguised himself in the
working-man's fustian coat and breeches and met Thoms,
who had pointed out the *Fair Trader* to him. 'They've
just finished unloading the incoming cargo,' he said. 'The
boxes of umbrellas are in the warehouse, waiting to be
taken on board.'

'Where's Allworthy?'

'Haven't seen him.'

This had been a blow. He had been so sure the man
would take the bait. Without Allworthy, nothing could be
proved.

'Don't worry, sir, I've taken steps to get him 'ere. The
ship's captain was persuaded to write and tell him there
was something wrong with the cargo and he was needed
to sort it out.'

'How did you manage that?'

Thoms laughed. 'I never did like the fellow, not even
when he was dealing in or'nary contraband, but guns!' He

spat expertly onto the cobbles. 'That ain't fair, not nohow, and so I told him. He didn't argue for long.'

Harry could imagine what persuasion was used. 'Where is he now?'

'Trussed up somewhere safe.'

'Will they load without him? I want the merchandise on board and our man with it.'

'Yes, the first mate will see to it when I give the signal.'

'Can he be trusted?'

'I think so. Come, I'll take you to him.'

The first mate, who was found in a tavern that looked out on the wharf, was anxious to save his skin and was more than willing to cooperate and turn in King's evidence. 'Start loading, but do it slowly,' Harry told him. 'I don't want it finished before the owner arrives.'

They were just taking the last crate on board when Allworthy turned up. Leaving his driver to see to the lathered horses, he left his carriage and hurried on board. Harry, who was determined to see it through to the end, signalled to the hiding Excise men and went on board. He smiled to himself, remembering Allworthy's shocked face and then his fury, most of which was directed against Harry himself. Gone was the fashionable man about town, the respectable gentleman known for his exquisite manners, here was a snarling beast, who fought for his life.

He drew a tiny pistol from his pocket, but before he could fire it, the first mate, who had been standing beside him, knocked it from his grasp. Harry thanked him and dived upon his enemy. Then they were trading blows, though not in the gentlemanly manner used at Gentleman Jackson's; here was a vicious rough and tumble with no quarter asked or given. Harry blessed his time in the ranks where he had learned to fight without rules. Allworthy managed to pull a short dagger from his boot, but by that time the Excise men had joined the fray and he was overcome, but not before he had nicked Harry's ear.

Once the prisoner was bound up, the Excise men went off to check the cargo against the manifest and open the crates, which indeed did contain guns. Harry was relieved; he would have looked a great clunch if there had been nothing but umbrellas in them. He returned to watch as Allworthy was formally arrested. 'All this for a woman,' he sneered at Harry, 'and a crippled one at that. I hope you find she is worth it.'

Harry kept his fists to himself with an effort and smiled grimly. 'Oh, I am sure of it. But tell me—what was your interest in her? Did you ever intend to marry her?'

'Of course. She is a Hemingford, after all, and I had Lady Carringdale's promise to raise her up in Society and me with her. The Denderfields would have had to recognise me.'

'Then I am glad she had the good sense to turn you down.' He turned to the Excise officers. 'When you take him in and make your report, do not mention my part in it. Give Thoms and the first mate the credit. I am off back to London.'

He would have to report to Garfitt first and then what? Could he go straight to Jane or ought he to wait until she had recovered from the shock, for shock it would be? Had Anne kept her promise to go and see her?

'A good day's work,' Garfitt said, when he was shown, still dusty from travel, into his office. He poured two glasses of wine and handed one to Harry. 'Make your report.'

Harry told him what had happened in a dry tone which in no way betrayed his loathing of the traitor, his excitement in the fight, his general satisfaction with the outcome.

'Good,' Garfitt murmured. 'But why keep your name out of it? You have done an excellent job for which you should be recognised. Do you not wish for a reward?'

'If there is a reward, I shall not say no to it, but I have my reasons for shunning public approbation.'

The colonel nodded. 'Miss Jane Hemingford.'

'I must protect her from gossip.'

'My dear fellow, you, above all people, should know what an impossibility that is.' He paused. 'But I am glad you are of that mind. The lady's connection with the traitor will no doubt be on everyone's lips, but there is no need for it to involve you.' He took his time refilling their glasses, before going on. 'A certain royal personage wishes to meet you to congratulate you, but I am to find out if he will be compromised by anything you have done. He does not want to be embarrassed by gossip.'

Harry laughed. 'If you are referring to the Regent, he is the biggest instigator of gossip in the kingdom.'

'We know that, but there is one rule for him and another for the rest of us. So, my dear Hemingford, if you can avoid gossip for the foreseeable future, you are to be rewarded by the Regent himself. I will send you word when to present yourself at Carlton House.'

Harry returned to the carriage in a thoughtful mood. Was Garfitt hinting that he should shun Jane if he wanted to be received by the heir to the throne? Regent or not, he could not, would not, do that. He would do whatever he thought right for Jane.

He was unprepared for the news Anne gave him when he arrived at Bostock House. She was at first concerned by the sight of him, worrying about the congealed blood on his ear and the purple bruise on his cheek, but he dismissed it with a wave of his hand. 'It is nothing. When

I have cleaned myself up, you will not even see it.' He had gone upstairs, washed and changed his clothes and then returned to the dining room where Anne had ordered a cold collation to be laid out for him.

'Well, are you going to tell me what happened?' she asked, as he tucked in. 'I know the man was arrested; it was in all the papers.'

'Then you know it all. He cannot harm anyone any more. Did you see Jane?'

'Yes.' She paused. 'Her father has died.'

He stopped eating. 'Hemingford dead? Oh, my poor, poor Jane. How is she?'

'Bearing it bravely. She is to go back to Bath with Mrs Lane, who has undertaken to give her a home. Her father left nothing but the contents of the house, which are to be sold.'

'She does not need a home. She has one with us.'

'So I told her, but she expects there will be even more gossip over Allworthy now he has been exposed...' She paused. 'She knows it was you.'

'Knows? Do you mean to say you told her?'

'No, I did not, but she heard it from the Earl of Carringdale. He heard it from the Home Secretary and now the Countess has done a complete volte-face and is saying she knew all along that Allworthy was a bad lot and she was doing her best to persuade Jane not to have him.'

His grunt of laughter was made more from frustration than amusement. 'And now, I suppose, it is all over town.'

'All over the nation, I should not wonder.'

'What am I to do, Anne?'

'I cannot advise you. Perhaps you should let her go to Bath, be patient for a little while.'

He laughed suddenly. 'That's what Clarence Garfitt was prosing on about. He said I must avoid gossip and I would receive my reward from the hands of the Regent himself. As if I cared a tuppenny cuss about that. But Jane... When is she due to go?'

'As soon as the contents of the house have been sold. The end of the week, I think.'

They were interrupted by the entrance of the Earl. 'Heard you were back,' he said, sitting at the table opposite Harry to watch him eat. 'Glad to see you are in one piece.'

'Thank you, sir.'

'And my new carriage?'

'Also in one piece.'

'Good.' He paused. 'Can't think what you are doing here, though.'

'Where else should I be?'

'I should not have thought it necessary for me to tell you that. Get off with you. Go to her, before she disappears out of your life again.'

It had been a long, long day and he had had no sleep the night before; he was fagged out and in no state to go calling. Besides, it was late. 'I'll go tomorrow when I have rested. I am not fit to be seen now.'

The old man laughed. 'No, you look as if you have been twenty rounds with Jackson and come off worst.'

Harry bade them both goodnight, went to bed and was asleep as soon as his head hit the pillow.

Jane, in deepest mourning, sat with Aunt Lane in the drawing room of the house in Duke Street, her mind and body numb. It was no longer her home; Mr Redmayne had called that afternoon and told her the house had been let and that as soon as the sale of her furniture had been completed, the new tenants wanted to move in. Most of the heavy pieces had gone already and the rest would go the next day. The upheaval, coming on the heels of her father's death and funeral and the arrest of Mr Allworthy, was almost too much to take.

In two days' time, she would leave London for Bath. She would be in the hands of her aunt and, though she loved her dearly, she was not sure that she would like living with her permanently. But perhaps it would be best to leave town. Everyone was talking about her, saying dreadful things about her and Mr Allworthy, as if she had known about his treachery! In spite of his attempts to avoid publicity Harry had become the hero of the hour and her treatment of him two years before was being dragged out again as a despicable act against a fine officer.

She had yet to say goodbye to Anne, but was reluctant to visit Bostock House for fear of encountering Harry, who must surely have returned to the capital by now. If they met, what could they talk about? They would only go over old ground again, saying the same things, finding no solutions, hurting each other. He had used her, just as everyone else used her and she was hurt by it, especially since they seemed to have been dealing so well together since the accident. He had even mentioned marriage, but in the face of the latest gossip, he would not wish for that.

She had to make a new life for herself; if that meant going to Bath as a companion to Aunt Lane, then so be it. She would make the best of it. What would she do there? Visit the baths, go to concerts, go calling, sit and sew? Would she be able to ride? The thought of not being able to get on a horse again decided her. She would rise early and go riding in the morning, but better not say anything to her aunt.

'Aunt, I am very tired,' she said. 'I think I will retire early, if you do not mind.'

'Of course not, child. Go along.'

She climbed the stairs, past the blank spaces on the walls where the pictures had once hung, past her father's empty room and on to her own room, where Hannah, who had been offered the post of Jane's personal maid by Mrs Lane, was waiting to help her.

'I can get myself to bed,' she said. 'I want you to go out for me.'

Amid protests that she should not be doing it, Jane sent her to the nearest stables to hire a riding horse to be brought to the house at seven the following morning. Now the decision had been made she was looking forward to her ride and hardly dare close her eyes for fear she would oversleep, although she had asked Hannah to wake her.

She was sound asleep when the maid shook her at six-thirty.

'You'll have me in trouble with Mrs Lane, you really will,' she said as she helped Jane into her habit and pinned up her hair. 'You are still in mourning and this habit is blue.'

'It is a very dark blue. And no one will see me.'

'There's any number of blackguards out there, waiting to pounce. It ain't safe for a man, let alone a woman.'

'Oh, Hannah, you refine upon it too much. I shall be perfectly safe on a horse and back before my aunt misses me; you know she never rises before eleven. Now, fetch my hat and watch for the stable boy. I don't want him knocking on the door and waking her.'

Ten minutes later she was trotting purposefully towards Green Park in the light of a new dawn, unaware that Harry had seen her and was riding behind her.

He had woken early and, unable to wait idly until it was a decent hour to go calling, had decided to go for a ride. His route from Cavendish Square to Hyde Park took him past the end of Duke Street and on a whim he turned down it, only to see Jane emerge alone. He reined in and watched as she mounted a hack being held by a stable boy and trotted off towards Grosvenor Square. He assumed she was making for Green Park and changed his own destination to follow her.

When she entered the park, she avoided the cows, heavy with milk, and, once clear of them, put her mount to a canter, and then a gallop. After the gloom of a house in mourning, it was wonderful to be out in the fresh air. It would be frowned upon by Society, which set such store on behaving in the accepted manner, but she was sure her father, if he could see her, would not mind. Several minutes later, she drew up by a group of trees and turned to see the man she loved trotting towards her. Her heart gave a great leap of joy, before settling back into its recent numb acceptance that she was fated not to enjoy the love she wanted and needed so badly.

'We are well met, Jane,' he called, drawing rein beside her. 'How are you?'

'I am well.' She looked far from well. She was pale as a ghost, there were dark circles under her eyes and the eyes themselves had an empty look as if her tears had drained the life out of them. He longed to comfort her, to put the sparkle back in them. He waited, his hands idle on the reins. 'How did you know I would be here?'

'I didn't. I saw you leave your house and decided to follow.'

'Why?' He looked exhausted and there was a dreadful bruise on his face. The newspapers had said Mr Allworthy had resisted arrest before being overpowered. Had he inflicted that injury?

'Why? Because you should not be riding out alone and ought to have an escort.'

She smiled wanly. 'I needed to get out of the house. It's not the same now and…' She paused. 'You heard?'

'About your father, yes. Jane, I am so very sorry for your loss.'

'He was ill, I knew he was working too hard. That damnable book…'

He smiled at her language. 'He wanted to finish it.'

'No, he did not. He knew when it was finished he would have no reason to live.'

'Did he finish it?'

'Yes. When I went into the library to tidy it just before the funeral, there it was on the desk, neatly tied with ribbon. There was nothing else on the desk, no papers, no books, not even a pen, all had been tidied away. It was as if he knew…'

'Oh, Jane, I am sorry, but he is at peace now.' He did not want to talk about her father, he wanted to talk about her and whether she would accept his offer of marriage, but politeness demanded he speak of the late Mr Hemingford first, to offer condolences.

'Yes.'

'Anne tells me you are going to Bath with Mrs Lane.'

'Yes.'

'Is that what you wish?'

She shrugged. 'She has offered me a home.'

His horse was becoming restive. He dismounted and tethered it lightly to a bush so that it could crop the grass. Then he turned back to her. 'Come, my love, dismount. I cannot talk to you while you are on the back of that animal.'

She took his outstretched hands and slid from the saddle. 'I am surprised you want to talk to me at all.'

He did not release her hands, but stood looking down into her upturned face, studying her features, the sorrowful eyes, the brows, the soft mouth, the way her hair sprang from beneath her riding hat, the way her white muslin neckcloth nestled at her throat. 'How can you say that?'

'It is all over, is it not?'

'What is?'

'Your mission. You have captured the traitor.'

'Yes, it is all over. The man will trouble you no more.'

'Trouble me? That is not why you went after him, was it? Not for my sake.'

'No, I was ordered to find a traitor. I had no idea it was Allworthy, not in the beginning.' He paused and went on gently. 'Jane, I never wanted to hurt you. I hoped you might never learn that it was me who uncovered his villainy.'

'Do you think I care a groat about that?' she said sharply. 'Do you think I was so enamoured of him that I would condone his wickedness? I rejected him, or had you forgot?'

'No, I had not forgot.' He was puzzled. 'Jane, what are you trying to say?'

'You should have told me, you should have trusted me. Instead, you went about it in secret, dashing off to Norfolk with never a word, while the tattlers did their worst. They said Mr Allworthy had called you out and I thought you had gone to fight him…' She was in tears now, beating her fists ineffectually against his chest. 'Secrets, how I hate secrets. That's what you did two years ago, tried to conceal the truth from me.'

He let her hit him; she was not hurting him and if it made her feel better, then he welcomed the battering. 'Jane, there is no comparison. Two years ago I was foolish enough to think I could buy preferment and there is nothing I regret so much as our quarrel. This time I was given the task of uncovering a traitor and that sort of work has to be done in secrecy. Even from you, my darling.' He took both her hands in his and kissed the fingers one by one. 'It is over now.'

She shivered at his touch. 'Is it? Do you know what Lady Carringdale is saying?'

He laughed, still holding her hands.

'That she knew Allworthy was a rogue and had been trying to persuade you to reject him, but that you were so beguiled by him, you would not listen. I cannot imagine anyone believing that.'

'She is saying I am a tease, playing you both off one against the other, and now I had my come-uppance because I was lamed and had neither of you. And my shocking behaviour killed my father. Oh, Harry, do you think it did?'

'No, of course not. And as for losing me, I am afraid you will have to try very much harder if you want to do that.'

She looked up into his face. The tears glistening on her lashes were making her green eyes sparkle. 'I do not want to lose you,' she said softly.

'I am not talking about being friends,' he said. 'Not that a man can't be friends with his wife...'

'But...'

'Jane, there can be no buts. I asked you to marry me.'

'And then agreed it was a joke.'

'I was hurt by your reaction. Jane, I need to know the truth. Will you marry me?'

She smiled. 'You know, that is the first time you have couched it as a question.'

'And are you going to answer it?'

'Are you sure that is what you want? It is not because you feel sorry for me?'

'Feel sorry for you! Why should I feel sorry for someone who can wind me round her thumb, who is not afraid to say exactly what she thinks, who can ride like the wind and smile like an angel and has my heart so firmly in her grip, there is no escaping?'

'Do you mean that?'

'I never meant anything more in my life.'

She tilted her head up to look into his face. He smiled and slowly lowered his head to kiss her lightly, then leaned back to look at her again, his expression a question. She answered it with a smile, and he kissed her again, more urgently. They clung together, as if making up for lost time, kissing and being kissed, oblivious to the two horses cropping the grass near them, the early birdsong, the distant lowing of cattle. He released her at last and leaned back to look at her. 'Now, are you going to answer me?'

She laughed, suddenly joyous. 'No, I think you should kiss me again first.'

He did. And then again, 'Have I earned my answer?'

'Yes, oh, yes.'

He grinned and tipped her chin up with his finger, so that he was looking into her eyes. 'And what is it to be?'

'Need you ask?'

'Say it then. Say, "Harry, I love you and will marry you."'

'Harry, I love you dearly, have always loved you, and I will marry you.' She smiled, her tears forgotten. 'Now it is your turn.'

He obliged and followed that with more kisses until she was breathless. She reluctantly left his side to fetch her horse. 'I must go home, my aunt will be worried.'

'Yes, of course.' He helped her mount and then untethered his own horse and sprang easily into the saddle. 'I will escort you. I must speak to her.'

'Oh, Harry, she will not be pleased,' she said, as they walked their horses back to the gate. 'I am in mourning; if I suddenly say I mean to marry you, it will set the tongues wagging even more.'

'Are you suggesting we should keep it a secret?' He spoke sharply, knowing she was right and hating the idea of any delay to the fulfilment of his dream. 'I collect you hate secrets.'

'There is no need for secrets. I am going to Bath the day after tomorrow and very soon I shall be forgotten. In due course, you may follow me there.' She turned and smiled at him.

'How long is due course?'

'Oh, I leave that entirely to your good sense.'

'You do not want me to speak to your aunt?'

'Not today. She will still be abed, I hope. I will tell her.'

'You mean I am to let you go to Bath without seeing you again? That is the outside of enough and not to be borne.'

'I must say goodbye to Anne. I shall call at Bostock House tomorrow for that reason. If you choose to be at home...'

They had reached the gate where she intended to part company from him. They must not be seen together, not yet, and though he railed against it, he knew she was right. 'Then I shall most certainly be at home and if I cannot contrive to spend a few minutes alone with you, I will eat this hat.' He doffed his headgear in salute. 'Until tomorrow.'

'Tomorrow,' she murmured, and turned away.

* * *

She had been right: Aunt Lane was not pleased. 'How could you?' she railed when she came down for luncheon and Jane told her of the meeting with Harry. 'You are in mourning for your dear papa and should not be going out at all so soon, but you have to creep out of the house like a thief in the night to go riding. And to meet Harry Hemingford of all people!'

'I did not go to meet him. I did not know he would be there.'

Her aunt ignored her. 'Oh, I know he is the hero of the hour, but that doesn't change things, does it? You still broke off your engagement to him and accepted another man.'

'I did not!'

'As good as. You didn't know he was a traitor when you went off to Cumbria, did you? You made yourself the talk of the town. There are those who do not believe in your loss of memory, you know.'

'Lady Carringdale.'

'She isn't the only one. Now you must disgrace me with this…this tarradiddle about marrying Harry Hemingford. You can't marry him.'

'Why not?'

'Why not?' Her aunt was almost shrieking. 'You are in mourning. Do you want to bring shame on your poor father's memory? And me? I shall be glad when we get to Bath and you learn to behave with a little decorum. If you had anyone else to turn to, I would not take you in.'

'I do have someone else—the Earl of Bostock.'

'And that would compound your folly. I have no doubt he is of the same mind as I am. As for that grandson of his…'

Jane was so happy that most of this diatribe went over her head. Her aunt would run out of breath and then she would explain that she was not planning to marry Harry immediately, but if her aunt was going to complain about him, she had to be stopped. 'Aunt, do not say it. Do not revile Harry or we shall have a serious falling out and I shall refuse to come to Bath with you. I love him dearly, I always have, he is the bravest, most honourable man I know and he loves me. I will not have a word said against him.'

'Well!'

Jane smiled. At last her aunt was speechless. 'Aunt, we have no intention of announcing our engagement yet. No one shall know of it but you and Anne and the Earl of Bostock, not until I am no longer in mourning and all this dreadful fuss about Mr Allworthy has died down. But I shall marry him. And do not think I will change my mind, because I will not. I would not have broken off the engagement before if I had not been persuaded it was the thing to do. I never stopped loving him.'

'Oh.'

'You do understand, don't you?' she asked softly because her aunt was sitting very still as if digesting this information.

'I suppose so. But if you are intent on going to Bostock House tomorrow, then I am coming with you. We will go openly in my carriage. I am not laying myself open to any accusations of neglect of my duty towards you.'

Jane reached over and kissed her aunt's cheek. 'Thank you, Aunt. I shall be glad of your company.'

How she was going to have any time alone with Harry, she had no idea, but somehow they would contrive it.

The house was empty, the packing all done and the bags and boxes, except what was needed for their journey, had been loaded on a wagon to be taken to Bath ahead of them, and, after seeing it all off the next morning, they set off for Bostock House in her aunt's carriage.

All three were there, Harry and Anne and the Earl, when they were shown into the drawing room. Anne ran forward and kissed Jane. 'Harry has told me. I am so happy for you both.'

Jane went forward and curtsied to the Earl. 'Come closer, girl,' he said. 'Let me look at you.'

She obeyed and he took her hand. 'Come to your senses at last, have you?' But his eyes were twinkling.

'Yes, my lord.' She looked round for Harry. He was standing beside a chair, his hand lightly on its back. There was a huge smile on his face as he made her a bow. 'Miss Hemingford.'

She laughed, dropped him a curtsy, then ran to take his hand. 'It is all right,' she said. 'Aunt Lane knows.'

'My lord,' Mrs Lane interrupted, addressing the Earl, 'I am at a loss… I did not think you would condone…'

He rose stiffly. 'Madam, I wish to talk to you. Be so good as to come with me to the library.' He held out his arm, obliging her to take it, and they disappeared from the room.

'What does he want with her?' Jane asked as soon as the door was shut on them.

Harry laughed. 'Goodness knows. Did she give you a hard time?'

'Only a little one. In any case it did not signify, I had made up my mind.'

'And you will not change it again?'

'Never.'

He took her hand and looked deeply into her eyes. 'Neither shall I,' he whispered.

Jane was aware of the soft rustle of silk and the closing

of the door and knew Anne had left them alone. 'Oh, Harry, we have wasted so much time.'

'And more still to waste if you go off to Bath.'

'I must. I want to do this properly, Harry.'

'Six months,' he said. 'I will give you six months before I come calling, and it will be the longest six months of my life.'

'What will you do?'

'I will not kick my heels, you may be sure of that.'

'Not guns?'

He laughed. 'No. I am to see the Regent next week. I believe I am to be reinstated in his regiment with promotion to Major.' He laughed. 'Properly earned, this time.'

She was alarmed. 'You are not going back to the war? I could not bear that. You might be killed. Oh, Harry, do say you are not going to fight.'

He laughed and kissed the tip of her nose. 'The only fighting I will be doing is with paper and words in the War Department offices. Colonel Garfitt tells me I am to interview prisoners of war and obtain intelligence.'

'Oh, then I shall have to congratulate you.' She smiled and stretched her arms up to put them round his neck, pulling his head down to hers. The kiss went on for a very long time. It was a foretaste of what she could expect in six months' time and the memory of it would have to last. It was a mixture of sadness and joy, hope and regret, but most of all an expression of a love that would last forever.

'Hurrumph!'

They sprang apart as the Earl re-entered the room, followed by Mrs Lane. The lady was looking decidedly pink and flustered. 'Jane, I must go. I have to say goodbye to the Countess. I am sure the Captain will see you safely home.' And with that, she turned and bustled out of the room before a footman could be summoned to conduct her to the door.

The Earl fell into his chair, startling Jane until she realised he was doubled up with laughter.

'My lord, what have you said to her?' Jane asked. 'She and the Countess are not exactly bosom bows these days.'

He mopped his eyes with his handkerchief. 'Oh, dear, the poor lady is devastated that she has been so blind.'

'Grandfather,' Harry said severely, 'what mischief have you been up to?'

'Someone had to do something. You seemed to be prepared to stand by and let the tattlers blacken Jane's name without doing a thing about it.'

'What could I do that would not make it worse?'

'No, you are right, it had to be me. I have just told the good lady...' he paused to chuckle again '...I told her that Jane knew all along that Allworthy was a villain, that you had taken her into your confidence and enlisted her help in nailing him. That was why she went to Coprise Manor, to find out what she could, and her information was vital to his arrest.'

'My lord!' Jane stared at him, unbelieving.

'I suggested that she would do well to correct those gossiping friends of hers before the name of Hemingford was irretrievably blackened. After all, Harry will be the Earl of Bostock one day.'

Jane went to kneel at his feet. 'Not for a long time yet,' she said.

He put his hand on her head. 'Go to Bath, child, I shall be waiting here when you come back. And so will Harry.'

'I know.' She took his gnarled hand and put it to her lips. 'Thank you, for everything.'

Harry raised her to her feet. 'Come, we will find Anne.

You must say goodbye to her and then I will take you home.'

She curtsied to the Earl and followed Harry from the room. She had been a long time finding that happiness which had so eluded her, but now it had come it tasted doubly sweet. Six months would soon pass. She would spend it making plans and dreaming of a reunion she knew would be everything she hoped for.

* * * * *

LET'S TALK
Romance

For exclusive extracts, competitions
and special offers, find us online:

f facebook.com/millsandboon

🐦 @MillsandBoon

📷 @MillsandBoonUK

Get in touch on 01413 063232

For all the latest titles coming soon, visit
millsandboon.co.uk/nextmonth

MILLS & BOON
A ROMANCE FOR EVERY READER

- **FREE** delivery direct to your door

- **EXCLUSIVE** offers every month

- **SAVE** up to 25% on pre-paid subscriptions

SUBSCRIBE AND SAVE

millsandboon.co.uk/Subscribe

MILLS & BOON

THE HEART OF ROMANCE

A ROMANCE FOR EVERY KIND OF READER

MODERN

Prepare to be swept off your feet by sophisticated, sexy and seductive heroes, in some of the world's most glamourous and romantic locations, where power and passion collide.
8 stories per month.

HISTORICAL

Escape with historical heroes from time gone by. Whether your passion is for wicked Regency Rakes, muscled Vikings or rugged Highlanders, awaken the romance of the past.
6 stories per month.

MEDICAL

Set your pulse racing with dedicated, delectable doctors in the high-pressure world of medicine, where emotions run high and passion, comfort and love are the best medicine.
6 stories per month.

True Love

Celebrate true love with tender stories of heartfelt romance, from the rush of falling in love to the joy a new baby can bring, and focus on the emotional heart of a relationship.
8 stories per month.

Desire

Indulge in secrets and scandal, intense drama and plenty of hot action with powerful and passionate heroes who have it all: wealth, status, good looks…everything but the right woman.
6 stories per month.

HEROES

Experience all the excitement of a gripping thriller, with an romance at its heart. Resourceful, true-to-life women and strong fearless men face danger and desire - a killer combination!
8 stories per month.

DARE

Sensual love stories featuring smart, sassy heroines you'd want as a best friend, and compelling intense heroes who are worthy of them.
4 stories per month.

To see which titles are coming soon, please visit

millsandboon.co.uk/nextmonth

JOIN US ON SOCIAL MEDIA!

Stay up to date with our latest releases, author news and gossip, special offers and discounts, and all the behind-the-scenes action from Mills & Boon...

 millsandboon

 millsandboonuk

 millsandboon

might just be true love...